**Her phone beeped and vibrated against
the coffee table.**

Mel turned and pounced on it before the screen even had
time to go dark.

Hey hot stuff, what are you doing?

Laundry, she texted back as a smile split her face.

Sounds thrilling. Want a distraction?

*Depends on what you have in mind. I'm about to start
matching my socks and that's the best part.*

I'll show you my best part, he responded a second later.

Mel took a deep breath feeling a little light-headed and a
lot turned on.

*Well, then get over here and show me... will there be a
hands-on portion of this demonstration?* she typed out. But
her finger hovered over the send button for a second. She'd
never sent dirty text messages. Well, there was no time like
the present...

"HOT! Richard's tempting second addition to her Country Roads series puts a clever spin on the small-town romance trope with great effect. The chemistry between her main characters is indisputable...a heartwarming story with clever twists that will please Richard's fans and win her new devotees."
—*RT Book Reviews*

UNDONE

"Richard's page-turner marks her as a contemporary romance author to watch."
—*Publishers Weekly*

"A fun, feel-good story and perfect for a quick, entertaining escape!"
—ABookishEscape.com

"4½ stars! These characters are rich and deep, so expertly written that they feel like friends, and the best news of all is that this small-town series is set to continue!"
—*RT Book Reviews*

Also by Shannon Richard

Undone
Undeniable

Acknowledgments

To Kaitie Hotard, no matter the distance you continue to be a constant source of encouragement and strength in my life. It's always a comfort to know you're just a phone call away. To Stephen Hotard, you've become a close friend over the last couple of years. Thank you for being such a good husband to my best friend.

To Sarah E. Younger, you are beyond wonderful. You've become my guru on all things book-related, and on more than a couple of things life-related. You help me work past the rough spots and never hesitate to lend a helping word or two (thousand). Thank you isn't enough for what you do for me.

To my editor Megha Parekh, you were so excited about Mel's story and your help during the planning and editing process was indispensable. You continue to make me a better writer and I love working with you. And to everyone I've worked with at Grand Central Publishing, especially my publicist Julie Paulauski and the amazing art department. I love my covers. They are beyond beautiful.

To David McCue, for working out the beginning of *Unstoppable*. Thank you for going over the dozens of scenarios and potential recovery methods for Mel. You helped me put my beloved character through the least amount of pain as possible. I'm forever grateful for your patience and your friendship.

To Marina Coleman, for talking me through things (both with writing and life) and just for listening. You are fabulous and I'm so grateful to call you a friend.

To William Isaacs, sometimes you find friendship in the most unexpected places. Thank you for answering more questions than I can count on topics ranging from the military to dog training, and a few things in between.

To Ken Kenyon and Kenny Miller, real-life handymen, who gave me more than a few tips on construction and building. You wear your hardhats well.

To Rachel Lacey and Annie Rains for making RWA 2013 so much fun. You guys are awesome, and I hope to have many more conferences laughing over a bottle (or two) of wine.

To Gloria Berry, for supporting my writing from day one, and for dragging me to frozen yogurt when I'm in desperate need of a mental break; nothing says happiness like Nutella goodness.

To my parents, for giving me life and all, and everything else you do because it's a whole heck of a lot.

To Katie Crandall, we were kindred spirits from the start. You share my love for one Fitzwilliam Darcy (and all things Jane Austen), sunflowers, Scotland, and strawberry wine. You named the ever adorable and lovable Teddy, and you helped me figure out a lot of what makes Bennett Hart tick. You are, as always, invaluable.

Unstoppable

Prologue

The Calm in the Storm

The pain was incredible. It was like someone had drilled a hole into her shoulder. And she was cold, oh so unbelievably cold.

She'd been shot. At least she was pretty sure she'd been shot. The gun had gone off and then someone had been screaming. Was it her that screamed? Was she screaming now? She thought she was. She felt like she was. Or was the screaming all in her head?

No. No, there was definitely something blaring. A loud, piercing noise, and it wasn't in her head. It was everywhere.

And she was flat on her back. When had she fallen? She didn't remember going down. Just opening her eyes to a world of pain.

"We're at Rejuvenate," a panicked voice said. "We walked in on Chad Sharp and Hoyt Reynolds breaking in, and they shot Mel. They shot her."

Okay, so she *had* been shot.

"Oh God, oh God, oh God," another panicked voice said. This voice was much closer. It was above her.

The room was dark. Blurred images moved around in a dim light, but she couldn't make them out.

Warmth was leaking out of her, spreading out over her shoulder. There was pressure, pressure, over the pain. Someone was trying to hold her together.

She closed her eyes. Maybe then the pain would go away. Maybe then she'd be okay.

"Mel, look at me," the panicked voice said.

She opened her eyes and tried to get past the pain. Tried to come back. Harper, it was Harper above her. She focused on Harper's face. There was blood smeared on Harper's cheek and she was crying.

The rest of the room slowly came into focus. The loud blaring was the alarm and Grace was on the phone, talking to someone.

"Mel, say something. Please," Harper begged.

"I'm scared," she whispered.

"I know, I know." Harper's voice shook along with her hands.

"Jax is here," Grace cried out, shooting across the room.

More voices, and the floor underneath Mel shook as people walked across it. And then someone was kneeling on the other side of her. Mel looked up into the last face she'd expected to see.

Bennett.

His piercing bluish gray eyes were intently focused on her.

"Mel, it's going to be okay," he said calmly as he put his hands over Harper's trembling ones. "Understand? You're going to be fine."

"Okay," she whispered as tears streamed from her eyes.

"I got it." Bennett looked up at Harper.

Harper nodded and pulled her hands out from under his. And then Bennett was in Mel's face, his calm, beautiful eyes staring straight into hers and his voice the only thing she could hear.

"Stay right here, Mel. I've got you. I promise."

Chapter One

The Scruffy Man and
the Curly-Haired Girl

It had been eight weeks since Melanie O'Bryan had been shot, eight weeks since she'd gone to a spa after hours and walked in on a burglary in progress. She'd been with her two best friends, Harper Laurence and Grace King. It wasn't like the three girls had done anything wrong; Harper was a massage therapist who worked at Rejuvenate and was able to go in and out of the spa as she pleased. They'd just been in the wrong place at the wrong time.

Mirabelle, Florida, was a small beach town. Its six hundred square miles boasted a population of about five thousand. Even though there were very few saints in that five thousand, the burglary spree that had hit the town had been out of the norm. Chad Sharp and Hoyt Reynolds had stolen hundreds of thousands of dollars from over a dozen businesses and houses.

No one had known who was behind the burglaries until Mel, Harper, and Grace had walked in on the one at Rejuvenate. Chad and Hoyt had gotten away that night, but their greed caught up with them, and so had the law. Now the two thieves were sitting behind bars, awaiting trial. With any luck they would be in there for a *very* long time.

Chad had been the one who shot Mel in the shoulder. The bullet hadn't hit anything vital, but she had required physical therapy for the past six weeks. She'd actually just finished her last session the day before. Her shoulder was still sore for the most part, but little by little she was getting back to a full range of motion.

Things were slowly getting back to normal for Mel. It was the middle of August and school was starting on Monday. The teachers had spent the last week planning, and Mel couldn't wait for her students to be back in the classroom.

It was just after four on Friday when Mel pulled up in front of her little two-bedroom house. It had belonged to her grandparents and she inherited it after both of them had died. Otherwise Mel wouldn't be a home owner; her salary as a math teacher at Mirabelle High School didn't bring in the big bucks. She'd always loved the little buttercream-yellow cottage, with it's robin's-egg blue shutters and doors.

Mel grabbed her purse and groceries from the trunk of her black Jetta. She had just enough time to put everything away, jump in the shower, and get ready for tonight before Grace and Harper came over. There was a crawfish boil over at Slim Willie's, and they were going to head over together. But only after they spent a little while catching up on each other's lives. They'd all been so busy lately that they hadn't really gotten to see each other.

Mel had been best friends with Grace since birth. Well, since two months after Mel's birth, as that was how long it took Grace to join the world. Their mothers had been best friends as well, so Mel and Grace hadn't had a choice, and really, they wouldn't have wanted it any other way. They'd been pretty inseparable over the years, and when Harper had moved to Mirabelle in the sixth grade, they'd eagerly accepted her into the fold.

Harper was now a massage therapist, and she'd been

booked solid all summer with clients. Mirabelle had a fancy little resort out on the beach called LaBella. They tended to draw in clientele with pretty thick pocketbooks. Harper also worked at Rejuvenate, the spa in downtown Mirabelle where Mel had been shot. Between the two places, Harper barely had enough time to think, let alone go get dinner.

Grace had been busy planning her wedding to her fiancé, Deputy Jaxson Anderson, and it was about damn time. The girl had been in love with her stubborn redhead since she was six years old, and they'd only just gotten together last April. It had taken Jax a while to figure out he was in love with Grace. The boy had always been ridiculously protective of her, but in his stupid-boy mind he'd thought he wasn't good enough for her. He'd finally gotten a clue.

Mel opened the door and walked into her house. The air conditioner provided a welcome relief to the humidity that was Florida in the summer. She locked the door behind her and made her way down the hall, dropped her purse on the dining room table, and went into the kitchen. She put her bags on the counter and headed for the cabinet, where she grabbed a cup and filled it with ice water. Once she downed half of it, she pressed the cold glass to her forehead.

In all truth, there was no point in taking a shower to wash off the stickiness from the day. As soon as she walked outside again, the heat was just going to coat her skin and frizz up her hair. Mel had long, honey-blonde corkscrew curls that were a royal pain in the ass to maintain.

But Bennett Hart was going to be at Slim Willie's, and even if it was just for five minutes, Mel wanted to look halfway decent. She might've had a small crush on the guy. *Small* meaning that whenever he was around she went all warm and gooey and felt like a freaking sixteen-year-old again.

But really, how could she not? He was gorgeous, all six feet and however many inches of him. And he had muscles everywhere. Toned arms and legs and abs of wonder. And don't even get her started on his eyes. They were some sort of icy gray-blue that sucked her in. He had dark blond hair that he kept cut close to his skull. He hadn't let it grow out when he'd gotten out of the military. But he had gotten a little more lax with shaving, and he now had perpetual five o'clock shadow on his square jaw. Mel had always been a sucker for a scruffy man.

Not to mention he'd been there the night Mel had been shot. But she'd liked him long before that fateful night at the spa. Him saving her life hadn't started those feelings.

When the 911 call had gone through to dispatch, the closest deputy to the scene had been ten minutes away, so the deputy had called Jax. He had been hanging out with Bennett that night, and both of them had rushed over to Rejuvenate.

Mel had never been more terrified in her entire life. The pain had been unbelievable, and she'd been on the brink of passing out when Bennett had showed up. He'd been so calm as he talked her past the panic. His voice had been the only thing that had grounded her.

Bennett had stayed at the hospital all through her surgery and waited to see her after. He'd also been around for the last couple of weeks, checking up on her recovery often and going to more than one of her physical therapy sessions with her. He'd dealt with his own recovery a couple of years ago after he'd survived being shot in Afghanistan. He'd been more than aware of what was going on with Mel, and he'd helped her out in more ways than one.

He'd given her something to watch during her recovery time, too. He'd gotten her hooked on *Lost*, and he'd spent more than one night sitting on her couch with her and watching episodes. And then Bennett just had to go and do something that made her like him even more. He was going to volunteer at the school, working with Mel and her students.

For the last year, Mel had wanted to do a hands-on project with her students to show them how math could be used to build things. The former superintendent, Keith Reynolds, hadn't given Mel or her project the time of day. But after more than one scandal had hit the Reynolds family, Keith had tendered his resignation over the summer.

As it turned out, Keith Reynolds was Grace's father. This little tidbit of information had been revealed in a very public way, at a dinner honoring the superintendent. Over the years, Grace and her older brother, Brendan, had been the center of more than a little bit of gossip in Mirabelle. The mystery of Grace's father had been a big part of it. It had also been a pretty big blow to the Reynolds family when it was discovered that their son, Hoyt, had been involved in all of those burglaries that had plagued Mirabelle.

So there was a new superintendent now. It had been only two months, but Fred Stafford was leaps and bounds better than his predecessor. The library at the high school was in desperate need of some new bookshelves, and Mel wanted to build them. She'd presented the proposal to Stafford, complete with costs and how she planned to raise the money. He'd approved it right away, thinking it was a fantastic idea.

Bennett had helped Mel with that proposal, and Bennett would help her out with the project. He was going to be at the school often, working with her and the students on a regular basis. For free.

But Mel had to keep telling herself that this didn't mean anything. This didn't mean he had feelings for her. No, he was just her friend. And so what if she had a *little* crush on him? Okay, so it was a *massive* crush.

Mel put the groceries away before she went into the bathroom and promptly stripped down. She hesitated in front of the mirror before she walked to the shower, her amber eyes dipping down to the scars on her right shoulder. One, the size of a dime, was where the bullet had gone in; the three around it, all surgical scars, were about the size of pencil erasers.

She reached up and touched the bullet wound, her fingers tracing around the small pucker on her skin. Even if her arm healed completely, the scar would always be there to remind her of that awful night.

Mel dropped her hand and got in the shower. The hot water poured over her, and as she stretched her arms up to wash her hair, the tight pain in her right arm made her wince. It might still hurt, but it felt loads better than it had.

When she got out of the shower she grabbed her blow dryer. Wrapped in her towel, she methodically dried her hair, doing her best to shape the curls into a manageable style. She put on a light coat of makeup, then went into her bedroom.

Mel stood in front of her opened closet, staring at her clothes and trying to figure out what she was going to wear. The winning combination was a flowing, knee-length, green cotton skirt and a white V-neck shirt. After she was dressed, she went into the kitchen to uncork a bottle of wine. If the girls were going to talk, they were going to be drinking as well. That was just how it was.

She grabbed three glasses from the cabinet, the corkscrew from the drawer, and the wine from the fridge. The kitchen had a view of the front yard, and as Mel finished pouring the wine she saw Harper's car pull up. Grace got out of the passenger side, and the two girls made their way up the front porch.

There'd never really been a chance for the three friends to share clothes growing up—or even now, for that matter. Grace came in at a whopping five foot four. She had light blonde hair and a heart-shaped face that framed her blue eyes and pouty lips. She was tiny, with an A-cup bust and a slim waist, though she did have a fairly round butt that she was proud of and that Jax was pretty fond of. She wore tight jeans that accentuated said rear and a cute, little hot pink tank top that only she could pull off. Said tank top would've looked more than somewhat scandalous on Mel and just downright indecent on Harper.

Harper had been a little overweight when she'd first come to Mirabelle, and most of the boys in school hadn't been very nice about it. But it had taken her only a few years to grow into her body. Now she was all curves. Men had absolutely nothing negative to say about how her D-cup breasts filled out a shirt or anything else. She was currently wearing a formfitting, light blue dress that made her violet eyes pop, and it looked incredible with her long black hair. Yeah, Harper didn't have any issues catching a man's eyes these days. Problem was, no one was catching her eye.

Both Mel and Harper were five foot seven, but that was where all the similarities stopped. Where Grace had most of her curves below the waist, Mel's were above. She had a decent C cup, no real butt to speak of, and thin legs. But at least she had good thighs and calves, so she didn't have a lot of complaints.

Mel put the bottle of wine on the counter and went to open the front door.

"Oh, no," Harper said as soon as she saw Mel. "Oh, no, no, no. You get your skinny ass in that room of yours and change."

"What's wrong with this?" Mel asked, looking down at herself.

"It's flirty. You don't want flirty. You want *sexy*." Harper grabbed Mel's hand and pulled her down the hallway.

"Yeah, you need to show off those legs of yours," Grace said as she shut the door and followed them.

"That's what's going to help you in your man-catching endeavors," Harper added.

"What man-catching endeavors?" Mel asked, coming to a sudden stop.

"Bennett," Grace coughed.

"Excuse me?" Mel, rounded on Grace.

"Oh don't even deny it," Harper said as she dragged Mel into the bedroom. "You *sooo* want to have that man's babies."

"Oh. My. Gosh. It isn't anything like that," Mel said a little bit too loud.

"Whatever you say. Now take off that skirt." Harper let go of Mel's hand and looked at her.

"You're being ridiculous. My skirt is fine."

"You don't want fine, you want *fine*." Except Harper pronounced it *fwine*. "And you wouldn't be this resistant if Bennett were asking you to take off your skirt."

Yeah, if Bennett were asking her to take off her skirt, she'd be completely naked in three seconds flat.

"Strip. Now," Harper demanded.

"I'm going to go get something for us to drink," Grace said and left the room.

"The wine's already poured and on the counter," Mel called out after Grace as she pushed her skirt down her thighs.

"Pretty pink panties?" Harper asked, raising an eyebrow.

"Just find me something to wear so you'll shut up."

Harper turned to Mel's closet and started looking through it. "No, no, no," she said as she pushed through the hangers.

Grace came into the room holding three glasses of wine. She handed one to Mel and smirked as she looked at Mel's undies. "Wow, those are nice. Were you planning on someone seeing those tonight?"

"Are the two of you quite finished?" Mel asked before taking a sip of her wine.

"We're never finished." Grace handed Harper a glass of wine and then sat on the bed.

"I see that teddy bear he got you is still on your bed," Harper said, turning to them. She took a drink of wine.

Okay, so Bennett might've brought Mel said bear when

she was in the hospital. And it was possible that she'd slept with it every night since. It was just because it was soft and cuddly and...

Yeah, she was pathetic.

"Look, it's just a silly crush, so let's not make anything of it, okay? We're just friends. Nothing's going to happen and I'll get over it."

"Uh-huh." Harper raised an eyebrow. "Just friends," she said slowly. "A friend who is helping you out with this little project at your school?"

"And by *little*, you mean this *huge* and quite extensive project. A project that is going to take months and lots of his time," Grace clarified.

"He doesn't have feelings for me." Mel was getting just a little bit exasperated. These two were like a freaking dog with a bone.

"How do you know? Have you asked him?" Grace asked.

"No, and I'm not going to. And neither are the two of you," Mel said pointedly, staring at her two friends.

"Who?" Harper tried to look mildly offended.

"Us?" Grace asked innocently.

"We would never." Harper turned back to the closet and resumed her hunt.

"What about her jean miniskirt?" Grace asked.

"Ohhh, that would look really good with this orange tank top or this green V-neck with the stripes. Take your shirt off, too," Harper demanded without even turning around.

"I'm going to need more wine." Mel took a fairly large gulp before she put her glass down and did as Harper ordered.

* * *

Bennett Hart had been back in Mirabelle for just over two years now. He moved back when he'd gotten out of the air force. He'd enlisted when he was eighteen and spent eight years in the service before he'd been shot down in Afghanistan. There'd been ten soldiers in the helicopter that day; only Bennett and his commanding officer had survived, and both of them had barely escaped with their lives.

Bennett had been shot in the shoulder, but the bullet that had ripped apart his body was nothing. He'd had his life ripped apart that day.

He knew just how lucky he was to be alive, but that didn't stop the survivor's guilt. How could it? He'd watched as his best friends, his brothers, had died, and there'd been absolutely nothing he could have done to save them.

He was still plagued by the nightmares and panic attacks. He'd wake up in a cold sweat, screaming as he fought with his pillows and sheets like they were the demons that had taken his friends. That day would haunt him for the rest of his life.

These days Bennett took things easy. Well, easier. There were a certain number of hazards that came with working in construction, but he wasn't being targeted on a daily basis. He'd picked up a thing or two in the military, and building schools and hospitals had stuck with him. Now he mainly worked on remodels with businesses and houses.

He was actually branching off a bit lately, doing more specialty jobs for his boss, Marlin Yance. There was a surprising demand for custom woodwork out at the beach houses, so Bennett had been pretty busy with those. He'd also been working on a few of his own creations.

Bennett had started restoring antiques and building his own pieces of furniture. So far it had mostly been for friends and family. He'd made quite a few things for Jax and Grace's new house, and he had a few customers here and there.

For Bennett, it was more than just a job. He liked working with his hands, liked creating things. It gave him a peace he'd been missing for quite sometime. Another thing that was giving him peace was being back in Mirabelle. It was good for him to live close to his dad and stepmom.

Bennett's parents had divorced when he was four. Bennett's mother, Kristi, had run off to Arkansas with a man with whom she'd had an affair for years. Now they were married with three children. Kristi sent a card every year on Bennett's birthday, which he never opened. Besides that, he'd had absolutely no contact with her.

Bennett's father, Walker, had remarried when Bennett was six. Jocelyn had been the one who packed Bennett's lunches when he was in school, taught him how to cook, and sat next to his father at all of his baseball games and his graduation. She'd always been much more than a stepmother to him; for all intents and purposes she was his mother.

Bennett had also fallen back in with a good group of guys whom he'd gone to high school with. Brendan King, Jax Anderson, and Nathanial Shepherd had all been a year older than him and they'd all played on the Mirabelle High baseball team together. The three guys had been best friends since preschool, or something like that, but they'd welcomed Bennett into their fold, and through them he'd gotten a whole other family.

It had been hard for Bennett at first, hard for him to let anybody into his life. When he'd first moved back he'd kept himself pretty isolated from everyone except his dad and stepmom. Losing his friends in Afghanistan had nearly destroyed him. It took him a while to realize that the country roads of Mirabelle weren't the same thing as the deserts of the Middle East. Yes, tragedies happened every day, but his friends weren't getting shot at.

Well, except for that one time a couple months ago.

Melanie O'Bryan was a sweet girl. Maybe just a little soft-spoken, but she had a quiet confidence. And she had this sassy sarcastic side to her that came out every once in a while. She'd drop these one-liners that tended to shock the hell out of him.

And damn, did she ever have a killer smile, one that made Bennett never want to turn away from her. She was a high school math teacher, and from what Bennett had heard she had the patience of a saint and was loved by her students. It wasn't that surprising. Mel was just a good person. A *great* person.

When Bennett had walked into that spa all those weeks ago and seen her bleeding out on the ground, it had taken everything in him to stay calm. All he'd been able to think was, *Not her.* But Mel was strong and she'd survived it, and Bennett thanked God for that every time she was around him, which was quite often these days.

Mel had a knack for holding his attention whenever she was in the same room as him. So it came as absolutely no surprise that he zeroed in on her the second she walked up onto the back deck of Slim Willie's.

The restaurant was more of an outdoor establishment with a deck that took up almost double the space as the actual building, which was pretty packed. The wooden tables were crowded with people digging into the food in front of them. The band played on a stage off to the side, and the dance floor already had a good amount of people on it. But even with all the commotion, Bennett only had eyes for one person.

Mel was wearing a skirt that showed off her killer legs and a purple-and-blue tank top that showed just a hint of cleavage. Her hair was down, and her curls framed her pretty face and ran over her shoulders and down her back.

Bennett was so distracted by Mel that he completely missed what Brendan had just said. The two men were standing at the outside bar waiting for a drink.

Brendan King was a mechanic at King's Auto, which he and his grandfather owned. Brendan and his wife, Paige, had just had their little baby boy, Trevor, two and a half months ago, and they were taking advantage of a night out. Paige's mother, Denise, was on babysitting duty.

"Sorry." Bennett cleared his throat and focused on Brendan. "What was that?"

Brendan turned and looked over his shoulder. Bennett let his gaze travel back to Mel. She, Grace, and Harper were joining the table where Jax and Paige sat. Mel looked up as she pulled out a chair, and her eyes locked on Bennett's. Her cheeks flushed a soft pink and she smiled at him. She waved and Bennett couldn't stop himself from smiling and waving back.

"I heard you two were spending a lot of time together lately. And that you'll be spending even more time together when school starts," Brendan said, facing Bennett again. "How's that going?"

"How's what going?" Bennett asked.

"You and Mel."

"There is no me and Mel."

"Oh, really? So you just get smiley for all the pretty girls?"

"I didn't get smiley." Bennett frowned as he looked at Brendan.

"Right."

"We're just friends," Bennett said as he tried to get the attention of one of the bartenders.

The two bartenders were giving a little too much attention to a group of about ten college girls. They were loud, bordering on obnoxious, and they were all processed to within an inch of their lives. Their dark tans were fake—too much time spent in tanning beds. Their makeup was on thick and their clothes were on light. They gave off more than a glimpse of their flat stomachs, and their breasts spilled out of their too-tight shirts.

They did absolutely nothing for Bennett.

His eyes automatically found Mel again. She had a natural, sun-kissed tan and her skin glowed. He wasn't even sure if she wore makeup or not. And he liked the way she dressed. Her clothes gave off just a hint of the sexiness he was sure lay beneath. She was modest, and real. She was beautiful.

"Just friends?" Brendan said skeptically. "Okay, whatever you say."

* * *

"You know he keeps looking at you," Grace whispered in Mel's ear.

"Shut up," Mel said, kicking her under the table. "He is not."

"Yes, he is." Grace pinched Mel's leg.

"Ow, don't pinch me." She rubbed the sore spot on her thigh.

"Then don't kick me."

"What are you two talking about?" Paige asked, leaning across the table.

Jax had gotten Grace's, Mel's, and Harper's drink orders before he'd joined Bennett and Brendan at the bar. So only Mel, Grace, Harper, and Paige sat at the table.

"Bennett," Grace said.

"Mel has a little crush," Harper added.

"What part of 'Shut up' do you not understand?"

The noise from the crowd and the music from the band were loud enough that there wasn't really a chance they would be overheard, but talking about Mel's crush in public made her nervous.

"Don't worry." Paige grinned. "I won't say anything."

Mel loved Paige and did trust her not to say anything. Paige had fit right in with their little group when she'd moved to Mirabelle over two years ago, and she'd quickly become a very close friend. She had long, dark brown hair that fell in messy waves, gray eyes, and freckles across her nose and cheeks. She was tall, and her running habit had kept her legs in amazing form; it had also melted off almost all of her pregnancy weight.

"He's really cute." Paige looked over at the bar for a second before she turned back. "You should totally go for it."

Cute? No. Bennett Hart was sexy as hell in a way that made Mel want to put her mouth all over his body.

Oh dear. I should not *be thinking about that.* "Can we *please* not have this conversation right now?"

"Oh look how red she's getting," Harper said. "She *really* likes him."

Yeah, *that* was why she was blushing, not because she was thinking about how lickable his abs probably were. "I hate you all."

"No, you don't," Grace said. "You love us dearly."

"That's debatable."

"Fine, no more harassing Mel...for now. But we will have this conversation later," Paige said.

"Count on it," Grace said with a grin.

"So school starts next week?" Paige asked.

"Yeah, on Monday. I'm looking forward to the kids being back. Sitting in that empty room all week was making me crazy."

Mel was glad they'd changed subjects, because when she glanced up again, Bennett, Brendan, and Jax were at the table, beers in hand.

"Here you go," Bennett said, sliding a bottle in front of Mel.

"Thanks." She smiled up at him.

"So what's making you crazy?" he asked as he took the seat directly across from her.

Mel didn't miss the matching smirks on Grace's and Harper's faces, but at least they kept their mouths shut.

"The kids not being there. It's too quiet."

"I'll bet. Too much quiet makes me crazy, too. Well, it's not going to be quiet when we're in that wood shop with the saw going."

"I would imagine not," Mel said, shaking her head.

"Jeez, this place is crowded."

Mel looked up to see Nathanial Shepherd and Tripp Black standing at the other end of the table. Nathanial, whom everyone called Shep, worked at his family's bar, the Sleepy Sheep. He was tall with thick, shaggy black hair and piercing blue eyes. His jaw was covered in what could only be described as ten o'clock shadow, and his arms were covered in tattoos. He had the whole bad-boy image down to a tee.

Tripp Black had moved to Mirabelle over a year ago when he became the fire chief. He had dark brown eyes and thick brown hair. He was also a man of the perpetual scruff.

"Yeah, good luck getting a drink unless you're going to flash something. But I feel like your legs could get you fast service." Brendan looked at Shep.

"Aww, come on, Brendan," Shep said. "You know you're the pretty boy around here."

"Who are you calling a pretty boy?" Brendan asked before he took a pull on his beer.

"You. You going to do something about it?"

"Nah," Brendan shook his head. "Because we both know the truth."

"That Jax is the prettiest of us all?"

"Exactly," Brendan nodded.

Mel wouldn't exactly say that any of the men around her could be termed pretty. *Hot* was a better word. Hot and incredibly built. Yeah, all of them were ridiculously good-looking, but none of them had ever inspired the feelings in Mel that Bennett had.

"I'm not even going to comment," Jax said, shaking his head, as he put his arm around Grace and pulled her close to him.

"That's because you have a maturity level higher than these two put together," Paige said, pointing to Shep and Brendan.

"I have no idea what you're talking about." Brendan pulled Paige in and gave her a loud, smacking kiss on the temple.

"We should start heading up for dinner." Grace indicated the ever-growing line behind them and turned to Paige, Brendan, and Bennett. "You guys should start. You too, Mel," she added with a wink.

Mel really wanted to glare at Grace, but chose not to draw attention to the not-so-subtle grouping. Instead, she got up from the table and followed behind Brendan and Paige, and Bennett fell in step by her side. She tried not to think about how that made her heart flutter a little bit.

It cost twenty five dollars to get into the crawfish boil, but the food was all you could eat, the live band was sure to provide hours of entertainment, and a lot of people had thought the price was worth it. The place was packed, and the line for food was already pretty deep when the four of them got to the end of it.

"So when do you guys start the project?" Brendan asked Mel and Bennett.

"The second week of school," Mel told him.

"So you raised enough money?" Paige asked.

"To build the first ten bookcases," Mel said.

Shep had been so kind as to let them do a karaoke night at the bar on Tuesday nights. There was a cover charge to get in, and there was a jar behind the counter for those who wanted to be a little more generous. People tended to get very generous when they were drinking.

They'd also had two movie nights out at the big barn, using a projector to show classics on the side of the building. A lot of people had come out for it, spreading their blankets out on the grass. Mel had even borrowed a popcorn machine, and they hadn't been able to make enough for everyone who wanted to buy it.

There were going to be some other fund-raisers in the weeks to come, so they still had time to get the rest of the money.

Brendan grinned at Bennett. "You ready for all of those teenagers and their hormones?"

"Really?" Paige asked looking at her husband. "You think you're any better than a sixteen-year-old?"

"I have no idea what you're talking about."

"Mmm-hmm." Paige shook her head at him.

"I'll be fine. I'm more concerned about them using the power tools," Bennett said, as the line shifted and they all moved up.

"You think I'd let any of my students lose a limb?" Mel asked.

"Well, I was concerned about *your* limbs, too," Bennett said with a smile.

Holy cow, was that man's smile lethal. Mel was pretty sure if she were using heavy machinery when he was around she'd probably lose those limbs he was so worried about.

But no pain no gain, right?

"I'm sure you were," Brendan said, looking at Bennett with what could only be described as an amused *I told you so* look.

And Mel *really* wanted to know what that was all about.

Chapter Two

Just Friends

Okay, so maybe Bennett had been full of shit when he'd told Brendan that he and Mel were just friends. Maybe he did think Mel was beautiful, and that her laugh was amazing, and that she had the warmest whiskey-brown eyes he'd ever seen. And maybe it was also true he did want to spend more time with her—a lot more time with her.

When Mel had first asked him to help with the project, she'd only wanted advice on planning it, but he'd quickly realized she was going to need someone to help out during the actual process. He might've agreed to help out a bit too eagerly.

But there was more behind it than just Mel. Mrs. Sylvester had been the librarian when Bennett had been in high school, and she was still the librarian now.

Bennett had always loved to read books. It was something that Jocelyn had passed on to him. He'd spent many an hour in that library. He felt like he owed something to the place, and he definitely owed something to Mrs. Sylvester. She was one of the kindest women who ever existed, and that library was her second home.

Mrs. Sylvester had always made suggestions to him on

what to read. She'd gotten him into murder mysteries and military crime, and told him which of the classics were up his alley. And she'd always been right. When he'd been overseas he'd filled his downtime with books, most of which had been sent to him by her. Those books had kept him from going crazy. And he wanted to do something to pay her back for what she'd done for him.

Yeah, he was looking forward to this project for many reasons. But if he was honest with himself, Mel was at the top of that list.

Not that this changed the fact that he just wasn't looking for a relationship. He'd come back to Mirabelle wanting a quiet, uncomplicated life. As he looked at the pretty, curly-haired woman sitting across from him, he had a feeling she would be a *big* complication in his life. She'd have to be—all women were.

He knew he should be smarter about this whole thing. Maybe put a little distance between the two of them.

But he really didn't like that thought.

Yeah, distance just wasn't going to happen. He'd spent all of dinner talking to her, watching her mouth move while she talked. She had a pretty mouth, soft and sweet. Her lower lip was slightly fuller than her top, and she was wearing some sort of gloss, and he was more than slightly curious as to what the flavor was.

"You want to dance?" he asked her, as half of their friends left the table to do precisely that. The band was playing country music, and the current song was one that Bennett had heard on the radio. It was fast, and the couples out on the floor were keeping up with the pace.

"Yeah," she said, smiling.

"Well then, let's go," he said, standing up.

He rounded the table and held out his hand for hers. She placed her soft, warm palm in his as she stood. He wrapped his fingers around her hand, held her close to his side, and guided her through the crowd.

When they got to the dance floor he spun her around and pulled her into him. He placed his free hand on her hip, while hers landed on his biceps just below where his T-shirt ended. Her fingers curled around the back of his arm. As they moved around the floor, he couldn't help but think about how her hand felt on his bare skin, and he wondered what it would feel like in other places.

The band started playing another fast tune and Mel smiled up at him, laughing as he spun her around. At the end of the song he dipped her backward and she stretched her head back, her hair falling toward the floor and exposing her neck. It took everything in him not to bury his face in that sweet spot just below her ear.

The band switched to a slow song, and Bennett looked at Mel, raising his eyebrows. She nodded, and he pulled her in closer. His hand drifted to the middle of her back as she leaned against him.

She was much smaller than him, maybe a hundred pounds lighter and half a foot shorter. The top of her head came in just under his nose. He'd resisted pressing his face into her throat, but only a stronger man than him could've stopped himself from pressing his nose into her hair. It smelled flowery; he was pretty sure it was jasmine.

When the song ended she pulled back and smiled up at him, her cheeks a little rosy.

"You want to get another drink?" he asked her.

She nodded, so he held tight to her hand as he led her to the bar. The group of half-naked girls was on the dance floor, so the bartenders were free from flirting it up with them. Bennett held up two fingers and pointed to the farthest bottle on the stand behind the bar. The guy nodded and pulled out two bottles from a massive bucket filled with ice.

Bennett pulled out some cash but Mel put her hand over his.

"I can get it."

"I don't think so," he said, shaking his head.

"Who bought my drink earlier?" she asked, raising her eyebrows.

"I don't know. We just paid for them."

"But you bought more than one."

"Yes, but that isn't the point."

"And what is the point?"

"That I asked if you wanted to get a drink and I'm not letting you pay for this." He pulled his hand out from under hers and handed the bartender the cash.

"Fine, but I owe you a drink."

"Fine." He grabbed both bottles and handed her one. "The next one's on you," he said, clinking the neck against hers.

They brought the bottles to their mouths and drank.

"Wow, that tastes good," she said, putting her bottle on the bar. She reached back and gathered her hair, then twisted it up to let the air get to the back of her neck. "It's so hot out here."

"You can't handle the heat?"

"No, I can. But my hair can't. I'm sure it's a mess," she said as she let go of her hair. It fell down, her curls expanding as they stretched down her shoulders.

"Nah." He shook his head and reached out. He wound one of her curls around his finger. "It's still beautiful."

Bennett might've had a small fascination with Mel's hair, *small* meaning that whenever she was around he had the urge to plunge his fingers in it and bring her mouth to his. He wanted to touch way more than that one soft strand but he pulled his hand back, letting the curl bounce up around her temple.

Her eyes warmed and her mouth curved up into a small smile. "Thank you," she said softly.

"You up for a few more dances?"

"Absolutely." She nodded then grabbed her beer and took another long drink.

"We'll finish these, and then I'm taking you back out there."

Bennett wanted her in his arms again, and he was pretty tempted to chug the damn beer to make that happen a little bit sooner than later.

* * *

Bennett didn't leave Mel's side for the next couple of hours, and she had absolutely no complaints about it. Whether they were dancing, walking through the crowd, or just standing around talking, his hand had a habit of finding its way to the small of her back. This was something else she had absolutely no problem with. She liked the steady weight of his palm on her, liked how he stood by her side and guided her around, liked that he touched her.

"You and Bennett look pretty cozy tonight," Harper whispered in Mel's ear as they headed toward the bathroom.

"We're just dancing."

"Uh-huh." Harper folded her arms across her chest and eyed Mel skeptically.

"Look," Mel whispered as they got in line. "I like him, all right. And I've liked him for a while now. But I'm just trying not to look too much into it, at least not until he makes a move."

"He's been making a move all night."

"By dancing? Well, if that's the case, then you and Shep are on the brink of a relationship yourselves."

"Me and Shep? I don't think so," Harper said, shaking her head. "You know I love the man dearly, and I'd be blind if I said he wasn't attractive, but Nathanial Shepherd is like a brother to me. Always has been, always will be. Besides, Grace told me he's still in love with Hannah."

"I've always thought that," Mel said, trying to get Harper onto a new topic of conversation.

Hannah Sterling had spent a summer in Mirabelle almost thirteen years ago, then left and had never come back. Mel had known Shep all her life and seen him with a fair share of women. And even though Mel had been only twelve at the time, she hadn't been oblivious to the way Shep had looked at Hannah. Nor had she missed the fact that he'd never looked at any other woman the same way since.

"Yeah, me too, but don't think I'm going to let you change the subject. You and Bennett have been doing way more than dancing. And that boy hasn't had eyes for any other woman tonight. It's just you."

"Harper," Mel pleaded. She really didn't want to turn this into something that it wasn't. She had a crush on him...and as far as she knew that was it. That was all there was, just her insignificant schoolgirl crush.

"I'm serious, Mel. You can bury your head in the sand all you want, but Bennett Hart is totally into you."

"Whatever you say," Mel said, trying not to think about the little flutter in her stomach.

But that feeling just couldn't be ignored, and if it was possible it intensified over the next ten minutes as they waited in line and finally used the restroom.

* * *

"Soooo," Shep said, coming up next to Bennett at the bar. "Are you going to deny there's anything going on with you and Mel? 'Cause Brendan said you claim to being only friends."

Bennett groaned internally. He just couldn't get a break

from these guys, could he? "When the hell did you have time to discuss that?"

"When you and Mel were out on the floor dancing a tad too close for *just friends*."

"You guys gossip like a bunch of old women," Bennett said, shaking his head.

"Yeah, we do," he said, placing his hand on Bennett's shoulder. "So here's the deal. Brendan, Jax, and I watched Mel grow up right alongside our little Gracie. And like Grace, we look at Mel as our little sister. Well, when I say *we*, I just mean *me*, in regards to Grace being *like* a sister. Obviously she is Brendan's *actual* little sister," Shep rambled on. "And as for Jax, he apparently didn't have brotherly feelings for Grace. But you get what I mean "

"Not really," Bennett said.

"You're a good guy, and really it would be great to see the two of you together, but don't hurt Mel," Shep said seriously.

"I don't know where this is going." Bennett started to feel more than a little uneasy. He didn't know if it was going anywhere at all. Yes, he was interested in Mel, but that didn't make them a couple. He wasn't even sure if he wanted that. Truth be told, he had no idea what he wanted.

"Just be careful." Shep removed his hand from Bennett's shoulder and took a step back. "Now I'm off to get a drink."

"Good luck," Bennett said. He started to make his way back through the crowd, his mind a bit of a jumble.

How the hell had everything snowballed so quickly?

Bennett had gone out tonight only to have a fun time with his friends. He'd only wanted to have some food, a couple of drinks, good conversation. He hadn't intended to focus all his attention on Mel. So what if that was what had happened? It didn't mean anything. He was just doing what felt good, what felt right. And at the moment that was being around Mel.

He wasn't doing anything wrong: just dancing with her, and maybe flirting a little bit, and enjoying the feel of her body under his hands. Where was the harm in that? He was an adult, and so was she. They were both capable of making rational decisions and not letting everything complicate matters.

Shep didn't need to be worried about it. It wasn't anything serious. It was . . . well, he had no idea *what* it was, and he didn't need to be worried about that, either.

* * *

When Bennett came back up to the table he slid another beer in front of Mel. She looked up at him, and he smiled back at her.

You're just friends, she reminded herself.

Harper didn't know what she was talking about. Bennett wasn't interested in Mel beyond friendship. So he'd danced with her and bought her a couple of drinks. That didn't mean anything.

"Thanks," she said as she grabbed the beer. "I thought *I* was getting the next round."

He just shrugged as he sat down. "Now I owe you two drinks."

"So you do. We'll just have to figure out how you can pay back your debts." He smiled as he lifted his beer to his mouth. "I think more dancing might be in order."

When they both finished their beers, Bennett and Mel returned to the floor. She wasn't sure how many songs they stayed out there for, but when they got back to the table, Brendan and Paige were getting ready to go.

"We're going to call it a night. Denise has Trevor all night, so we're going to take advantage of an empty house," he said with a grin.

"Brendan." Paige blushed as she smacked his chest. "Can you not announce stuff like that?"

"Stuff like what?" he asked innocently. "I meant we're going to get a full night's sleep without a crying baby. What did you think I was talking about? Sex?" He shook his head and tried to look shocked. "Your mind is always in the gutter."

"Shut up," she said, smacking him again. "That wasn't what you meant and you know it."

"I do," he said, grabbing her hand. "So let's go and take advantage of every second. Bye, everyone." He waved as he pulled Paige away from the table.

"Bye." Paige laughed and got in a quick wave before Brendan practically dragged her away through the crowd.

"Harper left, too," Grace said, as she and Jax got up. "She has an early appointment tomorrow."

"Oh." Mel looked down at her watch to check the time. Jeez, it was past midnight. "Well, can you guys give me a ride home?" she asked, looking at Grace and Jax.

"I can take you," Bennett said before either of them had time to respond.

"Are you sure?" Mel asked, turning to Bennett.

"Absolutely."

* * *

"So how far are you with *Lost*?" Bennett asked as he drove toward Mel's house.

"Um, well, I might've marathon-watched it last weekend, and I watched a lot during the nights this week. That show's addictive."

"It is," he agreed. He kept his eyes on the road as she shifted in her seat. He might not have looked at her, but he knew her eyes were on him, studying the side of his face before she told him what she was thinking.

"I only have two episodes left."

"Really?" He laughed.

"Hey, what do you expect? Every single episode ends at a cliffhanger. And they just keep killing everyone off. It's too much to handle most of the time."

"It's true," he said, nodding. "Well, if you can't handle it, maybe I should watch those last two episodes with you. What are you doing tomorrow night?"

"I don't have any plans," she told him. Bennett knew she was smiling—he could hear it in her voice.

"You want to come over to my house? I can make you dinner." They might've been hanging out a lot lately, but because she'd been recovering, he'd always gone over to her house. So this would be a change, especially if he cooked for her. They'd always gotten takeout before.

"You cook?" she asked.

"Yes, I cook. I'm a little domesticated. I do my own laundry and make the bed, too. I even put the toilet seat down."

"Well, aren't you impressive?"

"I like to think so," he said, as he parked his truck in her driveway.

"Hmmm, it'll be interesting to see what else you do," she said.

"Then it's a date?" He shifted in his seat so he could look at her.

She nodded slowly. "It's a date." Even though it was fairly dark in the cab, Bennett could see something change on her face. "And I'll bring wine, since you were so insistent on not letting me buy drinks tonight."

"I think I can handle that." He really wanted to lean across the seat and press his mouth to hers, but instead he unbuckled his seat belt. Mel mirrored his actions, and as she turned for the door he grabbed her hand. "Wait there," he said before he got out.

Bennett rounded the truck and opened her door. She

turned and slid to the edge of the seat; he put his hands on her hips and lowered her to the ground.

"Thank you."

"It's no problem." He shut the door and grabbed her hand. "A man's always supposed to open a door for a lady," he said as he turned and started to walk.

"Is this another part of you being domesticated?" she asked.

"Sure is."

"Your mother taught you well."

"She sure did."

He took her keys out of her hands when they got to the front porch. He unlocked the door and Mel went inside, finding the switch and flipping it.

"Well, Ms. Melanie O'Bryan," he said, handing her the keys. "As always, I had a lovely evening with you. So I'll see you at my house tomorrow. Six o'clock sound good?"

"I'll be there."

"Good night, Ms. O'Bryan," he said, pulling away from her.

"'Night, Bennett." Mel smiled and took a step back into the house.

Chapter Three

A Date? Or Not a Date?
That Is the Question

Friends. They were just friends.

It didn't matter how many times Mel repeated that to herself, she kept coming back to the fact that Bennett had called tonight a date. Those words had most definitely come out of his mouth.

Which was why Mel might've started getting ready at around three. She took meticulous time with her hair, and her curls were in an almost complete state of antifrizz. Her makeup was perfect. And she spent a good amount of time picking out her clothes.

Harper and Grace had told her to stay away from safe and flirty. They said she needed to play to her strengths, so she had. She chose a pair of bright blue shorts that showed off her legs, and a sleeveless black blouse that gave just a glimpse of cleavage. She was wearing leopard-print sandals with straps that wrapped around her ankles, and she'd given herself a pedicure, complete with pretty pink toes.

Not that any of this mattered, because it wasn't a date.

Mel had to stop doing this to herself. Had to stop thinking this was something. She hadn't even told Grace and

Harper about it, because they would've just filled her head with ideas. Ideas she desperately didn't need to think about.

Mel had never been the type of girl to inspire lust in a man. She wasn't sexy by any stretch of the word. She was a high school math teacher, for goodness' sake. What was sexy about that?

Nothing.

Mel had only had a handful of boyfriends in high school, and they hadn't been anything serious. She'd only ever had sex with one man. Justin Abrahams had been her college boyfriend. He'd been a year older than her, and they'd been together during her sophomore and junior years. He'd gotten a job in Birmingham when he'd graduated from the Florida State University Business School, and they'd decided to end things.

Mel had always known she wanted to move back to Mirabelle when she graduated, and Justin wasn't cut out for small-town life. It hadn't ended badly, and they were actually still friends. But she wasn't pining over him by any means. She just hadn't found someone she wanted to be in a relationship with.

Or she hadn't until a certain military man had come back to town.

Mel stopped by LauraAnne's Liquors on her way to Bennett's. She walked inside and headed straight to the refrigerated section. She looked through the glass doors and tried to figure out which kind of wine to buy. She had no idea what Bennett liked.

"Melanie O'Bryan. Look. At. You."

Shit, Mel thought as she closed her eyes. She opened them and slowly turned around. Harper was standing there, her arms folded under her ample chest. She looked Mel up and down and shook her head.

"You got plans tonight?" Harper asked.

Mel sucked at lying. She just couldn't do it. She wore her emotions plain as day on her face. Always had, and most likely always would.

"Why would you think that?"

"Because you're looking pretty freaking hot. I don't think I've seen those legs make this much of an appearance in, well, I don't know how long."

"They're just shorts," Mel said, looking down at herself. *Crap*, was she that obvious?

"Oh stop second-guessing yourself."

"I'm not second-guessing myself," Mel said, looking back up.

"Riiight. So what are you doing tonight?" Harper asked with a more-than-knowing smile.

"I'm having dinner with Bennett."

"A date!" Harper said excitedly, drumming her fingers together.

"It's not a date," Mel said seriously.

"If it walks like a date, quacks like a date, and drinks wine like a date, then it's a date."

"He's making me dinner and we're watching a TV show. That's it. It's nothing that we haven't done before."

"He's made you dinner before?" Harper asked, raising her eyebrow.

"Well, no. We just got a pizza or whatever before."

"Hmmm. I'd say making dinner for you is a pretty serious thing."

"And I would disagree with you."

"All right, but expect a big, fat 'I told you so' when you're wrong."

"Whatever you say, Harper. Now help me pick something out." Mel turned back to the wine.

* * *

Mel pulled up in front of Bennett's house just before six. She took a deep breath, grabbed the bottle of Chardonnay that Harper helped her decide on, and got out of the car.

Bennett lived in a town house on the northwest side of Mirabelle. There were about twenty of them in the small neighborhood. Like Mel's little house, these were far enough away from the water, so they hadn't been built on stilts. Mirabelle got its fair share of hurricanes. If any of the buildings by the water weren't built off the ground, they were pretty much guaranteed to flood when one blew through.

Bennett's slate-gray truck was parked in the driveway. Mel was a Southern girl through and through, and there was just something about a guy in a truck that drove her crazy. And Bennett in a truck? Yeah, there were absolutely no words.

Mel walked up to the front door and knocked. When he opened it a minute later she was struck dumb for just a second. He was wearing a button-up white shirt with the sleeves rolled up, and khaki shorts that showed off his toned, tanned calves. His feet were bare.

Why did she find his lack of shoes so freaking sexy? Why?

"Hi," she said, giving him a nervous smile.

"Hey." He beamed at her.

He was beaming? Right?

He pulled the door open wider and stepped back so she could come inside. The smell of garlic and oregano hit her nose, and she inhaled deeply.

"Something smells good," she said, turning to him.

"That would be baked cheese ravioli and chicken parmesan."

"That would've probably paired better with a red wine, but red wine gives me migraines, so I brought Chardonnay," she rambled.

"Chardonnay will work great." He took the bottle from her, then put his hand at the small of her back and led her through the hallway.

God, she loved it when he had his hands on her.

There was no clutter in the living room, and the walls were all painted white. The curtains on the windows were a simple green, and the carpet was a light brown. He had a huge black leather couch and a coffee table that looked like a steamer trunk. His TV was mounted to the wall, and a stereo system sat underneath it. That was pretty much it.

"You hungry?" he asked, dropping his hand from her back and going into the kitchen.

"Starving." She nodded.

Mel hadn't realized how hungry she was until she'd smelled what he was cooking. She hadn't really eaten that much all day; she'd been too nervous. Not that any of that nervousness had gone away. Nope. It was still all right there, fluttering around in her stomach.

The dining room was just an alcove off the kitchen, with a table that sat four. It just about fit into the small space. The table was set with plates, silverware, and two folded cloth napkins. A bowl of salad and another of garlic bread were in the center.

So he knew how to set a table. One more thing to add to the list of his domesticatedness.

"Do you need any help?" she asked, standing in the kitchen doorway. The kitchen was small, with barely any counter space around the appliances.

How did such a big man live in such a tiny space?

"Nope. It's all ready." He pulled two casserole dishes out of the oven and set them on the table. "So," he said as he opened a drawer and grabbed a corkscrew. "What did you do today?"

Besides obsess about tonight? Not much. "Got ready

for school on Monday, ran a few errands, cleaned. It was a thrilling day."

"Sounds it." He poured them each a glass of wine and put the bottle in the fridge.

"You?"

He handed her one of the wineglasses. "A lot of the same. I had to go to the store to get what I needed for tonight. And I cleaned up a little."

"So you can clean, too?"

"Yes, I clean. You keeping a tally or something?"

"Maybe," she said as she walked over to the table.

"Well, you can add this to it as well." He put down his wineglass before he pulled out her chair.

"I guess I can."

He helped her sit, and when her bottom was firmly in the chair he leaned over and put his mouth *very* close to her ear.

"So what number am I at?" he whispered.

"Umm," she said as her mind promptly went blank. "Five?"

He just laughed, his breath tickling her skin. He straightened, moved to his side of the table, and sat down. Mel was still trying to find her tongue as Bennett proceeded to load her plate with food.

Find something to say. Find something to say. Anything. Say. Anything.

"I thought you said you read a lot of books," Mel said, looking at his living room.

"I do."

"Where are they? You don't have any bookcases." She unfolded her napkin and put it across her lap.

"I haven't made the ones I want for myself yet. Right now my books are in boxes in a closet."

"You hide your books?" Mel asked in a mock-horrified tone, putting her hand to her heart. "That's an offense." She grabbed her silverware and started to cut into her chicken.

"I know, I know," he laughed. "This place is only temporary, though, so I haven't really settled in."

Mel took a bite of her chicken. It was moist and cheesy and just perfect. "Oh my gosh," she said after she swallowed. "This is amazing."

"Thank you." He looked pleased as he took a bite of ravioli. "Is that number six?"

"No." She shook her head as she reached for her wine. "Cooking was number one. That was the first thing you said you could do. You just proved you could do it."

Something flashed in his eyes, and if Mel wasn't mistaken—and she was sure she was—it looked like he wanted to prove some of his other skills to her. But she had a feeling that those skills wouldn't prove he was domesticated. Quite the opposite, in fact.

"So this place is temporary?" she asked, taking another healthy sip of wine. "Haven't you lived here for two years?"

"Yeah, I have. But it's not where I'm staying. It's too small. I want to buy a house soon. I just haven't found the perfect one yet. But it works for now. The garage is convenient, and I'm able to use it to work on pieces here as opposed to having to find some other space."

"I saw everything you made for Jax and Grace. It's all incredible." She took a bite of the ravioli. It had sun-dried tomatoes and basil in the sauce, and it was pretty freaking amazing.

"Thanks," he said.

"Did you make anything here?"

"That steamer trunk in the living room."

Mel looked over at it. Even from twenty feet away she could see his attention to detail. The hardware was antique, and the dark mahogany wood had been treated. It looked as if it had survived generations but at the same time it had been cared for.

"Wow," she said, turning back to him. "Did you restore it or build it?"

"I built it."

"I'm impressed. But then again, I normally am when it comes to your creations."

"Thank you," he said again. But this time he didn't look pleased so much as humbled.

God, she liked him more and more. This was going to be a problem. Who the hell was she kidding? It was already a problem. A massive one.

* * *

Eating dinner while sitting across from Mel was so much better than Bennett had imagined. She'd been a little nervous when she'd first gotten to his house, but she was fine now. They kept up the conversation with each other, and there weren't any of those awkward pauses where neither knew what to say. She told him what it had been like teaching the last two years. How much she loved what she did.

She had a lot of passion for her students, passion for life.

"So what about you?" she asked, as she put her napkin next to her empty plate. "Did those years in the military help train you to be a proper Southern gentleman? Or was it all your mother?"

Bennett couldn't help but grin. His stepmother had trained him long before he'd joined the military.

Jocelyn was a short woman, about five foot four, with red hair and bright blue eyes. She'd been taller than Bennett until he was about twelve, and then he shot up right past her. But it didn't matter that he was bigger than her; he'd always listened to her, not only because she was his mother in every sense of the word and that was what a good Southern boy did, but because what she said went. Always had, always would.

Even Bennett's father listened to her. But Walker was pretty easygoing, so he and Jocelyn worked well together. She wasn't overbearing or anything; she let Walker do his thing, and she did her thing, but nobody was going to take advantage of her. Ever.

Bennett had definitely gotten his temperament from his father. Well, at least he assumed he had. He hadn't spent enough time with his birth mother to really know what he'd gotten from her. Though she apparently didn't have any difficulties walking out on her family, so she was just easygoing in a different way.

"It was Jocelyn for the most part." He smiled at Mel. "You know she's not my birth mother, right?"

"No," Mel said, sitting back in her chair. "I had no idea. You always call her Mom."

"That's because I've considered her my real mother since she married my dad. She raised me. She's been there for most of my life. I wouldn't trade her for anything. My dad started seeing her when I was five, and even at that age I had no delusions that Kristi, my birth mother, was coming back. I might've been a little bit of a troublemaker when I was little. It had just been my dad and me for over a year, and I liked it that way. I didn't need another mother who was just going to leave."

"That's understandable."

"Jocelyn worked so hard to win me over, and once she did, I always wanted to prove myself to her."

"So that she wouldn't leave, too?" Mel asked softly.

"I guess." Wow, this conversation had gone in a direction he hadn't expected. Normally he'd probably be embarrassed about getting a little too sappy, but for some reason he liked sharing with Mel. And he found himself sharing more than he ever had before.

"That's sweet."

"Does that go on the list?" he asked with a grin, hoping to change the subject.

"Maybe," she said, finishing her wine.

"Let me clean up and then we can get started. I can only imagine how anxious you are to finish the series," he said, pushing his chair back.

"I'm only a little anxious." She stood. "And I can help you."

"That isn't necessary."

"Let me help, Bennett." She reached for the bowl of salad and walked into the kitchen. "If you get the stuff for me to put the food in, I can do that while you load the dishwasher."

"No matter what I say, you're going to insist on helping, aren't you?" he asked as he grabbed the dish of chicken.

"Yup." She looked over her shoulder and smiled at him.

"Then I guess it will have to work," he said, putting the dish down on the counter next to her.

"I guess so."

Bennett shook his head as he got some containers down from the cabinet and put them on the counter for Mel. When he stepped back, he couldn't stop himself from looking at her.

Her curly hair was long, going well past the middle of her back. Her shorts weren't indecent or anything, but they definitely hugged her tiny little bottom. Bennett pulled his gaze away, not wanting to get caught checking her out, and went back to gather more things in the dining room.

They cleaned the kitchen, and when everything was put away, Bennett led Mel to the living room.

"You ready for this?" he asked as he put the disc into the DVD player.

"As I'll ever be. I feel so attached to all of these characters, I just don't even know what I'm going to do when it's done," she said, as she settled down on the couch.

"I have a plethora of other series to watch. We can just start something new."

We?

Yeah, that little word had popped out *way* too easily.

* * *

Mel couldn't stop sniffling. Okay, so she got emotional sometimes. So what. But Bennett hadn't laughed at her tears, or been weirded out by them. On the contrary, he'd gone to get her some tissues.

The final scene ended and the credits began to roll. Mel just stared at the screen, not sure of how she felt.

"How you doing over there?" Bennett asked.

"I'm not sure yet," Mel said, still staring at the credits. "I think this is going to take some time to sink in."

"I know what you mean."

"Do you?" Mel asked, looking at him.

"Yeah," he nodded. "This show is a total mind fuck. Excuse the language."

Mel laughed. "You're excused. It is definitely that. But I'm going to miss it."

"Then we'll just have to fill that void. How about Monday night? I'll make you dinner again. I'm sure you're going to need a little pick-me-up after your first day of school."

"I'm sure that I'm going to as well."

"All right. Same time, same place."

"Same time, same place," she agreed.

* * *

Mel did need a pick-me-up on Monday. A big one. She had a *very* long first day of school. There was a Mrs. O'Ryan who taught English, and her classes had been mixed with Mel's, giving some students two math classes and no English, or two English classes and no math. But it wasn't just a quick fix for the students—their entire schedules had to be redone.

During Mel's second class of the day, her overhead projector stopped working. She requested a new one, but it wasn't coming in for two weeks. This meant she had to deal with one of the ancient ones, which was a royal pain in the ass. Then the bell system malfunctioned, and for about an hour it went off every five minutes. And right before the last class, the janitor had disturbed a family of raccoons in the storage closet, and the family had quickly run out into the halls. The students had been switching classes, and needless to say it had caused a bit of a panic.

By the time Mel got to Bennett's, she was exhausted and so looking forward to a home-cooked meal, a cold beer, and a hot man.

He provided all three.

And dinner had been amazing. He'd made apple and bacon pork chops with garlic-mashed potatoes and asparagus. Mel was stuffed.

"Pick something out to watch." He nodded toward the living room before he pushed his chair back and stood from the table.

"I can help," she said, standing.

"Come on, Mel, I know how tired you are, and this will only take a second." He indicated the plates. "By the time you find something, I'll have finished."

"I don't have the energy to argue with you." She grabbed her beer.

"Good," he said, as she headed into the living room.

Bennett kept all of his DVDs in the steamer trunk, so Mel walked over to it and knelt, popped the latches, and pulled up the lid.

Holy cow. It was filled with movies and TV shows, all

of them alphabetized. She recognized *Game of Thrones* and grabbed the box to read the back. When Bennett came into the room a couple of minutes later she stood and handed him the box.

"I've heard of this, and I'd wanted to watch it," she said.

He looked at it in surprise, and maybe a bit uncomfortably.

"Mel, there is *a lot* of sex in this show," he told her.

"You don't think I can handle it?" she asked narrowing her eyes playfully.

"Oh, I'm sure you can. I'm just telling you, it leaves *nothing* to the imagination."

"Well, your warning has been heard. Let's watch it," she said, as she stepped past him and took a seat on the couch.

"All right, but don't say I didn't warn you."

* * *

They were halfway through the second episode, and Mel was already hooked. Bennett hadn't lied when he'd said that there was *a lot* of sex. And it was more than a little awkward watching scenes that were fairly intense with him sitting right next to her.

And he was sitting *right* next to her. His arm resting on the back of the sofa and his leg pressed into hers. She really wanted to lean into him and use his chest as a pillow, but she refrained.

Well, really, she wanted to hide her face behind a pillow because she was the shade of a freaking strawberry. But she couldn't look away. One reason was because more often than not something important besides all of the sex was going on in a scene. And second, because she'd told Bennett she could handle it, and she didn't want to show weakness. So she watched, and even though she was completely into the show, she was aware of Bennett next to her the entire time.

And just like *Lost*, this one ended its episodes on a cliff-hanger every time.

"You've got to be kidding me," she yelled at the screen when the episode finished.

"So you're into the show, I'm guessing."

She turned and glared at him. "Does every episode end like this?" she asked.

"Pretty much."

"I don't think I can handle this again. Why didn't you warn me about this before?"

He laughed. "We can watch some more episodes this week."

"Yeah?" she asked, her frustration quickly giving away to pleasure.

"Yeah."

Huh. Before, he'd just let her borrow the DVDs and watch episodes with her every once in a while. This time he wanted to watch all the episodes with her. This was an interesting development.

"Well, then I'll cook. It's only fair," she said.

"It *is* only fair."

"When is good for you?"

"I have baseball practice tomorrow. How about Wednesday?" he asked.

"Wednesday is good. Six?"

"Sounds perfect. I'll be there."

"All right. I should probably get going," she said, more than a little disappointed. But it was getting late and she was exhausted.

Bennett stood and held out his hand. He helped her stand before he walked her outside. She unlocked her car with the remote, and he opened the door for her.

"I had a good time, Mel." He reached up and rubbed some of her hair between his fingers.

"Me too," she said, resisting the urge to bite her lip. "Thanks for dinner and the entertainment. It was a relaxing night after a stressful day."

She desperately wanted him to lean in and kiss her, and she thought he was going to. His eyes focused on her mouth for just a second before he took a deep breath and let go of her hair.

"Anytime. Drive safe," he said, taking a step back from her.

Mel got into her car, and though the night had been perfect, she was more than a little disappointed that it hadn't ended with his mouth on hers at least once.

Really? Was it so much for a girl to ask for?

Chapter Four

The Terrifying Reality of Teddy Bears

Bennett spent multiple nights that week with Mel, but he refused to look too much into it. They were just hanging out. Nothing more. No big deal.

They made some steady progress on *Game of Thrones*, granted there were only ten episodes per season, but still they were over halfway through the first season. The plan for that Monday night was for them to have dinner, Mel cooking for Bennett, and to celebrate the first day of the bookshelf project.

The supplies had been delivered to the school on Friday. Both Mel and Bennett had found multiple vendors around Atticus County who were willing to sell to them at cost. Some had been a little resistant at first, but they'd stood no chance against the sweet smile of one Melanie O'Bryan. She'd turned on her Southern charm, and they'd been putty in her hands.

On Monday morning, Bennett got to the school at six thirty. They were going to use the old wood shop building by the baseball field, so Bennett parked over there and headed inside.

Mr. Coryell had been the wood shop teacher when

Bennett had been in high school. He'd retired five years ago, and no one had been hired to replace him. It was a position that the former superintendent, Reynolds, hadn't thought important to fill. It was a shame, really, that the kids weren't given the option to take the class anymore. Mr. Coryell had taught Bennett a lot, and he owed his former teacher in more ways than he could count. It was because of that class that Bennett had a job today. More important, it was because of that class that Bennett had found his passion in life.

Creating something with his hands gave Bennett a peace that he'd never had before, and these days he was always looking for a little bit of peace.

When Bennett walked into the building, Mel was already there. She was leaning over the table looking down, but her head came up and she smiled wide at him.

"Hello," she said brightly.

"Hey," he said as he crossed the room. "You're rather cheerful in the mornings."

"Oh, Bennett." She shook her head. "I'd hate for you to think I'm even remotely a morning person. It's all coffee."

"Ah, a caffeine junkie." He stopped on the other side of the table.

"Don't you forget it," she said, holding out a to-go cup for him. "I brought you some, too."

"Looks like I'm now the one in your drink debt," he said, taking the cup.

"Just bring something tonight and we'll be even again." She picked up her own cup and brought it to her lips.

"Sounds like a plan." He took a sip of coffee. He'd already had some that morning, but Bennett had never been one to turn down caffeine. Mel had been generous with the cream and light on the sugar. Just how he liked it.

"I wasn't sure how you took your coffee, so I just made it like mine."

"This is perfect. Thank you," he said, then took another long drink.

"So you ready for your first day of teenagers?"

"Teenagers don't scare me."

She grinned. "We'll just see about that."

They spent the next twenty minutes getting everything ready, and at ten till seven Mel headed back to the school to get her first-period kids.

Mel was doing this project with her geometry and trigonometry classes. Bennett would be coming on Monday mornings to work with the geometry classes, which were first and second period. On Wednesdays he would work with the trig classes.

The bookcases were going to be simple. They had to be, because any fancy woodwork would've been too difficult for the students to do. Elaborate and showy weren't always the way to go, and more often than not they took away from the natural beauty. Sometimes something was just better the less you tried to change it.

Mel filed in with her students at ten after seven. Half of them looked like they were still fighting sleep, but they all looked fairly excited for the most part, except for a tall kid in the back who was standing a little off to himself. His arms were folded across his chest, and he looked thoroughly unimpressed. He was wearing jeans that hung down a little too low and a black T-shirt. His dark brown hair was long and shaggy, and his ears were pierced.

The only other kid that stood out to Bennett was Mel's little brother, Hamilton. Well, these days he wasn't so little. He'd already shot up past Mel, though he was a bit on the lanky side. Bennett had been around Hamilton a lot lately because of Mel, and he liked the kid.

"Everyone, this is Mr. Hart. He's the real expert behind this project," Mel told the class as she grinned at him.

Mr. Hart? That was his father. That title was going to take some time to get used to.

"Have any of you ever worked with wood before?" Bennett asked the class.

"Not that kind of wood," the tall kid said making a jacking-off gesture in the back.

"Dale Rigels," Mel said sternly. The smile that had been on her face a moment before was gone, replaced by a severe frown. She now looked at the kid with narrowed eyes and raised eyebrows.

Dale dropped his hand and looked down at his feet. Yeah, Bennett didn't blame the kid. If Mel had looked at him like that, she would've put the fear of God in him, too. Her *don't fuck with me* attitude was scary, and just a little bit hot.

"All right, let's get this out now," Bennett said, trying not to laugh. "I'm sure there will be a lot of opportunities for 'that's what she said' jokes, innuendos about sex, and so on. Let's try to keep those to ourselves. It's never the best time to tell a funny joke when someone is using a hammer or a power saw. Does everybody understand?"

The students nodded.

"But like I was saying," he continued. "When it comes to working with wood, you have to pay attention, because if you measure wrong and start to cut, you can't go back and fix it. Your actions are permanent, and as I'm sure you're all aware, we don't have unlimited supplies. So it's important that you stay focused and alert at all times.

"Half of you look like you could crawl back into bed right now and take a little nap. That isn't going to work when you're in this room. So you guys are either going to need to start going to bed a little bit earlier or eat two bowls of Wheaties to give you some energy. Does everybody understand that?"

The students nodded again.

"All right, now for the fun part. Math is used often in our everyday lives. You have to use it in cooking, budgeting your money, dividing your time up in a day, and a hundred other things that you wouldn't even think were related to mathematics. I use it every day in my profession, and if I didn't use it correctly I would be highly unsuccessful. So all of you are going to learn how math helps build things.

"Ms. O'Bryan has already divided you up into groups of four, and each group will work solely on their own bookshelf. Any questions yet?" he asked.

The students shook their heads.

"All right, let's get started," he said, clapping his hands.

* * *

Mel was more than a little amazed as she watched Bennett interact with the kids. He was completely confortable around them. When he talked, they listened. Maybe they just realized right off the bat that he wasn't someone to mess with.

She wished she'd been as smart to realize that from the beginning.

Today the kids were all going over the plans and deciding who was going to be their team leaders. Mel made a round of the class and headed over to the group where her brother was. She'd put Dale Rigels in his group in the hope that her brother might rub off on the troubled kid.

Dale hadn't had it easy growing up. His father had been killed in Afghanistan three years ago, when Dale was twelve. Mrs. Rigels worked hard to support her son, but Mel could only imagine how hard it was for a single mother. Dale had a tendency to get into trouble. He'd been caught shoplifting more often than she could count, and he smoked pot and drank beer, sometimes right on school grounds. He was heading down a bad path.

Mel was going to try her hardest with the kid this year, and she prayed she—or someone—would get through to him.

She approached Hamilton's table. Hamilton looked up at her and frowned. No, he was not happy with her.

Not. At. All.

Mel had been ten years old when Hamilton was born, and she'd been over the moon at having a baby brother. She'd always wanted a sibling, and Hamilton hadn't disappointed. He'd followed her around the second he'd been able to crawl, and they'd always been incredibly close.

Mel pretty much looked like their mother, except for her hair. She'd inherited their father's curly, light blond color. Hamilton was the opposite. He'd gotten their mother's dark brown hair, but he looked like their father with his freckled cheeks, Roman nose, hazel eyes, and poor eyesight. Though both Mel and Hamilton had their father's big smile, Hamilton's was somewhat lopsided.

Mel had also inherited their father's love for math. Miles O'Bryan was an accountant, and he took great pleasure in crunching numbers every day. Though the love for math was much stronger in Mel, Hamilton wasn't completely out of the loop. He was all about music, which used its own fair share of math.

Hamilton was in the high school band, where he played about six different instruments, all of them amazingly. He was just a little bit on the nerdy side with his black, framed glasses. But Mel had been around long enough to recognize his type. Once he grew into himself girls would be all over him, especially if he was a musician.

"How's it going?" she asked.

"Just grand," Hamilton said, not hiding his sarcasm.

Okay, so she might've paired him with Dale, but the other two girls in his group were sweet. He could just suck it up. It would be a learning experience for him, too.

"Good," Mel said, resisting the urge to ruffle his hair. He was already pissed off at her; no need to make it worse. "Who's going to be the team leader?"

"Kylee," Hamilton said.

Kylee Flint was a tall, pretty blonde girl with big blue eyes and long lashes. Her mother was the owner of the spa where Harper worked, the same spa where Mel had been shot. Celeste Flint was a bit of a free spirit, and it had most definitely rubbed off on her daughter, except when it came to school. The girl was hard-core when it came to her studies. She'd been in Mel's algebra class last year, and she'd gotten straight As.

"So what do you think, Dale?" Mel asked him.

"It's whatever." He shrugged his shoulders and looked thoroughly bored.

"Well, I think it's awesome," Kylee said, looking straight at Dale with a *you think you're so cool but you're not* look. Dale straightened a little bit in his seat.

Well, Kylee was definitely going to keep the boy in line.

"I do too," Ashley Rodriguez said, her shrewd brown eyes peeking out from under her auburn bangs. She was another girl not to be messed with, and Mel knew she wasn't going to take any crap from Dale, either. This was why Mel had put him in their group.

The bell rang, and everyone started packing up their stuff.

"So how did I do, Teach?" Bennett asked, coming up to Mel.

"Pretty impressive, actually."

"Don't sound so shocked. I can handle myself around the young'uns."

"I saw. Thanks again for doing this, Bennett. I'm going to go get the next class," she said, turning around.

But before she could start walking, he took her hand and

stopped her from leaving. She turned, more than a little startled, and looked up at him.

"I'm really glad I'm a part of this, Mel. You don't have to keep thanking me," he said seriously.

She could only nod. He let go of her hand, and as Mel walked back to her classroom she was at a complete loss for words.

* * *

Over the next three weeks Bennett quickly adjusted to his new work schedule. Really, it wasn't that much different. His Mondays started a little earlier. Normally he hadn't gotten to a construction site until about nine, and that was about the time he finished up with Mel and the kids.

On Wednesdays, he cut it a little short at work and headed over to the school just before one. Different groups of kids had started to stay late on Wednesday to work a little bit more and catch up on their shelf. A few of the kids wanted to work on other projects, and Bennett was more than happy to help them as long as they paid for the supplies.

He was having a good time with the project, and he was having a *really* good time with Mel. He looked forward to being in that wood shop with her and to regularly hanging out with her at night.

"You've been MIA lately," Tripp said to Bennett one Tuesday night. It was another karaoke night at the Sleepy Sheep, and since Bennett was so involved with everything he made a point of going to them.

But he flat-out refused to sing. Nope. That shit wasn't happening.

"Yeah." Shep sipped his beer behind the bar. "I feel like I only see you at practice and at games. What are you doing with all your free time these days?"

"I'm pretty sure it has to do with that pretty girl over there," Brendan said, indicating a spot behind Bennett.

Bennett didn't need to turn to see that Brendan was talking about Mel. She sat at a corner table with Grace, taking money, signing people up for karaoke slots, and helping them pick out which songs they wanted to sing.

No, Bennett knew exactly where Mel was, because he'd looked over at her not even sixty seconds ago.

"We're just friends." He was tired of saying that, but mainly because it wasn't true anymore.

"I've heard that before," Shep said.

"I've *said* that before." Jax shook his head pityingly at Bennett. "It sounds about as true coming out of your mouth as it did coming out of mine."

"Jeez, when Jax calls you out about being clueless, that's saying something," Brendan said.

"I really wish I could take offense to that, but it's sadly true," Jax said.

"But not anymore," Tripp said.

"Nope." Jax grinned. "Not anymore."

Yup, Jax had the grin of a very satisfied man. Something that Bennett was definitely not. Frustrated was a way more accurate word, and every time he even looked at Mel his frustration grew. Who was he kidding? All he had to do was think about her. Which was all the fucking time.

* * *

When Mel got home on Thursday, she started preparing dinner right away. She was making her grandmother's shrimp and grits for Bennett, and the meal involved a lot of prep work.

Mel lost all track of time, and by the time she was finished cooking she had only enough time to change. Her makeup was still okay, and her hair wasn't too frizzy. There really wasn't any hope of making her curls look any better. Besides, this was her, up close and personal.

She stripped the second she got in her room and grabbed a white linen button up shirt and a pair of cutoff jean shorts. Just as she was buttoning the snap, the doorbell rang. She headed down the hallway and when she opened the front door it wasn't Bennett on the other side.

"Hey," Grace said as she looked Mel up and down. "You going somewhere tonight?"

"No." Mel stepped aside so Grace could come in. "Bennett's coming over."

"I know. I ran into him at LauraAnne's about"—Grace dramatically looked at her watch—"ten minutes ago. He was trying to pick out a wine that you would like and that would go well with shrimp and grits. So he asked for my help. It was really rather adorable. But anyways, it got me to thinking. I know for a fact you don't whip out your grandmother Maris's shrimp-and-grits recipe for just anybody. That's only when you want to pull out the big guns."

Mel frowned. "And?"

"*And?*" Grace repeated incredulously.

"You know, you're a giant pain in my ass, Grace."

"I'm aware—and just so you know, you're just as big a pain in my ass. When are you going to admit you two are more than just friends?"

"When *he* actually does something. That's when, and not a minute before."

"All right," Grace said.

"So was this all you wanted during this little reconnaissance mission of yours?" Mel asked.

"Actually, no. I came over to get the second book by Ilona Andrews," she said opening up her purse, pulling out the first book and handing it to Mel. "I need to know when Kate and Curran actually get together."

Mel didn't comment on that, because they didn't get together for a couple more books. Which meant Grace was going to be waiting for a little while.

"Let me go grab it," Mel said, going into her living room and heading to her overstuffed bookshelf in the corner.

"You might as well just give me the third one, too," Grace said, following her.

"Really? I didn't think you'd have all that much time to read, what with Jax around. Is he demanding less of your time these days?" Mel grabbed the books and put the first one away. When she turned around, Grace was smirking at her.

"Oh believe me, that man still demands plenty of my time. These are for when he works late. A girl's got to be able to distract herself somehow."

"Brag much?"

"After being in love with him for practically my whole life?" Grace asked, her smile one of a cat that had just eaten the canary. "You better believe it."

God, what Mel wouldn't give to have that look on her own face.

"Are you done rubbing my nose in your sex life, or are we done here?" Mel asked.

"Oh come on, you're not going to let me hang out till he gets here? I just want to observe for a little bit."

"No," Mel said. But she didn't get her way, because the doorbell rang.

"Score." Grace lit up with glee.

Shit. "You better only say hello and then leave," she said, pointing a finger at Grace.

"What else would I do?" Grace asked sweetly.

"God only knows." Mel headed toward the front door and opened it.

And there stood Bennett holding a bottle of wine in

one hand, and the box set of *Game of Thrones* in the other. He was wearing a pair of jeans that Mel assumed he'd just changed into, because they were free of dust and dirt, just like his blue-and-white flannel shirt. Mel didn't miss the appreciative look in Bennett's eyes as he took in her shorts and legs. As Grace was standing right next to her, she was pretty sure Grace caught it, too.

"Hey Bennett," Grace said, stepping past Mel and walking out onto the porch. "I see you went with the wine I suggested. You won't be sorry."

"Thanks again," he said with a grin.

"I'll see you later." Grace gave Mel a significant look that said, *We'll be talking.* But she didn't say anything else as she headed toward her car, leaving Mel and Bennett alone on the porch.

* * *

Mel looked hot. Her crazy curls were all over the place, her cheeks were rosy, her eyes were warm, and her legs were barely covered by the sexiest cutoff jeans Bennett had ever seen. She was wearing a shirt that was only half-buttoned and he could see the very top of her breasts peeking out of a pink tank top.

"Hey," he said, walking into the house. For some reason completely unknown to him, he leaned down and kissed her on the cheek.

"Hi," she said, looking even more flushed when he pulled back. "Thanks for picking up wine." She nodded at the bottle in his hand before she turned and headed to the kitchen.

"It's no problem." He walked behind her, his eyes drifting down to her *very* tiny bottom, which was covered by those *very* tiny shorts.

"So am I going to be highly disturbed by the last two episodes in season two?" she asked.

"Nah, not like season one." He somehow managed to pull his eyes away to look where he was going.

"Well, nothing can be as heartbreaking as season one," she said as she entered the kitchen. Bennett followed and put the wine on the counter.

Mel had indeed been very sad and upset about that. A couple of the main characters had died, including her favorite character. He'd been part of a very dramatic love story that she'd been particularly invested in. And now with his death that love story was over. She had claimed she would never be the same. But the series was based on a series of books, and Mel didn't know that the author had a thing about killing his characters off. No one was safe.

"Yeah," he said, not too reassuringly.

Mel looked over her shoulder at him and narrowed her eyes, giving him the scary *don't mess with me* look. "You're holding back on me, aren't you?" she asked as she grabbed two bowls on the counter and went over to a steaming pot on the stove.

"Hey," he said, holding up his hands in defense. "You're the one who hates spoilers."

She started dishing out the grits. "Ugh. I do, but this show is too much to take."

"I tried to warn you." He reached over to the drawer next to him, and it stuck a little as he opened it. He grabbed the corkscrew and started twisting it into the bottle.

"No, you tried to warn me about all the sex. You didn't warn me that I'd have my heart ripped out on a regular basis."

"I didn't." Bennett looked up at her, unable to stop a smile from turning up his lips. There was just something about how passionate she was about these little things in life that did funny things to him. Made him feel things he'd never felt before.

"Are you laughing at me?" she asked, raising her eyebrows.

He shook his head. "I'm not. I promise. I'm sorry I didn't warn you."

"It's probably for the best, anyway. And good thing you weren't laughing at me. Otherwise you wouldn't be getting dinner."

"That's harsh." He turned back to the wine and popped the cork. He reached above him for the cabinet door. It made a loud squeak as he opened it. He grabbed two wineglasses and pulled them down.

"Sometimes it's necessary. Like when you're dealing with a bunch of teenagers on a daily basis." She put two bowls down in front of him, one with almost double the amount of food. She'd piled the grits with shrimp, bacon, chives, and cheddar cheese.

"That's true. But I've smelled and now seen what promises to be an amazing dinner. It would be more than a little cruel to deprive a starving man." He filled both glasses with wine and handed her one.

"Well, then we should get you fed." She smiled and grabbed her bowl from the counter, then headed over to the set dinner table.

Bennett grabbed his bowl and wineglass, and followed her.

They chatted over their meal as usual, and it had taken everything in Bennett not to moan around his spoon as he'd eaten. Never in his life had he tasted anything more delicious.

"You've without a doubt ruined shrimp and grits for me," he said, as he pushed his second bowl away from him. "I'll never be able to eat it again and not compare it to this."

"That's a compliment if I've ever heard one."

"It's the truth. I'm stuffed." He rubbed his stomach.

"No one forced you to eat that second bowl."

"I couldn't resist," he said, shaking his head. "Too much of a temptation."

"Really? I would've thought you were a man that was quite capable of resisting temptation."

"Sometimes."

"Hmmm." Her smile was making Bennett think of other tempting things. "Well, since you're quite done with dinner, I'll clean up and then we can move on to my heart getting trampled." She stood up and went into the kitchen. He watched her walk away before he stood up, too.

Bennett helped her clear the table and put the food away. If he didn't know any better, he'd think they'd fallen into a bit of a routine over the last month. He'd gotten comfortable with her, more so than if they were just friends. He liked being around her, maybe a little bit more than he should, and definitely more than he was ready for. But even that didn't excuse the idiocy of what he did next.

Mel stretched up on her tiptoes to reach into a cabinet above her head. She wasn't short, but the container she was trying to get was just out of reach. The more she stretched, the more her shirt pulled up, exposing the smooth, creamy skin of her back. Bennett couldn't stop himself from coming up behind her and reaching over her shoulder, but it had nothing to do with trying to be a gentleman and helping out a lady.

No, he wanted to run his hand across her skin and around to her stomach. He wanted to pull her back into him and press his face into her neck. He wanted to turn her around and push her back against the counter. He wanted to kiss her.

Mel jumped back into him as his arm skimmed over hers. He steadied her by placing his free hand on her hip. He grabbed the container, and when he set it down on the counter she turned and looked up at him.

"Thank you," she said softly.

He was so close to her. All he had to do was lean down a little bit and he'd be able to press his mouth to hers.

"No problem," he said, unable to look at anything but those soft lips of hers.

She was breathing unevenly. He was pretty sure he'd stopped taking in oxygen a while ago, because he felt a little light-headed.

He took a step into her, pushing her back against the counter, and her breasts came up against his chest. His eyes flickered up to hers, and what he found there made all rational thought leave his mind.

"Bennett," she whispered.

And just like that everything came crashing back to him. There was something about the breathy little hitch in Mel's voice when she said his name that terrified him. He cleared his throat and took a step back from her, his hands falling away from her body. There was much more than just a flicker of disappointment in her eyes this time.

Fuuuuck. He really didn't know what to do with this. Didn't know what to do with her.

"We should start the show," he said somewhat awkwardly, as he took another step away from her.

"O-okay," she said slowly. "Let me just finish putting this away."

"I'll go put the DVD in." Bennett promptly retreated out of the kitchen, like the coward he was.

* * *

Mel just stood there for a second, so thoroughly confused she didn't know what to do next. He'd almost kissed her. For real this time, not just a peck on the cheek. She hadn't imagined it.

Had she?

There'd been something in his eyes. Desire for her. She'd seen it before she said his name, and then it had disappeared with the blink of an eye. And then he'd run out of the kitchen like a bat out of hell.

It wasn't like she'd been the one to come up to him. No, he'd done that. He'd been the one to put his hands on her. He'd been the one who pushed his body against hers. He'd been the one to look at her mouth like it was dessert. She hadn't done anything.

Were all men this freaking baffling to the mind? Or was it just Bennett? Whoever said women were hard to understand was mistaken. Men were leaps and bounds more perplexing.

Mel grabbed her wineglass and refilled it. She was going to need something to get her through the rest of the night, because the man in her living room was frustrating as all hell.

When she went into the room, he was sitting at the far end of the couch, not in the middle where they normally sat. Well, if he wanted to put distance between them that was fine. Just fine. She wasn't going to be some needy, desperate girl that was pining over some stupid man who didn't want her.

Whatever.

So she sat on the opposite end of the couch and took a big drink of her wine. Too bad it had absolutely no effect in calming her ever-spinning mind.

* * *

Bennett wasn't even paying attention to the show. How could he when all he was thinking about was the woman who was sitting five feet away from him?

Normally Mel would make comments here and there during the show or ask questions because there were more than a few confusing story lines, but she hadn't said a word the entire hour.

And neither had he. What the hell was he supposed to say? *Sorry for not kissing you? Sorry for not knowing what's going on with the two of us? Sorry for being a candy-ass?*

Yeah, none of those seemed like appropriate things to say.

How was it that Bennett had fought in wars, and yet this beautiful woman scared the ever-living daylights out of him? He'd never been tongue-tied or nervous around women before. But Mel? Mel was an entirely different story.

He just needed to say something to her. Tell her he kind of liked her.

Kind of liked her? What, was he in the fifth grade or something?

His palms were sweaty and itchy, and he kept rubbing them on the thighs of his jeans. When the episode ended he jumped up from the couch and excused himself to go to the bathroom. He was too damn twitchy for his own good, and Mel had raised her eyebrows at him before he turned around and walked down the hallway.

Why was he making this so damn complicated? He was attracted to her. He liked spending time with her. He wanted to spend more time with her. So what was the big deal if they started dating? They could do that casually. It wasn't like they were going to get married or anything.

Married? No, no, no. Noooooooo.

Bennett wasn't ready for that. He wasn't sure he'd *ever* be ready for that. Marriage wasn't in his plan. Not to Mel. Not to anyone. He wasn't stable when it came to relationships. Really, he wasn't stable, period. It might've been a couple of years, but he wasn't over what had happened in Afghanistan. He'd never be over it. He'd forever be screwed up.

It wasn't something that Mel needed to be exposed to. She didn't need to witness his nightmares or the panic attacks that accompanied them. No one should have to deal with his fucked-uppedness, especially her.

He'd probably scare the ever-living shit out of her with one of his panic attacks. God knew he scared the ever-living shit out of himself.

Bennett was so far in his head that he wasn't really paying attention to where he was going. He pushed open the door and flipped on the switch, but instead of walking into the bathroom, he walked into Mel's bedroom.

The walls were a light green. The curtains, lampshades, and quilt spread across her queen bed were a bright blue. And right there, right in the middle of the pillows on her bed, was the teddy bear he'd gotten her when she'd been in the hospital.

* * *

Okay, so something was definitely up with Bennett. That much was obvious to Mel. He was fidgety and just…off. He'd never acted like this with her before, and she really didn't like it. She had absolutely no idea what was going on and she was going to ask him about it just as soon as he came back from the bathroom.

But Bennett was walking back down the hallway about ten seconds after he'd disappeared, and he looked like a man on a mission, a man on a mission to get the hell out of her house.

"Everything okay?" she asked, standing up.

"Yeah, I just have to go. I didn't realize how late it was, and I have to get up early tomorrow."

Mel's eyes flickered to the clock on her wall. They normally hung out until around ten and it was only eight thirty.

She didn't really know when that was ever considered late, but all right.

"I'll see you later." He turned and hightailed it toward the front door. Mel followed. When he stepped out onto her porch he turned. "Thanks for dinner."

"You're welcome," she said, still uncertain as to what was going on.

"Have a good night," he said before he turned and walked out to his truck.

Mel watched him for just a second before she shook her head and went back inside. She closed the door and locked it, then leaned against it, listening to his truck start up and back down the driveway.

"Well, that was delightful." She pushed off the door and went into the kitchen. She'd drunk a little bit too much wine tonight in an attempt to calm her nerves, and she needed some water. She filled a glass and sipped at it as she walked through the house turning off the lights.

What the hell had happened? Bennett hadn't even gone to the bathroom. She'd never even heard the door shut before he'd come back down the hallway looking panicked.

Had he just figured out he wasn't interested in her or...

Mel froze when she got to her bedroom. The door was open, and she knew for a fact she'd closed it. As she peered into her room, her eyes settled on the reason why Bennett had freaked and promptly peaced out.

He'd seen the stupid teddy bear.

Chapter Five

The Healing Powers of Friends…
and Wine, Lots of Wine

Okay, so Bennett was a coward. That resounding fact kept repeating over and over again as he drove home. There were few things that freaked him out these days. But when he'd seen that bear on Mel's bed it had scared the shit out of him.

The thing was, it had scared him so much because he'd liked seeing it there. He'd liked that something he'd given her was so close to her at night. That it meant something to her. That he might mean something to her.

He liked her. That much was obvious. And she apparently liked him.

But things wouldn't be casual with her, and when it came to a relationship he was incapable of doing anything serious. Really he'd been an idiot to think that something with Mel would be anything less. She wasn't a one-night-stand kind of girl. Not that he'd wanted a one-night stand with her. Bennett didn't work that way, not anymore. He'd been a little wild when he'd first joined the military, picking up girls in bars whenever he was on leave. But then the next morning would roll around and he'd feel more than a little empty.

He'd dated a couple of girls semiseriously over the years,

but the relationships had always ended when he'd been transferred to a new base or when he'd been deployed. Bennett had never been in love with a woman before. So whenever he'd left, he'd never looked back. Never had any regrets.

But Bennett knew he'd have regrets if he kissed Mel, if he walked her back to her bedroom and done all of the things he wanted to do . . . for many, many hours.

He was a bad man. Mel was too sweet for him, too innocent and vulnerable. Kind of like Bambi. The very last thing he wanted to do was hurt her. Who would want to hurt Bambi? Yeah, he needed to stay far, far away from her.

Which was going to be a bit of a problem, because he would be working on this project with her for the next three months. If Bennett was anything, he was a man of his word. So he was just going to have to suck it up and deal. Act like a man. *Be* a man.

She was just a pretty girl. Nothing more.

Except that wasn't exactly true. Actually it wasn't true at all. She was way more than just a pretty girl. She was his friend, his beyond-beautiful friend whom he wanted in ways that weren't friend appropriate.

Yup, he was so totally screwed.

* * *

Mel was more than a little humiliated over the whole teddy bear incident. Bennett had seen the damn thing, seen that she slept with it on her bed. Well, *did* sleep with it on her bed. Now, it was stuffed in the far recesses of her closet, where it was going to stay.

She was so done with all of this. So done with worrying about what one man's opinion of her was. So done with wanting that same man who obviously didn't want her. So done with everything that involved Bennett Hart.

It was just too damn bad she wasn't going to be free of him anytime soon. It was going to be a long semester. But she was an adult. She could do this. She could be around Bennett in a professional manner and get over her stupid little crush.

Because that was what it was: stupid and little. She'd get over this. Get over him.

Mel kept repeating this to herself over and over again as she tossed and turned in bed for a good four hours. She was determined that when, or in this case *if*, she fell asleep, she would leave Thursday behind her. Friday would be a new day, free of humiliation and rejection. It would be better.

But that just wasn't the case.

* * *

Friday dawned rainy and miserable. Mel was tired from her lack of sleep the night before, and in her pre-coffee morning haze, she managed to spill the entire pot all over the counter.

Mel wasn't what anybody would call a morning person. It usually took her two cups of coffee and a shower to even resemble a human being. She always set her coffeemaker at night, because to do it when she first woke up in the morning normally took skills that were beyond her. Today, it was pretty much mission impossible.

Somehow she managed to blunder through it, keeping only one eye open as she glared at the damn machine. When it percolated enough for one cup she carefully poured it and carried her steaming mug into the bathroom, where she was tempted for a second to bring it into the shower with her. Instead she set it on a shelf outside of the shower and took a healthy gulp in between shampooing and conditioning her hair.

Mel wasn't exactly sure why she spent any time on her hair that morning. By the time she got to school, the wet and humid day had made her hair take on proportions so large it needed it's own zip code. She threw it up into a bun that only somewhat managed to tame the mess that it was.

Good thing she wasn't trying to impress anyone today. No, it was perfectly okay that she looked like a freaking mess. And why should she care? She was Melanie O'Bryan, math teacher extraordinaire. Really she should just change it to *ordinaire*, because that was what she was, just an ordinary girl who couldn't offer a man anything more than friendship.

Okay, she was officially done throwing this stupid little pity party for herself. She was going to get over this whole Bennett thing. She just needed time and she would be past it. Yeah, that was all she needed, just a couple of days to get over him. But first she was going to need at least another cup of coffee to get through the day.

* * *

School got out around two o'clock. The day hadn't been as bad as Mel imagined it was going to be. The key was for her to stay busy, so the second she walked in the door of her empty house, she had a problem. She changed out of her dress and into an old T-shirt and a pair of shorts. She may as well do something productive, like clean.

Oh what a thrilling life she led, doing housework on a Friday. It was pretty hard for her to not feel just a little bit pathetic at that moment.

Her first room to tackle was the bathroom. As she scrubbed the tub, she decided she was tired of the pale purple walls and the shabby blue bath mats. She wanted something different. Something bold. Something that wasn't plain and boring.

She grabbed her keys and drove down to the hardware store. She headed straight back to the paint department, where she spent a good twenty minutes looking at all of her options. She finally decided on a deep red.

That was definitely a different color choice for her.

After she got her paint mixed, she went over to get the other supplies she needed—and who did she just happen to run smack into?

Bennett.

You have got to be kidding me! Her face flamed up and her stomach tightened painfully.

"Hey," he said, looking down into her cart. "What's the project?" he asked raising his eyebrows

Seriously? After fleeing from her house yesterday, he wanted to chat? Well, she didn't want to talk to him. She just wanted to crawl into a hole. And drink wine. She wanted lots and lots of wine.

"Painting the bathroom."

"Ah." He hesitated as he continued to look at her.

God, why was it so freaking awkward? They were friends. Or had been. Hadn't they?

"Well, I'll let you get to it." He took a step back and walked away.

Yup, even he knew how pathetic she was. It was going to be a long couple of days getting past the rejection from Bennett.

After Mel got the rest of her stuff and checked out, she threw it into her car and headed over to LauraAnne's Liquors. She scanned the parking lot before she went in, looking for Bennett's slate-gray Silverado. It wasn't there, thank God.

She bought two massive bottles of wine and headed home.

She shoved one bottle in the ice tray, put the other in the fridge, and started getting ready for her night of painting. By the time she went to get her second glass of wine, she already had the bathroom cleared out and all of the trim taped. She was just pulling the bottle out of the fridge when her cell phone rang.

"So how was last night?" Harper asked. "Did he fall in love with you over shrimp and grits?"

"Grace has the biggest freaking mouth."

"Hey," Grace's indignant voice came through the line. Apparently Mel was on speakerphone.

"Last night wasn't good," Mel said.

Both girls were silent on the other side of the phone for a moment.

"We're on our way over now," Harper said.

"And we've already picked up a pizza," Grace added.

"Great. The two of you can help me," Mel said.

"Help you with what?" Harper said slowly.

"You'll just have to see when you get here," Mel said, and hung up.

The two girls were on Mel's doorstep within ten minutes. Grace was holding the pizza. Harper had a bottle of wine in each hand.

Four bottles of wine for the night? Yeah, they were good to go.

"All right, spill," Harper said, as they followed Mel into the kitchen.

"You were both wrong about him. He is *soooo* not interested," Mel said as she grabbed three plates from her cabinet.

"There's no way," Grace said.

"Oh, there's a way. And I experienced it three times in less than twenty-four hours."

"What?" Harper asked, one of her eyebrows going up.

They sat at the dining room table and Mel launched into the story. They ate most of the margherita pizza and finished the first bottle of wine.

"Well, shit." Harper dropped her napkin on her plate.

"So to sum up, he's *not* interested." Mel got up from the table and went to get another bottle of wine.

"I'm still trying to work out how you got that he rejected you three times," Grace said.

Mel held up a finger. "Once when he didn't kiss me in the kitchen." She held up two fingers. "Twice when he ran out of here like his pants were on fire after he saw that stupid teddy bear." Her third finger popped up. "And three at the hardware store."

"I thought you said you hadn't wanted to talk to him," Harper said.

"That isn't the point." Mel grabbed the corkscrew and started twisting it into the cork.

"What is the point?" Grace asked.

"That it was awkward as hell and he couldn't wait to get away from me again. He isn't interested in me. But it's fine. I'm fine. I'll get over it."

"Just like that?" Harper asked, as she leaned back in her chair.

"Just like that." Mel pulled the cork free and an audible pop sounded throughout the kitchen.

"Bullshit," Grace said, shaking her head. "Don't try to act all tough and stoic in front of Harper and me. Sweetie, we got your number a long time ago."

"Look," Mel said, walking back to the table. "I don't want to do this, okay? I don't want to dwell on this man who obviously doesn't want me. Life's too short, and I know that for a fact." As she spoke, her voice got a little bit louder, a little bit more passionate. "I know what it's like to have your life flash before your eyes. And I'm not wasting it on a man who's not interested."

Harper and Grace didn't say anything. They just looked at Mel for a second, a little at a loss for words.

"So are we done with this?" Mel asked setting the bottle on the table a tad too forcefully. The bottle thunked loudly on the wood, and a little bit of wine sloshed over onto her hand.

"Yes," Grace and Harper said in unison.

"Good!" Mel grabbed the plates and went back into the kitchen. She loaded them into the dishwasher, fully aware that Grace and Harper were still staring at her.

"He's an idiot, you know," Harper said.

"What?" Mel asked, turning around.

"Bennett. He's a moron," Grace clarified. "He couldn't find anyone better than you, and if he's to blind to see it then it's his loss."

"Without a doubt," Harper added with a nod.

Grace and Harper were loyal to a fault. They were two of the best friends a girl could ask for, and if Mel didn't watch it she was going to get a little too emotional, which was definitely not what she needed at the moment.

"So what exactly are we helping you with?" Grace asked, mercifully changing the subject.

"Painting," Mel said pouring wine into all three of their glasses.

"And drinking, apparently," Harper said.

"This is going to be interesting," Grace said.

"Or at the very least entertaining." Mel held up her glass, Harper and Grace raised their glasses, and they clinked them together.

* * *

For three fairly tipsy women, they did a pretty good job of painting the bathroom. Maybe that was because they had done all the trim work at the beginning of the night before the alcohol really took effect. When they finished around midnight, they sat on the floor, leaning back against the bathtub, and stared at the brightly painted walls.

"I like this color," Harper said, stretching out her legs.

"Me, too," Mel agreed.

"Very fiery," Grace added.

"Unlike me." Mel took a sip of wine.

"That's not true." Harper leaned around Grace to look at Mel.

"Really? When have I ever been anything besides Little Miss Tame?"

Harper squinted her eyes like she was thinking really hard. "Uh, well, there was that one time you went skinny-dipping."

"I was with the two of you. That doesn't count."

"Yes, it does. And you're plenty spicy when you want to be," Grace said.

"Yeah, but not around men. I was never very spicy with Justin."

"That's 'cause he wasn't very spicy. He was just sweet. You need something beyond sweet. You need ho-o-o-o-o-t," Harper said.

"Drunk much?" Mel laughed.

"Maybe a little bit." Harper smiled, holding her thumb and forefinger an inch apart. "Grace and I are going to have to crash with you tonight."

"Lushes," Mel said.

"Takes one to know one," Grace said.

"Yeah, I don't think you could walk in a straight line at the moment. But like I was saying, you're going to find the right guy and he's going to set you off," Harper said.

"Riiight. I'll believe it when I see it." Mel rolled her eyes.

"Or feel it." Grace grinned stupidly.

"God, I hate you," Harper said with a frown.

"Yeah, for those of us who aren't getting any, you and your regular orgasms are too much to take sometimes," Mel added.

"Preach." Harper held her glass of wine in the air.

"Speaking of lover boy, is it going to be okay with him that you aren't coming home tonight?" Mel asked Grace.

"Is that *okay*?" Grace asked, raising her eyebrows. "I do not ask Jaxson Anderson for permission to do anything."

Harper smirked. "Or she just doesn't have to worry about it because he's working a late shift tonight."

"Or that. Hey, can we get out of the bathroom? The paint fumes are making my head spin."

"I think the fumes are coming from our breath," Mel said, getting up on her feet a bit unsteadily. When she found her balance she rolled her sore arm. She was left-handed, so she had done all of the painting with her good arm. But she'd still had to use her wounded right arm a little bit more than usual. It was tight and made her wince when she stretched it.

"What's wrong?" Grace asked, looking concerned.

"I'm fine. It's just sore. Part of the norm these days," she said, rubbing her shoulder.

"That shouldn't be part of the norm." Harper frowned as she stood up.

"I'm okay."

"If you say so." But Grace didn't look at all reassured.

"Is there more wine?" Harper asked as the three of them headed toward the kitchen.

"We have one bottle left," Mel said.

"Well, I say we finish this night good and proper and drink it," Grace said.

Harper sat on a stool at the bar. Grace followed Mel into the kitchen and hopped up on the counter. Mel went to retrieve the last bottle of wine.

"Is this the design for the bookcases?"

Mel turned around to find Harper looking at one of Bennett's sketches, which was on a stack of papers in the corner. It was with all of her other plans for the project.

"Yes." Mel frowned as she grabbed the corkscrew that was still on the counter.

"Let me see," Grace said, leaning across to get a look.

"Bennett might be an idiot when it comes to you, but he really knows what he's doing when it comes to this stuff." Harper pointed to the sketch.

"I know," Mel said miserably.

Harper and Grace looked up at Mel in unison.

"I like him," Mel said softly. "I wish I didn't. I wish I could just get over him. But I *really* like him. Enough to where the next couple of months are going to suck. *A lot.*"

"Oh sweetie," Grace said, reaching over and placing her hand on Mel's.

Mel sighed. "I just feel like the world's biggest idiot, you know? To think he'd ever like *me* back."

"Hey," Harper said. There was a certain sharpness in her voice that made both Mel and Grace jump. "Don't you go talking about my friend that way." She waved her finger at Mel. "The Melanie O'Bryan I know is beautiful and smart. But when you sit there and say that crap, you don't sound like any of those things. That man would be lucky to have you in his life. Luckier than he could ever dream. So don't you dare sell yourself short, because if you do, then everybody else is going to too. You said it yourself: life's too short."

Mel looked at Harper's serious face for a couple more seconds before a smile split her own lips. "You're right. You're absolutely right. Here." She put the wine bottle and corkscrew in front of Grace. "Open this."

Mel reached over and grabbed a yellow steno pad that was next to Bennett's sketches. She flipped to a blank page, then she reached over and grabbed a pen that was sitting in front of Harper. She pulled the cap off and wrote in big bold letters:

My "I Didn't Kick the Bucket" List

1) No more dwelling on things I can't change.
2) No more just thinking about the things I can change. If they can be done, do them.

"Three?" Mel asked biting the end of the pen and looking up.

Grace was pouring the wine and sliding now full glasses in front of everyone.

"Three is 'Don't give a flying fuck what anybody else thinks of you,'" Harper said, eyeing the list with approval.

"That sounds more like rules to live by than things to do," Grace said.

"It's both," Mel said and wrote it down.

"Then number four should be 'Get a tattoo,'" Grace challenged.

"I'm not scared to get a tattoo," Mel said.

"Really?" Grace asked. "Then prove it."

"I will," Mel said, writing it down. She followed it with number five: "Get a dog."

"Give me that," Harper said, holding out her hands for the pad of paper and the pen.

6) Spend the night with a man who knows exactly what he's doing between the sheets.

"Oh my gosh! Harper!" Mel said.

"What?" Harper asked, raising an eyebrow. "Can you honestly tell me you don't want to be with a man that makes you lose your ever-loving mind?"

"Well, no," Mel said, chewing on her bottom lip.

"That's what I thought." And with that Harper started writing again.

7) Be brave enough to take chances that you wouldn't normally take. Be impulsive.
8) Go bungee jumping.

Harper kept writing until she got to fifteen, and then Grace snatched the pad and pen.

16) Ride a motorcycle.
17) Don't let anybody hold you back.

And so the night went; the piece of paper got passed back and forth, and the list grew. It was going to take some time for Mel to do everything on it, and she couldn't wait.

Chapter Six

Up to Bat

Bennett spent Thursday night, all of Friday, and the better part of Saturday morning trying to distract himself, but it was useless. A certain curly-haired woman kept crossing his mind. He still felt like a complete and total asshole about what had happened the other night, but that didn't stop him from wanting to see her.

He'd spent quite a few nights with her over the past couple of months, and he'd more than liked spending so much time with her. He wanted to hear her voice. To talk to her about something. Anything.

But no, he was really trying to keep his distance. He was trying not to do something incredibly stupid, like getting involved with a woman who wouldn't be anything but a long-term relationship. Bennett just didn't do long-term. He didn't *want* long-term.

But no matter how many times he told himself that, he just couldn't get Melanie O'Bryan out of his head, and that had never happened to him before. In the past, if he couldn't be with a woman, he accepted it and moved on. Yet he wasn't moving on from Mel.

By Saturday, he felt like he was going more than a little bit out of his mind. But at least he had something to do for a couple of hours.

Last year, Bennett joined the Stingrays, which was a baseball team that Brendan, Jax, and Shep played for. He played his old position of third base. The league used the fields at the high school from July until September.

When Bennett got to the field that afternoon, Jax, Tripp, and Baxter McCoy were already parked in the lot. Baxter was a deputy sheriff like Jax. He'd come out of the closet a couple of months ago when he'd made his relationship with Preston Matthews public.

Preston had been outed by the abominable Bethelda Grimshaw. Bethelda had a blog in which she wrote awful things about the people in town. She liked to drag everyone through the mud, and she had absolutely no remorse about it. Really, she had no conscience. Her blog was one of those things that nobody claimed to read, yet everybody always knew what she was saying. One of those small-town mysteries.

Bennett got out of his truck and made his way over to the dugout.

"What's up with you?" Baxter asked.

"Nothing." Bennett dropped his bag on the ground and started searching for his cleats.

"Translation: you did something stupid," Tripp said.

"I didn't do anything," Bennett said, looking up.

"Yeah, that's not the way I heard it. You should watch out for Grace, by the way, 'cause she's going to be on your ass like a pit bull."

"Do mine ears deceive me, or is Jax gossiping?" Shep asked as he walked into the dugout.

"Not gossiping." Jax shook his head. "That was a warning. Believe me. When it comes to Mel, Grace will draw blood."

Shep frowned at Bennett. "What did you do?"

"Look, I didn't do anything," Bennett said, holding up his hands.

"That's the point, apparently," Jax said.

Everyone looked at Jax, more than a little surprised. Jax normally wouldn't have anything to offer up on the insights into women.

"What?" Jax asked, raising his eyebrows. "I live with a woman now. I've picked up on a few things."

"Huh. Who would've thought?" Bennett said.

Shep rounded on Bennett. "Don't think we've moved off you yet, buddy. What did I tell you about Mel?"

"Not to hurt her. Which is exactly what I tried to do."

"You want to explain that one?" Shep asked.

"Not really."

"Do you like her?" Baxter asked.

"Yeah, I do. But it's not as simple as that."

"It never is," Tripp said.

And didn't Bennett know that for a fact.

* * *

Mel finished stacking the boxes of chips in the corner of the concession stand and walked back out to her car.

The school was in charge of the stand during the games, and the teachers took turns supervising and helping the students run it. What were the odds that Mel would be scheduled for one of Bennett's games? She knew she couldn't avoid him. That wasn't possible, considering the circumstances. And she knew she just needed to get over it.

What was rule number one on her list? She wasn't going to dwell on things she couldn't change. She couldn't change Bennett and his lack of feelings for her, so she wasn't going to care.

Well, at least she was going to try not to care.

Mel closed the trunk of her car and leaned to the side, stretching her tight back and her sore arm. All three girls had slept in Mel's queen bed, and it had been a bit of a squeeze. They'd all woken up with headaches that morning and they'd been sipping coffee in the kitchen when Jax had showed up to get Grace. He'd given their rather disheveled looks a big smirk before he'd pulled Grace into his arms and kissed her like he hadn't seen her in days.

What Mel wouldn't give to have a man kiss her like that.

Nope, she wasn't doing this to herself. She shook her head, which made her slightly woozy, and leaned back against her car. She closed her eyes and took a moment to breathe before the chaos of the next two hours started.

"You okay?"

Mel opened her eyes to find Stu Corson standing in front of her. Stu was a fairly unassuming man, with thick brown hair and a nervous smile. He was about five years older than Mel, and he'd been the chemistry teacher at the high school for the past four years. He was helping Mel run the stand for the afternoon.

"Yeah." Mel straightened. "Just tired. It's been a long week." She gave him a small smile—it was all she could offer the man.

"You sure you're all right? I can handle the kids by myself if I need to."

She shook her head. "I'm okay."

"All right, but if you need to go just say the word."

"Will do." Mel turned and made her way to the front of the building, while Stu headed inside.

Six kids worked the stand with two adults. The kids got community service hours for college—and boy, did they earn those hours. The concession stand was nonstop busy throughout the entire game. A lot of people from around Mirabelle showed up for the men's baseball games. The men loved watching a live sporting event, and the women loved watching the men playing said sporting event.

There were a handful of attractive guys on every team. And the team that Bennett played on—the Stingrays? Every single man on that team was ogleworthy, so today was guaranteed to bring out the women in droves.

Mel unlocked the wooden coverings that were on the two windows over the counter. She pushed back the doors before she turned and looked out at the field.

Men from both teams were on the red dirt: the Stingrays in black and white, and the Bears in orange and brown. Mel spotted Bennett right away. He was throwing the ball back and forth with Baxter, his muscles rippling under his shirt. And damn did his thighs fill out those tight pants, so did his butt.

Dear God, the man was attractive. He was what Harper had described as ho-o-o-o-o-t, every single inch of him…well, Mel was pretty sure every single inch of him would be.

"Caught in the act."

Mel jumped, startled, and turned to find Preston Matthews standing next to her.

Preston was another incredibly good-looking guy, with his sandy blond hair and bright blue eyes. It was too bad he played for the other team, and Mel wasn't talking about sports. Preston was tall and muscular, but not nearly as muscular as Bennett. No, Preston was lean and had the body of a basketball player, which made sense, since he'd played basketball all the way through college. Now he was a lawyer at his father's law firm.

"I have no idea what you're talking about," Mel said, shaking her head.

"You're a bad liar, Mel. If you were staring at him any harder there would be steam coming out of your ears."

"I plead the Fifth."

"Which means you're guilty," he said with a grin.

"You're obnoxious."

"You're just mad because I'm right. Admit it."

"Fine, you're right. But it doesn't matter."

"Why?" Preston asked, throwing his arm around Mel.

"Because he's not interested."

"Well, then he's a moron," Preston said seriously.

"Thanks. And why are you here so early, anyway? The game doesn't start for another forty minutes."

"My adorable boyfriend forgot his glove, so I had to bring it to him. And now I'm going to harass you for a little while."

Mel couldn't stop herself from smiling her first genuine smile of the day. She hadn't seen a lot of Preston lately, and she was excited about getting to spend a little time with him. He'd been pretty busy with his new, and first, boyfriend. Mel couldn't be happier for Preston and Baxter.

"Come on," she said, heading toward the stand. "I'll buy you a soda."

"I don't think so. I'll buy *you* a soda."

"What is it with men and their refusal to let me buy drinks?"

"Who refused to let you buy a drink?" Preston asked raising his eyebrows.

"No one."

"Ah, Muscle Man Wonder. Well, that's one point in his favor."

"Muscle Man Wonder?"

"I think the nickname is apropos. I mean he was the reason you were drooling a minute ago?"

She slapped his arm. "I wasn't drooling."

"Oh, yes you were. And to answer your earlier question, men don't let women buy drinks when they are interested in them."

"You want to buy me a drink, and we both know you're clearly not interested. Much like you-know-who," she muttered under her breath as they walked into the stand. Three of the kids were already there, and Stu was assigning them jobs.

"Like I said before," Preston said, lowering his voice, too. "That man's a moron."

* * *

Mel was wearing those damn cutoff jeans again. The ones she'd been wearing the night Bennett almost kissed her. The sexy-as-hell ones. The ones that put dirty, dirty thoughts in his head and made it difficult for him to think of anything else besides sliding his hands up her bare thighs.

They really weren't indecent shorts or anything. Mel was fairly modest in most aspects in life, and her clothing choices were one of them. She was a teacher and she was working with her students in the concession stand, so the shorts weren't all that short. But for some reason they drove him crazy.

She'd journeyed out of the stand about halfway through the game and sat with their friends in the bleachers. Bennett couldn't help himself from looking over at Mel. Unlike him, she was actually paying attention to the game, so she didn't see him openly staring.

"Why don't you just make a move already?" Tripp asked Bennett, as they waited for their turn to bat.

"It's complicated," Bennett said, pulling his gaze from Mel. He focused on the game again as Brendan hit a ball clear into the outfield.

"That's just another way of saying *you're* chickenshit."

Bennett wasn't even going to deny it. "It's just a bad idea."

"*Scary* bad or *bad* bad?"

"That's part of the problem, I'm not sure."

"Yeah, but in my experience, in that situation the only way to figure it out is to try."

"And what happens when it turns out it was *bad* bad?"

"You get over it. But it's a lot harder to get over the regret of never knowing."

Bennett had a feeling that was going to be true, that he would always wonder when it came to Mel. But Bennett also knew something else, that the *unknown* was scary as hell. He didn't like unpredictable.

When Bennett went up to bat a minute later, he looked straight at Mel. That part of the stands was cheering him on, but he wasn't really paying attention to anyone else. Only her. But she wasn't cheering.

She was wearing sunglasses, so he couldn't see where she was looking, but he could damn sure feel her gaze. There was a blush creeping up her chest and cheeks, and he had a feeling it had nothing to do with the September heat.

How the hell was he supposed to hit a ball in these conditions?

Focus, focus, focus. Yeah, right.

Bennett stopped at the plate, and pulled up the bat. He looked at the pitcher who wound his arm and let the ball fly. Bennett swung and—

"Strike one!" the umpire called out.

The catcher threw the ball back to the pitcher. Bennett rolled his shoulders and brought the bat back up. The ball flew through the air and—

"Strike two!"

He was choking. He hadn't been close either time. He knew he wasn't focusing on the ball but on the girl behind him, the girl who had him thinking about a different game altogether. Well, maybe a similar game. There *were* bases involved.

Tripp's words repeated in his head: *It's a lot harder to get over the regret of never knowing.*

Bennett already had a number of regrets in his life, and

he didn't want any more. And when it came right down to it, he needed to figure things out with her, no matter his fears.

The pitcher's arm came forward and Bennett swung. The bat connected, and the ball sailed through the air and over the left-field fence.

Home run.

* * *

Mel watched Bennett round the bases. The man really was a sight to behold. When he got to home plate he headed into the dugout, and Mel stood up. Earlier, two extra kids had shown up, and it had gotten crowded in the concession stand. Stu had insisted that Mel go watch the game from the bleachers and take a break, but she would feel guilty if she left him in there the whole time.

"I should get back," she said to the group.

"Okay," Grace said. "You still coming tomorrow?"

Grace and Jax were having a barbecue, and everyone was going over to their place. Which meant Bennett would most likely be there.

Well, if she was going to get over him, there was no time like the present.

"I'll be there." She nodded and headed back to the stand.

"Good game?" Stu asked as Mel walked in the back door.

"Yeah." But she wasn't too sure. She'd been watching Bennett the whole time and not really paying attention to anything else.

Ugh, she still wanted him way too damn much.

Stupid man.

Mel grabbed a package of cups and stacked them by the drink machine. "How's everything been back here?"

"Busy," Ashley Rodriguez said, as she spooned some cheese into a nacho container. "But not bad at all."

"Good. There are only two innings left, so we're almost done for the day," Mel said, as she moved on to refilling the napkins.

Mel spent the next half hour helping everyone keep up with the line. The Stingrays won the game, 13–9. They served a small crowd of last-minute customers, and then they cleaned up. Mel went to the front to lock the windows over the counter. She pulled on the two wooden doors of the first window, but they wouldn't close all the way. She struggled with them for a minute before big, strong hands came around her and pulled them into place.

She didn't need to turn around to know it was Bennett.

His body wasn't pressed up against hers, but he surrounded her nonetheless. His arms brushed hers, the tiny little hairs tickling her, and the warmth of his skin spread across her body like wildfire.

"Thank you," she said softly. She still did not turn to look at him.

"No problem," he said close to her ear. He did not pull back.

She took out her keys to lock up but she fumbled with them, her hands unusually unsteady.

"Here." He took the keys from her.

When he finished he took a step back. Mel turned and looked up into his face. He was still wearing his baseball cap, and even though his eyes were shadowed, they still showed a fair amount of heat. Heat that was directed at her.

What the hell? "What are you doing, Bennett?" she asked.

"With what?" he asked, reaching up and pushing a piece of hair back from her face.

"Did you get the doors?" Stu called out.

Mel looked over as Stu rounded the side of the building. He stopped short when he saw how close to each other she and Bennett were standing. Stu's ears turned red as his eyes narrowed on Bennett. "Everything okay?" he asked, trying to look menacing. "Is this guy bothering you?"

The tension bubbling up in Mel's chest eased, and she had to stop herself from laughing. Was Stu trying to intimidate Bennett? Bennett's forearms were thicker than Stu's thighs. Bennett would crush the guy in a second. "Everything's fine," she said, stepping back from Bennett. "He was just helping me."

"Do you need help with the other one?" Bennett asked, pointing to the other open window above the counter.

"I got it." Stu pulled at the wooden doors but he struggled to close them. His feet slid in the dirt as he tried to get a grip.

"You sure?" Bennett asked. Mel knew he was trying not to crack a smile.

"Yes," Stu said as he continued to strain against the door. "Your help isn't needed here."

"All right then." Bennett gave Mel one last look, his mouth quirking up a bit. "I'll see you later."

"Later," she said, biting her lip to keep from laughing.

As Mel watched him walk away, she wondered if there was any man more complicated than Bennett Hart.

* * *

So the little guy had a crush on Mel. Okay, no big deal. Bennett could handle a little competition, not that it was a competition or anything. No, this wasn't going to be a problem. Not at all.

Except the thought of Mel with any other man annoyed Bennett.

No, it made him angry.

He didn't want her with anyone else. He wanted her with him. He'd gone over to talk to her. He needed to explain himself. Apologize for the other night. Tell her he'd made a mistake. That he'd been wrong to freak out.

Simple enough, right?

False. It wasn't simple at all. He'd failed. Struck out.

And she'd even given him an opening. She'd asked what he was doing. Yeah, he'd wanted her to clarify, but he was pretty sure she was talking about the two of them. Or what would be the two of them. If there ever was a chance for the two of them.

Damn, he'd never been this confused in his life.

But right before they'd been able to talk, the sweaty little man had come up and interrupted. And so Bennett had chickened out.

But not because of the sweaty little man.

It was because he had no freaking clue what he was doing with Mel. So it was about damn time he figured it out.

* * *

Mel finished up with everything in the stand, and when she got into her car it was the temperature of a small sauna. Her hair was in a ponytail, and the long strands were sticking to her sweaty neck. She hadn't washed her hair that morning, knowing that after spending an afternoon in the humid heat she would just have to rewash it. Sometimes her hair was more trouble than it was worth.

No. Scratch that. It was *always* more trouble than it was worth. So why continue to put up with it?

As Mel asked herself that question she drove by the Honey Comb Hair Salon. Grace's great aunt, Pinky Player, owned the place. Before Mel even realized what she was doing, she was turning into the parking lot. It was five till four, and the shop always closed early if they weren't busy. Maybe Pinky would squeeze Mel in.

Well, if she walked in that door she was going to be doing a lot of things on her list.

"Here you go, Harper. I'm being impulsive," Mel said under her breath as she got out of the car and headed up the steps of the building.

Honey Comb definitely looked like its namesake. The outside was painted a bright yellow, while the shutters, front door, porch, and roof were a burnt orange. The inside looked like bumblebees had decorated it. The walls were golden yellow, the floorboards and crown molding were black, and the floor was a pattern of pale yellow-and-black hexagon-shaped tiles.

"Why if it isn't Ms. Melanie O'Bryan," a sweet Southern drawl greeted Mel.

Pinky Player was more than a tad bit eccentric. She had overplucked eyebrows that she managed to make work with her bright eye shadow; she kept her strawberry blonde hair cut short, and she used some sort of product to spike it up all over her head. Mel wasn't sure what it was, but she suspected it had to be something stronger than gel, because Pinky rode her motorcycle whenever she could, and her helmet never messed up her rocker look.

"Hey Pinky." Mel took a deep breath and tried to reassure herself of this decision.

It was a little out of character for Mel to leave off the Mrs. when it came to an adult. She was raised good and proper in the South, after all. But Pinky had never wanted to be called anything but Pinky. Besides, she might've been in a happily committed relationship with one Reginald Reid for the past thirty-four years, but the two had never married. Not even after the births of their two kids.

"You have time to give me a haircut?" Mel asked.

Three stylists were still in the shop: Pinky, Janie Ashton, and Connie Applewood. Janie and Connie both had clients in their chairs, and Pinky was sweeping up around her station.

"For you? Always." Pinky smiled as she set her broom to the side. "Just the usual trim?" she asked as she grabbed a smock and headed over to the sink.

"Actually, no," Mel said following her.

Pinky stopped and turned around, her thin eyebrows raising high on her forehead. Pinky had been the only person ever to cut Mel's hair, and for the past couple of years she'd been trying to convince Mel to let her do something different.

"Really?" Pinky asked.

"Yeah." Mel nodded nervously. "Surprise me."

"Oh, this is going to be so much fun." Pinky smiled and rubbed her hands together before she settled Mel in the chair.

"You just made her day," Connie said as she snipped Veronica Harold's salt-and-pepper hair.

Connie had been working at the shop since Pinky had opened it thirty years ago. She dyed her short hair a reddish brown and streaked it with blonde highlights. Veronica and her husband ran Farmer's Pharmacy.

"Yeah," Veronica said. "Delta Forns was in here not ten minutes ago causing a fuss."

"Batty old woman," Karen Wilson said. Karen was the high school music teacher.

"Lean back, baby doll." Pinky guided Mel back and adjusted a towel under her neck.

"And Bethelda Grimshaw was in here this morning," Janie said.

Janie was a couple of years younger then Mel. She'd gone up to Tallahassee and studied at the Aveda Institute before moving back to Mirabelle, and Pinky had given her a job. Janie was tiny and curvy, with sunshine-yellow blonde hair that she kept short and usually curled.

"Oh God, that woman is horrible," Veronica said.

"I hate it when she's in here." Connie shook her head. "Because I have to watch every single thing that I say."

"Mmm-hmm." Pinky began to wet Mel's hair. "And you know how none of us like to watch what we say."

"I just don't talk," Janie said. "I'd hate to slip up and be the focus of her next big story."

"Wouldn't we all." Mel closed her eyes as Pinky shampooed her hair and massaged her scalp. As the suds were rinsed away with warm water, Mel's tension and fear washed away, too. She knew for a fact she was in good hands with Pinky, and she was excited for the change. So she just sat back and relaxed, and enjoyed the company of the women around her.

Chapter Seven

An Infuriating Man and
an Infuriated Woman

Mel was more than a little nervous and very excited as she pulled up in front of Jax and Grace's house. She hadn't gone anywhere after she'd left Pinky's shop the day before, so no one outside of the shop had seen the new haircut. And boy, was it different.

But Mel loved it.

Pinky had cut off a good twelve inches, and Mel's hair now lay at her shoulders. It had taken her about a half hour to blow-dry and style it that morning, which was a very nice change compared to the usual hour.

Mel was the last to arrive, parking right behind Brendan's black truck, which was right next to Bennett's gray one. She got out of the car and walked around to the trunk to grab the groceries she'd brought. A bottle of ketchup had fallen out of one of the bags and rolled to the back of the trunk. Mel bent over and leaned into the space, but the bottle was in the far left corner and she had to really stretch to get to it. Leaning on her right arm made her wince.

It was at this point that someone came up behind her. "Need help?"

Of course Bennett had to come right when her ass was in the air. Mel jerked her head up and banged it hard on the roof of the trunk.

"Shit," she shrieked, as pain radiated through the back of her skull.

"Are you okay?" he asked as his hands came up around her sides.

Oh, why did he have to touch her?

He helped her get out of the trunk, and she reached up and touched the back of her sore head.

"Let me see." He moved her hand and gently probed the back of her head. She flinched when his fingers found the spot.

"I'm fine." She tried to swat his hands away.

"Are you sure?" he asked. One of his hands gripped her waist while the other didn't move from her head. He took a step closer, bringing her body right up against his, and tilted her head back so he could look into her face.

"What are you doing?" she whispered.

"Checking your pupils and making sure you don't have a concussion."

He was so incredibly close to her, his mouth just inches away as he looked into her eyes. She was light-headed, and it had nothing to do with smashing her head.

Nope. It was because every hard inch of him was pushed up against her. And even though they'd been this close before, she still had no idea how to deal with it. How to deal with him.

"I'm sorry you hit your head," he said gently.

"Hasn't anyone ever told you not to sneak up on people?" she asked.

His mouth quirked to the side and she knew he was trying to hide a laugh. "I wasn't sneaking up on you."

"Uh-huh."

"At least I wasn't trying to. And I think you're okay." He moved his face back but kept the rest of his body plastered to hers.

"I told you I was fine."

He looked at her face for a second longer and froze. "You cut your hair."

"Yeah." She reached up and touched the curls at her shoulder.

He stared at her for a moment before he let go of her and took a step back. "It looks good. Really, really good."

"Thanks."

"You need help with your groceries?" He didn't wait for her to answer but leaned over and grabbed the ketchup out of the trunk with no problem. He tossed it into one of the bags, then grabbed all the bags in one hand and shut the trunk in one swift motion.

"Thanks," Mel said again.

Bennett stopped at his truck and grabbed a little bag before he shut the door. As Mel followed him up to the house, all she could think about was how the man never ceased to confuse the hell out of her. One second he was holding her and the next he was running away.

Again.

Yeah, this was getting ridiculous.

When Mel and Bennett walked into the kitchen, Grace was at the sink washing something under a steady stream of water. Paige stood on one side of the island cutting fruit, and Harper sat at the bar, holding a sleeping Trevor.

Grace spotted them first and her hands froze. "Holy shit," she said, her mouth hanging open.

Leave it to Grace to not mince words.

"What?" Harper asked following Grace's gaze. "Oh. My. Gosh."

"Wow." Paige looked up from her cutting.

It took Mel a second to realize what they were all going on about. She was still reeling from Bennett and his extreme weirdness.

Mel's eyes flickered to him for just a second. He'd set the bags down on the counter and was starting to unload them, keeping his back to all of the girls.

"What do you think?" Mel asked slowly, finding her bearings.

"I think it's awesome," Grace said, shutting off the water. She grabbed a towel from the counter and dried her hands as she walked over to Mel. "I haven't seen you with hair this short since we were five years old." She reached up and grabbed one of Mel's curls.

Bennett moved to the fridge and began stocking it.

"You look amazing. Not that you didn't look amazing before, but this is just . . . wow," Paige said in awe.

"Yeah?" Mel asked, a smile coming across her face. She just couldn't bring herself to keep Bennett out of her line of vision. He bent down slightly to move some stuff back on a shelf inside the fridge.

"Oh yeah." Grace nodded. "It looks *hot*."

"I'm sure you'll be *really* catching the guys' eyes now," Harper said a bit malevolently, giving a pointed look in Bennett's direction.

Crash.

Bennett's head had come up fast and hit the edge of the top shelf. "Shit," he said, taking a step back and rubbing the back of his head.

It took everything Mel had not to start laughing. "Do we need to check your pupils?" she asked him sweetly.

"No." If Mel didn't know any better, she would have sworn his cheeks had a little more color in them than they had a moment before. "I'll leave you ladies to those," he said, indicating the rest of the bags on the counter. "I ran to my truck to get the sauce for the wings, and Jax is about to put those on." He grabbed the small bag he'd pulled out of his truck and promptly vacated the room.

The second he was outside on the deck and the door shut behind him, all of the women burst into laughter.

"All right, I want the story of what just happened there between the two of you. You talk while I help them," Harper said. She stood and handed Trevor over to Mel.

"Talk about what?" Mel asked, adjusting Trevor in her arms.

There was no doubt about it—Brendan and Paige made beautiful babies together. He had Paige's wild dark hair and Brendan's light blue eyes. He was most definitely going to be a heartbreaker when he grew up, just like his daddy.

"What happened with you and Bennett?" Harper asked.

"What are you talking about?" Mel said.

"Don't think we didn't see the two of you talking after the game yesterday," Paige said.

"Or what just happened a second ago. I don't think he liked hearing about the possibility of you with other men," Grace said.

"Yesterday was nothing. He helped me with a jammed door. That was it."

"You two were mighty close." Paige looked up from her strawberry slicing.

"And by that you mean *he* was mighty close."

"Yeah, but you weren't moving away," Harper said, doing her one-raised-eyebrow thing that she did so well.

"No, you're right. He did that, too. He came up to me and then he was the one that walked away. Just like he always is."

"That was 'cause Short-N-Scrawny came up to you guys," Harper said.

"Stu isn't short and scrawny."

The other women stared at her in silent disbelief.

"Okay, fine, Stu is. But look, really it wouldn't have mattered if anyone had come up to us or not. Bennett—" Mel dropped her voice as she glanced out the window behind her to the deck outside. The guys were all gathered around the grill, and there was no way that any of them could hear her. "—Bennett keeps doing this. He gets close, then pulls away. Flirts, then bolts. Almost kisses me, then practically runs out the door. I'm not interested in playing this game of his."

"Oh, really?" Paige asked.

"Yes, really," Mel said firmly.

"You're going to be singing a different tune when he finally acts. You know how many times I was done waiting for Jax? Yeah, you can see just how much I stuck to my guns." Grace held up her left hand, which had a very nice diamond on it.

Mel shook her head. "You and Jax are different."

"Why?" Grace asked.

"Because that was a long time coming. You've been in love with him for most of your life."

"What about Brendan and Paige?" Harper asked.

"Yeah." Paige nodded. "Brendan and I moved pretty fast into things. I fell in love with him before I even knew what had happened."

"Again, you and Brendan are different. He didn't hesitate when it came to you."

"Oh Mel," Paige said, shaking her head. "All men are different, and they figure things out in their own time. And I think Bennett is right there."

"Right where?" Mel asked.

"Right on the verge of figuring things out."

"Hmm, we'll just see about that."

"Yes, we will," Grace said.

Trevor shifted in Mel's arms, and a second later he started to fuss.

"I think he's hungry," Paige said, wiping her hands on a towel. She rounded the corner and held out her hands for Trevor. "I'll be right back." The two disappeared into the guest bedroom.

"Here, can you take these out for the boys to grill?" Grace slid a plate full of hot dogs across the counter at Mel.

Mel frowned. "Are you just trying to get me in his line of sight or something?"

"I don't need to do that. He keeps looking through the window at you."

"No, he's not." Mel resisted the urge to turn around.

"Oh, yes he is," Harper chimed in.

"You two are giant pains in my ass."

"Yes. Fine. Whatever. Now get out there." Grace inched the plate even closer to Mel.

"Okay, okay, I'm going." Mel got down off the bar stool and grabbed the plate.

Brendan, Jax, Shep, Tripp, Preston, Baxter, and Bennett were all outside drinking beer. And the second Mel opened the door, seven sets of eyes landed on her. Why did she feel like she'd just been fed to the wolves?

"Mel, come over here." Shep grabbed the plate from her, threw an arm around her shoulder, and guided her over to the group. "Let me get a good look at this new haircut of yours." He passed off the plate to Jax, who was behind the grill. "Damn, girl, you're looking good," he added just a little bit too enthusiastically as he pulled her close.

"She sure does," Preston said, grinning hugely. She knew he was trying not to crack up.

"It's just a matter of time before somebody with half

a brain snatches you up." So Shep was definitely acting stranger than usual, and that was saying something.

Mel couldn't stop herself from looking over at Bennett, who was looking none too pleased. Shep pulled her so close she was literally plastered up against him. Apparently he hadn't missed the look, either.

Shep was like a brother to Mel, so she was used to them being this close without it meaning anything romantic. She was also used to him being an instigator. A big one. And based on the ever-growing frown on Bennett's face, Shep was succeeding. In spades.

"So how's the project going?" Baxter asked.

"Good," Mel said, trying to focus on the conversation around her and not on the glowering man in front of her. "The kids are really enjoying it."

Tripp clapped Bennett on the shoulder. "And I'm sure our boy Bennett here is working out. Anything he puts his hands on gets some pretty amazing results."

"Yeah, his expertise on the matter is evident," Jax said, waving a hand at his house. "He was the mastermind behind all of this."

"They were *your* plans." Bennett shrugged and took a sip of his beer.

"That *you* turned into this," Jax said.

"That you all helped with," Bennett countered.

"Oh, look at Bennett being all modest," Brendan said.

"I'm not being modest."

Mel wasn't sure how it was possible that the man could scowl any more than he currently was.

"Then are you saying you don't know what you're doing?" Baxter asked.

"I didn't say that." Yeah, Mel was wrong. He *could* scowl more.

"Well, I'm going to go back in and help them." Mel pulled

away from Shep and headed toward the door. She turned as she opened it and her eyes caught Bennett's. He was watching every move she made.

* * *

"Did you have fun with that?" Bennett asked Shep.

"Sure did." Shep grinned, looking pretty damn satisfied with himself.

Bennett had not had fun. Not. At. All.

The rational part of Bennett's brain had told him to calm the fuck down, that Shep and Mel were just friends and had been for years, for twenty-five long years. Shep wasn't the type of guy to not go after something, or someone, he wanted. If he had feelings for Mel that went anything beyond friendship, he would've done something about it a while ago. And besides all of that, Bennett had no claim to Mel whatsoever.

But the irrational part of Bennett's brain had wanted to punch Shep in the jaw. Or break his hands. Either one would've been highly satisfying. Especially with that smug expression that was still plastered across Shep's face.

"I found it amusing." Jax started to put the hot dogs on the grill. "And telling."

"Yeah, you must really suck at poker," Preston said.

"Oh, he does. He pretty much just gives his money away," Brendan said.

It was true. That was why Bennett avoided gambling.

"So you going to do anything anytime soon?" Trip asked. "You can't wait around forever."

"Someone's going to snag Mel up pretty soon. I would've by now if I didn't see her as a sister. But we all know that little scenario only tickles Jax's fancy," Shep said.

Jax looked up from the grill and pointed the tongs in his

hand at Shep. "I stopped looking at Grace like a little sister when she was eighteen years old and I figured out she was hot."

"Things I never, ever wanted to know," Brendan said, shaking his head.

"Yeah, from what Grace tells me, Jax doesn't do brotherly things to her now," Preston said.

"Seriously. Can we change the subject?" Brendan looked pained.

"Actually, if you're not going to do anything about Mel, I was going to give her number to one of my friends from law school," Preston said.

Bennett sputtered on his beer. He started coughing, and Tripp hit him hard on the back.

"I'll take that to mean he's going to do something about it," Baxter said.

Yeah, he was going to do something about it, all right. He just wasn't sure what.

When Bennett had walked outside earlier and found Mel with her tiny little butt in the air, he'd about lost his damn mind. And then he'd been so close to her again and he'd wanted to kiss her so much it was literally painful.

But he'd hesitated. Yet again. What the hell was wrong with him?

Every time he saw her he wanted her more. And how was it possible for the woman to get even more beautiful than she'd been before?

He'd been a huge fan of those curls stretching down her back, but damn if they didn't look that much more enticing bouncing around her shoulders. And they somehow seemed bigger, fuller. His fingers were just itching to plunge into them.

But that wasn't going to be a reality until he learned how to open his mouth and actually say what he needed to say to Mel.

Was it always this complicated when it came to women? He couldn't remember, but he was sure as hell going to have to figure it out.

* * *

Mel was beyond fidgety on Monday. Fidgety and irritated. She had no idea what the hell was going on with Bennett. That man turned hot and cold faster than she could blink. He'd acted so strange all through dinner on Sunday. Hardly talking to anyone, and whenever Mel would look at him he'd always be studying her like an incredibly difficult math problem that he just couldn't figure out.

It was beyond frustrating. *He* was beyond frustrating.

The man drove her crazy in so many different ways, some of them good...some of them not so good. Right now, the not-so-good was outweighing the good, by a lot.

He'd been fine this morning during the classes. He turned on a professional switch whenever the kids were around. He'd acted like everything was perfectly fine with him and Mel. Except it wasn't perfectly fine for her.

And she wasn't done for the day with Bennett driving her crazy. He had to come back because they were getting a delivery of the second shipment of wood. She'd told him she could take care of it. She had to wait for Hamilton to finish up with practice, anyway. But he'd insisted. She hadn't argued, because there was no point in arguing with a crazy person.

The final bell rang, and Mel decided to grade papers until Bennett got there. She got halfway through her pile before she leaned back at her desk and started chewing on the end of her pen.

Why was this so damn complicated? Why was *he* so damn complicated?

Mel's experience with men and relationships was certainly lacking, but really, she knew when she wanted a man. And boy, did she ever want Bennett. More than she'd ever wanted anybody else. And it was about more than his good looks . . . but did he ever look good.

It was about how great he was with her kids, listening to them and talking to them. He was actually having quite an impact on Dale. Dale was really into the project, and he was making a much bigger effort in class.

And then there was the effect Bennett had on her. Like how his smile made her go all warm and fuzzy. Or how when he looked at her, she felt like he was actually seeing her. He made her feel things she'd never felt before. Things she didn't know or understand. And it scared her, but the thought of not figuring out what it was scared her a lot more.

It wasn't like she thought Bennett was the guy she was going to spend the rest of her life with. She wasn't planning their wedding, or where they would live, or what they would name their kids. No, that would make her a little crazy, considering the fact that they'd never kissed or even been on anything that she would consider an actual date, or had a discussion about any of this.

Really, if their inability to get off the ground was any indication, then whatever they had going on wasn't going any further.

Any further than what? The inch it's moved in the two months since I got shot and he finally noticed me?

Okay, that might not be entirely true. They'd been friends before that. Well, he'd been her friend and she'd pined quietly.

Pined?

Yup, she really was pathetic, a pathetic little schoolteacher who fantasized about a hot muscled man. Muscles that she wanted to trace and memorize with her hands and tongue.

She was pretty sure he had some skilled hands, too. Hands she would have absolutely no problem with if they roamed all over her body.

How many times was she going to have to tell herself not to dwell on this man anymore? Well, to be fair, at that exact moment she wasn't dwelling, she was fantasizing. So she might as well indulge herself a little bit.

Or a lot.

She imagined what it would feel like to have Bennett's mouth on hers. What it would be like if he pushed her back against her desk, his hands going down to her hips where he would lift her up and sit her down. Then he'd make space for himself between her thighs while he lay her down and his body covered hers. His mouth would move from hers, and he'd kiss her jaw as he made his way over to her ear. One of his hands would travel up under her dress and he'd whisper her name as his fingers traced a slow torturous path up the inside of her—

"Hey, Mel."

Mel shot up in her chair to find Bennett standing in front of her desk. He was wearing a somewhat bemused grin as he looked at her. At least he wasn't frowning anymore.

"I thought I was meeting you over there." She stood up and smoothed the front of her dress. Her cheeks and chest were on fire.

"We were. But the delivery guys called me, and they're going to be ten minutes early. I called your cell but you didn't answer."

"It must still be on silent."

"No problem." He looked her up and down. "Whatever you were thinking about must've been something good."

She flushed and rounded her desk.

"So was it?"

"Was it what?" she asked as she headed toward the door,

trying to not look at him directly. He was ex-military, he could probably read her mind or something if she looked him in the eye.

"Good?" he asked as he fell in step beside her.

She cleared her throat uncomfortably. She was incapable of lying, and telling Bennett she hadn't been thinking of something good would be a bald-faced lie. And if she said yes, and he asked her what she'd been thinking of, she'd have to lie then, too. "Oh, you know, just thinking." She waved her hand in the air vaguely.

"Riiight," he said slowly.

Please no more questions. Please, please, please.

She held her breath for a couple of seconds waiting. He didn't say anything, so she exhaled, her shoulders relaxing.

"I'll have to get it out of you later."

She stopped dead and stared at his back in horror as he continued to make his way down the hall.

"You coming or not?" he called out, not turning around.

* * *

Maybe that was a bad choice of words, Bennett thought as he rounded the corner. Because if he got to put his vote in, they'd both be coming.

Really it wasn't his fault that he was having dirty thoughts. It was Mel's. When he'd walked into her classroom he'd been more than a little surprised to find her in the state she'd been in.

Her head had been resting on the back of her chair, her long slender neck exposed and looking incredibly kissable. All of her wild curls had been tied back into some sort of knot thing that Bennett really wanted to pull down. Her lips had been pursed around the end of her pen, which had put images in Bennett's mind of other things her lips could be wrapped around. Her lovely chest had been rising and falling rather quickly, and her skin had been flushed.

When Bennett had been in school, he hadn't had any hot teachers. So he'd never had any classroom fantasies. Yeah, seeing Mel sitting behind her desk looking hot and turned on had blown that out of the water. He'd had a fairly graphic image of them on the top of her desk.

She caught up to him just before he opened the doors to head outside. He held it open and she walked past him.

"Thank you," she said, still not making eye contact.

Bennett couldn't stop himself from grinning. Whatever she'd been thinking about must have been really good, and the fact that she wouldn't look at him led him to believe it had probably been about him.

Here's hoping.

He stared at her back as she walked in front of him. She was wearing some sort of green wrap dress, the tie just above her right hip. Bennett's fingers itched to pull at the bow. Instead, he watched her hips sway back and forth; the clingy material of her dress molded to her in all the right places.

The delivery truck got there just as Bennett and Mel arrived. Mel had told Bennett she could take care of the delivery by herself. But he'd vetoed that plan. First, he wanted to check the wood and make sure it was up to his standards. And second, he was finally going to talk to her, just as soon as he could get her alone.

When all of the wood was stacked in a neat little pile in the corner, and the delivery truck had pulled away from the wood shop, Mel and Bennett made their way back up to the school.

As they passed the library, a door opened and Mrs. Sylvester came out. She was in her seventies now, with dark gray hair and kind blue eyes. She wore a fuzzy blue sweater, thick glasses, and a big smile. She had her purse over her shoulder and her keys in her hand ready to lock up.

"Why, if it isn't Bennett Hart!" Mrs. Sylvester said. "How have you been, sugar?" She smiled wide and held out her arms for a hug.

"Good," he said, taking a step forward and wrapping his arms around her.

"Now why haven't you been to see me since you started working on that project?" She put her hands on his forearms and took a step back. "You too important to come visit your favorite librarian?"

The woman might be tiny, but when she peered up at him with that stern eye he felt like he was fifteen years old again.

"No, ma'am," Bennett said. "I just haven't had a chance to get over here. I promise to make it up to you when my schedule calms down."

"That's what I like to hear." She reached up and patted his cheek, her stern look melting back into a smile. "Melanie has told me how busy you guys have been." She gave Mel an indulgent smile. "Still as pretty as ever my dear. And you're looking good, too, young man. Have you still not found a nice woman to settle down with?" She gave Mel another significant look.

Bennett cleared his throat uncomfortably as he rubbed the back of his neck. "Uh, well, I uh...," he stuttered. "I'm not seeing anyone at the moment." He was very aware of Mel next to him.

"I'll let you two talk," Mel said, moving off rather quickly.

Shit. He needed to talk to her. But Mel didn't get very far down the hall before another teacher stopped her, a male teacher who was definitely looking her up and down as he started chatting her up.

"Well, you need to get on it. You aren't getting any

younger. You know," Mrs. Sylvester, whispered taking a step closer. "Ms. Melanie O'Bryan over there is single." She nodded to where Mel was standing.

The guy who was talking to her was wearing khaki pants and a polo. He wasn't scrawny like Stu; he was tall and filled out the sleeves of his shirt. He also had pretty-boy hair that Bennett suspected was gelled or moussed or some crap like that.

Bennett reluctantly pulled his gaze away from Mel when Mrs. Sylvester started talking again: "And I've heard a couple of the other single males at this school are interested in her. I'm just saying she's a mighty nice girl. She'd be a good catch for you. Maybe you should think about that as you spend time with her on this project." She patted his arm.

Bennett looked back up just in time to see Mel laughing. It wasn't one of her real down-to-the-belly laughs, not the one that he always tried to get out of her. Not the one that made all the tension in his body disappear. No, this one was small and polite. But the stupid schmuck in front of her must have thought it meant something else because he reached out and touched her elbow, and his hand slid up the back of her arm. She didn't move away from him, but Bennett could see the tension snap into her shoulders as her laugh died off.

"I'll see you later. I promise. I need to go take care of something," he said to Mrs. Sylvester.

"Atta boy," Mrs. Sylvester said, as Bennett walked off.

"Hey Mel." He came up behind her and put his hand at the small of her back. She didn't tense up with him; if anything she leaned into his hand, pulling away from Pretty Boy.

"Hey," she said, turning to look up at him. "Bennett, have you met Duncan Marsh? He teaches geography and is a football coach."

"Defensive coordinator," Duncan said, holding out his hand.

"Duncan, this is Bennett Hart. He works for Marlin Yance's construction company."

"Nice to meet you," Bennett lied. He shook the guy's hand while not moving his other hand from Mel's back. Duncan sized Bennett up and tried to squeeze Bennett's hand just a little too tightly.

Really, pal? I could snap you. It might be a bit of a challenge, but I could still snap you.

"Bennett is helping me out with the bookshelf project," Mel continued.

"Really?" Duncan asked, letting go of Bennett's hand. "So you're going to be around here for a while? With Mel?"

"Yup." Bennett nodded. "Until the end of the semester."

Duncan folded his arms across his chest. "You know, you could've asked me, Mel. I know my way around a hammer and a nail. And I'm sure coming down to the school all the time is a big inconvenience for Bennett here."

"Mel and I are old friends. We go way back." Bennett let his hand travel around to Mel's side and pull her in closer. "So it isn't an inconvenience at all."

Mel looked up at him, but Bennett didn't see her expression because he was still focused on Preppy.

"If you'll excuse us," Mel said, grabbing Bennett's arm and pulling him away.

He let her drag him down the hallway. When they were well away from the library she rounded on him.

"Are you kidding me with this?" she yell-whispered at him.

"Kidding you with what?" he asked.

"With whatever the hell it is you're doing!" she exclaimed. "You, Bennett Hart"—she poked him hard in the chest—"are the most frustrating"—*poke*—"most difficult"—*poke*—"back-and-forth man that I've ever"—*poke*—"met!" *Poke.*

"What did I do?" he asked taking a step back out of range.

She might be small, but she had some force in her, all right. And she had some other things, too. Her curls were coming down from her bun, her amber eyes were blazing, and the apples of her cheeks were bright red. She looked sexy as hell.

"We're 'old friends'?" she asked, gesturing between the two of them. "We 'go way back'? And by that do you mean the last two years? Because I don't recall us ever hanging out when you were one of the most popular seniors in high school and I was an eighth grader with braces and uncontrollable hair.

"And you know what else? I'm so sick of this game you insist on playing. I'm sick of your inability to make a freaking decision when it comes to me. You're hot and then you're cold. You're flirting with me then you're ignoring me or acting pissy about God only knows what. You freak out when we almost kiss then you proceed to have a pissing contest with some guy right in front of me.

"*That's* what you did, Bennett. If you're not interested in me, that's fine." She took a step forward and pushed him hard in the chest. "But leave me alone." With that she turned around and walked away.

Well, he thought, that had been enlightening.

Chapter Eight

No More Playing Games

Mel was shaking as she walked back into her classroom. Her hands were balled up into fists at her sides, and she just wanted to scream. She needed to get out of this place pronto. She needed to call Harper and Grace and have them come over so they could drink wine and bitch about life. She needed something to think about other than that ridiculous man, because if she thought about him for a second longer she was going to go crazy.

She needed to move on from him. She *had* to move on, because they weren't going anywhere.

What the hell was she talking about? There was no *they*. There was her, and there was him. That was it. That was how it was and how it was going to stay. She had to accept that and move on.

Move. On.

Please, just move on.

Oh God, who was she kidding? She'd never felt this way about any man before. Bennett was...well, infuriating to start with, but he was brave, smart, kind, funny, intense. There was nothing like having his full attention focused on her. He gave her way more than butterflies. It was like eagles were flapping around in her stomach whenever he was around. There were no flutters. They were freaking tidal waves.

Yeah, getting over Bennett was going to be way easier said than done.

Mel headed toward the supply closet at the back of her classroom where she locked up her purse in a filing cabinet. She grabbed the key and unlocked the top drawer, pulled out her purse, and slammed the drawer shut. When she turned around Bennett was standing in the doorway. Filling it completely. Mel stopped short and stared at him. His eyes were focused on her, the determination in them making all of the thoughts vacate her brain.

"I can't leave you alone." He came into the room and shut the door behind him. "And I'm not playing games." He crossed the small space. "Or at least I'm not trying to." He shook his head. "I think about you all the time." He stopped in front of her, took the purse out of her hands, and put it on top of the filing cabinet. Then he reached up and touched her cheek. His fingers fanned out as he pushed his hand to the back of her head and tilted her face up.

Holy hell, what is happening?

She looked into his eyes, and her knees went just a little bit weak. She reached back and planted her hands against the wall, trying to find some balance, something to keep her upright, because she really didn't want to miss this.

"Because I *am* interested in you, Mel." He cupped her face with his other hand and ran his thumb across her lower lip. "Very interested." He leaned forward and pressed his mouth to hers.

The kiss was soft and gentle at first, just his lips against hers. He took another step into her, pushing her back. When she hit the wall she gasped, and Bennett took advantage of her open mouth. He sucked her bottom lip into his mouth, and she couldn't stop the moan that escaped her throat.

She plastered herself up against him, against every inch of his hard body. Her arms wound around his shoulders; her hands skittered up the back of his head. She opened her mouth further and his tongue touched hers. Bennett groaned as their tongues began a thorough exploration of each other's mouths.

His hands were at the back of her head, his fingers deftly pulling out the pins that held up her bun. And then he was unwinding her hair, his hands plunging deep into her unruly curls.

"I've wanted to do this for so long," he said against her mouth. "These curls of yours drive me out of my mind."

"What stopped you?" She nipped at his lower lip.

"Pure stupidity," he said, as he claimed her mouth again.

Holy cow, can this man kiss. I feel it everywhere, and do I mean everywhere! He had her toes curling in her shoes, all manner of body parts tingling where they were pushed up against his, and his hands were magic in her hair. One of his hands drifted down to her side. He touched her hip for a second before his hand slid to the small of her back. He held her to him, but really, she wasn't going anywhere.

"Mel," a voice called out from her classroom. "Are you here?"

There were only a few things that could bring Mel back to reality with the snap of a finger. The sound of her little brother's voice was definitely one of them.

"Oh crap, it's Hamilton," Mel gasped, pulling back. Bennett's hand was behind her head, and it prevented her from hitting the wall. "I'll be right out!" she answered Hamilton, unable to completely cover up the breathy edge to her voice.

Bennett nodded. He let go of her reluctantly, and took a step back. "You're going to have to give me a minute before I can go out there," he said, clearing his throat uncomfortably.

"Oh," she said, nodding. "Um, okay."

Actually, she was going to need a minute, too. She knew her hair was everywhere, and she had a feeling Bennett's scruffy jaw had left its fair share of marks on her face. Not to mention her thoroughly swollen lips.

Soooo worth it.

She grabbed her purse from the cabinet and searched for a hair tie. She found one at the bottom and attempted to pull back her hair. It was useless. Bennett had done his best to untame every single one of her curls. He'd succeeded.

"Do you have a sweater or something?" he asked her.

"Nothing that will fit you," she said, looking up at him with a small smile.

"I meant for you." He indicated her chest.

"What?" she asked, looking down. Apparently Bennett wasn't the only one that had body parts rising to the occasion. Mel's nipples were standing at attention. Front and center. "Oh." She turned around and grabbed a cardigan from a hook on the wall. She put it on and turned back to Bennett. "Do I look presentable?"

"Sure." His eyes took a slow journey up her body, lingering in more than one place.

"You're not helping matters," she said, shaking her head.

"You don't say?" He finally met her eyes, and his mouth quirked to the side. "What exactly am I doing?"

Making her want to jump him, that was what he was doing.

"I'll see you out there." She walked past him, opening the door and stepping into the classroom.

And there sat her little brother, sitting at her desk with his feet propped up on the corner.

"What were you doing?" he asked, pushing up his glasses.

She frowned at him. "Hamilton, get your feet off my desk."

He dropped his feet and stood up just as Bennett came

out of the supply room. "Ahh, so it wasn't *what* you were doing, but more like *who* you were doing." It didn't matter that he needed glasses, because the boy missed nothing.

Mel wanted to deny it and say that nothing had been going on. But her inability to lie made that a problem, and she couldn't lie to her baby brother. She also didn't want to deny that something had *finally* happened between her and Bennett.

"Don't bother trying to hide it," Hamilton said, folding his arms across his chest and shaking his head as he looked between Mel and Bennett. "I'm not an idiot. It looks like someone took sandpaper to your face, and there's no helping your hair."

"You're a pain, you know that?"

"I'm your little brother—that's what I do. So Bennett, I see you *finally* made a move on my sister. You've wised up and you *will* be seeing her now?" He said it like it wasn't really a question, more like an order. He also attempted to give Bennett an intimidating glare.

If Mel weren't beyond mortified, she would've laughed at her little brother being protective of her.

"Hamilton," Mel said still trying to sound stern, "that isn't any of your business."

Hamilton just looked at Mel like she was crazy, then returned his gaze to Bennett. "So...are you?"

"Well, your sister and I haven't discussed that yet. But as far as I'm concerned, yes."

Mel hadn't realized she'd been holding her breath until she exhaled in relief.

"I've got a consult in half an hour with a client and then practice tonight," Bennett said to Mel. "Can I see you tomorrow?"

She nodded.

"When's your lunch?"

"Eleven thirty," she said with no small amount of thrill.

"You available?"

"Yeah."

"I'll bring lunch." He crossed the room and planted a soft kiss on her mouth, then he headed for the door. "Good seeing you Hamilton." He gave a final wave as he left.

Mel was more than a little stunned by the kiss, but not stunned enough to stop herself from looking at the amazing way his jeans molded to his butt.

"You're drooling," Hamilton said.

Well, it was an improvement from the panting she'd been doing five minutes ago.

* * *

Mel tried to have dinner with her family on a regular basis. Lately, her mother tended to hover over her the entire time she was there. Tonight was no different.

"You look too thin. Are you eating enough?" Corinne asked as she studied Mel.

It was always a little disconcerting for Mel when her mother scrutinized her. Maybe it was because Mel had her mother's eyes. They were the exact same shade and shape, and Mel always felt like she was looking into a mirror.

"Yes, Mom," Mel said as she helped herself to another piece of fried chicken.

"Have you lost weight?" Corinne pressed.

"Mom, I'm fine." Mel tried to change the subject. She'd actually lost ten pounds since the shooting, but it wasn't like she'd wanted to. It was because she hadn't really had an appetite for a while. But she was eating regularly again.

"Are you sure? Because—"

"Corinne, Mel's fine. She would tell us if she wasn't," her father said.

Miles O'Bryan wasn't a formidable man by any sense of the word, but his wife and children had always listened to him.

"Oh, all right," Corinne relented.

Thanks, Dad, Mel mouthed to her father.

No problem, he mouthed back. "So how's this project shaping out?" he asked aloud.

"Oh, yeah, I meant to ask you about that," Corinne said. "Superintendent Stafford came by our school the other day and he told me how impressed he is with you. I really like that man."

Corinne was a preschool teacher and had been for the last twenty-seven years. She'd never liked the former superintendent, Keith Reynolds. But that might've also had to do with the fact that Keith had screwed over her best friend. Corinne had known who Grace's father had been, too, but she'd been sworn to secrecy along with Claire's mother, Lula Mae.

Corinne had also despised Reynolds because he'd always treated the preschool grades like a day-care center. He'd had absolutely no concept whatsoever as to what went into teaching three- and four-year-olds. So not only had he been a prick in every facet of his life, he'd also been a moron.

"It's going really well. We're right on schedule, and the students seem to be getting a lot from it. Which was what I'd wanted."

"And Bennett?" her mother asked, saying his name with more than a little emphasis.

Yeah, Mel wasn't the only one who liked Bennett. Ever since the shooting, Corinne asked about him all the time. She'd been more than a little appreciative of him, having saved her daughter's life and all. She also hadn't forgotten that Bennett had sat in the waiting room with Hamilton for a good couple of hours after Mel's surgery. Yup, she'd been pushing her daughter in that direction for months, not that Mel had needed any more incentive.

"What about him?" Mel asked.

"How is he doing?"

"I'm pretty sure they were making out in the supply closet this afternoon," Hamilton announced to the table.

"What?" Corinne dropped her knife and fork on her plate. It clanked loudly.

"Thanks, Hamilton." Mel frowned at him.

He grinned. "Anytime."

"Are you two seeing each other?" her mother asked anxiously.

"Um, yes," Mel answered, suddenly finding her carrots fascinating.

"That doesn't sound very convincing," Corinne said.

"Don't worry, Mom, I asked him the exact same question," Hamilton said. "They have a lunch date tomorrow."

Mel looked at her little brother in horror. She didn't care how much she loved him. He was a dead man.

"Hamilton." Miles looked at his son over his glasses. "You do realize your sister works at the school you go to, and she is more than capable of paying you back for what you're doing right now?"

"There's nothing for her to tell. I'm an angel at school. You can ask any one of my teachers."

"Can we get back to the subject of you and Bennett?" Corinne said, absolutely refusing to get sidetracked.

"Mother, it just happened."

"I might be a little biased because he helped save your life, but I like him," Miles said. "If anyone wants my two cents."

"Well, of course we all like him. He's perfect for her," Corinne said excitedly.

"Okay, Mom." Mel put her knife and fork down. "Don't start planning a wedding and grandchildren. We just kissed. That's it."

"Looked like a lot more than kissing to me."

Mel kicked her brother under the table, hard.

"Ouch," he cried.

"Shut up," she said to him. "We are not going to make this into something before it is something." She looked around the table. "Does everyone understand that?"

"Yes," Miles said.

Hamilton scowled, continuing to rub his shin. Corinne pursed her lips, as if she was trying desperately not to say anything.

"I love that the only person to agree to this is the only person I'm not worried about."

"Fine, I won't say anything to him," Corinne said after a moment. "But you better keep us informed. No more of hiding what you've been doing."

"I wasn't hiding anything, Mom." Mel resisted the urge to bang her own head against the table. "I don't know what this is yet."

And the more she thought about it, the more nervous she got. Yes, Bennett had said that they were seeing each other now. And yes, he'd also kissed the ever-living daylights out of her. But when it came to her, the man hadn't been all that consistent. Who was to say he wouldn't wake up tomorrow and change his mind again?

* * *

Bennett had finally freaking done it. He'd finally kissed Mel. Whatever slim chance there'd been of walking away from her was completely gone now. He'd wanted to talk to her yesterday, to tell her he liked her. Tell her that he wanted to start seeing her. When he'd followed her into that closet he'd had every intention of doing so.

And then he'd kissed her and the talking plan had gone out the window. But he was pretty sure she'd gotten the message.

Bennett had kissed a number of women in his life, and it was safe to say that none of them even came close to Mel.

Not a single one.

No woman had ever drawn him in like she had. No kiss had ever made him feel like he was going to go crazy, made him feel like he was losing every single ounce of sense that he possessed. Yeah, after he'd pressed his mouth to hers, he'd been a goner.

She'd been soft and sweet. He'd forever remember that kiss, everything from her body pressed to his, to the smell of her hair, the taste of her skin. She'd been the clearest breath of fresh air that Bennett had inhaled in over three years—since before that, actually. She'd probably been the clearest breath of fresh air he'd ever taken in his life.

No, there was no way he was walking away now.

Bennett managed to stay focused at practice that night, which was saying a lot, because he kept hearing Mel's moans of satisfaction in his head. He wanted to get her to make those sounds again very, very soon. Preferably with both of them in bed and naked and her underneath him. But he tried to calm the hell down and pay attention.

Bennett had slipped only once, and he'd been lucky that Tripp was the one who caught him grinning.

"I'd be careful with that smile of yours if I were you. If the triplets catch you, they're going to pounce, and you're not going to know what hit you."

"I know." Bennett looked over his shoulder to make sure that Brendan, Jax, and Shep weren't within earshot.

"I'm assuming you finally did something?" Tripp asked.

"Yeah."

"Was it worth knowing?"

"It sure was," Bennett said.

And it really, really had been.

Chapter Nine

The Many Talents of Bennett Hart

At eleven o'clock on Tuesday, Bennett stopped by Café Lula, Lula Mae and Grace's café, to grab some lunch. He'd been relieved to find Lula Mae working the front and Grace baking in the kitchen. He wasn't sure what she knew, but he was pretty sure he would've gotten the third degree no matter what.

He walked down the hallway to Mel's class at eleven thirty-five. He'd just missed the last bell, and the halls were clear. He stepped into Mel's classroom and found her in much the same position he'd found her yesterday. Except, unlike yesterday, she was in no way turned on.

She had leaned her head back and her eyes were closed, and she was rubbing her temples. Her face was washed out and she looked exhausted.

"You okay?" he asked, coming into the room.

She opened her eyes slowly and winced before she shut them again. "No." She was on the verge of tears.

"Mel?" Bennett crossed the room and dropped the bags of food on her desk. "What's wrong?"

"I have a migraine."

"Bad?" he asked, crouching down next to her.

Bennett had never had a migraine, but his stepmother got them all the time. She'd be laid up in bed for hours in misery, lights and smells making her sick to her stomach.

"Yeah. The medicine hasn't done anything. It's just getting worse." She dropped her hands from her temples, as if she just didn't have the strength to hold them up anymore.

"Let me take you home," he said, rubbing the back of her hand.

"No, I'll be fine," she said, opening her eyes. She moved slightly and her face paled even more, which was saying something.

She abruptly lunged out of her desk and grabbed for the trash can at her feet. Bennett moved fast, pulling her hair back as she emptied her stomach. He rubbed her back until she stopped.

"I'm taking you home," he said.

"Okay," she said miserably, slowly getting to her feet. "I have to call the office."

"No, you have to sit down. I'll call." He reached over to flip the switch on the wall and made the overhead lights go off. Now the only light in the room was coming from the windows.

"Thank you," she mumbled, putting her head down on the desk.

Bennett continued to rub Mel's back as he called the secretary and told her they were going to have to find a sub for Mel for the rest of the day. Then he packed up Mel and her stuff, and walked her out of the school. She leaned into him and let him guide her. She had her sunglasses on, but he suspected her eyes were shut.

"What about my car?" she mumbled, as he helped her up into his truck.

"Don't worry about it. I'll take care of it."

"Bennett, I don't want to be an inconvenience."

"Mel, you're not an inconvenience," he said, brushing her hair back from her face and kissing her lightly on the forehead. "I got it."

"Thank you."

"It's no problem." He pulled back and closed the door gently.

And really she wasn't an inconvenience. He knew she was in a lot of pain, and all he could think about was making her feel better. That was all that mattered.

* * *

When Bennett pulled into the driveway, Mel started to move to get out.

"Just sit a second," he said, grabbing her purse and her bag.

"Okay." She slumped back into the seat.

Bennett went up to the house. He hesitated for a second, staring at Mel's purse. Her keys were in there somewhere, but a woman's purse was uncharted territory for him.

"Stop being a coward," he said, opening her purse and looking in.

He grabbed her keys that were lying on top of her wallet and unlocked the front door. He dropped her bags off on a chair in the hallway then went back out to get Mel. He opened the passenger door and reached across her to unbuckle the seat belt.

He slid one arm under her knees and the other behind her back. He pulled her into his chest and lifted her from the truck. She settled into his arms and rested her head on his shoulder.

He closed the door with his hip, taking care not to jostle her, and walked up to the house. He'd left the front door open, so he walked into the hallway and used his shoulder to shut the door. Mel burrowed into his neck, her hair tickling his skin. He liked having her in his arms, but the circumstances sucked.

He carried her to her bedroom and set her down on the bed.

"You want to change?" he asked as he went over to her window, closed the blinds, and drew the curtains.

"Yes, please," she said, kicking off her flats. "T-shirts are in the top drawer, shorts in the second."

Bennett went over to the dresser and pulled open the top drawer on the left. Mel must've meant the top drawer on the right; this one was filled with bras and panties, and man, did she have an assortment. She had every color of the rainbow and varying shades of every color. There were polka dots, stripes, and hearts. Lace, satin, cotton, and variations of those materials mixed. The most intriguing pair of panties was cream and tan leopard with cream lace all around the edges. He was also a pretty big fan of the red lace thong. Not to mention the number of bras made with more lace and satin.

"The other drawer," Mel said, sounding pained. He wasn't sure if it was because of her migraine or the fact that he'd just seen all of her unmentionables.

Bennett shut the drawer and moved to the other side. He pulled out a gray T-shirt and grabbed a pair of shorts. "Do you have more medicine you can take?" he asked, handing her the clothes.

"There's some in my bathroom. It's the only prescription in the cabinet. It usually knocks me out. Could you get me some Gatorade from the pantry, too?"

Bennett headed to the kitchen and got what she needed. When he walked into her room a couple of minutes later she was already changed. She was underneath the covers, her knees drawn up to her chest. He sat down next to her.

She attempted to open her eyes again before she moaned and quickly closed them.

Yeah, Bennett had wanted to get her moaning in bed, but this wasn't what he'd had in mind.

"Here," he said, taking her hand and giving her the pill.

She sat up and put the pill in her mouth before she held out her hand for the glass. She took a couple slow sips before she gave the glass back to him and lay down.

"Come here." He grabbed her shoulders and adjusted her so her head was in his lap. He gently touched her temples and began to move his fingers in slow circles.

"That feels good," she said. A little bit of relief crossed her face. "You really are good with your hands."

"You haven't seen anything yet."

A small smile crossed her mouth. "Thank you for taking care of me."

"It's no problem," he said as he continued to massage her temples.

He looked around her room, and his eyes landed on the pictures on her dresser. There was one of her, Grace, and Harper at the beach. They were standing at the water's edge, smiling as a wave crashed around their feet. Mel was wearing a red bathing suit top that stopped just above her belly button, and black bottoms that somehow made her legs look longer.

There was another of her and Hamilton. He was probably eight or nine at the time. They were sitting on a couch, Hamilton's arm around Mel's neck as he pulled her in and kissed her on the cheek. There were more frames in the room, but Bennett couldn't really make out the pictures in the dim light.

Mel had a painting over her bed of a big, blooming flower that was the exact same shade as her bedspread. Bennett recognized the signature at the bottom as Paige's. Brendan's wife was an artist. Her work was on display at a couple places around town where people could buy it.

Mel's bed wasn't covered in useless pillows. She had four regular pillows and a small one with a green-and-white zig-zag pattern. But the bear that he'd given her was no longer on the bed. He hadn't seen it when he'd come into the room. He'd have to ask what happened to it.

It didn't take very long before Mel's breathing changed, and he knew she'd fallen asleep. He gently moved her head to the pillow and left, shutting the door behind him.

He went into the kitchen and pulled out his phone, more than a little wary about what was about to happen as he dialed.

"Bennett Hart, don't tell me you messed this up," Grace said.

"Your confidence in me is overwhelming."

"That's because I don't have confidence in you at the moment. I know you're supposed to be eating lunch with Mel because she told me that was the plan. I also know that you picked up lunch from here because Grams told me, so there obviously was no problem with the food. So what did *you* do?"

Okay, so maybe he didn't have the best track record when it came to Mel. But he wasn't going to mess things up now.

"I didn't do anything. Mel had a migraine, so I drove her home."

"You're still at her house?"

"Yes, she's asleep. The *reason* I'm calling you is because I'm trying to find out how long these put her out for and how she normally feels afterward. She threw up at the school, so I'm pretty sure there isn't anything in her stomach. Will she want to eat when she wakes up?"

"Wait, she got sick in front of you?"

"Yeah."

"And what did you do?"

"Held her hair back."

Grace was quiet for a second before she cleared her throat. "Good job. You've passed the first round, but I'm still holding judgment for the second."

Bennett couldn't help himself from smiling as he leaned back against the counter. Grace might be a tiny little thing, but she was a real ball buster when she wanted to be.

Good luck, Jax.

"To answer your earlier question, she usually sleeps a migraine off in about four or five hours. And she likes mac and cheese after she's been sick. But it isn't any old mac and cheese. It's my grandmother's recipe."

"Are you willing to share this recipe?"

"You going to make it from scratch?" she asked, sounding a tad bit skeptical.

"Are you doubting my cooking skills?"

"According to Mel, you're pretty talented in the kitchen. So I'll just have to ask her if you do the recipe justice."

"You do that," he told her.

"I'll bring the recipe and ingredients by around three. I'm assuming you're staying there and playing Nurse Nightingale."

"Absolutely. And hey, if you have time do you think you could drop me off at the school so I can get her car?"

"Sure. See you later, Bennett."

"Bye."

Bennett called his boss next. He told Marlin he'd be taking the rest of the day off, which was fine with Marlin as they weren't ready for Bennett to start the custom cabinetry portion of the current job.

When Bennett hung up, he leaned back against Mel's counter and looked around her kitchen.

What was he going to do for the next couple of hours? He needed to be quiet, so watching TV was out of the question.

But there was no way he'd be able to do that for four hours anyway.

He pushed off the counter and went to get a glass out of the cabinet. When he opened the door it made the same audible squeak it always did.

Well, he could fix the cabinets, because this definitely wasn't the only one that was messed up. Some of them were hanging more than a little bit crooked. And then he could fix the drawers, because those weren't in the best condition, either.

Bennett went out to his truck to get his tools, and when he came back inside he got to work, doing his best to stay as quiet as possible.

He made fast progress with the cabinets, and then he moved on to the drawers. It was when he opened the fourth one that he found something interesting. It must've been Mel's catchall drawer, because it was full of pens, hair ties, rubber bands, notes, and coupons. Right on top was a yellow piece of paper.

"My I Didn't Kick the Bucket List" was scrawled across the top in Mel's handwriting, and both sides were covered in things to do. Most of them Mel had written down, but two other people had joined in with ideas. Most likely Grace and Harper.

1) No more dwelling on things I can't change.
2) No more just thinking about the things I can change. If they can be done, do them.
3) Don't give a flying fuck what anybody else thinks of me.

Bennett couldn't help but smile. The thought of Mel saying fuck was more than slightly amusing to him.

4) Get a tattoo.

Where was she going to put it? The possibilities were endless, and so very intriguing. He moved on and froze when he read number six.

6) Spend the night with a man who knows exactly
   what he's doing between the sheets.

That one wasn't in Mel's handwriting, but it was on the list nonetheless. Did that mean Mel hadn't been with someone who knew what he was doing? Or that she hadn't been with anybody at all?

Bennett looked up and over to the side of the house where Mel was currently sleeping.

No, she couldn't be a virgin...could she?

He shook his head, trying to clear the images that were now flooding his brain. All he could think about was the fact that he'd be happy to participate in task number six.

More than happy. Ecstatic even.

Bennett continued reading, trying to figure out what else he could participate in when it came to this interesting and oh-so-very informative list.

* * *

When Mel woke up her head was only slightly tender from the beating it had taken. She was still out of it, but at least she could function.

She'd started getting migraines when she was in elementary school. They'd been quite frequent all the way until high school, when they started coming more sporadically. Sometimes the medicine worked, but more often than not her best bet was to take the antinausea medicine and sleep it out.

But she'd been pretty good lately. She hadn't gotten one

in a while. Certain things triggered her migraines. A big one was drinking too much caffeine when she hadn't had enough sleep, and as Mel was a coffee addict, it tended to happen. It had been a real problem in college during finals week. Another trigger was the scent of some perfumes or cleaning products. Which was what had happened today.

She'd gone to the computer lab with her fourth-period class, and the carpets had just been sprayed with something. The second she'd walked in she'd known she was in for it.

Ugh, why did it have to happen today of all days? Not only had she had to cancel her lunch with Bennett, but she'd also thrown up in front of him. And if she remembered correctly, he'd seen her underwear drawer.

Awesome. Just awesome.

But he hadn't run away. He'd actually taken care of her, and very effectively at that. His hands were magic. She'd known they would be. And now that she'd really experienced them, she wondered what other amazing things they were capable of.

She really hoped she'd get to find out, and soon.

She rolled over and slowly sat up. She was a little lightheaded, but at least her head wasn't spinning anymore and the nausea was blissfully gone. She was actually kind of hungry.

She glanced at her clock to find that it was just after six in the evening. She'd slept for over six hours, but she was still tired and groggy, and so thirsty her tongue was like sandpaper. She grabbed the glass of Gatorade by her bed and drank it slowly, trying to test the waters of her stomach with something easy before she tried actual solids.

When she finished she got up from her bed, still a little unsteady on her feet, and made her way to the door. She hadn't expected Bennett to stay, so her heart jumped a little bit—okay, a lot—when she stepped out into the hallway and heard a drawer shut. But then she smelled an oh-so-heavenly scent.

Lula Mae's mac and cheese.

"Bennett?" she called out as she walked into the living room. Her voice was still a little sleep worn.

He ducked beneath the cabinets over the bar so he could see her. "Hey," he said, smiling at her. "You feeling better? 'Cause you look better."

She had to still be asleep. This was surely a dream. Bennett Hart was cooking in her kitchen. Cooking her mac and cheese, otherwise known as the food of the gods.

"Yeah, I feel better," she said as she walked into the kitchen. "You stayed and cooked me dinner?"

"Well, I wanted to make sure you had something to eat in case you were hungry." He turned to open the oven. The muscles in his back strained at his T-shirt, and his pants pulled tight across his butt as he pulled out a casserole dish filled of golden goodness.

Mel wasn't sure which had her drooling more.

He put the dish down and pulled off the oven mitt. He tossed it on the counter and then crossed over to her.

"You feel good enough to eat?" He reached out and ran his hands up and down her arms.

"Yeah," she said softly, looking up into his face.

"What about other things?"

"Hold that thought," she said, putting her hand over his mouth.

"You okay?" His mouth moved under her hand, and his forehead wrinkled in concern.

"Yes, I'm fine. I just need to go brush my teeth." She took a step back from him and hurried to the bathroom.

She'd thrown up and then slept for the last six hours. No way was she going to kiss that man before she brushed her teeth.

Absolutely not.

* * *

Bennett grinned as he watched Mel scamper off to the bath room. It didn't matter that she'd been sick all day. He still found her incredibly beautiful, and way sexy in her T-shirt and tiny little boxers. He was also a pretty big fan of her bed head. He hadn't thought it was possible for her hair to get any bigger, or any sexier. Boy, had he been wrong.

Bennett continued to make himself busy in the kitchen, grabbing plates and silverware and setting the dinner table.

She came out of the bathroom about five minutes later, looking wide-eyed and refreshed. She definitely looked better than she had earlier. The color was back in her face and the pain was gone from her eyes. The only thing Bennett wasn't a fan of was that she'd tried to tame her hair by pulling it into a bun at the back of her head.

Well, he'd fix that in a second.

"Do you need help?" she asked, looking around.

"No." He reached out for her, bringing her to his chest. "Can I kiss you now?"

She only had time to nod once before he put his mouth over hers.

She sighed as her body relaxed into his. She opened her mouth and he took full advantage, dipping his tongue inside and tasting her minty tongue. He reached up and pulled her hair down, and his fingers dove into its gloriousness. He let his fingertips work into her scalp and she moaned, pressing her body closer to his.

And then her stomach made an audible growl.

"Oh." She pulled back, her cheeks flaming in embarrassment. "Sorry."

"Why are you apologizing? Being hungry is a good thing after the day you had."

"Yeah," she said, giving him a small smile. "The problem is I'm hungry for something besides food, too."

"Oh really now? Well, we can make out a little bit later." He grabbed her hand and pulled her over to the table.

"Hmm, that sounds promising."

He pulled out her chair and helped her sit. Then he took the seat next to her.

"I still can't believe you did all this." She looked at the food in front of her.

"I've cooked for you before." Bennett scooped a generous amount of the mac and cheese onto her plate.

"Yes, but you stayed and took care of me," she said softly.

"I wanted to be here, Mel."

"You must've been bored. What did you do besides slave away making me dinner?" She grabbed two slices of bread and put a piece on each of their plates.

"Well, I put that fan up in the living room."

"What?" she asked, turning around.

After Bennett had finished reading Mel's very fascinating list, he'd finished with the drawers and fixed a leak under her sink. Then he'd found a fan in a box in the corner of her living room. Bennett had been at Mel's house a number of nights, and he'd noticed that whenever the fan was on, it wobbled back and forth and made a very noticeable noise.

The new fan was blessedly quiet.

Mel turned back to him, her mouth slightly hanging open. "Are you kidding me with this stuff?"

"It was no problem," he said, waving off her words.

"I'm sure for you it wasn't. That probably took you, what, thirty minutes? It would've taken me hours."

"It was no problem," he repeated.

"You've done a lot for me today. Taking care of me, cooking me dinner, putting up the fan." She reached across the table and touched his hand. "Thank you."

"You're welcome," he said, flipping his hand and letting his fingers curl around hers as he squeezed lightly.

She gave him one of her heart-stopping smiles as she squeezed his hand back.

"What else did you do?" She pulled her hand from his and properly dug into her food. "Oh. My. God." She closed her eyes as she pulled her fork from her mouth and chewed. "This is perfect." Her eyes slowly drifted open.

"Really? Well, be sure to tell Grace. She didn't think I'd live up to the mac and cheese standards."

"Oh you do. Believe me, you *soooo* do." She took another bite, looking as if she were in heaven.

* * *

After dinner, Bennett propped up Mel on the countertop while he cleaned up. He refused to let her help. But she wasn't going to complain; she got to watch as he moved around her kitchen. As he opened and closed her cabinets, she noticed a few very audible squeaks were missing.

"So what else did you do besides fix my cabinets?" she asked.

He snapped a Tupperware container shut and grinned. "The leak under your sink."

"Jeez, is there anything you didn't do for me today?" she asked, amazed.

"I was trying to stay busy, and you have quite a few things that you need done around this place."

"Well, feel free to help me anytime."

"Oh, so you approve of the adjustments? You don't think I'm a shoddy craftsman?" he asked, raising his eyebrows.

"You appear to know how to use your tools." The second it was out of her mouth her face turned bright red.

Bennett walked across the kitchen and made a space for himself between Mel's thighs. "I can assure you I know how to use all of my tools. And I'm pretty good with my hands, too." The gleam in his eyes led Mel to believe he had something very specific in mind, something that probably had very little to do with squeaky hinges.

"I experienced a little bit of those magic hands earlier. I just wasn't coherent enough to appreciate them."

"All in good time."

"Is that a promise?"

"Mmm-hmm." He buried his face in her neck. "Do you know how incredible you smell?" he asked as he nipped at her skin gently. "Because on a scale of one to ten you're about a fifty-nine."

"Are you kidding me? I'm a freaking mess."

"No, you're not." He began trailing kisses up her jaw until he got to her mouth. He nibbled on her lower lip, pulling it down with his teeth and then soothing it with his tongue. "Melanie," he whispered against her mouth before he pulled back. "I'm so damn glad I cornered you in that office."

"Took you long enough."

Bennett laughed, his eyes lighting up as he reached up with one hand and tunneled his fingers in her curls. "You know, your hair is so damn sexy right now that I barely know what to do with myself."

"Yeah, I've noticed you have a bit of a fascination with it," she said, running her hands up his chest.

"It isn't a *bit* of a fascination. It's much, much more."

"Is that so?" she asked as she wrapped her legs around him. He'd be able to untangle himself if he really wanted to, but he didn't look even remotely interested in stepping away.

"Yeah," he drawled out slow and lazy. "There are a lot of things I like about you."

"Hmmm, such as?"

"Well, there is the matter of these legs of yours." He traced her knee with his fingertips before he slowly walked them up the top of her thigh. "And then there's these shorts."

"What's so impressive about the shorts?"

Bennett pulled back and looked at her like she was crazy. "All right, woman, let me explain something to you."

"Woman? You did not seriously just say that. I will have you—"

"I did say it, and—"

"Bennett Hart, you're going to have to—"

She didn't get any further than that, as Bennett effectively silenced her with his mouth.

Mel had kissed a few boys in her day, but really, they were nothing compared to Bennett. He took full possession of her mouth. His tongue moved against hers, twisting and pulling and tasting. All the while one of his hands gripped her thigh, his fingertips rubbing just underneath the hem of her shorts. And his other hand hadn't moved from her hair; he held her to him and made it impossible for her to escape. Not that that was even a possibility in her current state.

No, she wanted to hold this man close to her for as long as possible.

He pulled back, his mouth hovering just above hers. "So, what were you saying?"

"Huh?" she asked, more than a little dazed.

"You said I was going to have to . . . to what?"

Oh, who the hell cared? She just wanted his mouth back on hers.

"This." She grabbed the front of his shirt and pulled him back to her, getting exactly what she wanted.

Chapter Ten

Brave and Beautiful

Mel was supposed to be at the Sleepy Sheep for karaoke on Tuesday nights, but loud music wasn't going to be good with her head. Bennett had called Harper and Shep earlier that day, and they'd both said they would take care of it.

Just one more thing Bennett had done for her.

After he finished cleaning the kitchen, they spent the evening sitting on her couch and kissing for a good couple of hours, a task that in no way hurt her head.

Bennett had baseball practice on Wednesday night, so there were sadly no hours of making out. This was not the case for Thursday. Bennett made Mel dinner at his place, and they watched the season two finale of *Game of Thrones*. And instead of starting the third season, they got horizontal on his couch, where they stayed until well after midnight.

On Friday afternoon, Mel met up with Grace, Harper, and Paige at Annie Madison's seamstress shop. The dresses for Grace's wedding had come in, and all of the girls were getting fitted. When they were finished, they all went to dinner and called it an early night.

Mel was more than a little anxious for Saturday. Bennett

was taking her out on an official date. She was going to his game, and then the rest of the day would be a surprise. All he'd told her was to bring her bathing suit.

Mel wasn't on concession duty, so she was able to sit on the bleachers with everybody else and watch the whole game—especially Bennett.

Really that man should just live in those tight pants. He should get a pair in every color and wear nothing else. However, Mel was pretty partial to him in a nice pair of jeans. Who was she kidding? He looked good in everything, and she was damn sure he'd look good in nothing too.

The Stingrays ended up demolishing the Marlins, 12–3. Bennett had been on a roll. He scored three of those runs, and in the eighth inning he hit a grand slam to add four more.

"You're my good-luck charm." He kissed Mel lightly on the mouth before he took her hand and led her to his truck. She'd gotten a ride with Harper so she could just leave directly with Bennett. "The last two games I've gotten home runs."

"I think it's your pure talent," she said, as he put their bags in the backseat.

"Nah." He grinned. "It's me just trying to impress you. Did it work?"

"I'll hold out on judgment till the end of the day," she said before she turned around to get into his truck. His hands were suddenly on her hips, where they lingered for just a second longer than necessary after she was safely seated.

"Looks like I might need to step up my game." He stepped up and leaned into the cab. His mouth came down on hers, but this time it wasn't quick. She opened her mouth under his, giving him access to dip his tongue inside and find hers.

Someone wolf-whistled and Bennett pulled back, looking over his shoulder. Mel peeked behind him to find Shep and Tripp standing a couple of yards away and giving the two of them a round of applause.

"You two have fun now," Shep said with a wink.

And now Mel was blushing. Blushing bad.

Bennett just shook his head before he turned back to make sure Mel was comfortable in the truck. He stepped back and shut her door before he rounded the front and got in on his side.

Before they could go on their date, Bennett needed to take a quick shower because he was all hot and sweaty. Well, hot was a given, because that was always the case. But Mel wasn't exactly sure how she was going to handle him being naked in the shower. Hot and naked in the shower, with her under the same roof.

"What are you thinking about over there that's got you so quiet?" he asked, glancing at her. He was wearing sunglasses, but they did nothing to change what she always felt whenever he looked at her.

Can't lie. Can't lie. Can. Not. Lie.

"Uhhh...you know, this and that."

Like how lathered soap would look dripping down your chest.

"Care to elaborate?" he asked.

"Not particularly." She fidgeted in her seat and looked back to the road.

"Well, I have a pretty good idea."

"What?" She looked at him. He was grinning. Full-on, sexy-as-hell, mind-blowing grinning.

What had they been talking about?

"You have that same dreamy, turned-on look you had the other day when I found you in your classroom," he said.

"What?" she repeated, shocked and embarrassed. "How did you..." She trailed off.

The man did read minds.

Bennett laughed. "Your breathing gets all shallow and your cheeks get red."

"No it doesn't, and no they don't." She covered her cheeks with her hands. They felt as if they were on fire.

"You know, you do the same thing to me," he told her.

"Really? Because I don't see your cheeks getting all red or your breathing changing."

"Yeah, you have different effects on me."

"Oh yeah?" she asked, turning and leaning against the door. "So you think about me?"

"Yeah."

"And what are those thoughts?"

Bennett pulled into his driveway and shut the truck off. He turned and stared at her, his mouth in a crooked grin. "I'll tell you mine if you tell me yours."

"Oh look at that, we're at your house." Mel unbuckled her seat belt and promptly fled from his truck.

Okay, so she was a coward. It was what it was, because she was *not* going to tell him any of her dirty thoughts. Because there were many. *Many*.

Bennett grabbed both of their bags and met her at the door. "I'm going to find out sooner or later."

"Oh, really?"

"Yup." He unlocked the door.

"Well, we'll just see about that," she said, narrowing her eyes playfully.

"I guess we will." He pushed the door and held it open for her.

She walked inside, and, a second after the door shut behind her, Bennett's hands were on her waist. He kissed her neck, just a simple little peck that made her skin tingle.

"Do you need anything before I get in the shower?" he asked.

"I'm good," she said, shaking her head.

"Come on, you can get changed in my bedroom." He kissed her neck one last time before he let go and made his way down the hallway.

His bedroom? She was going to be naked in his bedroom?

Mel followed him into a room at the end of the hall.

Bennett's bedroom was much like the rest of his house: clean and organized. His king-sized bed was on the wall opposite the door. It had a navy blue comforter, and the headboard was made from an antique door that had been painted gray. The nightstands and dresser had been made to match. It was all simple and beautifully made, but of course it would be. She had no doubts that Bennett had made it.

"I won't take long," he said, putting her bag down on the end of his bed. He walked over to his dresser and pulled out some clothes. "My underwear drawer is the top left one in case you want to get even with me for seeing all of yours." He grinned before he left the room, shutting the door behind him.

Mel couldn't help but smile as she went over to the bed and unzipped her bag. She pulled out her bathing suit and started to undress.

Yup, it was more than a little strange standing in Bennett's room sans clothes, and maybe just a little bit thrilling. She had an image of him in the room with her. His hands at the front of her shorts, unbuttoning them and pulling them down her hips.

God, what was wrong with her? She was thinking about sex entirely too much these days. But who could blame her? The man inspired thoughts, and they just happened to be of a sexual nature.

Whatever.

Mel shook her head and forced herself to snap back to reality. She really needed to not think about such things, especially with Bennett in the freaking shower.

Mel grabbed her blue bikini bottoms and shimmied into them before she put on the matching top. She pulled on a pair of yellow water shorts and a white tank top. Then she shoved her clothes in the bag.

As tempted as she was to check out his underwear drawer, she decided to pass. It would've just added more fuel to the fire. But she did look around his room. It was clutter free. Surprise, surprise.

There was nothing on the white walls and very few items on the few pieces of furniture in there. Each of his night-stands held a lamp, and the one to the left had an alarm clock.

Mel wondered if he favored the left side of the bed. It would be interesting if he did, because she favored the right. Not that they would be sharing a bed anytime soon.

There were two pictures on his dresser. One was of him and his parents when he was in high school. The other was of him and a group of guys. They were all in fatigues and standing somewhere in the desert.

She knew Bennett had been shot down in Afghanistan and that he'd almost died. She also knew that only he and one other man had survived, that eight of his friends had been killed. She'd never talked to him about it. It was prob ably too soon in their relationship to ask, but she wanted to know what had happened to him.

She just wanted to know *him*.

* * *

Bennett had wanted to surprise Mel with their date. She hadn't hounded him about what they were doing, which was nice. She could handle not knowing what the plan was. He just hoped she was going to have a good time.

The first stop on the agenda was lunch. The Floppy Flounder was a landmark in Mirabelle. They had the best fish on the Gulf Coast, and their hush puppies were killer. The restaurant was right on the beach, and people would often come in their bathing suits and eat out on the deck.

"I haven't been here in forever," Mel said as they made their way up the front steps. "And I've been craving it like crazy."

"Perfect." He smiled as he opened the door for her.

"Welcome to the Floppy Flounder," a young girl behind the hostess stand said after they walked in. "Outside or inside?"

Bennett turned to Mel.

"Outside," she said.

"Outside," he repeated to the girl.

They followed her through the restaurant and out to the back deck, which overlooked the water. Clouds were forming in the distance. It didn't look like it was going to get too bad, but if the wind kept blowing in the same direction it was now, those clouds would be heading straight for them. He just hoped the weather would hold out long enough for them to be able to do what he planned.

"Stacey will be your waitress, and she'll be with you in a moment." The girl handed them menus before she walked away. The waitress arrived a few minutes later, and got their drink and meal orders quickly, as they'd both already known what they wanted.

"So." Bennett leaned back and looked at Mel. "I'm finally on an official date with the much-coveted Melanie O'Bryan."

"Coveted?" she laughed. "Where did you come up with that?"

"You have a couple of admirers."

"No, I don't," she scoffed.

"Really? 'Cause I've seen you around the sweaty little man and pretty boy."

"Who?" Mel asked.

"Stu and Duncan," Bennett clarified, maybe a tad bit grudgingly. He didn't like either of those men. He just had a feeling, and maybe that feeling stemmed from the way they looked at Mel, but either way he didn't like them.

At all.

"You're kidding, right? They're just friends."

"No, I'm not kidding," he said. "Both of those guys are interested in *way* more than being friends with you."

"If you say so." She laughed, sitting back in her seat.

"What's so funny?"

"You. You're jealous."

Jealous? He wasn't jealous. Just protective of what was his.

What was his? Where the hell had that come from?

"I'm not jealous," he said. "And those guys *are* interested in you."

"Whatever you say," Mel said, as their sweet teas were delivered to the table.

"I'm glad you find this amusing."

"Oh, but it is amusing. I've never had a man jealous over me before."

"You done yet?"

"Not even close. You're really adorable when you get all jealous." She reached across the table and took her drink.

"Adorable? I am *not* adorable."

"In a manly way, of course."

"I don't think there is such a thing," he said, unable to stop himself from smiling. He was getting used to that effect when she was around, and he had a feeling it would always be like that with her.

* * *

Lunch was incredible, and it had more to do with the fact that Bennett was sitting across from Mel than with the food she was eating. Though the food was pretty amazing, too. When they finished, they walked back to the truck. Bennett grabbed the cooler and led her down to the dock.

"So I thought we could go Jet Skiing," he said, coming to a stop in front of a Jet Ski that was bobbing up and down in the water.

"I've never been before."

"I know."

"How do you know that?" she asked, tilting her head to the side.

"All right, so don't get mad."

"Nothing ever starts off well with those words," she said, suddenly nervous.

"I found your list."

"My list?"

Oh, please not the *list. Oh please, oh please, oh please.*

"Yeah, your 'I Didn't Kick the Bucket List.' I believe 'Go Jet Skiing' was number twenty-seven."

"Oh. My. God," she whispered, mortified. She put her hands up to her flaming cheeks and stared at him in horror.

There were a couple things on that list that involved sex. And even though she'd vowed to be over Bennett when said list was written, he'd been in the back of her mind the whole time. And there were a ton of other ridiculous things on there. Things that proved just how inexperienced she was in multiple aspects of life.

"Hey." He grabbed her elbows and pulled her in close to him. "Don't be embarrassed. I thought it was pretty awesome, and pretty informative."

"Oh, I'm sure you found it very informative," she said, not moving her hands from her face. "When did you see it?"

"On Tuesday."

"So while I was sleeping, you were snooping?" she asked, not successfully hiding the edge to her voice.

"I wasn't snooping. I found the list when I was fixing the drawers in your kitchen. Are you mad?"

"Yes. No. I don't know. I wasn't exactly sober when I

wrote it, so I feel like I said a lot more things than I'd normally share with the public. It's like you reading my diary or something." Not to mention a significant number of those things on that list were Harper's and Grace's ideas, and they tended to be a lot more daring. Mel *had* agreed to every single thing they'd written down, but still this was just horrifying. "You read the *whole* thing?"

"Melanie, don't overthink it." He brought his hands up to hers and pulled them from her face. "I saw it as an opportunity to get to know you more. To learn a little bit of what goes on in here." He tapped her temple. "I read it without even thinking, and I'm sorry if that was going too far."

He looked so sincere as he said it. She didn't think he'd ever lie to her, or do anything to hurt her. His words counted for a lot. Probably way more than they should have this early on.

"I wasn't lying when I said I thought the list was awesome. It's really brave, too, to want to do all those things you've never experienced before."

Brave? He thought she was brave?

"Am I forgiven?" he asked, looking intently into her eyes.

"Umm, yes," she whispered.

His mouth turned up in a smile, and a second later it was on hers. All Mel could really think about was the way his tongue moved against hers. When he pulled back a minute later, the heat that was now in her face had very little to do with embarrassment.

"You ready?" he asked.

She nodded and he pulled back from her.

"Good, come on," he said, pulling her to the edge of the dock. "I borrowed this from one of the guys I work with." He lifted up the seat and put the cooler inside. Then he slipped off his shoes and put his keys in a mesh pouch on the side. "You have anything you need to put in?"

"Just these." She slipped off her flip-flops and handed them to him.

He put those in and gave her a life jacket before he started to put his on. Then he shut the seat and held out his hand.

"Ready?"

"Yes," she said putting her hand in his.

He helped her sit, the Jet Ski rocking underneath her, and then he got on in front of her.

Holy shit, she was straddling him.

She wrapped her arms around his waist and held on, not only because she didn't want to fall off when they got going, but also because she just wanted to touch him.

"Let's go," he said, pushing off from the dock before he turned the engine over.

When they were in the clear he rolled his wrist and they took off. She gripped his waist hard, her palms going flat against his stomach. He had a six-pack, and it was glorious.

Yes, she'd seen him with his shirt off at the beach before, but it was a whole new experience touching him. Feeling every inch of his defined muscles.

* * *

Every time Bennett hit a wave, Mel's thighs tightened around him and her fingers moved against him. She was tracing his abs, and damn, did he love the way it felt. But it was driving him crazy.

They hit another wave, and as it splashed up around them she laughed. God, he loved that sound.

He wasn't sure how long they drove around for because he completely lost track of time. When he pulled into a small cove, the dark clouds he noticed earlier were rolling in. He'd kept an eye on them, and he hadn't seen any lightning nor heard any thunder. They were just rain clouds, so he figured they were good to not call an end to the afternoon.

Bennett pulled up to a public dock and secured the Jet Ski before he got off and helped Mel up.

"You thirsty?" he asked.

"I could use a drink." Her hair was windswept and her cheeks were flushed.

Bennett lifted the seat and grabbed two waters from the cooler. "You want to go for a swim?"

"Yeah." She pulled the string on her shorts and let them fall to the dock. She put her water down and took off her sunglasses before she grabbed the hem of her shirt and pulled it up over her head.

Bennett's mouth went dry when he saw Mel in just her bikini, so he chugged the rest of his water. He'd seen her in a bathing suit before, but he didn't remember ever liking it this much. It wasn't one of those teeny tiny numbers that was only held together with string. The straps were thicker, and the triangles that covered her breasts were bigger than postage stamps. Again, she somehow pulled off modest and sexy all at the same time.

Bennett put the empty bottle next to hers and took off his sunglasses. He pulled off his shirt and dropped it on the dock next to hers.

Mel smiled as her gaze dropped to his abs, then she took a step back and dove into the water. Bennett followed, diving in and surfacing a couple feet from her. He swam toward the shore until he could stand and the water lapped at his shoulders. He wiped the water from his eyes just as Mel swam to him. She slipped her arms around his shoulders, and he pulled her legs around his waist.

"Hey," he said, sliding his hands to her lower back.

"Hi." Her hands came up to the back of his head.

He kissed her slowly. She opened her mouth to his and

when his tongue touched hers, her entire body tightened around him.

Bennett wouldn't have been able to stop the groan that came out of him if he'd tried. Nor was the water cold enough to calm the certain parts of his body that he needed calmed.

Then the skies opened up, and the water came down all around them. Mel pulled back and looked around. The rain was cooler than the ocean water and the contrasting temperatures felt good—not as good as Mel's body wrapped around his, but good.

Mel stretched her head back further and looked up at the sky, exposing her neck as her ponytail dipped back into the water. She closed her eyes and the raindrops landed on her face, catching in her eyelashes.

Damn, she was beautiful.

Bennett moved one of his hands from her back and reached up to trace the bullet scar on her shoulder. Her head came up and she looked at him. There was an uncertainty in her eyes that he really didn't like seeing.

"How's your arm?" he asked.

"It's better. Still healing, but I don't think those scars are going to fade that much more." She looked away from him.

"Melanie?" As he said her name softly, he moved his hand to her chin and gently pushed up.

When her eyes met his they were filled with sadness. "It's just a constant reminder of that night. I wish I could forget it ever happened."

"We all have scars. Some of them are just more visible than others." He took one of her hands and placed it on his left shoulder. Her eyes dipped down, and her fingers traced the multiple scars from his bullet wound and surgery.

It was interesting to him that when they faced each other their scars were mirror images.

"They make us stronger. They change and shape you into

something, but they don't take anything away from what you are. Every part of you is beautiful," he whispered right before he leaned down and pressed his mouth to her shoulder, kissing every single scar.

When he looked back up he saw tears in her eyes, but she was smiling.

"Thank you," she said and returned the gesture. No one had touched Bennett's scars since they'd healed, and the fact that Mel was the first felt right. Her sweet little mouth felt like heaven no matter where it was on his body. She spread kisses up his shoulder and to his neck, licking the water from his skin.

And then her mouth was on his again. This was another instance where time seemed to get away from them. Bennett wasn't sure how long they stayed out there, but when he pulled back the rain was coming down harder. He looked at the clouds in the distance and knew that it was only going to get worse.

But if anything, the impending bad weather was the exact opposite of how he felt, because at that moment he'd never felt better.

* * *

When Bennett pulled into his driveway, the rain was coming down in sheets. The clouds were a dark gray, almost black, and they stretched out across the sky, with no reprieve in sight. Their clothes had dried slightly on the ride back to the house, but they were both completely soaked again by the time they got inside. The cold air from the air conditioner made goose bumps crawl across Mel's skin. She started rubbing her arms.

Bennett put his hand at the small of her back and led her down the hallway. She shivered under his hand.

"Come on. Let's get you warmed up," he said as he opened the door to the bathroom.

He moved his hand from her back and went to the shower. He flipped the handle and water started streaming out. She watched him as he tested the water a couple of times until it warmed up.

One date. They'd had one date, and she already knew she was in for the count with this man.

God, nothing could describe how he'd made her feel when they'd been out there on the water. She'd never experienced anything like when he'd held her and kissed her scars. And then he'd gone and told her she was beautiful.

It hadn't even been a week since he'd kissed her, since they'd started seeing each other. But she knew without a shadow of a doubt that she wanted him, that she wanted him right then and there.

Mel had never been one to really follow through with impulsive decisions, but she wasn't going to run away from this one.

Life was too short.

She crossed the small space to Bennett and ran her hands around his waist. She pressed her body into his and stretched up to kiss his neck. He turned, and she caught the look of surprise on his face a second before she put her mouth on his.

His arms came around her and his hands were in her hair. He pulled back after a moment breathing hard.

"Mel?"

"You read the whole list, right?"

"What?"

"Number six was to find someone who knew what they were doing in bed. Do you think you'd know what you were doing in the shower?"

"You're serious?" he asked, his eyes going hot.

"What do you think?" She let her hand slip to the front of his swim trunks. The second she touched him through the wet fabric his nostrils flared and he took a sharp breath.

Apparently it wasn't always true that a man shrunk when he was cold and wet. Well, at least not with Bennett, because this man was hard and his erection more than filled her hand.

"I think we can start in the shower, but I promise you, I'm not going to stop until your legs are shaking."

"Really?" she asked, sliding her hand up and down. "Prove it."

Chapter Eleven

Fall into Me

Bennett moved so fast that Mel didn't even see it coming. She was pinned up against the wall and his mouth covered hers. His hands worked up under her tank top and he touched her through her bikini top. She was still cold and his warm hands felt incredible on her breasts.

He bent down and grabbed her thighs, pulling her legs up around his waist, their mouths never separating. He turned around and set her on the counter.

His hands went down to the hem of her shirt and he pulled it up over her head. He was untying the straps at her neck and back before her shirt even hit the floor. He pulled the material away, and when she was completely bared to him he took a deep breath and just looked at her.

He reached up and cupped her naked breasts in both of his hands, now touching her with no barriers. He ran his thumbs across her nipples. Back and forth. Back and forth.

She leaned her head back against the mirror and moaned.

"Got to love that sound," he said right before his mouth descended and he sucked one of her nipples into his mouth.

She brought her hands up to the back of his head and

arched up, pushing herself further into his mouth. He switched sides a minute later, providing her other breast with the same delicious torture.

And then he was working his way back up, kissing the space between her breasts and nibbling a path up to her neck. But before he got to her mouth he pulled back from her and reached to the side.

He opened the second drawer and pulled out a box of condoms. He opened the box, pulled out a string of them, and ripped one off before he leaned to the side to set it on the ledge of the shower.

Mel reached down and grabbed the hem of his shirt. She pulled it up and off, and threw it to the ground. She ran her hands down his chest, tracing his muscles with her fingertips.

Bennett closed his eyes and tilted his head back, breathing deeply. She continued her southward journey, and when she got to the top of his shorts his head snapped up and he stilled her hands. "Wait a second. You first."

He pulled her off the counter and into his arms. Her naked chest was pressed up against his, and she didn't think she'd ever felt anything so perfect before. His chest hair tickled her nipples, turning her on even more.

His hands moved down her back slowly, and when he got to her shorts he pushed them down her hips, dragging her bikini bottoms off with them. Her clothes fell around her feet and he helped her step out of them, taking a long look at her naked body.

"You're so fucking beautiful."

"*Fucking* being the appropriate word," she said. Her hands went to the tie on his shorts, and she pulled at the knot.

Bennett grinned as she pushed his shorts down his hips. "Why, Melanie O'Bryan, look at the mouth on you."

"Is that all you want to do with it? Just look?" she asked

as she reached down and took him in her hand. She also took the opportunity to look at him in all of his naked glory.

Damn he was beautiful, too. Every single, defined inch of him.

"No," he groaned from deep in his chest, as she began to stroke him. He grabbed her face and pulled her mouth to his, and his tongue worked her mouth in much the same rhythm in which her hand was working him.

After a minute, he stilled her hand and pulled it away. Then he grabbed her hips and walked her backward toward the shower. He helped her up, and the second they were both inside he had her pressed against the wall. The water rained down around them, making everything hot and slippery.

There wasn't a single inch of Mel's body that was cold anymore.

Bennett reached down to the apex of her thighs. He slid a finger inside of her and then two. He stroked her for a minute before he dropped to his knees.

"Bennett?" Mel said his name with more than a little bit of uncertainty. She had a feeling about what he was going to do, and she wasn't all that sure she was ready for it.

"Shhh." He bent his head down as he parted her with his fingers.

Mel gasped when his mouth came down on her and she forgot how to talk when he added his tongue into the mix. No man had ever put his mouth on her like this before, and holy shit she'd never known what she was missing. This was perfection. She was going to go off just like this, with his fingers and mouth working her like magic. But that wasn't really how she wanted it to go, at least not this time around.

"Stop." She gently pushed him away.

"What's wrong?" he asked looking up at her, water dripping down his nose.

"Nothing, I just, I want you inside me."

He didn't say anything, just stood up and reached behind him to grab the condom. He opened it and rolled it on and then he was pulling her legs up and around his waist and sinking into her. Mel couldn't stop the moan of pleasure that escaped her lips. And neither could Bennett apparently, because one rumbled through his chest. He felt so incredible inside of her.

He stilled, waiting for her to adjust around him. She nodded and he started to move. In and out. In and out.

He knew *exactly* what he was doing, and he took his time doing it. She felt like a freaking live wire, and she was going to go off any minute. Everything felt so good. *He* felt so good. She didn't want it to end. She wanted to feel him moving inside of her for just a little bit longer.

She tried so hard to hold off, but her climax was inevitable.

"Bennett," Mel gasped his name as she pulled her mouth from his. She looked into his eyes as she came around him, saying his name over, and over, and over again.

He followed a second later, her name on his lips.

* * *

Bennett was slumped against the shower wall. His face pressed into Mel's neck as he held her up, her body still pulsing around his.

There weren't words for what had just happened.

He'd never had sex like that before, so all consuming and flat-out amazing. And he'd sure as hell never come harder in his life. He was surprised he was still standing.

He was *still standing, right?*

He'd told her that her legs would be the ones shaking, but damn if she hadn't done it to him. He pulled back and looked into her face. Her expression mixed shock and satisfaction, which mirrored what he felt.

"You okay?" he asked.

"Am I okay?" She laughed. "I'm so far past okay. That was..." She shook her head, at a loss for words. "*Incredible* doesn't seem adequate."

"I know what you mean." He grinned and he brushed his mouth over hers.

He slowly let her legs drop, and when she was able to stand he took a step back from her, pulling out of her. He took the condom off, stuck his hand out of the shower, and threw it into the trash can. And then he came back to her, wrapping his arms around her and pulling her body flush against his.

They took their time in the shower. Bennett grabbed the soap and lathered it up, then ran it across every inch of her body. He loved touching her. Loved how she responded to everything. Loved how she responded to *him*.

He washed her hair, his fingers massaging her scalp. The second he was done rinsing the soap away she had her hands on him.

"My turn," she said, giving him a wicked grin as she grabbed the bar of soap.

Yeah, by the time she was done with him he was ready to have her again, but he didn't want it to be in the shower. He turned the water off and grabbed the towel on the rack next to the shower. He wrapped it around his waist and stepped out.

"Give me a second," he said, quickly leaving the bathroom and stepping out to the linen closet.

He grabbed two clean towels and came back to her. She was still standing in the bathtub, dripping wet, and so sexy he couldn't handle it. He was going to need all night to learn every facet of her body.

Bennett couldn't fucking wait.

He dropped the towels on the counter and helped her step out of the bathtub. He grabbed a towel, unfolded it, and

held it out for her. She turned and he wrapped it around her.
He lifted her wet hair from her shoulders and gently ran the
towel through it. When it wasn't sopping wet anymore, he
grabbed the other towel and moved in front of her.

"Come here," he said, taking a step back and bringing
her with him.

He unfolded the towel as he sat down on the edge of the
tub. He dried her breasts first, then her belly. He moved the
towel behind her and dried her bottom, then moved down to
her thighs.

When her legs were dry, he grabbed her waist and pulled
her between his thighs. He kissed her breasts, running his
tongue underneath them.

"I thought you were supposed to be drying me off." She
rubbed her hands across the top of his head.

"Am I not?" he asked, looking up at her.

"No, quite the opposite, in fact."

"Really. Well, this involves some further investigation."
He moved his hand between her legs.

"Ahh, Bennett," she moaned, as he slid two fingers inside
her.

Yup, she was wet all right.

He moved quickly, getting to his feet and picking her up
in one swift movement.

"Oh," she gasped, startled.

Her towel fell from her shoulders, and Bennett's fell
from his waist. It wasn't like they were going to need those,
anyway. He adjusted her in his arms so he could grab the
condoms from the counter, and then carried her to his bedroom. He set her down on her feet so he could pull the covers
back. Then he kissed her as he laid her back onto the bed.

He really wanted to take his time exploring her body. He
wanted to put his mouth all over her. But she wanted to put
her hands all over him, and there was only so much he could

take before he had to be inside her. He reached out to the nightstand and tore off another condom.

Mel decided she was going to help him put it on, though all she really did was drive him crazy. They were both breathing heavy and shaking when it was finally on. Their need for each other was so strong, it was like they hadn't even done anything in the shower.

Bennett had wanted to go a little slower this time, but that plan was shot to hell the second he was inside her again.

She was so damn ready for him.

She bent her legs, planting her feet at his hips and changing the angle of their bodies, making him go deeper. She apparently didn't want slow, either, because she was arching up into him and matching his movements.

Her head fell back onto the pillow, her eyes closed in what looked like pure ecstasy. Bennett buried his face in her neck. He couldn't help himself; it was at the perfect angle, begging for his mouth, and tongue, and teeth. He nipped at her skin and then soothed it with his tongue. Mel's hands were at his back, her fingernails digging into his skin, urging him on harder and faster.

And then she was crying out as she came around him. Bennett's control snapped and he let go, letting everything overtake him.

He didn't want to collapse onto her, so he rolled and brought her with him. She was sprawled across his chest, her hand on his pec and her fingers playing with his chest hair. He rubbed one of his hands lazily up and down her back. His other hand cupped her bottom holding her against him.

They lay there slowly catching their breath, and after a minute he looked down at her. She smiled at him, and damn if it didn't knock the breath out of him all over again. He pressed his mouth to hers, kissing her gently.

She hummed and drew back to look at him. "Well, I

can cross number six off the list," she said, looking quite satisfied.

Bennett knew he'd never appreciated that satisfied look on a woman's face quite as much as he did when it was on Mel's. And he never wanted anyone else to put that look on her face. Just him. *Only* him.

"Yeah?" he asked, smiling. He was feeling pretty damn pleased himself.

"Oh yeah. Well, now that that's done. I should get going." She put her hands on his chest and attempted to push herself away.

"What?" He frowned and tightened his grip on her to keep her from moving. "You're leaving? You can't be serious." He was in no way finished with the night. In no way finished with *her*. He wanted her again, and again, and again.

"I wasn't," she said with a grin.

Relief washed through him. She was just messing with him. Well, two could play at that game. She squealed as he rolled over and pinned her to the mattress. Her hands were stretched up above her head.

"You think you're funny, do you?" he asked raising his eyebrows.

"Well, see, I don't have a private list of yours to read to figure *you* out, so I've got to use other means."

"You want me to write down that I want you to stay?" he asked above her lips. "I'll paint it on the fucking walls." He kissed her, not so gently this time. No, he ate at her mouth. When she was good and breathless and writhing beneath him, he moved to her neck, kissing and licking his way up to her ear. "Stay with me, Melanie," he whispered.

And the moaned *yes* that came across her lips a second later was enough to make him hard all over again.

* * *

"Oh. My. God."

Mel stared at her reflection in the mirror, her mouth hanging open, horrified with what she saw. Her hair was about three times the size it normally was. Her curls were a frizzy mess that stuck up all over her head.

Mel and Bennett might have spent another hour rolling around in bed. His wandering hands and delicious mouth had a way of making her forget everything. She'd never experienced so much pleasure in such a short amount of time. He had absolutely no difficulty setting her off.

Justin's odds had been about one in four. Maybe it was a chemistry thing that they'd been lacking. Mel wasn't sure, but whatever she'd been missing with Justin, she had with Bennett. In spades.

"It really isn't that bad," Bennett said from behind her.

She looked up at his smiling reflection, *soooo* not amused.

"You did this." She turned around to look at him. "You and those wandering hands of yours."

"I can't help myself," he said. He turned them so that he was leaning back against the sink. He widened his stance and brought Mel between his thighs. "It's instinct for my hands to go to your hair. Just like I always want my mouth on you." He moved in to kiss her. But she dodged his mouth. Never one to be deterred, he kissed her throat instead.

"I look like a freaking poodle."

"I'm going to have to strongly disagree with that." He nibbled on her neck.

His hands came down to her thighs, and he pushed up the very large T-shirt she was wearing. He'd let her borrow one of his and it read AIR FORCE across the chest. He'd worn it so many times that the gray fabric was ridiculously soft, and it felt good on her naked skin and bare breasts.

She hummed, unable to keep up her annoyance. It was

impossible when he had his mouth on her. "Well, if you want a repeat performance in the shower you're going to have to buy me some conditioner."

"Mel, I'll buy you a whole damn case," he said just under the hollow of her ear.

He was wearing only a pair of boxers low on his hips, so his chest was completely bare. She put her palms flat against his stomach, her fingers going back and forth on his abs. As he kissed her neck Mel rested her head on his shoulder, and then she saw their reflection in the mirror.

"Oh, my God," Mel said in another horrified whisper as she got a good look at his back.

"What is it this time?" He pulled back so he could look at her face.

"I, uh..." Mel trailed off as the heat rose to her cheeks. "I might've gotten a little carried away earlier."

"What are you talking about?" he asked, raising his eyebrows.

"Bennett, I scratched you."

"What?" He looked over his shoulder at the mirror. "Holy shit," he said as he got a look at the dozen or so scratch marks she'd made across his back. "I must've done something right." He looked back at her, grinning like an idiot.

Something? He'd done *everything* right. But she wasn't going to tell him that. He didn't need any more of an ego boost at the moment. No, not with that self-satisfied look that was plastered across his face.

"Looks like I'm not the only one who can't control myself."

"You're enjoying this, aren't you?" she asked, still completely mortified.

"Yup. And I'm enjoying this, too. Enjoying *you* underneath my hands." And those hands started an upward journey underneath her shirt. He ran his fingers across the swells of her breasts. "You are *soooo* soft," he groaned, moving his hands down her sides and around to her back, and continuing south. He palmed her bottom and pulled her against his body. "I don't think I'll ever get over how your skin feels."

Ever? Ever was an awfully long time...and Mel wondered exactly how much of it she was going to get to spend with Bennett.

Shit. She was already in this too far. She was so totally screwed, both literally and figuratively, the literally being the much better part of the deal.

But she needed to talk to him, to explain things. Like how she'd never just jumped into bed with a man before. She needed to tell him that this was more than just lose-control-sex for her, tell him that she really liked him.

He had asked her to stay, and she thought it might have meant something. But what did it mean? She had no idea. Did he just want more sex? Or did he want to spend time with her? *Be* with her?

"Bennett." She leaned back to look at him.

"Yeah?" He reached up and pushed away one of the many wayward curls behind her ear.

"Are you going to make me dinner now?" she asked, chickening out.

Yup, she was going to stay in the moment for just a little bit longer, and worry about her little heart later.

He gave her a slow, lazy grin that made her think of about a million other things besides food. "Absolutely," he said, grabbing her hand and leading her into the kitchen.

* * *

After they finished eating and cleaned up, they lay down on the couch and started watching the third season of *Game of Thrones*.

His body was curled around hers, his front to her back. They were snuggled up under a blanket, and Bennett's hand drifted under her shirt. He cupped her breast, his finger running back and forth across her nipple.

"Are you trying to distract me?" she asked.

"Hmm, maybe. Or I'm trying to comfort you." He kissed her neck. "You seem to be a little stressed out about what's happening on the screen."

"I'm always stressed out by what's going on in this show. I'm always so nervous they're going to kill somebody else off," she said as the credits began to roll.

"Well, if you don't want to watch anymore..." He let go of her breast and pulled his hand out from underneath her shirt. He reached over her and grabbed for the remote.

"Hey," she said, swatting his hand away.

"You're the one who said it was too much for you."

"I can handle it." She looked over her shoulder at him.

"I'll just bet you can." He grinned as he pressed his mouth to hers.

Mel turned in his arms, one of her legs riding up between his, and she stretched up to kiss him. "Is this what it's like?" she asked running her hands across his chest.

"What what's like?" he asked as he put his hand low on her belly. She'd borrowed a pair of his drawstring pajama pants, and he inched his fingers under the band at the top.

"Always wanting someone."

"I have no idea." He shook his head. "I've never wanted anyone this much." His fingers continued to travel down to the promised land.

"It scares me," she said, nervously biting her lip.

Bennett stopped his downward journey. He pulled his hand out from her pants and slid it under her body, wrapping it around her and holding her to him.

"Melanie," he said softly, and he reached up with his

other hand and cradled her face. He pulled her lip out of her teeth with his thumb.

"It's just . . . it's never happened like this before. Earlier . . . I've never done anything like that."

"Anything like what?" he asked.

"Initiating sex. Bennett, I haven't been with very many men," she tried to explain.

He'd picked up on the fact that she was a little inexperienced from the list, but if he hadn't read it he wouldn't have had any clue. She'd been incredible in bed, and in the shower for that matter. Yeah, he'd figured out that she wasn't a virgin real quick.

"How many is not very many?"

"Including you? Two."

Two? That wasn't what he was expecting.

"You've only been with one other guy?" he asked, more than a little bit shocked.

"Yes," she said slowly. "He was my boyfriend in college. And we'd dated seriously for a while. But I was never impulsive with him, and things were never quite that . . . um, explosive."

"Meaning?"

"Well, I . . . you know . . . finished. But not like *that*. Not like how it is with you."

"Mel, I'm not going to lie to you, I've been with more than two women. But nothing's ever been like how it is with you." He shook his head. "And I mean more than the sex."

"Yeah?" she asked.

"Yeah," he said. "That wasn't why I wanted you to stay."

Her mouth quirked to the side in a shy smile, and Bennett couldn't help but lean in and kiss her again.

"You know what else?" he asked.

"What?"

"It's been a little while for me. I haven't been with anyone since before the crash, over three years for sex or a relationship of any kind with a woman. Letting you in was scary for me, too."

Terrifying would have been a more accurate word. But holy hell, was being with her worth it. And damn, was he glad he'd been prepared. The condoms had been an impulse buy the day before. He hadn't needed one in years.

"What made you get over your fears?"

"Who said I've gotten over them?" he asked.

"You're still scared of little old me?"

"Well, you can be pretty vicious. I've got the scratch marks to prove it." He grinned.

She punched him in the chest. "Shut up. I still can't believe I did that." She shook her head, a slight blush creeping up her cheeks.

Bennett didn't think he'd ever get over how beautiful she was. Even in this moment, with no makeup, her hair a crazy mess, and wearing his oversized clothes, she was simply the most stunning woman he'd ever seen. And she had more passion in one of those crazy curls of hers than most people did in their entire being, and she'd shown him more than he'd ever imagined.

He wasn't sure how ready he was for it, for her. But it was too late now. He was starting this relationship with her, and he was going to have to stop being a freaking coward.

He leaned in and kissed her again, trying to get past this new wave of fear. He pushed his tongue into her mouth while her hand wound around to his back, her fingers lightly moving across his skin as she traveled down. Her hand slipped under the back of his boxers, and she was grabbing nothing but his bare backside.

Bennett groaned, and a second later she was disentangling herself from him and getting off the couch.

"What?" He looked up at her, confused.

"Come on." She held out her hand to him. "Let's go back into your room, where there's a bed. And condoms."

"Good plan," he said, quickly getting up. He took her hand and let her lead him down the hall.

* * *

Bennett wasn't exactly a *wham, bam, thank you ma'am* kind of guy, but he'd never been one to cuddle after sex, or while sleeping, for that matter. He wasn't much for cuddling, period.

Whenever he'd slept in a bed with a woman before, he'd made a point of staying on his side of the bed. And when that didn't happen before he fell asleep, he somehow always made it to his side of the bed at some point during the night, wanting to be alone even subconsciously.

This was not the case with Mel.

Shocking.

No, Bennett woke up in much the same position he'd gone to sleep. Both he and Mel were still firmly stationed in the middle of the bed, his arms wrapped around her while she used his chest as a pillow. One of her legs was thrown over his, her thigh inching close to very dangerous territory. Her hand was curled around his neck and there was more of her hair covering him than the actual blanket, which she'd stolen.

Bennett had been more than a little nervous before he'd fallen asleep. His nightmares were fairly unpredictable, and he'd hate to have one when she was in the bed with him. They were more than traumatizing to him. They'd probably send Mel running for the hills. But she wasn't running, at least not yet.

Mel moved in her sleep and her thigh inched up higher. This was a problem. It didn't matter that he'd had sex with her four times. His need for her hadn't even been touched, and his body was more than prepared for round five. Painfully so.

Bennett shifted, trying to get out of her oncoming path without waking her up. He was unsuccessful.

She opened her eyes and gave him a warm, sleepy smile that was now officially the sexiest thing he'd ever seen in his life.

"Morning."

"Morning," he said, brushing the hair back from her face. "You sleep okay?"

"Yeah. What time is it?" she yawned.

Bennett rolled slightly and looked at the alarm clock. "Almost nine," he said, staring at the clock in disbelief. He hadn't slept that late since before he'd joined the air force.

"Mmm." She burrowed closer to him, put her lips on his chest, and trailed open-mouthed kisses across his skin.

Well, round five it is, he thought as he rolled her onto her back.

* * *

Functioning without coffee was not a possibility for Mel. Well, it hadn't been before. Apparently a Bennett-induced orgasm was leaps and bounds beyond caffeine, and it could quite possibly make Mel a morning person. Or help her leap tall buildings in a single bound.

Problem was, all of those orgasms had come at a price, and Mel could feel it in places all over her body.

"Holy cow," she groaned as she stared up at Bennett's ceiling. She was still trying to catch her breath and work up enough strength to move.

Yeah, that wasn't going to be happening anytime soon.

"What?" Bennett asked. He was sprawled out on his back next to her, breathing just as hard.

"You've worked muscles on my body I didn't even know I had."

He rolled to his side and pressed up close to her. He ran his hand up her hip and to her stomach, his fingers spanning her belly. "Is that so?" he asked as he burrowed his face into her neck. "Do you need me to massage those sore muscles for you?"

"I think if you were to massage the muscles that are sore, we'd wind up doing things to make it worse." She turned her head to look at him.

"Probably." He grinned right before he pressed his lips to hers. "I'll get you some Tylenol."

He rolled out of bed and Mel closed her eyes, letting her body sink into the mattress. She dozed off briefly. When Bennett came back into the room he was carrying two mugs.

"I figured you needed something to wash the pills down with. And what better than coffee?"

Bennett was wearing a pair of boxers low on his hips. Mel, on the other hand, was still entirely naked, so she pulled the sheet up as she sat to keep her breasts covered.

"Mmm," she said. "You know me so well."

"I'm trying." He kissed her on top of the head before he handed her a cup and sat down. "And what's with this?" he asked, raising an eyebrow as he tugged at the sheet.

"Seriously?" She tried to hold the sheet up and not spill her coffee.

"Yup." He grinned, tugging at the sheet again until it fell into her lap. "Let's see how daring you can be to sip coffee with me just like this."

"*Daring?* You just want to stare at my breasts." She shook her head.

Sitting and having a conversation with her breasts on display was *soooo* not something Mel would ever do, but if he was going to challenge her, she most definitely wasn't going to show fear.

"You got it. Besides, it isn't like I haven't had my mouth all over them for the last day."

She rolled her eyes. "You're such a guy."

"You say that like it's a bad thing. I didn't hear you complaining before," he said, waggling his eyebrows at her.

"If my entire body didn't hurt right now, and we didn't have steaming cups of hot coffee in our hands, I'd grab that pillow and smack you in the face with it."

"Big talk for such a little girl."

"You did not just call me a little girl," she said, trying so hard to give him an intimidating glare. It was taking everything in her not to smile.

"I sure did."

"You just wait, Bennett Hart."

"You going to show me what you're made of?" He leaned into her and pressed his lips to hers.

"Yes," she said, against his mouth. "But maybe just a little bit later, when it doesn't hurt so much to move."

"Sounds like a plan." He sat back and took a sip of his coffee, watching her over the rim as he did so.

Mel brought her cup up to her lips, too, blowing the steaming liquid before she took a tentative sip.

It was perfection.

"So, speaking of plans, what are you doing for the rest of the day?" Bennett asked.

"I'm going to lunch with Grace, Harper, and Paige at one."

"So I only get you for three more hours?"

"Not even that. I have to go home and deal with this mess," she said, pointing to her hair.

She didn't even want to know the state that it was in after two more rounds of hot sex with Bennett *and* sleeping on it.

"What about tonight?" he asked.

"You mean you're not tired of me yet?"

"God, no."

The emphasis in his words made Mel a little giddy... okay, *a lot* giddy. But she couldn't help it—she hadn't had enough of him, either.

Chapter Twelve

The Perils of Wild Sex

The Tylenol Mel took had little to no effect on her muscles. She was pretty sure she was walking funny.

She'd spent plenty of time in the shower that morning, letting the hot water work its healing powers on her body. The problem was her right shoulder was acting up a little bit more that usual, which made the task of combing her hair a bitch and a half.

But whatever. Every single pain was *soooo* worth it.

Mel pulled into the LaBella parking lot to find Grace, Harper, and Paige all standing next to Mel's yellow bug.

LaBella was the same resort that Harper worked at a couple days a week, and they had a rather expensive little restaurant called LaBouche. The only reason the girls ever ate there was because Harper got an employee discount.

Mel had more than a little trouble getting out of her car, and she was pretty sure that all three women caught her wincing.

"Had a good night, did we?" Grace smirked.

"Maybe." Mel smiled. She couldn't help it; that man was magic.

"Seriously?" Paige asked, more than a little surprised.

"Yeah? Seriously? I was just joking. Did you and Bennett..." Grace trailed off and raised her eyebrows.

Mel hummed in response. Or was it a purr? Too close to tell.

"You've got to be kidding me." Harper threw her arms up in the air. "Am I the only one who isn't getting hot sex?"

"Looks like it," Paige said with a smirk.

"Hey, let's not be so loud. One never knows who's around." Mel looked behind her. As far as she could tell, no one was in the parking lot.

"Come on," Grace said as she headed toward the building. "Let's get seated and then you, Ms. O'Bryan, need to spill."

* * *

Bennett tried to work out at the gym on a regular basis. He went that afternoon because he needed to do something to distract himself. All he wanted was Mel, and he wasn't going to get to see her for a couple of hours.

His mind was still completely blown by what had happened the night before as well as that morning. He'd never expected their first date to end in bed. Not in a thousand years. She'd shocked the hell out of him in the bathroom when she'd pressed her body up against his.

And the sex? There were no words for how incredible it had been. He still couldn't believe she'd been with only one other person besides him. They'd found their rhythm pretty quickly, and she'd matched him in everything.

And now he couldn't get her off his mind no matter how hard he tried. *Hard* being the operative word, because every time he thought about being inside her that was exactly what happened. No woman had *ever* had this kind of effect on him, thus the need for the gym.

When Bennett got there, he put his bag in a locker and grabbed his gloves. He went out into the main workout area, and as he made his way across the floor he spotted Shep and Tripp lifting weights. He nodded at them before he headed over to one of the punching bags and let loose.

After the accident, it had taken Bennett a while to work up to using a punching bag again. He still couldn't do it for as long as he had before, but he was grateful for the fact that he could do it at all.

"You letting out some frustrations there, pal?"

Bennett stopped and turned to find both Shep and Tripp behind him. He'd been going at the bag for a good thirty minutes, and sweat was pouring down his face. He used the sleeve of his shirt to wipe at his forehead before he bent down to grab his water bottle.

"Something like that," Bennett said before he shot a stream of cold water into his mouth.

"You seem tense," Tripp said.

Sure, if *tense* meant "horny."

"Hmm, I don't know if *tense* is the word I'd use." Shep studied Bennett. "But there is definitely something going on with you."

"Did your date with Mel not go very well?" Tripp asked.

"No, it was good."

More like perfect. He couldn't have planned for it to go better.

"So you didn't fuck it up?" Tripp asked, surprised.

"No, I didn't," Bennett said.

"Well, there's a first time for everything," Shep said with a grin.

"You two are assholes, you know that?"

"We're aware," Tripp said. "So you up for a game of basketball? Preston is going to be here in about five minutes. He thinks he's going to mop the floor with us."

"So it will be the two of you against Preston and me?" Bennett asked.

"Yup." Shep nodded.

"I'll take those odds any day," Bennett said. "You two are toast."

"We'll just see about that, Hart," Tripp said, as the three men made their way to the basketball court.

* * *

As it turned out, Tripp and Shep were a pretty good team out on the court, and they gave Preston and Bennett a run for their money. But Preston and Bennett pulled it out in the end.

The four guys headed back to the locker room to grab their bags. Though Bennett was just going to get a shower at his place, he had to change his shirt because it was soaked with sweat. He peeled it off and grabbed a dry one from his bag.

When he turned around the three men were staring at him: Shep with a smirk, Tripp with raised eyebrows, and Preston with his mouth hanging open in complete shock.

"Well, shit. I didn't think she had it in her," Shep said.

"Her? I didn't think *he* had it in *him*," Tripp said.

"What are you talking about?" Bennett asked.

"Did Mel seriously do that to your back?" Preston asked.

Oh. Fuck.

"We aren't talking about this." Bennett threw his nasty T-shirt in the bag and zipped it up. He was not turning Mel into locker room talk. Besides, Bennett didn't brag about his conquests. Not that Mel was a conquest or anything. She was so much more than that.

Tripp grinned. "Message received."

"Good." Bennett grabbed his clean shirt and put it on.

"Though you'd think he'd be a little bit more relaxed given the circumstances," Shep said.

"Nah," Preston said. "Gentlemen, what we're looking at here is a man who's falling hard and doesn't know what to do with himself."

"We aren't talking about that, either." Bennett grabbed his bag and headed out of the locker room.

But damn if Preston hadn't hit the nail on the head.

* * *

After lunch Mel went to the Piggly Wiggly to get groceries. She was making dinner for Bennett at her place. The menu was a whole roasted chicken, rice with gravy, and artichokes. Okay, so she was still trying to impress him with her cooking. Whatever—she felt no shame.

She was just pulling the chicken out of the oven when her cell phone rang.

"Hey, Mom," she said as she leaned her head to the side. She used her shoulder to hold the phone to her ear while she went to the fridge and started pulling out ingredients.

"How was your date with Bennett?" Corinne asked, not even bothering with saying hello.

"It was good." Mel couldn't help but smile. It had been *way* beyond good, but Mel wasn't going to go into those details with her mother.

"Where did he take you?"

"To lunch at the Floppy Flounder and then Jet Skiing. He made me dinner, too."

"Oh did he now?" Corinne's voice went up a few octaves. "He's been making dinner for you a lot lately. So is there anything else going on? Is it getting serious?"

Well, they were sleeping together, but that was information her mother just didn't need to know.

"I think it's getting there." Dear God, she hoped it was. The doorbell rang as Mel dropped butter into the pan.

"When are you seeing him again?" Corinne asked as Mel walked to the front door.

"He's coming over for dinner now," Mel whispered right before she opened the door.

Bennett grinned at Mel as she stepped aside to let him enter. She shut the door behind him and turned.

My mother, she mouthed, and he leaned in and pressed a quick kiss to her lips.

"Oh, really!" Corinne said excitedly.

Bennett put his mouth close to the receiver. "Hi, Mrs. O'Bryan."

"He's there now?" Corinne asked, positively giddy. "Tell him I said hello and ask him what he's doing tomorrow night. You should bring him to dinner with you."

"She says hello," Mel said. Then she grabbed Bennett's hand and led him into the kitchen.

"You didn't tell him what else I said. Invite him to dinner."

"Mom, I have to go. I'll talk to you later." She hung up and put the phone down on the counter. "Hey," she said to Bennett.

"Hi." He put his hands on her waist and pushed her back against the counter. "Dinner smells good." He pressed his mouth to hers and nibbled on her bottom lip. "You smell better."

Mel's phone buzzed on the counter. Instinctively both she and Bennett turned to look at it, and there prominently displayed on the screen was a message from Mel's mother.

Invite him to dinner tomorrow!!!

"Crap." Mel reached out and flipped the phone over. She turned back to Bennett and looked up at him nervously.

"You don't want me to come to dinner?" He tilted his head to the side as he reached up and ran his finger down the side of her face.

"You want to come? To dinner? With my parents? More importantly, with my mother?" she asked, unable to stop her eyebrows from going up. "She's going to try to get as much information out of you as possible."

"Is there something we should be hiding?"

"Well no, but . . . I didn't know we were there."

"Where?"

"At 'dinner with the parents.'"

"It isn't like we haven't met each other's parents before. Tell her I'll be there." He reached for her phone and handed it to her.

"O-okay." Bennett didn't move as she took the phone and texted a quick response to her mother: *We'll be there at seven.* She hit Send and put her phone on silent before she set it back on the counter facedown.

"You need help with dinner?" He was acting so cool and collected. Like having dinner with her family wasn't a big deal at all. Like it wasn't a *huge* step. They'd only just started seeing each other. But fine, if he was going to be calm, she would be, too. No problem.

"No, you can just stand there and look pretty." Mel reached up and patted his face.

"Look pretty?" he asked as his forehead wrinkled in confusion.

"Mmm-hmm." She put her hands on his chest and pushed him back. She stepped around him and went to the stove. The butter was almost melted, so she scooped out some flour and added it to the pan.

Bennett casually leaned against the counter, one leg crossed over the other and his arms folded across his chest. He looked at her, grinning.

"What?" she asked as she stirred the flour in.

"Nothing. I'm just standing here and looking pretty."

That he was. That he was.

* * *

Bennett was really beginning to appreciate the wonder that was a warm, soft, naked Mel in his arms. She was curled against his side, one of her legs thrown over his and her hand lazily moving around his chest.

They'd had another rather exciting go-round in Mel's bed, and it was almost eleven. They both had to get up early the next day, but Bennett really didn't want to go to sleep yet. He was enjoying this way too much to miss a moment of it.

"So what happened to the teddy bear?" he asked, moving his hand down her back.

"Hmm?" She looked up.

"The teddy bear I got you when you were in the hospital. I saw it on your bed a couple of weeks ago—"

"I knew that was why you freaked out." She put her hands on his chest and pushed herself up into a sitting position.

"I didn't freak out."

Mel just raised her eyebrows at him.

"Okay, maybe I freaked out a little bit."

Her eyebrows climbed up even higher.

"Fine. A lot. But I wasn't prepared for that."

"Prepared for what?" she asked.

"You."

He grabbed one of her hands and pulled her back down to him. She was now splayed across his chest. She moved her legs so that she was straddling him. Her face hovered just inches above his, her hair spilling forward like a curtain on either side.

"I wasn't prepared for how much I liked you. But I was able to distance myself from it a little bit. Or so I thought," he told her. "And then I saw that bear and it made everything real."

"And when exactly did you accept reality?"

"When I realized that not figuring out what was going on between us would be one of the biggest mistakes of my life. Life's too short."

"It is."

"So where's the bear?" he asked again.

"In my closet."

"You didn't get rid of it?"

"No. I thought about it for a minute. But it meant a lot to me," she said, kissing the tip of his nose.

"And why's that?"

"Because you mean a lot to me."

Bennett wasn't sure how it was possible that Mel's words could simultaneously leave him warm and satisfied, but also just a little bit unsettled. But he didn't want to think about the latter. Not right now.

He rolled so that they were on their sides, then he tucked her in next to his body, wanting her to be as close to him as possible.

* * *

On Monday morning, Bennett headed home. He hadn't brought a change of clothes so he needed to run back and get a quick shower. He left as a very sleepy Mel was getting in her shower. He would have liked to have joined her, but then they would have been late. Plus, she wasn't exactly coherent. The girl really wasn't a morning person, but she was pretty adorable in her tousled state.

It was six thirty when Bennett pulled up to the wood shop building. He noticed Dale Rigels right away. The kid was hanging out by the door, and he was staring down at his shoes.

"Hey," Bennett said as he got out of his truck. "You're a little early today."

Dale just shrugged his shoulders, still not looking up at Bennett.

"Since you're here, do you want to help me set up?"

Dale just shrugged again. Bennett went to the front door

and put the key in the lock. He went inside and turned on the lights. When he turned around Dale was standing in the doorway, his hands shoved in his pockets. This time he was frowning at Bennett.

"What do you want me to do?"

"Can you put two pieces of plywood from that stack over there at every station?" Bennett asked, pointing to the corner.

Dale just nodded and got to work, not saying a word as he went back and forth across the room.

Bennett had known Dale's father. Vince Rigels had been a good guy, even though he was a marine. Bennett and Vince had shared a couple of beers with each other over the years when they'd been home on leave at the same time. Bennett had been in the hospital from his own near-death experience when he'd found out that a roadside bomb had killed Vince.

Dale wasn't a bad kid, he really wasn't. But he needed a role model to look up to, one who didn't wear his pants around his knees. Bennett had seen him hanging out with some of the older kids at the school—the same kids who continually got busted for drugs and alcohol.

"Do you stay after school every Wednesday to help out in here?" Dale asked after about ten minutes.

Bennett had been pulling out the tools they were going to need for the day and setting them up on the station. He leaned back against the table and looked at Dale.

"Yeah. Some of the groups need a little bit more time to keep up with the schedule."

"I heard you were letting kids work on some things that weren't related to the bookshelves. Like personal projects or whatever." Dale shuffled his feet back and forth on the dusty concrete.

"I am. Was there something you wanted help with?"

"Nah. Just curious." Dale turned around and headed back for the pile of wood.

"You know, you're really doing good with this project. You listen to what I say and figure out what to do before you act."

Dale paused for a second as he reached for two pieces of wood. "You should tell my mom that. She doesn't think I can listen for shit."

"Well, do you?"

He didn't say anything as he walked to another station and put the wood down. He looked at Bennett before he answered. "I hear what she says loud and clear. I just choose not to do what she says."

Bennett had to resist the urge to smile. "I'd argue that isn't listening. You have to follow through with it. What else does she say?"

"She doesn't like my friends."

"Do you know why?" he asked.

"She thinks they're bad influences. But she doesn't get it."

"What doesn't she get?" Bennett asked.

"That sometimes you just have to forget."

Well, Bennett understood that perfectly. "Maybe you should try doing something that doesn't mess with your mind."

"You telling me you don't have a beer every once in a while?" Dale asked, narrowing his eyes.

"No, I do. But I'm also an adult."

"You don't get it, either." Dale shook his head at Bennett, frustration evident in every feature of his face.

"Kid, I get it more than you could imagine."

"Whatever." He rolled his eyes as he turned away from Bennett again.

Bennett really hated that *I don't care* attitude, and he really wanted to say something but before he could a group of girls came into the room talking and laughing. One of them was the little blonde in Dale's group, Kylee something. The second Dale saw her his shoulders straightened and he made an attempt to pull his jeans up. Now Bennett only saw half of the skull and crossbones that were across his butt.

Well, that was interesting. The little punk had a crush on the girl. Maybe if he took those damn earrings out and wore pants that weren't five sizes too big, she'd give him the time of day.

Maybe.

Mel walked into the room a minute later, looking rather bright-eyed with two cups of coffee in her hand. She smiled as she crossed the room and handed him one.

"Well, you look wide awake," he said, taking the cup.

"The coffee just needed to set in first."

Bennett looked around to make sure that none of the kids were around them. "I don't remember you needing coffee yesterday to wake up," he whispered before he took a sip.

"Well, yesterday I had a very different wake-up call," she whispered back.

"That you did. We missed out on that this morning."

"If we'd only gotten up twenty minutes earlier."

"That was an oversight on my part. It won't happen again."

"Good to know." She smiled mischievously as the first bell rang. "I'm going to go get ready for class. I see that you've already got everything ready. So you can just stand there and look pretty again." She patted his shoulder before she walked away.

Bennett couldn't help but grin like an idiot.

"Dude, you've got it *bad* for my sister."

Bennett looked to his left to find Hamilton shaking his head.

"And?" he asked, raising his eyebrows. "Didn't you want to know what my intentions were?"

"Your intentions are written plain as day on your face, and it's rather disturbing as it's directed toward my sister. Maybe you should calm it down there, buddy."

" 'Buddy'?" Bennett asked. Geez, these kids liked giving him a hard time.

"Yeah, you should get some practice in before you have dinner with my parents. I don't think my mother would appreciate you drooling over Mel instead of the meat loaf."

"Don't worry, little man. I'll learn to control myself."

"Little man?" Hamilton asked, getting all puffed up.

"Yup, you're smaller than me."

"Everyone is smaller than you. You're freaking Goliath."

"I wasn't always. I was kind of small until I was around your age. And then I started lifting. You can work out with me sometime."

"Seriously?" Hamilton asked, looking just a little bit excited.

"If you want."

"Hell, yeah," he said loudly.

A couple kids looked over at them, as did Mel from the other side of the room. She merely raised her eyebrows at him.

"Sorry," Hamilton said to Mel, somewhat abashed, before he turned back to Bennett. "Hell, yeah," he said again, so only Bennett could hear.

"Sounds like a plan." He clapped Hamilton on the back and looked up to find Dale watching the two of them. If Bennett didn't know any better, he would have sworn that Dale looked envious.

* * *

Bennett's mother had a bit of a green thumb. Jocelyn was out in her garden every chance she could get. She'd just picked a ton of peppers, squash, tomatoes, and eggplant, and she'd told Bennett he needed to come by the house so she could give him some. He hadn't been by the house in a couple of days, so he stopped by on Monday after work. He wasn't supposed to pick up Mel until six, and then they'd head over to her parents' house together.

"Mom. Dad," Bennett called out as he walked in the front door

"In here, Benny," Jocelyn called out from the kitchen.

It didn't matter how old or big he was, Jocelyn still called him Benny.

He walked down the hall to the back of the house to find his mother at the stove stirring a pot. The smell of marinara sauce hit him, and his stomach growled audibly.

"Hey, sweetie." She beamed at him as she covered the pot and wiped her hands on her apron. It was the same apron Bennett had sent her his first Christmas away from home. It said: *I'd tell you the recipe, but then I'd have to kill you.*

"Hey, Mom," he said, crossing the kitchen to her. She took his face and kissed his cheek before he wrapped her up in his arms. "Dinner smells good." He let go of her and took a step back.

"You want to stay. I have more than enough."

"Nah, I'm good. I'm going over to Mel's parents' house for dinner."

"You're what?" she asked.

"It isn't that big of a deal, Mom."

"Isn't that big of a deal?" She was beyond incredulous. "Have you ever gone home to a girl's house before?"

Bennett raised his eyebrows. He'd been to plenty of girls' houses, but he wasn't about to discuss that with his mother.

"I meant to meet her parents," she said, smacking his shoulder. "Because I know for a fact that you've never brought one home to meet us."

This was true. He'd never been serious enough with anyone in high school, and bringing a girl home after he'd joined the military would've involved some traveling, since he'd never been stationed close to home.

"I know, I know. But again, I don't see what the big deal is. You knew we were dating."

"I knew you went on *one* date." She glared up at him. "I want you to bring your girlfriend *here* for dinner. And soon." She poked him hard in the chest.

Girlfriend? Yeah, that seemed like a pretty accurate title for Mel. It was just a little weird for Bennett, because he hadn't referred to a woman as his girlfriend in about five years.

"All right, all right," he said, holding up his hands in defense. "I'll invite her over here."

"Tomorrow, then."

"We can't tomorrow. It's the last karaoke night at the bar."

"Wednesday?"

"I have baseball practice."

"Thursday?" she said through narrowed eyes.

"Thursday should be fine. Let me just check with Mel."

The severe look disappeared from her face. "Good," she said, clapping her hands together. "Is there anything I should make specifically? Or not make? She isn't a picky eater, is she?"

"No, Mom. She isn't picky at all and she'll like whatever you make her."

"So things are going well between the two of you?" she asked as she went to the pantry and pulled out a canvas bag.

"Things are going very well." He leaned back against the counter and watched Jocelyn load up the bag with veggies.

"Oh geez, you're just like your father, a man of few words. Can I get a little bit more than that, please?"

Bennett laughed at her obvious frustration before he conceded and gave his mother more information, but only a little bit. Really there were a lot of things he had to leave out, because he just wasn't going to talk to his mother about his sex life.

Chapter Thirteen

Dinner with the Family

Mel wasn't sure why she was so damn nervous. She'd brought home guys to meet her parents before—not a lot, but there'd been a few. And she'd never felt as antsy or anxious as she did right at that moment.

"You okay?" Bennett asked.

"Yeah."

He was watching the road, but he glanced at her for a second. "I can hear your mind turning all the way over here."

"I'm worried about my mother," Mel told him.

"Why?"

"Because she tends to say what's on her mind. And I have more than a small feeling she isn't going to filter herself around you."

"So what's in store for me tonight?"

Our wedding plans, probably. "Uhhh," Mel said, completely unsure of what to say.

"Oh, come on. Just tell me. Wouldn't you rather me be prepared than surprised?"

"My mother thinks a lot of you—" Mel began.

"Naturally."

Mel rolled her eyes at him. "She tends to make things into something before they become something. Or makes them bigger than they are. And this is new, and I'm really worried she's going to say something to scare you off."

"Melanie," he said seriously. He reached across the console to take her hand, lacing his fingers with hers. "There is nothing your mother is going to say that will scare me off."

"You say that now."

"I'm serious." He brought her hand to his mouth and kissed the back of it. "I don't scare off that easily."

"Really? Because I remember a certain teddy bear that freaked you out to the point of fleeing my house."

"Hey, that was different," he said, sounding mildly offended, as he rested their still-joined hands on the console.

"How?"

"That was me freaking out about something that you'd done, not something that somebody else had done. But I'm cool as a cucumber these days—something you should be, as well."

"After tonight I'll be fine."

Bennett cleared his throat. "About that. I stopped by my parents' house today, and when I told my mom I was eating over here, she pretty much demanded we have dinner at their place sometime this week. So you free on Thursday?"

"To have dinner with your parents?" she asked, surprised. "Um, yeah."

Why was that even more terrifying than dinner with her parents?

Bennett let go of her hand as he pulled into her parents' driveway and put his truck in Park. He turned it off and moved to look at her. It took him about a second to correctly read the plethora of emotions on her face.

"Wasn't one of the things on your list to not dwell?" he asked her.

"It was to not dwell on things I can't change."

"All right, well, we can't change dinner tonight, and we can't change dinner on Thursday, so stop overthinking it."

"I overthink everything."

"Not always." He leaned across the console and came in very close to her face. "If I remember correctly, you were a little impulsive on Saturday."

"Saturday I was *very* impulsive."

"Well, just keep calm and think of Saturday," he told her before he pressed his lips to hers.

She might've moaned just a little bit when he nibbled on her lower lip. "That isn't going to make me calm," she whispered against his mouth.

There was a tap on the window and Mel pulled away from Bennett. She turned around to find Hamilton on the other side, looking thoroughly disturbed.

"Come on. Time to face the music." Bennett got out of his side of the truck.

Hamilton opened Mel's door, his look of disgust not moving an inch as she got out. "You two need to get a room," he said, shaking his head.

"Shut up," Mel said.

"Ooooh, Ms. O'Bryan you just said *shut up*. I'm soooo telling."

Mel looked over Hamilton's shoulder to find Nora Ross. Nora's hands were perched on her hips and her lips were pursed together as she gave Mel a look of sheer mischief.

The Rosses had moved in next door to the O'Bryans about ten years ago. Nora had been four and Hamilton had been five. They'd been best friends ever since.

Nora had shoulder-length light brown hair and big green eyes. She was also a tiny little thing, just under five feet, and she'd be lucky if she cleared it in the next year or two. But even though Nora was short, she was going to be curvy, with a narrow waist and a chest that was already just a little bigger than Mel's.

She was stunning even at fourteen, and she was going to cause her parents more than a little heartache when she went to high school next year.

The two families had always been very close. Nora's aunt Beth had been Mel's roommate for two years in college. And even though Beth was still living up in Tallahassee with her boyfriend, she and Mel still talked on a regular basis.

"What are you doing over there, Miss Priss?" Mel asked putting her hands on her own hips.

"Where else am I supposed to be?" Nora countered.

"Over here giving me a hug."

"Oh, well, that I can do." She dropped her hands and walked over to Mel, throwing her arms around Mel's waist and squeezing tight.

"How are you doing?"

"Good," Nora said, stepping back. "You haven't been around a lot lately."

"That's 'cause her new *boyfriend* is keeping her busy," Hamilton said.

"Hamilton, you're going to get a girlfriend one day and you're going to be falling all over yourself," Bennett told him.

"Kind of like you are?" Hamilton asked.

"I've got no shame."

Mel turned and looked up at Bennett. Yup, cool as a cucumber. And he hadn't even flinched when Hamilton had called him her boyfriend. And why that was such a big deal to her she had no idea. They were sleeping together, for goodness' sake.

"Anyways," she said, turning back to Nora, "you coming to dinner at our house tonight?"

"No. Mom and Dad are going out to dinner, so I have to watch the rug rats."

Colleen and Kevin Ross had waited a few years between

their first and second kids. Nine years, to be exact. They'd had Grant five years ago, and then Penny had come along last year.

They all talked for a couple more minutes before Nora headed home. Mel, Bennett, and Hamilton approached the O'Bryans' front door. Mel took a fortifying breath before they walked inside.

"It's going to be fine," Bennett whispered into her ear.

"You say that now."

They walked through the living room toward the kitchen. Mel's mother was putting the meat loaf on the dining room table and her father was looking in a drawer.

"I can't find those salad things," Miles said as he pushed all manner of kitchen utensils around.

"That's because they're not in the drawer by the stove, darling."

Miles straightened and looked at his wife. "Well, then, where are they?"

"In the drawer by the fridge."

"Because you keep lettuce in the fridge and not in the stove?" he asked jokingly.

She turned to him, putting her hands on her hips. "Exactly," she said.

"I'll leave you to your kitchen logic."

"As it should be." Corinne turned and saw Mel, Bennett, and Hamilton standing on the other side of the kitchen, and her face broke out into a huge smile. "Right on time." She crossed the room and hugged Mel, kissing her on the cheek before she let go and pulled Bennett into a hug. "I'm so glad you could come." She put her hands on Bennett's shoulders. "I'm so glad you and Mel are finally dating. She's always so shy when it comes to guys."

"Thank you, Mother." Mel's face was already starting to turn red.

"What? You are. You have to take some initiative with men. I did with your father."

"Hey," Miles said. "I resent that. I took plenty of initiative."

"Only after I got his attention. He had his nose shoved so far in those books of his that he was sneezing ink."

"All right, Mother, how about we start dinner now. Do you need any help?"

"No. Let me just get the wine."

"Oh, I brought some." Bennett held up the bottle.

"Well, aren't you thoughtful." Corinne beamed at him as she took the bottle and went to open it.

"I think my mom might have a crush on you," Hamilton said to Bennett under his breath.

Bennett laughed.

"He's serious," Miles said.

"Why don't you guys go sit down?" Corinne made a shooing motion toward the table as she opened a drawer looking for the corkscrew. "And I heard that."

"Teacher ears are intense," Hamilton said to Bennett. "Between my sister and my mother, I get away with absolutely nothing."

Bennett shook his head. "Tough break, pal."

"Yup."

"So how you doing, Bennett?" Miles asked as he held out his hand.

"Doing pretty good these days." Bennett nodded toward Mel as he shook Miles's hand. "How could I not be when I've been spending so much time with your daughter?"

"That's what I like to hear."

Miles ushered the group to the table as Corinne came back with the bottle of wine in one hand and the bowl of salad in the other. Bennett and Mel went to the opposite side of the table, and he pulled out the chair for her.

"Thoughtful *and* a gentleman," Corinne said.

"Oh geez," Hamilton mumbled as he sat down.

"You could take some notes," Corinne said to her son as she poured the wine.

"Who am I trying to impress?"

"Well, there's Nora," Miles said.

Hamilton frowned at his father. "We're just friends. Always have been, always will be."

"We'll just see about that." Mel grinned at her little brother. She'd always secretly wanted Nora to wind up with Hamilton, but either both kids were oblivious or they really were just friends. Either way, Mel wasn't giving up hope yet.

"Shut up." Hamilton stuck his tongue out at Mel.

Mel stuck hers out at him. "You just wait. You're going to wake up one day and have feelings for her and not know what happened."

Out of the corner of her eye she caught Bennett looking at her. He was wearing a bemused expression.

"Everyone start serving yourselves," Corinne said, indicating the table filled with food and effectively pulling Mel's gaze away from Bennett. "So, tell us how the project is going." She lifted the lid off the container of potatoes and dished a little out onto her plate.

"What, are my daily updates not sufficient enough?" Hamilton asked.

"You're only in one class. I want to hear about all of them."

"Yeah, and whenever she bombards me with questions they're always about the two of you." Hamilton waved his fork in the air between Mel and Bennett. "I've had more to report back lately."

"Oh geez." Mel closed her eyes.

"What? I'm just curious. My daughter refuses to tell me anything," she said to Bennett. "I've had to resort to other means."

"The project is coming along real nice," Bennett said as he helped himself to a slice of meat loaf. "We're right on schedule, and we should be finished by the end of the semester."

"Well, that's promising," Miles said as he passed the salad bowl to Hamilton.

"Yeah, we just need to raise the last little bit of money. But I think we'll be good. We've gotten a lot for the mud run that's this weekend, and the last little bit should be secured with the auction at the fall festival," Mel told them.

"And how are all of the kids responding? Are you getting them excited?" Corinne asked.

"I think so," Mel said as she put a dab of potatoes on her meat loaf and took a bite.

"There are actually quite a few who are coming in on Wednesday afternoons to work on other projects. It's a real shame they dropped the wood shop class. I think a lot of kids could benefit from it. I know I did when I was in school. If it hadn't been for that class I wouldn't be in the profession I'm in now. And it helped me when I was in the air force."

"It's all because of that horrible man, Keith Reynolds. I'm so glad he's gone," Corinne said more than a little angrily.

"Mom hated him," Hamilton said.

"I did not *hate* him," Corinne explained to Bennett. "I just despised him with every fiber of my being."

Truer words could not be spoken. Corinne wasn't exactly the most forgiving of people, and Keith Reynolds had never done anything to be even remotely redeemable. Ever.

"Knowing the little I do about the man, I find that to be completely justifiable," Bennett said.

"Well, maybe the new superintendent will see how the class benefits the kids and bring it back," Miles suggested.

"I hope so. I can already see a noticeable difference in some of the kids, especially Dale Rigels. I think it really brings something out in him." Mel reached for her wineglass and took a healthy drink before she dived back in to her mashed potatoes.

"Yeah, he isn't as bad as I thought he was going to be. I was real pissed when you put him in my group."

"Hamilton, language," Corinne snapped.

"Ticked! I was ticked when you put him in my group."

"Believe me, that didn't escape my notice. I thought you could be a good influence on him. He needs some better friends."

"No kidding." Hamilton nodded.

"It couldn't have been easy losing his dad. I know his mother Virginia has been having a really tough time," Corinne said.

"Maybe he'd like to work out with us," Hamilton said to Bennett.

"Maybe. You want to invite him?"

"Work out?" Corinne looked between Hamilton and Bennett.

"I told Hamilton I'd show him how to work out if he wanted to bulk up."

"Bennett thinks I'm too scrawny for my own good."

"Well, this will be interesting," Miles said with a chuckle.

"Hey, are you doubting me? 'Cause I can do this."

"I'm not saying you can't. I just said it was going to be interesting."

"I was small like Hamilton when I was his age. Well, maybe just a tad bit bigger." Bennett grinned. "I think he's got just enough fire in him."

"As soon as you say the word I'm ready to start," Hamilton said seriously.

"Wednesday after school. We can start at three after everyone leaves, and you can invite Dale. I think it's a really good idea. If he decides to come, tell him we'll be running."

* * *

Dinner with Mel's family was a breeze. Hamilton was hilarious, and Miles was very laid-back and easy to talk to. Sure Corinne seemed to say whatever she was thinking, but Bennett was used to that with his own mother. He could handle strong-willed women, and though Mel wasn't one to always voice her opinions, she was pretty strong-willed in her own right. He just didn't think she knew how strong she was.

When Bennett pulled up into Mel's driveway he parked next to her car and turned his truck off. He turned to her as he put his hand on the back of her headrest.

"So, do you want to come in?" she asked, tilting her head to the side.

"For coffee?" He twisted a curl around his finger.

"Sure." She glanced at her watch. "In about eight hours."

"Sounds like a plan," he said with a grin.

They were in her house about two minutes later, and about five minutes after that they were in her bed.

* * *

Bennett was more than a little pleased to see Dale show up with Hamilton at three on Wednesday. Both of them were wearing gym shorts, T-shirts, and sneakers, though Dale's looked a little bit more worn out than Bennett would've liked.

"You two ready?" Bennett asked as he threw his gym bag into the backseat of his truck and shut the door.

"Yup," Hamilton said.

Dale just shrugged.

"Then let's go." Bennett led them over to the track that ran around the football field.

They did stretches until Bennett thought they were

loosened up enough to hit the pavement. He didn't push himself as hard as he normally did, wanting the kids to keep up with him, and they did for about half an hour until Dale fell back, breathing hard.

Bennett stopped and turned around. Hamilton was pretty short of breath and red in the face.

"You two gone about as far as you think you can?"

Both of them nodded.

"Let's go cool it down, then," Bennett said.

They walked onto the field and stretched out again. When they finished, Dale fell back on the grass and looked up at the sky. "You're brutal, man," he said as he threw his arm over his eyes.

"You haven't seen anything yet, buddy," Bennett said from his position on the grass. He stretched his legs out in front of him and watched the two kids recover.

"Maybe it wouldn't be so hard for you if you stopped smoking weed," Hamilton said as he grabbed their water bottles.

"I don't see you doing much better than me, asshole." Dale dropped his arm and sat up. "And I haven't smoked anything in weeks."

Hamilton handed Dale a bottle and eyed him speculatively for a second. "That's good, because I can guarantee you there was no way you were going to get Kylee. She doesn't put up with that stuff."

Dale's eyebrows shot up in surprise and his body froze. "I don't know what you're talking about."

"Sure you don't," Hamilton said with a smirk. "You know you can hang out with me sometime if you want."

Dale's body relaxed at the change of subject, and he shrugged. "Sure."

"You doing anything tonight?"

"No, my mom's working late."

"You want to come over for dinner?" Hamilton sat on the grass a couple of feet from Dale.

Dale shrugged again. "Sure."

"Can you stop with all of the noncommittal 'I don't care' crap?" Hamilton asked. "It gets really old."

Bennett tried not to laugh. He was getting pretty sick of that crap from Dale, too.

"Maybe I *don't* care."

"Maybe," Hamilton said as he lay back and closed his eyes. "But I think you do."

Yeah, Bennett had to agree with Hamilton. He was pretty sure Dale did care, cared a lot.

* * *

Mel had dinner with Harper, Grace, and Preston on Wednesday night. She got back around seven and started doing laundry in between grading papers. She'd fallen a little behind on her normal day-to-day tasks, being a little distracted with a certain man.

She and Bennett hadn't actually made plans to see each other that night, so she wasn't exactly sure if he would be coming over after practice. He might need some space after spending four nights in a row with her.

So the ball was in his court as to what would happen tonight.

If anything did happen.

God, she hated playing games so freaking much, but she didn't want to be this pathetic clingy girlfriend who couldn't spend a night away from her new boyfriend.

"Oh, this is so stupid," she said as she slammed the door of the dryer shut and turned it on. "I want to see him. This shouldn't be so damn complicated."

She grabbed the basket full of clean laundry and headed

for the living room. She put the basket down on the couch and played the episode of *Friends* she'd paused. She folded about three things before she reached over and checked her phone.

Nothing.

"Soooo stupid," she said, beyond frustrated with herself.

He'd stayed at her house the night before, so she'd woken up with him, and they had seventh period in the wood shop. It wasn't like she hadn't seen him today. Why was she being so ridiculous?

She just needed to distract herself. She eyed the pile of laundry in front of her. Yeah, this sure as hell wasn't going to do it.

Her phone beeped and vibrated against the coffee table. Mel turned and pounced on it before the screen even had time to go dark.

Hey hot stuff, what are you doing?

Laundry, she texted back as a smile split her face.

Sounds thrilling. Want a distraction?

Depends on what you have in mind. I'm about to start matching my socks and that's the best part.

I'll show you my best part, he responded a second later.

Mel took a deep breath, feeling a little light-headed and a lot turned on.

Well, then get over here and show me…will there be a hands-on portion of this demonstration? she typed out. But her finger hovered over the Send button for a second. She'd never sent dirty text messages. Well, there was no time like the present. She bit her lip nervously as she hit Send.

Bennett had been responding right away, so when a minute went by with nothing, she started to feel a little nervous. But there was a knock on her front door a moment later.

Mel put her phone down on the coffee table and walked across her living room with a quickness. She peeked out of the peephole to find Bennett standing on her porch. She opened the door and before she could even say hello he was on her, pushing her back into the hallway and closing the door with his foot.

"So let's talk about this hands-on portion," he said against her mouth. He walked her backward until she hit the wall. "How much hands-on are we talking about?" His mouth was on her neck now, and his hands were traveling down her sides to her hips.

"How much can you handle?" she asked.

"At this point? Very little," he whispered against her collarbone as he pressed his very prominent erection into her thigh.

"It doesn't feel very little." She slipped her hand between them and cupped the front of his jeans. "You really do go from zero to sixty, don't you?"

Bennett laughed as he pulled back and looked at her. "Zero? I haven't been at zero in weeks. Though that text message of yours would've done the trick all on its own. I had no idea you could be so dirty, Ms. O'Bryan."

"You started it."

He grinned. "That I did."

"Do you intend on finishing it?"

Heat flared up in his eyes as he reached down and grabbed her thighs.

"Oh," she gasped, startled, as he picked her up.

Her legs automatically wrapped around him and he pulled back from the wall. He adjusted her in his arms as he reached for the door and flipped the locks.

He carried Mel to her bedroom and did finish it. And her. Twice.

* * *

There was just something about pillow talk with Mel that Bennett couldn't get enough of. She was curled up against him, her hands playing back and forth on his chest. He had his hands on her back and he was working his fingers up and down her spine. She was so soft and warm in his arms. He'd been thinking about this all damn day...well, this and the other things that they'd already accomplished.

She shifted against him, one of her legs riding up between his.

"I'm glad you came over," she said, looking up at him.

"I told you I was. Didn't I?" He slipped his hands down to the small of her back and pulled her closer to him.

"No." She shook her head shyly.

"I didn't?" he asked, confused. "I thought before I'd left after seventh period..." He trailed off as she shook her head again. "Well then, why didn't you call me or text me?"

Mel shrugged and bit her lip.

He brought one of his hands up and pulled her bottom lip out of her mouth. "Talk to me."

"I don't want to be *that* girl."

"*What* girl?"

"The clingy, needy one."

"I don't think you're either of those things." He brought his mouth to hers and kissed her.

"Okay," she said against his mouth.

"I mean it, Melanie."

A sweet smile came across her lips. "I really like it when you call me Melanie."

"Is that so?"

"Yeah," she said, as she snuggled into his chest.

"Well, then good night, Melanie. Sweet dreams." He kissed the top of her head and wrapped his arms around her.

"Night, Bennett," she sighed contentedly, her breath washing out over his skin.

Bennett held on to her, appreciating everything about the woman in his arms as he fell asleep.

Chapter Fourteen

Baseball Lessons

On Thursday night, Mel met Bennett at his place before they headed over to his parents' house. She was a little fidgety in the car, but she wasn't nearly as jumpy as she'd been before dinner with her family.

"How you doing over there?" Bennett reached over and gently squeezed her knee.

"Good." She smiled as she turned to look at him.

He could see she was telling the truth, too, not that he thought she would lie to him. Bennett had quickly picked up on the fact that Mel wore her emotions on her sleeve, and besides, lying just wasn't in her nature. "Good, because you have nothing to worry about."

"Me? Worry? Never," she said sarcastically. "I have absolutely no idea what you're talking about."

"Riiight." He looked back to the road. To be honest, he was a little nervous. Not because he thought his parents would say something to embarrass him, and he definitely wasn't concerned whether or not they would like Mel. They'd met her plenty of times, and they were already big fans. Plus it was Mel—what wasn't there to like?

No, he was nervous because this was a pretty big step for him.

"You know, I've never brought a girl home to meet my parents before," he told her. He wanted her to know this meant something to him. That she meant something to him.

She shifted in her seat to face him. "Never?" she asked, sounding surprised.

"Nope." He pulled into his parents' driveway and put his truck in Park. He turned to look at her and found a very sweet smile playing across her lips.

"What?" he asked, unable to keep himself from smiling, too.

"It's just, I'm not the only one crossing things off a list."

For some reason that little statement took him back for a second. But it was true. He was doing a lot of things he'd never done before with Mel, and they hadn't been together for all that long.

"That's true. You ready?"

Mel nodded.

"Then let's go."

As always, Bennett got out first and walked around to the passenger side to help Mel get out. He snuck in a few quick kisses before he grabbed her hand and led her up to the house. The second they walked inside Jocelyn was there, throwing her arms around Mel.

"Oh it's so great to have you here dear." Jocelyn beamed as she took a step back to look at Mel. "You're positively stunning." Then she looked up at Bennett. "She's stunning, Benny. You better tell her this all the time."

"I do," Bennett said. "Believe me."

"Come on, darling." Jocelyn grabbed Mel's elbow and led her down the hall. "Benny, your father is outside. He insisted on grilling steaks, so why don't you go help him?"

"Will do," Bennett said as he watched his two favorite women walk away.

Mel looked over her shoulder. *Benny?* she mouthed at him, grinning.

Yeah, so that one hadn't skipped her attention. Not that he'd expected it to. Bennett just shrugged at her. He had nothing.

Mel's grin widened as she turned back around.

Bennett headed outside to find his father flipping the steaks. The coals sizzled as juice spilled out of the meat. "Hey, Dad," he said as he shut the door behind him.

He looked a lot like his father. They were the same height, though Walker was about fifty pounds heavier and had a bit of a beer belly. He also had a very thick beard and mustache that matched his graying hair.

"Hey," Walker said. "Is your pretty little lady inside with my pretty little lady?"

"Yeah," Bennett replied. "I'm almost positive Mom is giving her an earful."

"Would you expect anything else?" Walker asked as he closed the grill.

"Nope."

"Your mother has been in a fuss for the last couple of days about this. You'd swear royalty was coming or something."

Bennett chuckled.

"That's a sound I've heard very little of lately," Walker said, giving Bennett a significant look.

"Oh, come on. I haven't been that bad."

Walker just raised his eyebrows at his son.

"All right, I admit it. The last few years have sucked. But it's getting better."

"Due in no small part to that young lady in there."

"How would you know?" Bennett asked, raising his own eyebrows. "You haven't even seen us together."

"Yeah, but I've seen *you*. I remember how closed off you were when Kristi walked out on us."

Bennett let out a sigh. He never liked conversations about his birth mother. She was long gone and she could stay that way forever, for all he cared.

"It took you some time to warm up to Jocelyn, but once you did you were putty in her hands."

"And you think I'm putty now?"

"Son, I know a malleable man when I see one." Walker grabbed his beer from beside the grill and tipped it back.

"I don't think I've ever been called 'malleable' before," Bennett said unable to stop the smile that turned up his mouth.

"Well, the fact that you're smiling these days is proof positive that something's changing, and for the better."

Yeah, things were definitely better with Mel. But this wasn't all that shocking. How could things not improve when she was around, when he was spending so much time with her, waking up next to her, making love to her? What man wouldn't be smiling?

"Anyway, it's good to see you happy again. That was all I meant."

"Thanks, Dad," Bennett said, clapping his father on the shoulder.

"You mind refilling me?" Walker asked as he handed Bennett his empty beer bottle.

"On it." He grabbed the bottle and headed for the mini-fridge in the corner.

The backyard was an oasis for both Jocelyn and Walker. Jocelyn had her massive garden on the back side, and Walker had his very equipped porch. The grill was built into the back wall, with slate counters on either side that could handle the outside weather. The back wall housed a minifridge, which was always stocked with beer, and a sink. Above the sink hung all of Walker's grilling utensils.

Bennett grabbed two beers, and as he straightened he heard laughter coming from the window to his right. He looked over to see Mel and Jocelyn in the kitchen. Both women held glasses of wine. Jocelyn was at the stove, sautéing what Bennett could only presume to be mushrooms and onions, while Mel leaned back against the counter.

Mel looked up and made eye contact with him through the window, and her sweet little mouth quirked to the side. As he smiled back at Mel, Jocelyn turned around and caught the moment between the couple. She said something to Mel that made her blush, but he could tell by the relaxed set of her shoulders that it didn't make her uncomfortable.

Bennett really wanted to know what Jocelyn had said. He'd just have to ask Mel later.

* * *

"He adores you," Jocelyn said. "I've never seen my son act this way before. He's had a rough couple of years since he came back. You've definitely had a positive impact on him."

"I can't have had that much of an impact. We haven't even been dating for two weeks." Really? Had it been only that long? Mel felt as if it had been months since Bennett had cornered her in that supply closet and kissed the breath out of her.

"Oh sugar," Jocelyn said. "My son has been sweet on you for some time now. He would drop your name every once in a while, and you better believe I noticed it when the frequency picked up."

"When did that start?" Mel asked, very intrigued.

"Around last April."

That was about the time Mel had asked him for help with

the project. Of course, at that time she'd been trying to get Superintendent Reynolds to approve it, and it had been an epic fail.

"He was beside himself when you got shot," Jocelyn continued. "You also better believe that his spending more time with you didn't escape my notice, either."

"Is that so?"

"It is," Jocelyn replied. "And him bringing you home to meet us isn't small potatoes. He's *never* brought a girl home before."

"He told me that." Mel still found it all a little hard to believe.

She glanced out the window again. Bennett wasn't on the other side like he had been last time. No, this time he was across the porch standing next to his dad. Both of them had beers in their hands.

"You know," Jocelyn said, bringing Mel's attention back into the kitchen. "Bennett was always a pretty happy kid growing up, but when he came back here, some of the light had disappeared from his eyes."

"I know it was hard for him, with the accident and everything."

"Has he told you about it?"

"No." Mel shook her head. "I know the basics, that the helicopter was shot down and that only two made it back alive. But I haven't asked him anything about it. I figure he'll tell me when he wants to."

"You're good not to push him. He's never done very well with that. When it comes to Bennett you're going to need patience."

"Boy, do I know that."

"He's worth it," Jocelyn said seriously.

"I know that too. I really do." Mel looked straight at Jocelyn, not flinching from the woman's intense gaze. Mel really wanted Bennett's mother to understand just how much she cared about that man. Even in such a short span of time she was already so in over her head.

"That's good to hear, because I think you're good for him. I'm starting to see my son again, the happy one who wasn't always haunted. His demeanor has lightened significantly since he's started to spend more time with you. Bennett beams now, and going to war or not, my son *never* beamed before."

"He makes me incredibly happy, too."

Jocelyn smiled. "That's what a mother likes to hear."

She moved on to a less a serious subject, and the two women chatted as Jocelyn cooked the vegetables on the stove. Mel helped her finish setting the table, over Jocelyn's protests. By the time the men came in with the steaks, everything was ready.

"Hey," Bennett said to Mel. "My mother telling you about all of my bad traits?"

Mel shook her head. "I think she's trying to talk you up so that I'll like you more. She keeps going on about all of these past achievements. I had no idea you got first place in the potato sack race in fourth grade. That's quite an accomplishment, and I don't know why you'd hide that from me."

"Well, I don't like to brag about it or anything. You know, big heads and all."

"I don't see why not. She also showed me some of your paintings from second grade. You sure had a thing for pink."

"Hey, I was making those for my mom—what do you expect?"

"That you would've made them blue, as that's my favorite color," Jocelyn said from behind them.

Bennett turned to his mother. He slid his hand around Mel's side and pulled her close. "Well, I know that now. Does that count for anything?" he asked.

"Mmm, maybe," Jocelyn said. Her mouth turned up as she took in the pair of them standing so close. "Dinner's ready. Why don't you show Mel into the dining room?"

"Yes ma'am," Bennett said as he started to pull Mel away.

"And Bennett." Jocelyn put her hand on his arm to stop him. "I loved everything you ever brought me, pink and all." She smiled warmly.

"I know, Mom." He leaned down and planted a kiss on her cheek.

There was just something about how Bennett interacted with his mother that made Mel feel all warm inside. But everything he did had that effect on her.

* * *

They got back to Bennett's house just before nine. He'd asked her to stay the night at his place, so she'd brought a change of clothes for work the next day. Bennett grabbed her bag from the trunk of her car while she grabbed the dress that was hanging in the backseat.

"Hold on—I need that other bag, too," she said, pointing to a black satchel. "My papers are in it."

The Braves were playing the Cubs tonight. Normally Bennett would've stayed at his parents' house to watch it with his dad, but Mel really needed to grade tonight. So Bennett would be able to catch the last couple of innings while she did what she needed to do.

"Got it," he said, grabbing the strap and pulling it up around his shoulder.

Bennett closed the trunk and led the way up to his house. Mel hadn't been there since that first night, and he was glad she was sleeping over. She followed him inside and he handed her the satchel and took the dress from her other hand.

"Make yourself comfortable," he said, pointing to the couch. "Let me just put this in my room."

When he came back, the TV was on and the game was playing. Mel was unzipping her bag and pulling out a stack of papers, and she had a red pen in her mouth. She put the papers on her lap and looked up at him. Then she pulled the pen out of her mouth and pointed to the screen with it. "I don't have good news for you."

Bennett turned and read the score. The Braves were down, 4–1.

"Damn." He sat down on the couch and pulled off his boots.

"They still have three more innings. Maybe they can pull it out." She settled back against the couch, pulling her legs up underneath her.

"Maybe." He stretched out and put his feet up on the steamer trunk. He wrapped his arm around Mel's shoulders and pulled her into his side, where she settled in for the duration of the game.

* * *

"You've got to be kidding me," Bennett later said to the screen for the umpteenth time.

Mel was trying not to laugh at him, really she was, but he was so aggravated. She'd seen him watch games, but he'd never been this upset before. Maybe Mel had just never seen him watching a game where his team was losing.

The Braves hadn't improved much on their score. It was now 7–3 in the ninth inning. The odds were not in their favor.

Fifteen minutes later Mel finished grading her last paper. She put it down on the stack in her lap and looked up at the TV just in time to see the last Braves batter strike out.

"Oh, come on," Bennett groaned. "Well, that's that." He shook his head as he grabbed the remote and turned off the TV.

He leaned back against the sofa and closed his eyes. "That was just painful. They were all over the freaking place tonight."

Mel put her papers on the steamer trunk. She turned to Bennett, put one of her knees on the sofa and threw her other leg over his lap and straddled him.

"What's this?" he asked, the frown on his face disappearing.

"You look like you could use some comforting." She ran her hands up his chest, to his shoulders, and around to the back of his neck.

"If this is comforting, I could always use some."

"Is that so, *Benny*?" she asked as her mouth twitched up at the sides.

"I knew that was coming." He shook his head. "You've been waiting all night to say something, haven't you?"

"I have no idea what you're talking about, Benny Boo, Boo Boo Boo."

Bennett moved so fast that Mel didn't even see it coming. She was suddenly on her back, her arms pinned above her head. Bennett was firmly stationed between her thighs, preventing her from moving even an inch.

"Call me Benny Boo one more time," he said right above her mouth. It would've been very easy for Mel to be intimidated by this massive man on top of her, especially with the current scowl on his face, but there was a twinkle of mischief in his eyes that let her know he was playing just as much as she was.

"Benny—" but she didn't get any further than that as he covered her mouth with his.

His tongue slid between her lips, and the kiss turned hot and hungry in a second. Mel's head fell back against the couch cushion as Bennett started to move against her. She could feel his erection growing on the inside of her thigh. There was just something about him getting hard against her that turned her on even more. She wanted to reach down and touch him, but her hands were still pinned up against the armrest.

"You won't be calling me Benny Boo in a second," he said as he kissed her neck and nibbled on her skin.

"And why's that?"

"Because I'm going to make you forget how to talk."

His lips were back on hers a second later and he worked her mouth as his hands traveled down her arms and to her sides. When he got to the hem of her shirt he pushed it up until it was over her breasts, then his fingers were working around to the clasp at her back. He had it undone and her bra and shirt off in the next moment. It hadn't been hard for him to pull it off, because she hadn't moved her arms from above her head.

Bennett's mouth disappeared from hers as he moved down her body. He kissed the space between her breasts before he took one nipple in his mouth.

"Ahh, Bennett." She arched up into him and her hands came up to the back of his head.

He just hummed into her breast as his hands went to the snap on the front of her jeans. The zipper was down a second later, and his hand was slowly working down underneath her panties.

She gasped as he parted her and slipped two fingers inside.

"Well, the Braves might've been off tonight, but *you* definitely know how to play first and second base," she said as she writhed against his hand.

"Mmm-hmm," he hummed as he switched to her other breast. He went at her for a good minute before he reared up on his knees. "Let's move on to third." He reached for the top of her jeans and pulled them, along with her panties, off her legs in one swift movement. "Perfection," he said as he settled back between her thighs. He pulled her legs up and over his shoulders, and then his hands were running beneath her bottom and he was lifting her up to gain better access and dive deeper.

"Bennett," she moaned as she gripped the top of his head. His hair was too short for her to hold on to anything.

Mel still couldn't get over the pleasure that Bennett was capable of with his mouth. And after he added his fingers to the mix, it was just a matter of time before she was bucking and coming hard. He kept his mouth on her throughout her orgasm, giving her everything he had.

* * *

Mel was out of breath as she lay on the couch. Her eyes were closed and her smile was one that radiated a postorgasmic glow.

"How you doing over there?" Bennett asked as he sat up.

Mel didn't say anything. She just opened her eyes slowly and gave him a warm, sexy smile. Bennett got up from the couch and looked at the naked woman still sprawled across it.

"Where do you think you're going?" she asked when she found her voice.

"I'd like to go in there." He nodded down the hall toward his bedroom. "I was hoping for a home run."

"Just give me a second. I'm still trying to remember how to stand."

"Mel, I just don't have time for that." He leaned over and picked her up in one fell swoop.

"Well, if you insist," she said as he carried her to his bedroom.

Bennett hadn't slept in there since last Saturday night, and as he remembered their first night together he found himself wanting her so bad it was ridiculous.

He set her down on the bed and took a step back as he started to unbutton his shirt. Mel stood before he even got through two buttons and she pushed his hands away. She looked up at him as her fingers worked their way down.

"So I was thinking."

"About?"

"I want a shot at third base, too," she said as she finished with the buttons and pushed the shirt off his arms, not looking up at him.

"What?" he managed to choke out, which was an accomplishment as he'd nearly swallowed his tongue.

Bennett had always been a pretty big fan of oral sex, both giving and receiving. But he'd never been one to ask for it. He might've gone down on Mel a couple of times, but reciprocating was her decision.

He reached up and gently pushed her chin until her gaze met his. "Are you sure?"

"Yes, but I've...umm, never done it before," she said, looking slightly nervous. "And to be completely honest with you, you're the first guy to have done it to me."

Well, as she'd only been with one other guy, neither statement was all that shocking. But still, the idea that she'd never done this to a man before, and that she wanted to explore him, was almost more than he could handle at the moment.

Almost.

"Okay, but if you feel uncomfortable, stop."

"Okay. I've...uhhh...done a little research on the matter," she said as she reached for the front of his jeans. "But you know there's only so much you can get from reading. So do you have any tips?"

"Tips?" he managed to ask. He was having a little bit of trouble hearing at the moment. Blood was pounding in his ears, which was an accomplishment because he thought it had all rushed to the bulge that was currently straining the front of his pants.

"Yeah, tips, pointers, suggestions." She stretched up on her toes and lightly pressed her mouth to his as she unbuttoned the snap on his jeans and pulled down the zipper. She didn't touch his erection, which was both good and bad.

"Hands are good," he said against her mouth. "The tip is important and supersensitive. But really just do what feels right, and I'm more than likely to respond to what I like."

"I think I can do that." She pulled back and looked at him as she pushed his pants and boxer briefs down his thighs. And then she dropped to her knees in front of him, keeping eye contact the entire time.

Holy. Hell.

She helped him pull everything off his legs. When he was completely naked in front of her, she sat up and kissed the very tip of his erection.

"Not like this," he said, reaching down and grabbing her arms to pick her up. "I really don't think my legs would hold out through the whole thing." He gently pushed her onto the bed and kissed her as he rolled to his back.

She settled on top of him and her lips left his. She kissed his neck, and then her warm, wet mouth was moving slowly down his sternum. Her hands traveled down his chest to his stomach where she traced his abs with her fingertips. All the while her body was pressing into his erection, her soft, sweet belly rubbing against him and driving him out of his fucking mind.

"*God. Melanie.*" His voice came out pained, which wasn't all that surprising, as he was trying his hardest not to move and create more friction between their bodies. This was her show, and he needed to be patient and endure the sweet torture of everything she was doing.

Now her mouth was on his stomach, and her tongue was

delving into the dips and grooves of his abs. He wasn't sure if he was even going to make it to the good part. But he also didn't want to miss a second of it. He reached over and grabbed another pillow to stack behind his head.

Watching her was going to make it so much more difficult to hold out, but he couldn't pull his eyes away. And really, why would he want to? Because a second later she opened that perfect little mouth of hers and covered him.

Bennett couldn't stop his hands from coming up to the back of her head, but it wasn't to thrust himself deeper. No, he just needed his hands in her hair, wanted to feel her as she moved over him. Her tongue ran up the underside of his penis as she took him deeper into her mouth.

She moved over him eagerly, and then she threw her hand into the mix. Yeah, he wasn't going to last long at all. Maybe a minute . . . or thirty seconds.

"*Melanie*," he groaned, closing his eyes and trying to breathe past the release that was building. He had a second of sanity cross his brain, and he reached down to pull her up his body. He wanted the home run. He didn't want to get off at third base.

He rolled her underneath him as his mouth came down hard on hers. He reached down and grabbed her thighs, holding on to her as they moved together. When he couldn't take a second more. He pulled back and reached for the nightstand to grab a condom. He had it on and was sinking into her in record time.

He gripped her thighs again as he thrust into her over and over again. She gasped his name and the breathy edge to her voice made the pressure in his entire body crank up even further. This was what he wanted, this right here. Her underneath him, his name coming from her lips, her fingers digging a path into his back.

Mel was losing control again in his arms, and he loved

that he was the one who could bring out the wild side in her. Loved that she trusted him enough to completely let loose.

Bennett let go of one of her thighs and brought his hand between their bodies. His fingers found her sweet spot, and it took only a couple of moments for her to let go, and thank God because Bennett was holding on by a thread.

He came about three seconds later, letting go with an orgasm so powerful he couldn't breathe. He pulled out of her and rolled to his back, bringing Mel with him. He stared up at the ceiling trying to catch his breath.

They rested for a minute or two. She stacked her hands on his sternum and rested her chin on top. They just looked at each other for a second, and when Bennett reached up to push her hair out of her eyes she smiled. God, did she smile.

"We can play baseball anytime you want," she said.

Bennett burst out laughing, unable to stop as he wrapped his arms around her and buried his face in her hair.

* * *

The mud run was scheduled for the first weekend in October. It was very successful in the fund-raising department, and it went off without a hitch. Well, sort of. Since Mel was doing all of the behind-the-scenes aspects for the day, she hadn't planned on getting involved in the messy part. But those plans hadn't exactly happened.

Everything was fine until after the awards ceremony at the very end of the event. Bennett, along with Hamilton, dragged Mel into the first obstacle filled with mud, which was still very wet and sticky.

It took a lot of time in the shower for Mel to get clean. But she wasn't complaining as she had Bennett scrubbing her back and washing the mud out of her hair. He'd followed through with his promise to buy her conditioner. There was a bottle in the shower and several more under the sink in the bathroom.

They spent Saturday night and most of Sunday curled up on his couch watching the rest of season three of *Game of Thrones*. The second to last episode had left Mel speechless for all of about five minutes, and then she'd proceeded to rant about it.

For the rest of the night.

Bennett apparently thought it was cute, which was lucky for her. *Really* lucky, because she still wasn't over it on Monday morning.

"I just don't understand what they're going to do now," she said before she took a long pull on her coffee.

"Well, maybe you should read the books. Then you'll find out."

Bennett was stocking all the stations in the wood shop, and watching him was a lovely way for Mel to start her day.

"Yeah, I don't think so. The books would just make me crazier. Maybe when everything is all said and done. Besides, he still hasn't finished writing them, so I'm just going to have to wait anyway."

"Impatient much?" he asked as he crossed the room.

"I think I've proved my patience, pal."

"Are you referring to me?" He raised his eyebrows as he grabbed her coffee cup and put it on the table behind her. Then he proceeded to cage her in against the table.

"Yes. And what do you think you're doing?"

"Oh, you know, kissing you." He leaned in and pressed his mouth to hers.

Mel was not one to resist Bennett, and as he'd taken away her caffeine she was going to indulge in one of her other favorite pick-me-ups. Well, not her favorite, as she had some modesty and they were in public and all.

There was a knock and someone cleared their throat.

Bennett and Mel pulled apart to find Mitch Bolinder, the principal of Mirabelle High, standing in the doorway.

Mel liked her boss. He listened to the teachers and cared about the students. He'd always been a pretty nice guy, so the frown that was currently across his face wasn't one that boded confidence.

"We have a bit of a problem, and I need to talk to the two of you."

"What problem?" Bennett asked.

Mitch sighed as he looked at the two of them and shook his head. "I don't take stock in anything that Bethelda Grimshaw writes about, but more than a couple of parents have called in regarding her newest article."

Mel's stomach dropped. "What article?" she asked barely loud enough for Mitch to hear her.

"This one," he said crossing the room and handing her a piece of paper.

THE GRIM TRUTH

THERE'S NO SUCH THING AS A FREE LUNCH...OR BOOKCASE

Curley Q might seem like one of Mirabelle's sweet and innocent little darlings, but she's just like the rest of them. This isn't all that surprising considering who her band of whorish and immoral friends are, Little Coquette, Brazen Interloper, and Flamboyant Peacock being just a few.

Q has been seen in the company of a certain ex-military man. Apparently, Lumber Jack's years in the service didn't teach him anything about self-control or morals. It's very disappointing. It appeared that after his near-death experience, and after the death of his fellow soldiers following a helicopter crash, that he had his head on straight. Well, appearances can be deceiving.

Q has been harassing dozens of Mirabelle's residents to try to raise funds for this unnecessary bookshelf project at the school. Not to mention she's been asking our hardworking businessmen to practically give their materials away. But it looks like she's paying for some of the services provided with a few resources of her own.

Apparently Lumber Jack isn't opposed to Q's form of payment, either. The two have been getting down and dirty in public as well as behind closed doors. They made a rather indecent public display of themselves over the weekend, when they pretty much groped each other while mud wrestling.

Who would've thought that Q would stoop to such low levels to get a little help? I for one am shocked, and I don't think I'm the only person. Q is a teacher, so what exactly are her students learning from her? What are they learning from this man who's more than willing to trade his labor for sex? What happened to honor? Because he apparently has none.

Chapter Fifteen

Way More Complicated Than
a Teddy Bear

Mel stared at the piece of paper in a daze. She couldn't even process the words she'd just read. Her mind was racing too fast for her to catch up. It was the tension radiating off the man next to her that finally pulled her out of her head.

But before she could open her mouth, Mitch was talking again.

"Look, I don't believe it. I know you two are in a relationship, and that isn't breaking any rules of any kind. I also know both of you well enough to know that this is a load of garbage, which is what I've told everyone who's called, and it's what I will continue to tell them."

"Thank you," Mel said, but Bennett was still silent.

"I just thought the two of you should know," Mitch said before he left the shop.

"Bennett." Mel reached out for his hand but he pulled away before she had a chance to grab it.

"I need to finish getting ready."

"Can we talk about this?"

At that moment Dale and Kylee came into the room

talking. They stopped when they saw Bennett and Mel, reading the tension that was in the room.

"Later," Bennett said as he moved off.

Mel closed her eyes as he walked away. The article sucked, beyond any shadow of a doubt. But she was way more concerned about the effect it had on Bennett. That stupid cow had questioned his honor, and Mel knew him well enough to know he wasn't going to deal well with that. Not at all.

* * *

Mel didn't hear from Bennett at all that day. No text messages, no calls, no nothing. He'd barely said good-bye before he left, but at least he'd said something about her coming over to his house after she had dinner with Grace, Harper, and Paige.

Mel would've canceled, but they were doing stuff for the wedding, and as Mel was the maid of honor, she needed to be there. Besides, Bennett needed to work on a desk he was restoring for a customer. He was going to be busy for most of the night anyway, and sitting in the house alone would've made her go a little crazy.

It was helpful for Mel to talk things over with her friends. Grace and Paige had been all over Bethelda's blog in the past. They spent a good portion of the night bashing Bethelda in every way they could, which was helpful on so many levels. But they'd only had two words of wisdom on how to deal with the article.

"Ignore it." They pretty much said it in unison.

"It's just going to make you crazy," Paige said.

"And you can't change it," Grace shook her head.

And when it came to what other's thought about it, Mel really hoped she'd be able to just ignore it. But she was fairly certain that Bennett wouldn't. She had to talk to him about it, because how he felt wasn't something she could ignore.

When she got to his house the front door was unlocked, so she let herself in and headed for his garage. She pushed the door open to find him sanding the top of the desk. He looked up at her, frowning.

Well, this was promising.

"Hey, what time is it?"

"Almost ten. You get a lot done?" She leaned against the doorjamb and folded her arms across her chest.

"Yeah."

"Can we talk?"

"Mel, it's not important. I don't care what that woman had to say."

"Except you *do* care."

Bennett didn't say anything as he reached over for his water bottle and unscrewed the cap. He looked away from her and took a long drink. Too long.

"Bennett."

"I really don't want to talk about it," he snapped at her.

Mel couldn't stop herself from flinching back at his tone. She'd never heard him raise his voice.

"Shit, Mel, I'm sorry."

"You weren't the only one she made up lies about."

He sighed. "I know."

"I can go home if you want to be by yourself tonight."

He crossed the space and grabbed her by the waist. "Look, I'm sorry, I didn't mean to raise my voice at you. I don't want you to leave. I want you here. I just really don't want to talk about the article."

"Can I say something? Please? You don't have to respond. Just listen to what I have to say."

He nodded.

"You're upset," she said, running her hands up his chest. "I know you are, because I care about you, but I'm not stupid. I'm upset about what was said, too. That woman questioned a lot of things about me, but at the end of the day I was way more concerned about how this was affecting you. And I'm trying to talk to you about it, and you won't talk to me."

"Mel—"

She put her hand over his mouth. "I want you to *want* to talk to me—I'm not going to force it out of you. What she said was bullshit. You have more honor in here"—she put her hand over his heart—"than most could ever dream of. And all I'm asking is for you to let me in."

She leaned up and gave him a soft kiss. "I'm going to get ready for bed." She turned and started to pull away but Bennett grabbed her hand.

"Mel."

She looked over her shoulder as she pulled her hand away. "You have to want to, Bennett."

* * *

Bennett felt like an asshole as he watched Mel walk away. But he hadn't been lying when he'd told her the article wasn't something he could talk about. It had pissed him off for many reasons, but Mel didn't understand the real reason he'd been so upset.

Today had marked three years since the crash, and he hadn't realized the day until he'd seen that stupid article. He had no idea how he could've forgotten. The very fact that he had made him feel like what Bethelda wrote was true.

How was he supposed to tell Mel something like that? That he wasn't the man she thought he was? He couldn't, so he chose to say nothing. Now Mel was upset, and he really didn't have the first clue how to fix it, because he couldn't talk about it.

Not now, not ever.

Bennett spent another hour out in the garage trying to

clear his mind. It was mission impossible. By the time he went into his bedroom, Mel was asleep. She was curled up on the far side of the bed, wrapped around a pillow, and facing away from where he would sleep. It made his chest ache.

Even though it was slowly getting cooler outside, it was still warm and he'd been sweating as he'd worked in the garage. He headed for the shower, hoping the hot water might clear his head.

No such luck.

When he crawled into bed ten minutes later, he couldn't stop himself from curling up behind Mel. She rolled over in her sleep and snuggled into him, her breath washing over his chest.

As he held her, he tried like hell to turn his mind off, but he couldn't. Images from three years ago were playing in his head like a movie. The helicopter crashing, the screaming, and the gunfire playing on a loop and ringing in his ears. And then he was laying flat on his back, the sun blazing down as he choked on the grit in his mouth. The pain in his arm exploded and he touched the spot, holding his hand in front of his face and seeing blood.

Bennett woke up breathing hard. Mel was still curled into his side, and by some miracle he hadn't woken her up.

He watched her sleep, counting her breaths as his calmed, and it was then that he realized he hadn't had a panic attack. The nightmares were a sure trigger to send him over the edge, but not this time. Not with her in his arms.

"Melanie," he whispered against her mouth. He ran his hand down her back and then slipped it up under her shirt before he ran it up again. "Melanie."

She stirred and slowly opened her eyes. It took a second for reality to come to her. "Bennett?"

He didn't say anything as he covered her mouth with his. She gasped in shock before she opened her mouth wide and let his tongue in. He rolled so that she was beneath him and she moved her legs to accommodate his hips between her thighs.

Sometimes words weren't necessary.

Bennett had never been one to find comfort in words, and he still wasn't. But he did know that he could find comfort in Mel, in her kisses, in her sweet sighs, in the way she moved with him. This was what he wanted. She was what he needed.

* * *

Okay, so they hadn't exactly talked.

Who was Mel kidding? They hadn't talked at all. No, they'd had hot sex. *Really* hot sex.

She'd laid in bed for a while that night waiting for him to join her, and the longer he'd been absent, the more of a void she felt. Like some sort of chasm was forming between them.

She was shocked that she somehow managed to fall asleep, but it was nothing to the shock of him waking her up. He'd said her name with a desperation she'd never heard before, so she gave in to what he needed. And, to be honest with herself, she'd needed it, too.

And though things might've been resolved for Bennett, they weren't in any way resolved for her. She was never one to sweep things under the rug, but the morning after, he'd acted like everything was fine. She wasn't sure how much, or how hard she could push him yet. She'd told him how she felt, that she wanted him to let her in. So the ball was in his court, and she was just going to have to pull out her handy-dandy patience again.

He would talk when he was ready. But when the hell was that going to be?

* * *

Mirabelle's Fall Festival was customarily held during the third weekend in October. Mel had volunteered at a booth for the high school the last couple of years. This year she was in charge of a silent auction for the bookcase project. People were in and out of the booth the whole weekend, and Bennett kept her company for a majority of it.

When he hadn't been there, Grace, Harper, and Paige were coming in and out of the tent. All three of them had put up items to bid on, and they were beyond curious as to how it was going. Harper was there at the end of the festival on Sunday to help Mel wrap things up, so she got to see who the winner was for the five massages she would be giving.

"Who is this Brad Nelson guy?" Harper asked as she looked at the list.

"That guy over there," Mel said, nodding toward the booth across the way.

The guy was blond but clean cut in a Clark Kent way, which meant he immediately stood out around the men of Mirabelle. He wore khaki pants and a buttoned-up white shirt with the sleeves rolled up to his elbows. He had muscles behind those clothes of his, too; his shoulders filled out that shirt, and his biceps were clearly evident through the material as well. His thick hair was slightly tousled from running his fingers through it. He also had dark brown eyes and a big smile that showed off his perfect teeth.

"Oh. My. God." Harper stared, her mouth hanging open just slightly.

"You're drooling," Mel whispered.

Harper turned to Mel with more than a slight look of skepticism on her face. "Tell me you weren't."

"What?" Mel shrugged. "He's cute, but I like the man I've got."

"Just because you're with Bennett doesn't mean you're blind."

Mel just laughed and shook her head.

"God, I get to put my hands all over that body of his." Harper was hardcore lusting over the guy, something that surprised Mel.

"Wow, I haven't seen you respond to a guy like this in a while," she said.

"Oh, I'm responding all right," Harper replied.

"I thought you couldn't date clients." Mel raised her eyebrows at her friend in mock disapproval.

"I can't, but it doesn't mean I can't appreciate what the good Lord blessed him with. Do you know anything about him?"

"Bennett talked to him a little bit. He's from Orlando, and he's the general contractor the county just hired to fix the bridges and roads around here."

"So he's going to be around for a while?" Harper asked excitedly.

"It would appear so."

"Well, things are about to get interesting." Harper grinned hugely as she drummed her fingers together and looked Brad Nelson over for a little bit longer.

* * *

The baseball league season was over, so Bennett now spent a couple nights a week at the gym with Hamilton and Dale. Mel had noticed a big improvement in Dale over the last couple of weeks. He'd stopped acting out in class and was doing his homework regularly, and he was starting to get pretty good grades. He was also wearing pants that actually stayed up around his waist.

Mel was pretty sure this had something to do with

Bennett as well. She could've sworn she'd seen the belt that was now holding up Dale's pants poking out of a shopping bag in the backseat of Bennett's truck last week. She was happy she was no longer seeing Dale's underwear. She was also happy he'd pulled out those earrings.

And so was Virginia Rigels, Dale's mother.

It was the fourth weekend in October when Dale's mother came to the school. Class had just gotten out, and Mel was packing up her bag when there was a knock on the door.

Mel looked up to see Virginia's round, smiling face. She was a very pretty, small, and curvy woman, but those curves had diminished as of late. Mel had met with her at the beginning of the year, and she'd seemed more than tired and stressed. It was understandable as she'd been working two jobs, one full-time and the other part-time. Today, there was definitely less strain around her hazel eyes.

"Do you have a second?" Mrs. Rigels asked as she reached up and pushed a lock of her dark brown hair behind her ear.

"Absolutely. How are you?" Mel crossed the room as she waved Mrs. Rigels in.

"I'm good." Virginia reached out and grabbed Mel's hands. "I can't thank you enough."

"For what?"

"For Dale. My son is coming back. And it's because of you, this project, your little brother, and Bennett, that wonderful, wonderful man of yours. I just can't thank you enough."

Mel knew there was a little color coming to her cheeks. "I don't need any thanks. Dale's a good kid," she said.

"Not everyone thinks that." She shook her head sadly. "My son misses his father dearly. I mean I miss Vince every day, and it hasn't been easy, but Dale couldn't move past it. He's needed something, or someone, many someones, and you were the catalyst behind that. He's happy. You don't understand how good it is to see my son again. Thank you."

The smile that turned up Virginia's face was so genuine, so sincere, so beyond anything Mel had known.

"You're welcome." Mel was lucky she'd been able to say that much, because she was at a complete loss for words.

* * *

Mel headed home still in a bit of an emotional daze. Virginia Rigels's words had affected her more than she'd been prepared for.

When she walked in the door she headed for the kitchen to figure out something for dinner. She opened the fridge and stared at the food inside for way longer than necessary and came up with absolutely nothing.

"So takeout it is," she said as she shut the door. The cold air rushed out and surrounded her. Fall had come to the South and it was cold outside. Mel hadn't turned the heater on yet, so it was fairly chilly in her house as well. She shivered as she headed for her bedroom in search of a thicker sweater and a pair of jeans.

As she threw her dirty clothes into the laundry basket, she noticed it was overflowing. She had a little while until Bennett got there, so she decided she'd be productive. She sorted out her darks, a couple of things of Bennett's in the mix, and started a load. Just as she was closing the lid on the washer, Bennett's big truck pulled up. He'd barely gotten it into Park before he was out the door and running up the steps.

"Hey," she called out when he walked in.

"Hey," he said, meeting her in the kitchen. He kissed her quick on the mouth before he grabbed her hand and started pulling her to the door. "Come on, I want to show you something." He was jittery with excitement.

"All right."

When they got to the edge of her porch he turned and made her stop. "Stay right here, and close your eyes. No peeking," he said seriously, but then he grinned.

"Okay." She closed her eyes, curious about what he was up to.

The door of his truck opened and a moment later it closed.

"Hold out your hands."

She stretched out her arms and a second later she was holding something soft, warm, and wriggly. She didn't wait for Bennett to tell her to open her eyes. There was a chocolate Labrador puppy in her face, licking her cheeks.

"Oh my gosh. He's adorable. He is a he, right?" she asked holding the puppy up so she could see his belly. Yup, he was a boy all right.

"Yeah," Bennett laughed.

Mel cuddled the puppy to her chest. He licked her again and then bumped his head up against her jaw.

"Oh, aren't you sweet?" She scratched him under his chin as she sat down on the porch steps. She pushed her legs together and laid the little guy tummy side up, scratching his round belly. His little body writhed in ecstasy.

Bennett took a seat next to her and scratched the puppy's head. "I got him for you."

Mel's hands stilled and she turned to look at him. "You got me a dog?"

"Yes," he said a little bit nervously. "It was on your list to get a puppy. But look, if you don't want him—"

Mel didn't let Bennett finish. She reached up and grabbed his chin, and kissed him, slowly, so he would get an idea of just how much she loved the gift.

"I'm keeping him," she said against his mouth before she let go and turned back to the puppy in her lap. The little thing had greenish-brown eyes that made her melt into a big old puddle when they were on her.

Yeah, like there was a chance in hell she'd be able to give him up. Not in a million years.

"Well, you sure are needy," she said as the little puppy tried to climb up her chest and get in her face. He licked her cheek and barked. "Okay, enough of that." She laughed as she wiped her mouth, set him down in her lap, and started scratching his back.

"I went to pick one out two weeks ago. And when the breeder showed me the litter, this little guy"—Bennett rubbed his hand back and forth over the puppy's head, making his ears flop—"came right up to me and sat on my boots."

"So, really, he picked you," Mel said.

"Yup."

"Well, he apparently has very good taste." The puppy started to crawl up Mel's front again, wanting to be in her face.

"He looks like that teddy bear you got me." Mel glanced at Bennett quickly before she turned back.

The puppy barked and squirmed.

"Teddy?" she asked him. "Do you like that?"

He barked again.

"How about Theodore and we call you Teddy?" she asked him.

He lunged for her face and licked her from her chin all the way to her hairline.

"Seems like he's a pretty big fan of the name to me."

"Yeah." Mel nodded, wiping her face. "So Teddy it is."

"I'm going to get the guy who trained Tripp's firehouse dog to train him. That way he'll be able to protect you when he's bigger."

"You worried about me?" she asked, looking at him. He'd been looking at Teddy, but his eyes met hers with a fair amount of seriousness in them.

"Always." He leaned in and pressed his mouth to hers, sucking on her bottom lip for just a second. "I'm glad you like him."

"I love him."

There was something about saying that word while looking at Bennett that had Mel's heart flying up into her throat. Yeah, this little dog wasn't the only thing she loved. She was in love with the man, too.

* * *

They wound up ordering Chinese food for dinner. Mel went with Bennett to pick it up, letting Teddy snore in her lap while Bennett drove. She couldn't believe Bennett had bought her a dog. And not only that, he'd also bought all of the other things that a new dog owner needed, and many other things that weren't all that necessary.

He'd pulled out multiple bags from the backseat of his truck. They were filled with a hunter green collar and matching leash, dog bowls, toys, food, treats, a brush, two doggy beds, a crate, and a gate.

"So you really like him?" Bennett asked.

"I told you, love at first sight." She rubbed Teddy's back. He snuggled further into her lap.

"Well, he's apparently a pretty big fan of you," Bennett said as he came to a stoplight.

"I can't believe you did this, Bennett. He's the best gift I've ever gotten." She leaned across the seat and he met her in the middle.

"You're welcome," he said against her mouth.

When they got to the restaurant, Bennett left the truck running and ran inside. Teddy stirred when the door shut and stretched his tiny body.

He wasn't going to stay this small for long. He had big

paws for such a little guy, and he was going to grow into them. Good thing she lived on a fairly big piece of land, so he was going to have plenty of space to run around.

"You know," Mel said, scratching Teddy behind the ears, "you're not the only one who I'm in love with."

He sat up and looked at her, his head tilting to the side.

"Yeah," Mel sighed. "I'm in love with that man who bought you, but he doesn't know it yet. I don't think he's all that ready to know."

He still wasn't ready to talk to her about certain things, so he sure as hell wasn't ready to hear that she was in love with him.

Teddy got up on his hind legs, putting his paws on Mel's chest and getting in her face.

"I know you'd like to think it wouldn't be this complicated. That when you love someone you could just tell them. This is not the case," Mel said, looking into his adorable little-puppy face.

Teddy leaned up and licked her nose.

"I know, it's much simpler for you."

He licked her again.

Bennett opened the door and climbed in the truck, he put the bag of food on the floor of the backseat. Teddy attempted to sneak under Mel's arm and go for the food.

"I don't think so, little man." Bennett put his hand out to block the great escape. "That's not for you."

"Nope, that sweet-and-sour chicken is mine." Mel grabbed Teddy and held him up in the air. He wriggled in her hands and licked her face again. He apparently loved the kisses, too. "All right," she said, holding him to her chest and snuggling him under her chin. "I'm willing to share a piece."

* * *

Bennett and Mel pretty much spent the entire weekend puppy-proofing Mel's house and getting Teddy acclimated to his new environment. He followed them everywhere, tripping over his big feet while he did it. He also cried at night, a lot. He might've been across the house, but he had a set of lungs on him that managed to travel the distance and get through two doors.

Teddy really didn't like being by himself. And Bennett knew just how much the constant crying was upsetting Mel.

"Ugh, I hate this," she said as she rolled over for about the hundredth time on Sunday night.

"I know." He pulled her to him, her back up against his front and buried his face in her hair.

"You're sure this is what they said you should do?"

"Yes, puppies are supposed to sleep on their own. They have to cry it out. He'll stop in a little bit, just like he has for the last two nights."

"It's a stupid rule," she said pouting just a little bit. She started running her fingers up and down his forearms. Her soft touch on his skin never failed to make his entire body start tingling.

"I know." He smiled in her hair. "But would you rather he be crying in the room with us?"

"No. I'd rather he was sleeping in the bed with us."

"What happens when he gets to be seventy-five pounds? All three of us going to still fit?"

Her hands stilled and she didn't say anything.

"Mel?"

"I...uh, I guess not." Her voice was soft, just barely above a whisper.

"Mel?" he repeated her name. "There's something else going on up there." He pressed his mouth to the back of her head.

She rolled around in his arms and looked up at him.

There was a dim glow coming from her alarm clock and he was just able to make out the smile turning up her mouth. "You just made a valid point is all."

"And me making a valid point is so shocking?"

"Well…"

Bennett just raised his eyebrows.

"I'm kidding." She stretched up and placed a kiss on his mouth. "'Night, Benny Boo," she whispered as she snuggled against his chest.

Bennett let out a small laugh as he wrapped his arms around her and closed his eyes to blessed silence.

* * *

Teddy slowly began to adjust to life in his new home. He was most definitely a little ball of energy. Bennett and Mel started getting up even earlier so they could play with him for a good while before they were out the door to work. It was the Tuesday before the Thanksgiving holidays, and fall had come in full force. The chilly weather had been consistent over the last couple of weeks, and it was there to stay for a little while.

Every morning, Mel would sit on the porch wearing sweats, wrapped in a blanket, and clutching a cup of coffee. She'd watch Bennett as he ran around the yard with Teddy. He bounded through the leaves and pounced at Bennett's feet, leaning on his front paws with his little brown butt in the air as he searched for what Bennett had just thrown.

Teddy's mouth wasn't quite big enough for the tennis ball that Bennett had bought, so they played fetch with one of the squeaky toys. More often than not, he would lie on the dog pillow in whatever room they were in and chew, and chew, and chew. The constant squeaks could be heard throughout the house.

The dog sure did like to make noise, but Mel loved that her house wasn't silent anymore. It hadn't been for a little while now with Bennett constantly being around, but the addition of Teddy was a good one. He quickly became part of her life, and she couldn't imagine going back to how it had been before him.

He'd done okay by himself during the day. He hadn't gotten up to too many hijinks in the laundry room. Though he'd somehow gotten a hold of one of Bennett's socks and made a meal of it.

This morning, she sat on the porch steps and watched as Bennett threw the little toy off in the distance, and Teddy sprinted off after it, stumbling through the yard as he went. Bennett came up behind Mel and sat down, putting his legs on either side of her body. She pressed back into him and sighed contentedly as he wrapped his arms around her.

"You a functioning human yet?" he asked as he buried his face in her neck.

"Mmm-hmm."

"Good. Time to share the wealth." He grabbed the cup of coffee from her hands and brought it to his mouth.

Mel looked over her shoulder at him with raised eyebrows. "You're lucky I like you, pal."

"Come on Melanie, sharing is caring."

"Not when it comes to my coffee."

"I'll make it up to you," he said as he leaned in, his lips hovering right above hers.

"You better."

He covered her mouth with his and dipped his tongue inside. He tasted like coffee: warm, delicious. They hadn't been kissing for that long when a loud squeak came from somewhere around Mel's feet. She pulled back from Bennett and turned to find Teddy. He came up on his back paws and stretched, trying to climb up Mel's leg.

"Hey buddy," Mel said, reaching down and picking him up. She held him as much as possible. He was growing at a steady rate, and pretty soon she wouldn't be able to hold him anymore.

Teddy got up in Mel's face and licked her cheek.

"I can't believe how big he's getting." Mel flipped Teddy onto his back and scratched his belly. As usual he writhed around, one of his back legs kicking up and thumping against her thigh.

"Well, enjoy it while you can, because he won't be sitting in your lap much longer."

"I know," she said, more than somewhat sadly. "He's just so cute at this size."

Bennett chuckled as he reached around her and scratched Teddy's belly, too. "I'm sure he'll still be plenty cute when he's full grown. *And* he'll be way more useful. Bigger is better when it comes to being a guard dog."

Mel looked over her shoulder at him, her eyebrows raised. "What exactly is happening that I need protecting from?"

"I don't know. But we should cover all our bases."

She grinned. "You know all about covering bases, don't you?"

"Sure do." He put his lips to hers again, working her mouth with his before he pulled back. "We should go back inside and get ready."

"But I don't want to. I'd much rather stay right here in your arms all day. I don't want to go to work."

"In about ten hours you'll be free for five whole days."

"Mmm. True."

"And we can spend an entire day in each other's arms."

"Promise?"

"Promise," he said, kissing the tip of her nose.

Mel put Teddy on the ground before she stood up. Bennett was on his feet a second later, and the three of them walked inside. Mel headed toward the shower while Bennett put Teddy away in the laundry room. Just as she was lathering up her hair under the steady stream of hot water, Bennett entered the shower behind her. He pressed his naked body to hers as he pulled her hands away and finished washing her hair.

* * *

Bennett's commanding officer, Danny Provo, and his family were coming down to Mirabelle on the Wednesday before Thanksgiving. They were spending the holiday with Bennett, Mel, and their families. Danny lived in Georgia with his wife and three kids, and on Friday they were continuing their journey south to Disney World.

Danny was the only other survivor of the helicopter crash that claimed the lives of the other eight soldiers. He'd left the air force at the same time Bennett had. After the crash, neither of them could go back, not after everything they'd seen, and especially not after everything they'd lost. But Danny's outlook on life was a lot different than Bennett's. Bennett just wanted to escape. Danny, on the other hand, wanted to get back to his life, to his wife and two sons.

Alex and Blake had been seven and four years old when Danny had gone home for good. He wanted his sons to know who he was, wanted to watch them grow up for more than a few months out of the year. For Danny it just wasn't good enough, and almost losing his life made him see his priorities differently. He'd been home exactly one month when his wife, Cindy, told them that they were going to have another child.

June Provo was now a happy and healthy two-year-old with a set of lungs on her that could rival an air horn when she got worked up. But she was incredibly sweet, and she had the tendency to curl up in whichever adult's lap was free and fall asleep, her head on their shoulder. She had soft blonde curls and the biggest blue eyes framed by blonde lashes. Everyone was putty in her hands.

It took June about three seconds to become entirely fascinated with Mel. Bennett wasn't at all surprised; Mel was pretty damn fascinating, if he did say so himself.

"You got hair like mine," June said to Mel. June was currently in Cindy's arms, but she was squirming to get to Mel.

"I do," Mel laughed.

"Wanna play," June said excitedly.

"Careful, Peachtree," Cindy said as she passed June to Mel.

Cindy was from Georgia, and she had a thick Southern accent that made her fit right into Mirabelle. She had blonde hair and blue eyes just like her daughter, but June's curls hadn't come from either of her parents. Not that anyone would be able to tell what Danny's hair looked like, as he kept his shaved short just like Bennett. Another thing that Danny hadn't passed off to his daughter was his thick, muscular frame.

No, sweet little June was tiny like her mother, and June was pretty much destined to be short, since Cindy was five foot three and Danny was about five foot nine. Even though Danny had been smaller than all the soldiers he'd commanded, no one had ever messed with him. When he talked, everybody listened. It was because of Danny that Bennett had survived that crash. Bennett owed the man his life.

"Pweeeeetty," June said as she bunched Mel's curls up in her teeny-tiny fists.

"Yours are very pretty, too." Mel smiled.

"What's your name?"

"Mel."

"I'm Juuuune." She looked over her shoulder at her mother. "Mommy, I like Mel. Can she stay and play?"

"I see she's just as shy as ever." Bennett laughed as he watched Mel bouncing and talking to the little ball of energy.

"Yup," Danny said, looking over his shoulder where Alex and Blake were currently playing with Teddy on Bennett's tiny front porch. The boys were Danny in miniature form, except they had their mother's blonde hair.

As Bennett was sharing a bed with Mel every night, they were going to stay at her house, and the Provo family was going to have free rein of Bennett's house for the next two nights.

It had been a couple of months since Bennett had seen Danny. Danny had come down to Mirabelle last May to go fishing. Bennett normally went up to Georgia at the beginning of hunting season to spend a few days up in a tree, but this year he'd passed on the trip. He hadn't been able to pull himself away from Mel for even a day.

"Well, Miss June, are you hungry?" Mel asked the toddler in her arms.

"Yes, ma'am." She nodded vigorously and her curls bounced up and down around her temples.

"Lunch is ready," Bennett said, waving toward the house. "We can unload everything after we eat."

"Sounds good to me. Lead the way," Danny said.

* * *

On Thanksgiving morning, Bennett woke up wrapped around Mel. Her perfect little butt was pressed against a very critical part of his anatomy. And said part was *very* up and ready to go.

The curtains on the window were closed, but he could see just a hint of light around the edges. He peeked over Mel's shoulder to get a look at the alarm clock on the nightstand. It was just before eight. The Provos weren't coming over until ten. So they had plenty of time.

Bennett almost always woke up before Mel, like 99 percent of the time, so he knew when her stirring got to the point where she was on the brink of consciousness. He moved his hand from where it was wrapped around her waist and slid it up her side to her back, and then to her shoulder. He brushed her hair away and kissed her neck.

She hummed as her body rubbed against his. "I see you're up," she said groggily. "Or should I say I *feel* that you're up." She moved against him some more and made him groan.

"You having fun?" he asked through his kisses.

"You have no idea."

Oh, he had a pretty good idea, and two could play at this game.

Bennett brought his hand back down to her waist and he slid it between her legs. He slipped two fingers past the elastic of her panties. She was arching against him as he slid his fingers inside of her and started moving them in and out. Maybe he hadn't thought this plan out very well, because he was just making her body rub up against his more. Yeah, there was no way he was going to be able to hold out very long with the way her body was moving against his.

He pulled his hand from between her thighs. "Don't move," he whispered in her ear. "Stay like that. Just. Like. That."

He rolled over and grabbed a condom from the nightstand, kicking his boxers down his legs while he did so. He opened the wrapper and was rolling it down his erection in seconds.

"Well, aren't you fast?" she asked as he started to work down her panties.

"Let's just hope you don't say that about what's next."

Mel laughed but it was cut off in the middle as he reached under her shirt and grabbed her breast, running his thumb across her nipple. He pulled her shirt over her head before he kissed her shoulder and neck. He moved against her and she pushed her little bottom back, grinding it against him.

"Baby," she said breathlessly as one of her hands came up to the back of his head.

He dropped his hand from her breast and guided himself inside her. He moved slowly, taking his time. When he started nibbling on her ear she turned her head, her mouth found his, and their tongues met somewhere in the middle.

Bennett wound his arm around her waist to the apex of her thighs, and he touched her as he moved inside her. She moaned into his mouth, and her body started to writhe against his. They stayed like that for a little while, rocking against each other.

"Bennett, please," she begged, pulling her mouth from his.

He picked up the pace, pressing his face into her neck as he really started to move. And then Mel was saying his name as she burst. He got in only a couple more thrusts before he followed her over.

They lay there for a minute or two, basking in the afterglow of another spectacular orgasm.

"Morning," she said, looking over her shoulder and smiling at him.

"Morning," he laughed, kissing her. He brought his hand to her thigh and moved it up to her hip and then back down. Up to her hip and then back down.

"God, I love your wake-up calls," she said dreamily.

Bennett's hand stilled and everything inside him froze. Those last couple of words had come out of Mel's mouth slowly, so slowly that for a fraction of a second he thought she said something else.

He thought she said she loved him.

He wasn't ready for that. Was he? Was he ready for her to love him? Did he love her? He loved waking up next to her, loved coming home to her at the end of the day, loved *being* with her. But that wasn't the same thing.

He'd never been in love before, so he wasn't sure what to expect. He knew it was something entirely different from what he'd ever felt before. He just didn't know what that *something* was, and the thought of figuring it out was terrifying.

He just wasn't ready for it. Not yet.

Mel's eyes slowly opened wide as she looked up at him. "What?"

He shook his head. "It's nothing."

"Bennett?" She tried to turn more to see his face, but as he was still inside her it made things difficult.

"It's nothing, Mel. Just still waking up. I'm going to go make some coffee to speed up the process."

"Okay," Mel said, her eyes still searching Bennett's face for something.

She wasn't going to find it, though. He had no idea what was going through his own head, so she wasn't going to find an answer, either.

"I'll be right back." He kissed her on the mouth one last time before he pulled out of her. He grabbed a pair of sweats from his dresser before he went into the bathroom.

After he was cleaned up and dressed, he splashed his face with water. He looked at his reflection in the mirror for a second, water dripping off the end of his nose. Nope, he wasn't finding any answers there, either.

Chapter Sixteen

Distance

Something was up with Bennett. Mel couldn't put her finger on it, but she knew. She'd seen something in his eyes after they'd made love that morning, something that scared her more than a little.

Not scared in the sense that he'd hurt her. Well, not physically at least. No, that thought had never entered her mind. But that look in Bennett's eyes said he might be running for the hills, which would ultimately destroy Mel.

She replayed everything from that morning over and over again, and the only thing she could come up with was that the word *love* had come out of her mouth. But she hadn't said she loved him.

She *did* love him, so much so that it was beyond ridiculous, but she hadn't told him yet. She wasn't exactly sure *why* she hadn't told him. Maybe that was something she needed to really evaluate later, but right now all she could think about was that look of fear that had been there plain as day in his eyes.

* * *

As Bennett's parents had the biggest space and the most accommodating kitchen to cook for so many people, they'd all gone over there on Thanksgiving Day. Dinner had already been eaten and put away, and everyone was waiting for their food to digest before they moved on to dessert.

All the guys were in the living room, watching the football game on the big-screen TV. Alex and Blake were again playing with a very hyper Teddy, and continually asking their father for a puppy of their own during commercials. The women were talking and playing cards at the dining room table. And as she had for the last two days, June was in Mel's lap, alternating between helping Mel play cards and coloring a picture in front of her.

Whenever Bennett and Mel had been with the Provos, June refused to leave Mel's side. The little rug rat was Mel's shadow, and something about seeing the two of them together both fascinated Bennett and added to the unease that was growing in his mind.

Not that Bennett had a problem with kids. He didn't. Not at all. He just wasn't ready to start having them yet. And it wasn't like he thought Mel was ready, either. But multiple times Bennett had to do a double take when June was in Mel's lap, either playing patty-cake, reading a book, or doing whatever else the little girl wanted.

Bennett could see Mel doing the exact same thing with a daughter of *their* own, and it scared the ever-living shit out of him. The idea of the two of them creating someone to raise was way more than Bennett was ready for. Yeah, they had Teddy at the moment, and Bennett was just as attached to him as Mel was. He couldn't imagine a custody battle over the dog, couldn't imagine walking away from Mel.

The thought of not being with her at all anymore was painful.

Shit.

Bennett rubbed his face a couple of times, like he could clear the image of not being with Mel, but it was there front and center in his brain, and he couldn't make it go away. He didn't know what to do with it.

He stood up and headed for the kitchen, but veered off and quietly slipped out the back door to the porch. He needed some fresh air, and the chilly afternoon provided it. He went over to the fridge stocked with beer and pulled one out.

"You can get me one of those, too." Bennett turned as Danny stepped outside and shut the door behind him.

Bennett reached in for another and handed it to his friend.

"What's eating you?" Danny asked before he brought the bottle to his mouth.

"Nothing," Bennett said.

"I'm pretty sure that's the first time you've ever lied to me."

Bennett turned away from his friend and looked out at his parents' backyard. They stood there for a minute in silence before Danny finally said something else.

"You were fine yesterday. So something had to have happened between now and then that flipped the switch."

"Did you know? Did you know with Cindy from the beginning that you were going to marry her?"

Danny chuckled and shook his head. "No. I was an idiot. A complete and total idiot when it came to women, and when it came to Cindy I was so far out of my league that I was on fucking Pluto. I told you we were high school sweethearts. Right?"

Bennett nodded.

"She was a year younger than me. So her senior year was my first year enlisted. She wrote me all the damn time, and every time I called she picked up. But then that second year rolled around and I told myself I didn't want the long-distance thing. That I wanted to see what other options I had. She went off to college to get her degree."

Danny took a sip of his beer before he continued. "I

came crawling back to her three years later. It was the summer after her junior year, and I went home to Georgia for my leave. All I knew was I had to get her back. And do you know what she said to me?"

"What?"

"She said she knew. She knew I was the one. Had always known that I was the one. And those three years we were apart? She didn't once test the waters with anybody else. Didn't date anybody. Didn't even kiss a random stranger. She knew. She knew I would come back and she didn't want anybody else but me. Do you have any idea what it was like to hear her say that?"

"Humbling?"

Danny chuckled again. "Understatement of my life. That woman never once stopped being loyal to me, and I was this piece of shit that didn't deserve her. I still don't deserve her. She's given me a love greater than anything I've ever known, she's given me my kids, she's given me my life."

Bennett didn't know what to say, so he just sipped his beer. Really how did someone respond to that?

"You want a word of advice?" Danny asked. And before Bennett even had time to say yes Danny was giving it. "Don't fuck this up with her. I've only been here for two days, but it took me about a minute to realize that girl in there is someone you need to hold on to."

Bennett knew that for a fact, too, he just wasn't sure how to do it or if he was even remotely ready.

* * *

Bennett tried like hell to push his concerns about his and Mel's relationship to the back of his mind. Things were going well, and there was no need to tip the apple cart. Their relationship was working the way it was. There was absolutely no need to worry.

So why was he questioning it? Why was he worrying?

He had no fucking clue, so he chose to ignore the nagging feeling. And distraction was the best policy.

As promised, Bennett and Mel spent the entire Saturday after Thanksgiving, and a good part of Sunday, in bed. Sex with Mel was a pretty freaking fantastic distraction. A lot of sex with Mel blew the questions of their relationship completely out of Bennett's mind.

And there'd been *a lot* of sex.

But by Monday they were back to the real world. The bookshelf project was pretty much finished that first week in December. They just had a few final touches, and after Wednesday all of the wood was stained and ready to go. Even though the shelves were finished, they weren't going to be put in the library until that last Thursday before Christmas break, which wasn't for another two weeks. There was going to be a big reveal at the awards ceremony that happened at the end of every semester and the math classes were going to be recognized then.

Since the bookshelves were finished, Bennett was able to start focusing more time on his projects again. He needed something to occupy himself. Idle hands meant an idle mind, and that wasn't good for his distraction method.

Bennett had bought a beautiful old barn door years ago that he wanted to turn into a dining room table for himself, but he'd envisioned the table to be bigger than just the one door. He'd been looking for another barn door to use as the other half for a while now. He hadn't expected to find one that would match perfectly, nor had he wanted to. He had an idea that was going to require two fairly different doors, but he wanted to make them meld in the middle. He'd have them transition smoothly from one design to the other.

Jax was still looking for random pieces here and there for his and Grace's new house, so he was going to auctions with

Bennett. They took a day trip up to Tuscaloosa on the first Saturday in December, and there Bennett finally found the perfect counterpiece for the table project he'd had in mind.

The concept wasn't something he'd done before, but he was pretty excited about it. So excited that over the next week he spent hours out in his garage without taking a break. He threw himself completely into the project, and his distraction method was successful. Bennett tried not to think too much about the fact that he was spending less time with Mel. He still saw her every day. Still woke up next to her every morning and went to bed next to her at night.

Time was cut down a little bit, but once the table was finished they'd pick up their routine again...that was until he found another project.

Whatever. It wasn't anything.

Their relationship was fine. Perfectly fine.

* * *

Bennett had been staying over at Mel's house every night ever since Teddy had been in the picture. But with the late nights he was now spending working on the table, Mel and Teddy had taken to staying at his house more often than hers. Teddy was almost completely potty trained, and he'd moved out of the crate a few weeks ago. He still had to stay in the laundry room during the day, but at night he was allowed to sleep on an oversized pillow on the floor in the bedroom.

Mel believed Bennett had pretty much invested stock in the dog accessories market with the amount of things he'd bought for Teddy. They'd just done an even split of everything and both his and Mel's houses had been good to go. It made things a whole hell of a lot easier, too, because depending on where they were staying, all they had to do was pick Teddy up.

The Saturday night of Grace's bachelorette party, Bennett

was on puppy duty. Which meant that Teddy was probably going to stay curled up in the corner of the garage on a pillow while Bennett worked on the table.

Bennett's new obsession hadn't failed to escape Mel's notice. He was definitely less present physically. Their time together had taken a drastic cut. She might've been in the same house with him, but for the most part they weren't even in the same room. And then when they were in the same room he wasn't always present then either. He was... distracted.

Mel wasn't used to Bennett being like this. Their relationship had moved pretty fast in the beginning, but it had stabilized pretty soon after that. Now she didn't know what was going on.

Even though they'd had a lot of sex that weekend of the holidays, Mel wasn't oblivious to the fact that something was up with Bennett. The sex had been good—fantastic, really—but it had been like he was searching for something. Searching for answers that Mel just couldn't give him, and at the end of it all, she'd felt more than a little out of sorts. She didn't know what was going on, and it scared her.

And things had continued to change over the next couple of weeks. She really didn't want to be that girl that whined about her boyfriend not spending every waking moment with her. He was so excited about what he was doing, and she knew it, but she missed him. She didn't quite understand *why* she missed him, but that was how it was right now.

She didn't see him at school anymore. And that was how it was going to be, because the project was done and there was no need for him to be there. But he usually picked up lunch once or twice a week and they'd eat together, and that wasn't happening anymore, either. There was also a significant drop in time they spent cuddling on the couch.

But that wasn't the worst of it. No, it was something else

that she missed the most, something that was more than kind of killing her. There was no more pillow talk at night. Bennett tended to pass out pretty quickly, and though he still held her close, she missed those conversations so much it was painful.

What she didn't get was that they were seeing each other less than normal, so shouldn't it be the other way around? Shouldn't they have more to talk about? Not less?

Mel didn't really know what to do. She prayed it was just a phase, a little blip in the relationship. It wasn't like everything was always going to be perfect, that was a completely unrealistic expectation. Maybe once the table was done things would go back to normal.

Maybe.

Mel got ready for the bachelorette party at her house. She just had so many more clothes options there, and it took a couple of tries to find the right outfit. The winner was a little black dress that pretty much hugged every single curve she had.

She had plans for this dress when she got back to Bennett's, thus the matching red lace bra and panties she was planning on him peeling off her.

Yup, *big* plans.

Mel had never been all that good at seduction, but she was going to try tonight. She'd continued to add stuff to her "I Didn't Kick the Bucket" list over the last couple of months, and so had Bennett. His additions were: "Make out in a movie theater," something that shockingly enough neither of them had done; "Go to the shooting range," which had actually helped alleviate some of her new fear of guns; and "Dance a striptease for him."

Maybe a little spice was what they needed. A little pick-me-up. Not that their sex had become all that less frequent or any less exciting. But that didn't mean Mel couldn't try to keep things a little interesting.

Mel picked up her carload of women before she headed over to the first destination of the night. Paige was driving a carful, too, with Grace included. Everybody was carpooling to have as few vehicles out as possible. First, they went to Caliente's for dinner, where the margaritas were free-flowing. After that they headed over to Café Lula, where Grace had a good and proper lingerie shower. Paige had been in charge of decorating. She'd forgone the penis motif in favor of lots of feathers and glitter, all of it pink, black, and silver.

Grace got enough naughty undergarments to keep Jax well and busy for weeks. She wasn't going to be the only one enjoying those gifts, either. If anything, the shower had been more for Jax's benefit.

There were more drinks being served at the café, mainly wine and champagne, and enough had been drunk by all that the girls had to walk over to the Sleepy Sheep, but that had always been the plan. Jax was going to pick Bennett up at around midnight. The two of them were then going to drive over to the bar. Tripp was going to do the same thing for Brendan, and Shep was obviously going to be at the Sleepy Sheep already. Between the five men, they were going to make sure all of the women got home safely.

Mel was feeling awfully good by the time they got to the bar. She'd only had the one margarita at dinner, and after that she'd stayed consistent with wine . . . and possibly a glass or two of champagne.

Shep had let them set up the karaoke machine again, and they had free rein. The patrons at the bar were more than slightly entertained by the spectacle of the night. The girls weren't obnoxious; they were just really giggly and obviously having a good time.

Somehow, Mel wasn't exactly sure but she had a strong feeling it had to do with the amount of alcohol she'd drank, Grace managed to pull Mel along with Harper and Paige up onto to stage. They proceeded to belt out a resounding rendition of "Summer Nights" from *Grease*. Mel and Grace sang the girls' part, while Harper and Paige had given the guys more than enough justice. And then just because they could, and an encore had pretty much been demanded, they stayed up on stage and sang "Living on a Prayer." Bon Jovi would've been proud.

As the bar filled with applause and the girls bowed to the cheers, Mel looked up to find Bennett grinning at her and clapping his hands together enthusiastically. She quickly, and rather carefully in her towering red high heels, got down off the stage and crossed over to him. He held his arms open for her and she pretty much jumped into them.

"Holy shit, you look hot," he whispered into her ear. He pulled back just a little so he could look down at her. "What are the chances you'll keep those shoes on for a little while when we get home?"

"Will I be standing?" she asked as she ran her hands up his chest.

"Nope."

"Then abso-fucking-lutely."

Bennett laughed, his head falling back and his face pointing toward the ceiling. When he pulled his head back down he was grinning widely. "Never a dull moment with you."

"With you either. You're early."

"Shep called us and told us we should head down. And good thing too, I would've hated to miss the show."

"That good?"

"Better. I didn't know you could sing *and* dance."

Mel stretched up so she could put her mouth to his ear. "I was thinking I'd cross another thing off my list tonight. If I remember correctly you added something that had to do with dancing."

When Mel pulled back, Bennett's eyes were so hot she

thought she might need to go fan herself. "You're serious?" He sounded like he was struggling to talk.

"Mmm-hmm. Now go have a beer with Shep. We should be done in a little bit."

"It's going to be a long wait."

"But well worth it."

"I have no doubt." He grinned.

Mel turned around and before she could walk away she felt a light little tap on her bottom. She jumped and looked over her shoulder at Bennett who tried to look innocent, but failed miserably. She headed back over to the table of women in the corner. She took a seat next to Harper, who was giving her a rather big smirk.

"What?" Mel asked.

"You are *soooo* gone for that man."

"And?"

"Nothing, you're just really freaking lucky."

"Yeah." Mel nodded, but that little bit of doubt as to what was really going on with Bennett flared up for just a second.

Mel must not have hid her reaction very well, because something flickered in Harper's eyes and she was reaching across the table for Mel's hand.

"Hey. Is something going on?" Harper asked.

"No," Mel said a bit too quickly.

Harper merely raised one of her eyebrows in that *don't mess around with me* way.

"I don't know. Things just feel . . . off. But our relationship is still kind of new. So maybe we just need some time to find our bearings. I'm sure it's nothing."

"Okay," Harper said slowly. "But if that man hurts you, you better believe I'm going to be the first in line to bust his balls."

Mel laughed. "I don't think that's going to be necessary. But thank you."

"Anytime, babe." Harper grabbed her wine and took a sip. She turned slightly over her shoulder and glanced at the bar, and her face flushed more than a little.

"What was that?" Mel asked making a move to turn and see what Harper was looking at.

Harper reached out and grabbed Mel's arm. "No."

"What?"

"Don't look over there."

"Why?"

Harper bit her lip nervously as she looked at Mel. "Do you remember that guy who won the massage package? Brad Nelson?"

"The blond Clark Kent you were drooling over?" Mel asked, leaning in closer to Harper.

"I wasn't drooling," Harper said a bit too loudly.

Some women at the table looked over at them for a second before they returned to their conversations.

"Yes, you were. But anyway, what about him?"

"He asked me out."

"When?" Mel asked, intrigued.

"After the third massage. I told him I couldn't date clients, so he said he'd wait until those last two massages were done, and then he'd ask me out again."

"And?" Mel was just about coming out of her seat.

"His last massage was Thursday. He called me yesterday, and we have a date tomorrow night."

Mel punched Harper on the shoulder. "I can't believe you didn't tell me this before."

"Hey, what do you want from me? I wasn't sure if he was going to ask me out again, and there was no need in getting my hopes up."

"You weren't sure? He would've been completely stupid not to ask you out again. Holy cow, Harper. This is big. Really big, because it takes a lot for a guy to catch your eye."

"Well, he's caught it all right. He's sweet and funny and God, that man's body is perfection." Harper paused for just a second before she looked at Mel. "Do you have any idea what it's been like to have my hands all over him and to force myself to stay professional?"

"No," Mel giggled. She could only imagine what that would be like. She tried for a second to imagine herself giving Bennett a full-body massage without getting all hot and bothered. It wasn't possible, so Mel gave Harper all the props in the world for what she did on a daily basis. "I expect a phone call tomorrow."

"You'll get one." Harper gave Mel a very uncharacteristic nervous smile.

"It's going to be great." Mel squeezed Harper's hand. "Because you're great. And anyone would be beyond lucky to have you."

"Thanks." Harper leaned forward and gave Mel a quick kiss on the cheek. "And just so you know, Bennett is beyond lucky to have you, too."

Chapter Seventeen

Pillow Talk

After Bennett dropped off the three fairly intoxicated women, he headed back to his house. Mel was still in a pretty good mood, and she was singing along to a song on the radio. Out of the corner of his eye he could see her little black dress slowly working its way up her thighs whenever she moved. She was wearing a coat, but it did absolutely nothing to cover up those fantastic legs.

He really wanted to know exactly what she was wearing underneath that dress...and she had promised to do a little dance for him.

When they got home, Bennett went outside with Teddy and waited somewhat impatiently for the pup to find a pile of leaves to relieve himself on. Teddy bounded up the back steps and not a moment too quickly, because when they walked inside Bennett almost tripped over his feet.

Mel's little butt was in the air, swinging back and forth as she leaned against the counter and scrolled through her phone. She'd lost the jacket, but she was mercifully still wearing the red high heels.

"Perfect," she said before she turned around and caught

him staring at her. "I found the perfect song. I believe I promised you a dance." She grinned.

"I believe you did."

"Sit down." She indicated the couch with her hand before she crossed the room to hook her phone up to his stereo.

Bennett kicked off his boots before he did what he was told. It was only a moment before the room filled with a steady beat, and a woman's somewhat breathy and incredibly sexy voice.

Mel extended her hands above her head as she slowly danced her way across the room. Her body moved in rhythm to the music, and Bennett was more than a little amazed at how smooth she was, especially on those heels.

God, she was sexy. Every single thing about her. He knew for a fact that she had no idea how fucking desirable she was, and if anything that made him want her even more.

She dropped one of her hands to the back of her head and pulled out the clip that was holding up her hair. Her curls fell down around her shoulders and began to expand out. Both of her hands were in her hair now as she continued to whirl around the room. Her dress clung to her like a second skin and every undulation of her body was evident under the material.

Moments like this made Bennett know just how lucky he was. This was a side of Mel that she didn't let out very often, and the fact that she shared this with him meant the world to him. She let him see every side of her, and she wasn't self-conscious or nervous. She owned the room.

Hell, she owned *him*.

She was standing in front of him now, and she stepped between his knees. Bennett spread his legs wide so she would have plenty of room between his thighs.

She leaned forward, the top of her dress pulling down and showing more than just a hint of cleavage. She put her hands on his knees and ran her palms up his thighs. They traveled in when they got to his waist, but she only lingered at his abs for a moment before her journey continued up. Then her hands were on his chest and then up over his shoulders.

She was no longer touching him as she used the back of the couch to keep her balance.

Her face hovered above his, and their mouths were inches from each other. She looked at him for a second, staring into his eyes, before she came in for a kiss. Only their mouths touched.

Bennett desperately wanted to grab her hips and pull her down on top of him. But if he touched her she would be underneath him in a matter of moments. So Bennett put his hands down next to him on the sofa, gripping the cushions as if they were a lifeline to sanity.

And he thanked God he kept his control, because a second later Mel lowered herself between his thighs, and her hips started to swivel to the music. Her pelvis was perfectly in line with his growing erection, and the up-and-down movement she was making was driving him out of his mind. But damn, did it feel incredible.

She pulled back from his mouth and turned around, leaning back against his chest as she rubbed that perfect ass against him. She grabbed his hands from their death grip on the couch and put them on her hips. She turned her head to look at him, and as she stretched up he leaned down, wanting her mouth.

Their lips parted and their tongues met, and her body didn't break rhythm for a moment. She pulled his hands from her hips and dragged them across her body, up her sides and to her chest.

Bennett groaned deep when she tightened her hands over his, making him squeeze her breasts.

Her hands were gone from his a second later, and one of her palms was slipping up to the back of his neck, and then her nails were lightly scouring the back of his head. Her other hand was on his thigh now, and she was using it to keep her balance as she began to move against him harder.

Bennett wasn't exactly sure how long they stayed that way for. She'd put the song on repeat, and it was starting over from the beginning when she pulled herself up off him and turned around again. She pushed his thighs together, and a second later she was climbing up onto his lap. She pulled her dress up so that is was easier for her to move, and Bennett saw a flash of red before she was lowering herself onto his lap.

She used his shoulders to keep her balance, and his hands automatically went to her hips. She looked down at him with that secret smile he loved so damn much. She knew she was driving him crazy and she was enjoying it.

But who was he kidding? He was enjoying the hell out of it, too.

"Baby."

"Hmmm?"

"I think I've reached my limit."

She leaned forward, her mouth hovering above his. "Then take me to bed," she whispered before she carefully crawled off his lap and got to her feet. Her dress was up over her hips and she was wearing a red lace thong. She didn't miss his slow, lingering gaze, and her smile widened. She crooked her finger at him as she took a step back. "You coming?"

"In moments, most likely," he said as he got to his feet and took the few steps to her.

She grabbed his hand and led him to the bedroom. And the view from behind wasn't bad at all.

Nope, it was beyond glorious.

When they got to his bed she turned around. "Undress me."

Bennett didn't have to be told twice. He reached down to the hem of her dress that was now at the top of her hips. It was some sort of stretchy material that made a zipper pointless, so all there was for him to do was work it up her body.

He let his hands linger in more than one place on the journey, but he was pretty damn impatient to get inside of her, so it didn't take that long for him to work it all the way up.

Mel extended her arms above her head and Bennett pulled the dress free from her arms. Her hair went up with the motion and it scattered back down to her shoulders in a rush.

She stood before him wearing a red lace bra that matched her thong and those killer red heels. He had to stop and stare for a moment to take her in fully, to appreciate everything about the moment, appreciate everything about her.

"God, Melanie," he said with no small amount of admiration.

He kissed her again, his hands roaming all over her body, and she did the same thing with him, undressing him in the process. His shirt was over his head and his pants and boxer briefs were on the floor in less than a minute. He undid her bra, and threw it on the floor with all of their other clothes, and then he was pushing her back on the bed, leaving her legs draping off the side.

She extended her arms above her head and stretched across the bed. Bennett reached down for one of her legs and pulled it up. He placed a kiss on her calf before he placed it on his shoulder. He placed her other leg on the same shoulder before he reached down to her hips and dragged the scrap of lace off her legs.

She was completely naked except for the shoes.

He grabbed a pillow before he pulled her legs up, lifting her hips off the bed. He placed a pillow underneath her before he lowered her.

He bent her knees toward her chest, then he pulled them apart and placed each of her heeled feet on the edge of the bed. He grabbed a condom from the nightstand. She watched him as he opened it and rolled it on, but her eyes closed in bliss when he slid inside her.

Bennett had to stop and close his eyes for a second, too, because the sight of her spread out like this in front of him was almost too much for him to handle.

Almost.

When he found a thread of control he opened his eyes, grabbed her feet from the bed, and wrapped her legs around his hips. He started to move in and out of her, and her legs tightened around him, drawing him in as she pumped her hips up to meet him. Her heels dug into his butt, but he couldn't have cared less.

He wasn't going to last much longer, not with the way she was moving. He could see everything, and it was stimulation overload to the max. So he would just have to overstimulate her. He brought his hand between their bodies and found the magic button that he knew was going to set her off.

She gasped, and her body arched off the bed when his fingers circled and applied pressure just the way she liked. "Bennett!" she cried out about a minute later as her body pulsed around his.

He took that as his cue and clutched her thighs, moving into her with more determined thrusts. He was right on the edge when Mel started coming again, or maybe her orgasm just hadn't stopped. He wasn't sure, and at the moment he didn't really care, because he was letting go with everything he had, and the force of it was enough to knock his legs out from under him. He had just enough time to pull out of her body before he fell forward and rolled, dragging Mel on top of him.

They lay there for who knew how long, their legs tangled up and hanging off the bed.

"Holy shit," Bennett said, still a little out of breath. "What the hell was that?"

"I don't know." She shook her head as she snuggled into his chest sleepily. "But I liked it."

"Me, too." He leaned down and kissed the top of her head. He lay back on the bed and stared at the ceiling for a moment, replaying the last twenty minutes in graphic detail.

"Mel?"

"Hmmm?"

"How did you know how to give a lap dance? More research?"

Mel laughed, her warm breath washing out across his skin. "There are so many things that can be found on the Internet."

"Please tell me you didn't Google lap dances."

Mel sat up, placing her palms on Bennett's chest and looking down at him. She gave him her secret smile again. "No, I didn't," she said. "I like to dance, always have, so I just went with it. So I did okay?"

This time it was Bennett's turn to laugh. "Beyond okay. I'd give you an A."

"An A, huh?"

"Yeah, but if you want to get that A plus, you can practice on me whenever you want. You know what they say: practice makes perfect."

"They do say that." She reached up and covered her mouth as she yawned.

"Come on. Let's get you to bed." He tapped her lightly on the bottom. Mel pulled her legs out from between his before she slowly got to her feet. She put her hand on the bed as she leaned to the side and kicked off her shoes.

As Bennett sat up, he looked down at the shoes in admiration.

"What?" Mel asked, putting her hands on her hips.

"I was just think we should get those shadow-boxed and hang them on the wall."

Mel laughed as she bent down to grab them. She straightened and walked across the room, dropping them by the dresser. "That's entirely up to you, but if you do that then I won't be able to wear them anymore."

"You make a valid point."

"I always do." She opened the second drawer and pulled out one of his T-shirts. She slipped it over her head, and it fell down to the tops of her thighs. "I'm going to go get some water and lock up. I'll meet you in bed in five minutes." She turned around and walked out of the room, the shirt pulling up just short of the swell of her ass.

Teddy got up off the pillow and followed her down the hallway. Bennett hadn't even realized the pup had followed them into the room. To be quite honest, he'd been more than a little distracted ever since Mel had told him to sit down on the couch.

Images of her dancing across the living room came back to Bennett, and he couldn't help but smile as he got out of bed and headed for the bathroom. When he was finished cleaning up and brushing his teeth, he opened the door to find Mel coming down the hallway, Teddy still on her heels. She handed Bennett a glass of ice-cold water before she switched places with him and went into the bathroom, locking Teddy out.

Teddy looked at the door for a moment somewhat pathetically before he turned and headed for the bedroom. Bennett followed and got into bed. It was only a couple of minutes before a fresh-faced Mel appeared in the doorway. She yawned again, and Bennett pulled back the covers for her. She turned off the light and climbed into his open arms, snuggling into his chest.

"'Night, Benny Boo."

"Good night, Melanie." He kissed the top of her head and ran his hands up and down her back, then trailed his fingers through her hair.

As Bennett lay there holding her, he thought about how much she meant to him. About how much she'd changed.

This one small woman had made a huge impact on him, on his life, on *everything*.

He'd never in his wildest dreams thought that anything like this could happen to him. He'd pretty much written love off entirely.

Love. Yeah, that was what it was, all right. He was definitely in love with her. He had been for a while now. He just wasn't sure when it had happened, but somewhere along the way he'd fallen. The thing was, he was pretty sure it hadn't been a gradual descent. No, he'd fallen off a cliff. He'd just been too scared to realize it. But there was no more denying it, no more avoiding it anymore.

Why was he such a freaking coward when it came to her? She was the strong one in this relationship. She was the one living her life like there was no tomorrow.

Bennett wasn't sure how long he'd been lying there thinking, but Mel's breathing had deepened. She was asleep. The love of his life was asleep in his arms, and for some reason that he didn't quite understand he had to tell her how he felt then, because he wasn't sure when he was going to say it again.

"You are the greatest thing that has ever happened to me," he whispered against her hair. "And I know you're the greatest thing that *will* ever happen to me. *Ever*." He pressed his lips to her temple. "I love you, Melanie O'Bryan. More than anything."

* * *

He loved her. Mel had heard the words come out of Bennett's mouth.

I love you, Melanie O'Bryan. More than anything.

She'd been dozing, just on the brink of sleep. Bennett had been playing with her hair and she hadn't wanted to miss it.

She hadn't been ready for sleep to claim her, so she'd fought it for as long as possible.

She'd been there just on the edge of losing consciousness when he'd started talking. When he'd whispered the sweetest words she'd ever heard.

He loved her.

She wanted more than anything to be able to say it back to him, but she couldn't. He'd told her when he thought she couldn't hear him. She wanted him to tell her when he *knew* she could hear him. When he was looking her straight in the eye.

It wasn't so much to ask for . . . was it?

No, it wasn't. So Mel would have to wait until Bennett was ready to say it. She could do that because she knew the truth, so she would just have to be patient to hear those words again.

So, patient she would be.

And besides, even though he'd said he loved her when he thought she couldn't hear the words, he'd still said them. Those words had meant something to him. She meant something to him.

* * *

Sunday morning brought warm and sunny weather. It was in the high sixties as opposed to the low forties that had come and stayed for the past couple of weeks. Bennett had the brilliant idea to borrow Tripp's motorcycle and take Mel on a ride down the coast.

"We can cross another thing off that list of yours," he said, as they cleaned up from their pancake breakfast. Both of them had been ravenous when they'd woken up that morning, which wasn't all that surprising given the events of the night before.

Mel looked at Bennett, stunned for just a moment. The fact that he was just as determined as she was to get things crossed off her "I Didn't Kick the Bucket List" meant more to her than she could accurately express in words.

God, she loved him.

She grabbed the front of his shirt and pulled him close so she could kiss him and he had her backed up against the counter in a second.

He grinned down at her. "What was that for?"

"For just being you," she said before she kissed him again.

They were on the road less than an hour later. The cold air slapped around them but it wasn't all that bad. Mel had many things going for her to keep her comfortable. One, she was bundled up in a warm jacket. Two, she had Bennett as a pretty solid buffer. Three, and most important, she was wrapped around him, and the man radiated heat.

They packed a picnic and had a very secluded lunch on the beach, where they made out for a good long while. The night was spent at Mel's house, where they made beer bread, one of Bennett's special recipes, and clam chowder, which they made from ingredients bought during their expedition along the coast.

On Monday after school, Bennett spent the afternoon with Dale and Hamilton at the gym. Mel was glad that he was continuing to work with the boys. There was a noticeable difference in both of them physically, which went along nicely with Dale's emotional transformation. Dale needed that time, and she knew Bennett enjoyed it as well. Bennett had a soft spot for both boys, but she knew he felt a certain responsibility to make sure Dale was okay.

"You think Virginia is ready to date?" Bennett asked Mel, as they lay in bed on Monday night.

Mel was running her hand back and forth across his chest. "Why? Are you interested in her?" she asked raising an eyebrow. "Do I need to be jealous?"

"No." He laughed, putting his hand at the small of her back and pulling her closer to him. Neither of them was wearing an article of clothing, so her body was flush against his. "I only want you. But I think Dale needs a male figure in his life. A stable one, and Virginia's still young enough and she's a good woman. And very pretty."

"Did you have someone in mind?"

"Not at the moment. Do you?"

"No, but I'll get back to you if I have any sudden inspiration."

"Sounds like a plan," he said.

* * *

It was just after five o'clock on Tuesday, and Bennett was loading his truck. It was his last day on the Lancing job so he had to make sure he got all of his tools. Eric Lancing was a football player for the Orlando Force, and he'd decided he wanted a summer beach house in Mirabelle. So he'd built one. Or, more accurate, had one built.

Bennett had met Eric on a handful of consultations over the summer. Even though Eric was rich and famous, he seemed like a pretty decent guy. He was from a small town in south Alabama that wasn't too far from Mirabelle, and he was a good old Southern boy through and through. The guy was in his late twenties, and he'd been a star running back even before he'd made it pro. He'd been the Heisman Trophy winner during his junior year of college at the University of Alabama, and he'd been a pretty big reason they'd gone on to win the championship that year.

Eric had spared no expenses when it came to his three-story mansion. It had six bedrooms, seven bathrooms, a state-of-the-art kitchen with appliances to rival a five-star restaurant, and a living room that would comfortably seat twenty. There was a Jacuzzi on the back porch and hardwood floors throughout. About sixty percent of the back of the house was comprised entirely of windows.

He'd spent millions, and part of that money had gone to Bennett's custom woodwork, which was evident in every room of the house. And after months spent working on the place, Bennett was finally done.

"Bennett," someone said as they clapped him hard on the shoulder. He turned around to find his boss, Marlin Yance.

"I just took a look around. I see you're all finished up."

"Yes, sir," Bennett said as he shut the hitch of his truck.

"Now what have I told you about calling me sir?" Marlin asked, raising his eyebrows.

Bennett grinned. "It's just habit."

"And good manners. That's one of the things that will help you keep that young woman of yours around."

"God, I hope so. I'm not exactly sure what else I've got going for me."

Marlin just laughed. "Anyway, you did a great job up there. If I didn't know any better I'd say you were going to start your own construction company. Give me a run for my money."

"Nah," Bennett said, shaking his head. "I like the custom work too much. I wouldn't want to deal with all the other stuff."

"Well, when you start your own company for that wood work of yours, don't jack your prices up so much that I can't hire you."

"That won't happen, sir."

Marlin just shook his head. "Did Annette tell you your next job?"

"Yes, I'm at the Henderson farm for the rest of the week."

"Let me know if you need anything," Marlin said before he turned to leave.

Marlin was a great guy in his late fifties. His hair was

thin and graying, and he had a slight beer belly working its way over the top of his jeans, but he was still doing pretty good for himself. He'd gotten divorced about ten years ago when his wife had had an affair. Bennett had seen him dating here and there, but Marlin was too gun-shy to start anything serious. Once burned and all that.

"Hey Marlin," Bennett called out. "You seeing anybody lately?"

Marlin turned back, his forehead wrinkled in confusion. "You asking me out?"

"No, I'm quite happy with Mel." Bennett laughed. Really, that was a huge understatement. He was more than *quite* happy with her. He was *beyond* happy. "Do you know Virginia Rigels?"

Marlin's expression went from confusion to intrigue in seconds. "Yes I do. She's a bit young for me."

"Can't be more than ten years."

"Yeah…" Marlin nodded. Bennett could tell he was thinking about it.

"I've spent a lot of time with her son lately. They're both pretty great. But it was just a suggestion."

"One that I'll keep in mind. Have a good night with that girl of yours," Marlin said before he headed off.

Bennett found himself grinning as he got into his truck. Mel sure as hell had changed him, and for the better. He'd never in his life played matchmaker, and it surprised the hell out of him that he was playing it now.

Bennett was just pulling into Mel's driveway when his cell phone rang. He put his truck in park and looked at the display. It was Danny. "Hey man, what's going on?" Bennett asked.

"Bennett," Cindy sobbed. "Danny was in an accident."

Chapter Eighteen

Bleeding Out

Mel was just pulling the chicken out of the oven when the front door opened. Teddy got up from the floor and bolted for the door.

"Hey babe," she called out as she pulled the oven mitts off and threw them on the counter.

Bennett didn't respond as he crossed the room. When he walked into the kitchen, Mel's smile disappeared from her face in an instant.

Bennett was white as a ghost and he looked like he was going to be sick.

"What's wrong?" She crossed the room to him and put her palms flat on his chest.

Bennett's hands came up to cover hers. He swallowed hard, like he was trying to remember to talk. "Danny was in an accident at work."

Danny was a forklift operator for a massive warehouse, so Mel knew that any job-related accident was going to be serious.

"What happened?"

"Some new guy wasn't paying attention and dropped a crate on him."

"Oh, God." Mel's hands tightened and she fisted Bennett's shirt.

"He's in surgery. It's going to be awhile. I have to get up there."

"Do you want me to go with you?"

"No," he said almost immediately. She couldn't help but flinch at how quickly he said it. His eyes focused on her face and some of the panic in his eyes cleared for a second. "Melanie, I don't know what's going on yet, and you have tons of stuff you have to take care of here."

Shit. He was right. She was in the middle of finals week, and the awards ceremony was in two days. That project had been her baby from the beginning, and it had meant the world to her and, more important, to the kids. She really couldn't miss it.

"Bennett, he's your best friend. I want to be there for you."

"I know, and I appreciate it. But let me get up there and figure out what's going on. I need to go home and pack. I need to get on the road. If I leave now I'll still probably make it there before he's out of surgery. The lift crushed almost half of his body," his voice cracked.

"Bennett." She pulled her hand out from under his and reached for his face, running her thumb across the stubble on his jaw.

He leaned down and pressed his mouth to hers. His lips were soft as they moved over hers and she tasted his tongue for just a second before he pulled back and rested his forehead against hers.

"Call me when you get there."

"It's going to be late," he said, shaking his head.

"I don't care. Call me."

He kissed her again, and Mel walked him to the door. She

stood in the doorway, Teddy sitting at her feet. He seemed to sense the somber mood so he sat quietly with her, the two of them watching as Bennett pulled out of the driveway and drove away.

* * *

The drive to Athens, Georgia, should've taken Bennett six hours. He made it there in just over five.

It was almost midnight when he got to the hospital. He found Cindy and the kids in the nearly empty waiting room. June was asleep on her mother's lap, while the boys slept on a couch across from her. Cindy was awake and staring at the TV in the corner. She might've been looking at the screen, but she wasn't watching. Her eyes were bloodshot and unfocused.

"Cindy," Bennett whispered her name as he came into the room.

She looked over at him and some clarity came into her eyes. "Bennett," she said, sounding a little relieved. "You're here."

She stood up, and June stirred only a little as Cindy laid the child down on the chair. Bennett wrapped his arms around Cindy, and she seemed so much smaller than normal as she broke down into sobs.

"He's still in surgery," she said when she managed to talk. "He went into cardiac arrest from the blood loss."

Bennett looked into her tear-stained face. "He's going to be fine. Your husband is the strongest man I know, and he's not going to let anyone or anything keep him from you or those kids. Do you hear me?"

Cindy just nodded as she reached up and wiped at her face. "Thank you for coming."

"Where else would I be?"

Cindy's little brother, Cory, had joined the air force, too.

He was currently stationed in Germany, and their parents had gone over there to spend some time with him during the holidays. They were trying to get back, but as a significant portion of Europe was being plagued by a snowstorm, they weren't going anywhere anytime soon. As for Danny's family, his mother had died when he'd been in high school, and his father was in a nursing home battling Alzheimer's. Bennett was the closest family they had.

They didn't even have a strong network of friends in Athens. They'd only just moved there a couple of months ago when Danny had gotten the supervising job at the warehouse.

"What do you need me to do?" he asked her.

"For now? Just sit with me."

"That I can do." He leaned down and kissed her on the forehead. He needed to calm his own fears for the time being, needed to be her rock. But who the hell was going to be his?

* * *

Mel had been dozing fitfully. Every time she'd start to nod off, she'd jerk awake and look at the alarm clock. It was after midnight and Bennett still hadn't called. She wanted to call him, but he'd said he would call her. So she waited.

But she wasn't waiting very well. She hadn't spent a night away from him since that first time they'd slept together, and she hated being alone. It had taken her about two minutes before she'd invited Teddy up onto the bed with her.

The puppy hadn't needed a second invitation. He was currently curled up next to her side, his head resting on her stomach. She was on the brink of sleep again when her phone finally rang, vibrating the bed. She grabbed for it eagerly, making Teddy jump.

"Hey," she said relieved. "How's Danny?"

"Still in surgery."

"And Cindy?"

"She's holding it together."

"And you?"

"I'm fine, Mel." He paused for a second before he continued. "You need to go to bed. You're going to be exhausted tomorrow."

"I wasn't going to fall asleep until you called me. I'm glad you're safe."

"At least somebody is safe," he said not keeping the contempt out of his voice.

"Bennett, don't."

"He might not make it, Mel." There was so much pain and anger in his voice that it made Mel's heart break.

She sat up in bed, clutching her chest. "Bennett, there are too many what-ifs in life. It's impossible to know how everything is going to play out, so all you can do is pray that it's the one you want, and not focus on the rest."

"But that's not how I do things. I've always had to prepare myself for the worst-case scenario."

"Not this time, baby. This time you focus on the best; it's the only way to survive it. Danny is going to pull through this."

"Mel I . . . I have to go." There was something about the way he said it that led her to believe that wasn't what he'd planned on saying.

"Will you please promise me that you'll call me if anything happens, or if you just need to talk? I don't care what time it is."

He sighed heavily into the phone.

"Promise me," she demanded.

"I promise." He didn't sound too pleased about it at all.

"I'll be here." But she wished more than anything that she was *there* with him.

"Okay," he agreed. "Now please go get some sleep."

"'Night."

"'Night." And with that the phone disconnected.

* * *

Danny's surgery had been a long and extensive one. The forklift had broken his left leg, left arm, and more than a few ribs. He had multiple internal injuries, including a collapsed lung, and a ruptured spleen that they'd had to remove. And then there was the matter of his head injury. He'd fallen backward when he'd been hit and cracked his head on the cement, and now he was comatose. He might've been out of surgery but he was nowhere near out of the woods.

Bennett hadn't been prepared for what he saw when he walked into that hospital room. The man in the bed only had a vague resemblance to Danny. The top of his head was bandaged, and his eyes were black and blue. His arm and leg were in casts, and the rest of his body was wrapped in bandages. He looked like he was being held together by the white cloth.

Danny might've been short, but he definitely wasn't a small man. That wasn't the case now. He looked diminished somehow in that little bed, diminished and vulnerable.

It took everything in Bennett to not go running from the room screaming and crying. He was back in the desert, next to that burning wreckage of a helicopter, watching his friends die before his eyes and unable to do a damn thing to stop it. Bennett didn't do helpless. He couldn't do it, couldn't handle it.

This wasn't happening to him again. Danny had been the strong one. Danny had been the one to save Bennett's life.

Bennett couldn't do what Mel had told him to do. He couldn't only focus on the best possible scenario. No, because all he could think about as he looked at his best friend, who saved his life, was that he was keeping watch at Danny's deathbed.

* * *

Bennett was exhausted, so he headed over to the hotel around three to get a few hours of sleep before he took over the night shift. He hoped Cindy would actually be able to pull herself away when he got back. She was going to make herself sick if she kept up the pace she was at. She hadn't slept in over thirty-two hours.

Bennett had left the kids in the waiting room, huddled around a small DVD player. Alex might've been only ten, but Bennett was impressed at how well he was looking after his little brother and sister. He was going to be a big help in the next couple of days, especially for his mother.

Bennett pulled out his cell phone and called Mel. He'd talked to her that morning and given her an update on Danny's post surgery status, but he needed to hear her voice again.

"Hey," she said almost immediately. The phone had barely gotten through the first ring.

He closed his eyes and let that one little word wrap around him. Her voice was like a light in the darkness.

"Hi."

"How is he?"

"Still hasn't woken up. But there was a lot of swelling in his brain, so it's going to take some time. Tell me about your day."

"All right," she said and proceeded to talk to him about everything and about nothing. When he got back to the hotel room the only thing he bothered to do before he lay down on the bed was take off his shoes. After that, he listened to the sound of Mel's voice until he passed out.

* * *

Mel was barely able to focus on anything. Her thoughts were consumed by what was happening 350 miles north of her. She'd talked to Bennett multiple times over the last two days, and there hadn't been any real progress since Danny had gotten out of surgery.

Mel really wanted to be there for Bennett and the whole Provo family. But she was hesitant after Bennett had said *no* so quickly the first time she'd suggested it, that and the fact that he hadn't mentioned anything about her going up there.

Mel tried her hardest to hold it together, but the fact that Bennett wasn't going to be at the ceremony after he'd put so much of himself into the project was killing her. And it was more than just Mel who felt Bennett's absence. The kids were asking about him constantly.

At six o'clock on Thursday night, everything was ready to go. The bookshelves were all up, and filled with books. Grace and Lula Mae made more than enough finger foods, which were laid out on the back tables. A massive bowl had been filled with green punch which had red berries floating on the top.

Families were filing into the library, laughing and talking about the upcoming Christmas vacation. It all made Mel feel hollow. People's lives were going on, while this tragedy had happened. It was all *wrong*.

Hamilton came up to her. "I know this sucks for you."

"He should be here," Mel said softly.

"I know." Hamilton frowned. "He helped with a lot more than just the bookshelves."

"I know. Dale's an entirely different kid."

"Right?" Hamilton grinned. "You know he asked Kylee out."

"Really?" Mel asked, intrigued.

"Yup, and his mom has a date with Marlin Yance this weekend."

"Seriously?"

"No joke. Mrs. Rigels took us to get pizza last night and Mr. Yance was there. And before he asked her out he asked for Dale's permission."

"What did Dale say?"

"Yes. I think he was too shocked to say anything else. It completely made Mrs. Rigels's night."

This time Mel couldn't help smiling. It was Bennett. She just knew he was behind that one.

"You heard anything new about Mr. Provo?"

"I talked to Bennett earlier today. There hasn't been a change. I just wish I was up there with him."

"You going to be able to get through this?" Hamilton asked, nodding toward the podium.

"What other choice do I have?"

"You've got a lot of choices. You could run for the hills. But I don't see you doing that."

"Is that right?"

"Nope, not my sister. She's the bravest person I know."

Mel was at a complete loss for words as Hamilton pressed a quick kiss to her cheek. It probably wasn't the best time for Mel to forget how to talk as Principal Bolinder was making his way to the podium to start the ceremony, because she would be speaking soon.

Hopefully she'd be able to pull herself together by then.

Only a few chairs were lined up against the back wall, because there were so many people and they needed as much space as they could get. The room was packed, but everyone quieted down as Principal Bolinder began to speak.

Since the bookshelves were the big part of the ceremony, they were saved for the very end. Mel thought she'd been okay, but when Principal Bolinder called her name, she wasn't sure how she was going to do it.

"You got this," Hamilton said next to her, squeezing her hand tightly before he let go.

Mel made her way to the podium to a room full of applause. She looked out at the crowd seeing her parents, friends, and colleagues, her students, and so many people from the town that it was ridiculous. They were all beaming at her.

It took everything in her not to lose it. How was it that in a room filled with people she felt so freaking alone? This wasn't where she was supposed to be. She was supposed to be with Bennett.

"This project..." She paused, the catch in her voice obvious to everyone in the room. She cleared her throat and tried again. "This project has been months in the making. There were many people involved, many people who thought that it was a worthwhile idea and who wanted to be a part of it. This wouldn't have happened without the combined efforts of many people in Mirabelle. To all of the benefactors, the parents, and the kids, and to everyone who gave a moment of their time or money toward this project, thank you.

"Since I was a little girl, I've had two loves in my life that have always stayed with me: math and books. This project has been near and dear to my heart for many reasons, but the fact that it took math to make something that houses books? Well, it makes it that much more special to me."

And then there was the fact that I fell in love with the man of my dreams while doing it.

Mel had to take a moment to collect herself after that little thought.

"I know I wasn't the only person this project had an impact on, and I'd like to recognize a few people." She went through her list, giving out the awards that she and Bennett had come up with together. She saved the one that meant the most for last, and Dale had looked humbled when he came up to accept his award for Most Improved.

Mel watched him walk back to where his mother was standing with Kylee and her family. Virginia beamed at her son as she pulled him into a big hug. When she let go, Kylee was by his side, stretching up to give him a kiss on the cheek.

Bennett. This had all happened because Bennett had helped.

"I can't end this without mentioning the man who was at the center of this project. Bennett Hart volunteered his time and energy into this project without once asking what was in it for him. He couldn't be here tonight." She paused again, trying to swallow past the lump in her throat. "But I know he would say how proud he was of all the kids and how honored he was to be a part of it. Thank you again to everyone, and Merry Christmas."

Mel took a step back from the podium and the room broke out into applause again. When she went to walk away Mrs. Sylvester came up and stopped her.

"You know we really can't end this ceremony just yet. Ms. Melanie O'Bryan, your students have something they want to give to you."

Dale and Kylee moved to the side of the room where double doors led out to the hallway. They pushed them open and there stood a bookshelf.

"All of your students had a hand in making that," Mrs. Sylvester said to Mel. "They all wanted you to know how much this project meant to them, and they wanted you to have something to remember what you did for them."

It was a very similar design to the ones that had been made for the library, but it had a little something extra to it. The wood wasn't the same. No, they'd used beachwood, and though they'd kept the natural wood for the outer part of the case, the shelves were turquoise and green. Mel didn't need to get a closer look to know that Bennett's hands had been all over that bookshelf.

He'd made this with the kids. He'd done this for her. And she needed to do something for him. She needed to be with him. Now.

* * *

On Friday night, Bennett was reading a book to Danny. It was around nine o'clock when Cindy walked into the room sans kids.

"What's going on?" he asked, standing up from the chair next to Danny's bed.

"That wonderful woman of yours is what's up."

"Huh?"

"Mel got here about two hours ago."

"She's here?" Bennett asked beyond confused. He'd talked to her two hours ago. She'd said she was picking up dinner. She'd failed to mention the part where she'd driven six hours to get it.

"Yes, and she brought food. I cannot tell you how great it was to sit and eat a meal that wasn't McDonald's. She's watching the kids for me so I can be here."

"She's here?" Bennett repeated.

"Yes." Cindy tilted her head to the side and studied Bennett's face. "She didn't tell you she was coming?"

Bennett shook his head.

"Well, she's here. You want to go see her?"

How was it that going to see her hadn't been his first instinct? No, he didn't want to see her. Not like this. Not when his world had just been ripped wide open again and he didn't have the option of just hanging up the phone to prevent her from hearing it. He was barely holding it together, and the little he was able to hold on to was solely for the benefit of Cindy and the kids.

Mel wasn't supposed to be there. He'd told her not to come.

Part of him wanted to laugh that she hadn't listened to him. Of course she hadn't. But he couldn't laugh because he was so pissed at her for coming.

She shouldn't be here.

"Yeah." Bennett nodded slowly. "I, um... I'll go see her."

He had no idea what he was going to say to her, but he'd go see her.

Cindy gave him a look as he crossed the room, but she didn't say anything. Bennett walked through the stale hospital halls toward the elevator. He didn't get any inspiration in there, or when he walked outside and crossed the parking lot. So he decided to walk for a little bit longer in the cold air.

Somehow it turned into an hour and he still didn't have anything. He finally made his way over to the hotel room, and he stood outside and stared at the door for a good minute... or five.

The kids were in that room, so he needed to not get upset. And it wasn't just for their sake. Mel had good intentions in coming up here. She wanted to help. She just didn't realize that Bennett couldn't take her help right now.

He pulled out the card and ran his thumb across the top for a minute, trying to figure out what was going on in his head. But he had no fucking clue.

He stuck the card in the slot, and when it beeped he opened the door.

Alex and Blake were asleep on one of the beds. Their heads were at the foot of the bed; they'd been watching cartoons on TV, which was still on. Mel was asleep on the bed he'd been using, curled around a sleeping June.

He was still frustrated at her for being here, but it didn't stop him from what he did next. He pulled off his boots before he crawled in bed behind Mel, and curled up around her. She sighed in her sleep and pressed back into him.

He wasn't sure how long he lay there watching Mel sleep, feeling her warm body up against his. But at some point his exhaustion got the best of him—not all that surprising, as he hadn't slept for more than four hours straight since Monday night.

He was back in the helicopter. Everyone was there, all the guys. They were flying to the forward operating base, and everyone was laughing about something Santiago said. He was talking about his wife. She was six months pregnant with their son, and she'd gone on and on in a letter she wrote him about her weird cravings.

Santiago didn't think her cravings were all that different from her normal eating habits. "She's Italian," he said into his headset so that everyone could hear him. "Apparently it's normal to put hard-boiled eggs on pizza. To me that is strange. Caramel on potato chips? That's nothing."

Without warning, the side of the helicopter was ripped open by gunfire. They started losing altitude quickly. And just like that, Santiago was gone.

Bennett woke up breathing hard and covered in sweat. He swung his legs over the bed and hung his head between his knees. His heart was still pounding out of his chest and he couldn't take full breaths. He hadn't had a panic attack in months.

He started taking slow, steady breaths, counting as he did so. When his breathing evened out he closed his eyes and started curling and uncurling his toes. When he had the feeling back in his hands, he did the same thing with them.

The damn nightmare had been more real than it had ever

been before. Bennett had felt like he was back there in that hot, dry desert. He'd tasted the sand in his mouth, could feel the grit grinding between his teeth.

He took another deep breath before he lifted his head. The room was empty, and sunlight was streaming through the window. He looked over at the alarm clock. It was eight in the morning. He'd slept for almost nine hours.

"Shit," he said, rubbing at his face. He stood slowly, making sure his legs were steady and headed for the bathroom.

The hot shower was good for clearing his head.

* * *

Mel sat across from Alex and Blake as they munched on pancakes at the Denny's down the road. June, sitting at her side, dipped powdered-sugar-covered French toast sticks into syrup.

Mel had been a little nervous about what Bennett's reaction was going to be to her being up there, but after this morning, her nerves had diminished.

She'd been more than a little surprised to wake up that morning with him curled around her, his face pressed into her hair and his mouth on her neck. Mel could count on one hand how many times she'd woken up before Bennett. He'd had an alarm clock hardwired in him because of his time in the military.

She'd done her best to pull away from him without waking him up, and she'd succeeded. The next mission impossible had been the kids, but they'd expertly gotten ready that morning without making a sound.

"Mewanie," June said. "Can I see Daddy today?"

"Not today, sugar."

June looked at Mel and pouted. "Why not?"

"He's hurt."

"Daddy doesn't get hurt. He's Superman," Blake said.

If only that were true, she thought.

Mel ordered Bennett and Cindy some breakfast to go, and then the four of them loaded up in Cindy's SUV and went back to the hospital. When they got there, they met Cindy in the hallway as she was heading back to Danny's room from the bathroom.

"Mama," June said, letting go of Mel's hand and running down the hallway.

"Slow down, Peachtree." Cindy bent down and held her arms out for her daughter. June didn't listen and she flew right into her mother's arms.

"Can I see Daddy?" June asked.

"Not today."

"Why not?"

"He's sleeping and trying to get better." Cindy tried to keep the pain out of her voice.

"All right." June pouted some more. "Here's breakfast for you and Uncle B."

"And coffee that doesn't taste like sludge," Mel said under her breath so the nurse down the hallway couldn't hear.

"Sounds like perfection," Cindy said, smiling.

"Is Bennett here?" Mel asked as she handed Cindy her coffee. Dylan was holding her box of food, and Alex had Bennett's.

"He's with Danny now. I'm going to go eat this in the cafeteria with the kids."

"I'll take Bennett his." Mel held out her hand for the white polystyrene box that Alex had, and then she headed down the hallway.

When she got to the room she peeked in the open door to find Bennett sitting next to Danny's bed, staring off into space.

Mel knocked lightly and Bennett looked up, a frown plain as day on his face. He was not happy to see her.

"Hey," she said softly. "I brought you food."

Bennett stood up and crossed the room to her. "Thanks," he said as he took the box and coffee from her outstretched hands.

That was it. One word. That was all she got.

He didn't pull her into his arms. Didn't kiss her. Didn't touch her. His eyes were cold. Distant. Not anything she'd ever seen before.

"I'm going to spend the day with the kids. Get them out of the hotel room. Out of the hospital."

"I'm sure Cindy will appreciate that," he said as he set the food down on a table.

"All right." She looked at him for a minute, trying to figure out what to say. "Bennett, I—"

"I'll see you later." He leaned in and quickly kissed her on the forehead, before he turned around, effectively dismissing her from the room.

* * *

There was some small part of Bennett that felt bad about how he'd treated Mel. But he was able to push it to the side. He couldn't focus on her right now. All he could concentrate on was his best friend and not losing his damn mind.

With Mel watching the kids, Bennett and Cindy were able to spend more time at the hospital with Danny. Bennett gave Cindy the night watch again on Saturday, and much like the night before, Bennett spent an hour walking around outside in the cold trying to think. But nothing was processing.

He'd pretty much avoided seeing Mel all day. There was something about her being so close that made him even more on edge. Why? He had no freaking clue, but he hated how he was treating her. He knew she deserved better.

When he got back to the hotel room it was after midnight

and everyone was asleep again. He lay there next to Mel watching her sleep. He could handle her being close like this, when she was asleep and not able to see how weak he really was.

The helicopter was losing altitude. They were falling, plummeting toward the ground, but somehow they landed. Bullets were piercing through the cabin like it was paper. The glass from the cockpit shattered and Markel and Redding were gone—they never even had a chance to get out of their seats.

Bennett and Denham were out last. He lifted his gun and aimed in the direction of the gunfire, getting off a few good shots. He headed for the other side of the helicopter, and as he rounded the corner the bullet hit him, sending him flying back.

He was screaming as he woke up in bed. The pain in his shoulder was real, or it sure as hell felt like it. He couldn't breathe past it. Could barely hear anything above the gunfire that was echoing in his head.

"Bennett! Bennett!"

Mel's voice was coming through like static, but it was too hard to focus on. The blackness was swallowing him. Eating him alive.

He wasn't sure if it was just instinct or something else entirely, but he moved his legs over the edge of the bed. He dropped his head between his thighs and started taking deep breaths. He wasn't sure how long he sat there for, but at some point he realized Mel was kneeling behind him on the bed, rubbing his back in circles.

"It's okay," she was whispering over and over again.

It was those two words that set him off. Everything wasn't fucking okay.

"Stop," he said barely above a whisper. He needed her hands to not be on him.

"What?"

"I said stop."

She backed away from him as he got up and crossed the room. He turned around and Mel was looking at him, wide eyed and more than a little scared. She was still kneeling on the bed. Her hair was dripping wet and she was wrapped in a towel.

She didn't say anything. She just looked at him.

"Where are the kids?"

It took her a second to respond, like his question threw her off. "Cindy's parents got here early this morning. They came by and got the kids to take them to breakfast." She continued to look at him like he was a stranger. "Bennett, what was that?"

"A bad dream."

"What kind of bad dream?"

"The kind I don't want to talk about."

"Are you okay?"

"Am I okay? My best friend is lying in a hospital bed with half of his body broken. If he makes it out of this, his life will still be completely ruined. So no Mel, I'm not *fucking* okay." He did nothing to mask the harshness in his voice.

Mel got up from the bed, concerned, and took a few steps toward him, and then stopped when her eyes connected with his cold ones. "I know what's going on isn't easy for you. That's why I'm here."

"You have no idea what's going on with me. You shouldn't have come."

"What?"

"You shouldn't have come," he repeated. "And with Cindy's family here, you don't need to be here anymore."

"I came for you."

"I don't need you." He said that with so much finality that

she flinched back, her eyes going all wide and wounded. His chest started to hurt, and he knew it wasn't from the remnants of his nightmare. But he couldn't care about Mel's feelings. He needed her to leave. He needed to be alone, so he had to drive his point home. "Go."

She looked at him in complete and total shock, but a moment later it was replaced by a look of resignation that Bennett had never seen before.

"I don't know who this is standing in front of me right now, but you're not the man I know, not the man I..."

She wasn't choked up, but it was obvious she couldn't finish what she was about to say. Bennett didn't want to think about her unspoken words. And even in her silence she stood there calmly, so calmly in fact that it threw Bennett a little off guard when she started talking again.

"The man *I* thought you were, the man *I* know, would never talk to me like that, no matter what he was going through."

"Then I'm obviously not that man."

"I made a serious mistake."

"Like I said, I didn't ask you to come up here."

"That wasn't what I was talking about," Mel said abruptly, her hand coming up in the air to stop him from saying anything. "I meant everything. Everything we had, everything that ever involved you. It was all a mistake. A *lie*. I don't...I don't know who you are. I was wrong, so *very* wrong to ever think I actually knew you. You never let me all the way in. Not really. And you were never going to, were you? No matter how much I asked, no matter how patient I was, no matter how much I begged for you to just let me in, you were never going to?" Her hand dropped from the air as she looked at him for the answer.

Bennett didn't say anything. He just slowly shook his head.

"I waited all this time for something that was never going to happen. Well, I'm done waiting. I'm done with trying to get something out of nothing. I'm done with everything. I'm done with you, with us."

She might've been standing there almost completely naked, but she was so strong, stronger than he would ever be. He knew it as he watched her wet hair drip down and soak into the towel. He was being a complete and total asshole. He knew that, too. But he couldn't do it. He couldn't be with anyone, and he especially didn't deserve her.

"Well, I'm glad you figured it all out." He reached down and grabbed his boots from the floor before he walked out of the room. And if his world wasn't completely broken before, it most certainly was now.

Chapter Nineteen

Can't Stop

The drive back from Athens was without a doubt the longest six hours of Mel's life. She hadn't shed a tear, not even when Bennett had walked out of that hotel room. She'd been too much in shock. She was still in shock. She had no idea what had happened.

She'd just gotten out of the shower when Bennett had started screaming. She'd run into the room to find him flailing around in the bed. He'd woken up about a second later, and the fear that was evident in every fiber of his being had almost made her break down into tears. She'd never seen him like that.

But that had been nothing to the next five minutes. No, what followed had been way worse. She hadn't been scared that he was going to hurt her physically or anything. She thought she knew him enough to at least know that. But he had hurt her. Hurt her worse than anything or anyone had ever hurt her before.

She'd thought he loved her. She'd heard those words come out of his mouth. But they'd been a lie. Just like everything else.

It had *all* been a lie.

The thought of going home to that empty house was more than Mel could take. She'd left Teddy with Grace and Jax while she'd been gone, but she wanted him with her. It didn't matter that he was a present from Bennett. She couldn't have cared less about that fact. It didn't take anything away from how much she loved Teddy and how much Teddy loved her—unconditionally, in fact.

The problem was getting Teddy, which meant she was going to have to see people.

Mel pulled up in front of the house and put her car in Park. She sat there for a good couple of minutes as the hot air leaked out and the cold air took its place. She was trying to fortify herself, but the colder she got the less fortified she felt.

"Now or never." She pushed open the door and made her way up the front steps to the house.

Jax opened the door, Teddy bouncing around his feet. The second he got a good look at her his face fell. "What happened?"

Yup. That was it. That was all it took for everything in Mel to completely fall apart.

"Shit, Mel. Come here." He grabbed her and pulled her into the house, wrapping his arms around her as she sobbed into his chest.

It was done. Her and Bennett's relationship was done. Over. She'd never seen it coming.

They just stood there for a minute, or two. Actually, Mel had absolutely no idea how long they stood there. But Jax's hands were running up and down her back. Teddy was whining at their feet, and he climbed up Mel's legs and pawed at her. When she was finally able to breathe regularly she pulled back from Jax and wiped at her face.

"What happened?" he asked, running his hands up and down her arms.

Mel shrugged and shook her head, biting her trembling lip. "He didn't want me there. He doesn't want me at all."

"He's an idiot."

Mel laughed, but it was harsh and bitter, and directed at herself. "I'm pretty sure *I'm* the idiot."

"You're not." He shook his head. "Grace isn't here. She had to go do something with Paige for the wedding. But she'll be back soon. I can call her."

"No, don't do that. I'm actually going to just get Teddy and go."

"You should stay, Mel. Don't go home. Don't go and be by yourself. It's not going to help. It's just going to make you feel worse."

"You the expert on the matter?"

"Yeah I am. 'Cause when Grace and I broke up, being by myself almost killed me."

"Well, you don't sugarcoat anything, do you?"

"Come on." He put his hand at the small of her back and led her through the house. "Take a hot shower. You'll feel better."

Mel just looked at him and raised her eyebrows.

"Physically, at least."

"I don't know if that's possible."

"Well, we have wine."

Mel burst into laughter, but this time it was real.

"Give me your keys," he said when they got to the bathroom. "I'll go get your bags."

He turned to walk away and Mel touched his arm, stopping him. "Thank you."

"No thanks necessary. You're my almost wife's best friend. She'd kill me if I didn't take care of you."

"That's true." She let go of his arm and turned, pushing the door of the bathroom open. But this time it was Jax who stopped her from walking away. "You're my friend, too,

Mel. And I think you deserve the world." He leaned down and kissed her forehead before he stepped back. "You're not the stupid one. He is." And with that, he walked down the hallway.

Mel took the longest shower of her life. She was pretty sure she'd used every drop of hot water in the house, probably all of the hot water in Mirabelle. By the time she got out, Grace still wasn't home.

After crying in the shower she really wanted to lie down; her head was killing her. And after being in hot water for so long, she was freezing in the cooler air. She went and crawled into a bed in one of the guest rooms and Teddy snuggled up next to her. Mel ran her fingers through his fur and he shifted closer to her, putting his cold little nose right up against her throat and breathing out hard. It tickled and Mel laughed.

And just like that she was crying again.

God, the whole thing was so stupid. Why couldn't she stop? Why couldn't she stop caring? She wanted desperately to fall asleep, but it just wasn't coming. The sweet relief of oblivion refused to claim her.

The door creaked open and a few seconds later the bed dipped. Mel knew it was Grace who was crawling under the covers next to her. Knew it was Grace's arms that were wrapping around her.

"Oh Mel," Grace whispered. "I'm sorry. So, so sorry."

Mel was sobbing now. Sobbing so hard she couldn't breathe.

Grace just held her through it, held Mel until there were no more tears. They lay there in silence for only a moment before Grace said something.

"I'm not going to feed you some line of bullshit that it's all okay and you're going to feel better, because then I'd be lying to you, and I'm not going to do that."

"Good," Mel said through a voice that barely sounded

like hers. She rolled over so she could look at her best friend's face.

"Oh, sweetie. I know it hurts. Believe me, I know just how much." Grace reached up and ran her thumb under each of Mel's eyes.

"He said he loved me."

"When?"

"The other night. He thought I was asleep. But he said it, Mel. He said it. And then today . . . I don't even know who he was today."

"What happened?"

"I don't even know really. It happened so fast. I mean he was distant the whole time I was up there, but that I understood. His friend is beyond hurt. Bennett's worried about Danny, so I wasn't going to overthink his mood. It wasn't about me, at all. I got it, completely and totally. But then this morning, I don't know what happened."

"Mel?"

She told Grace how it had all gone down: Bennett's dream, his anger, his dismissal.

"Did he hurt you?" Grace asked.

"Physically? No." Mel shook her head. "But the way he talked to me . . . I never thought he could be so cruel. Not him. Not ever."

"Oh, sweetie."

"I still love him, Grace. I love him so much."

"Did you tell him?"

"No. I was too much of a coward."

"You're not the coward, Mel. You're *incredibly* brave," Grace said.

"It hurts. I never thought something could hurt like this." The tears made a magical reappearance at that moment, and Grace reached out and wiped them away.

"Another thing I'm not going to tell you is that Bennett

isn't worth your tears. I've never cried so much as I have over Jax, and if anybody were to tell me he wasn't worth it, I'd claw their eyes out with my bare hands. Bennett might not be worth it, but he might be worth everything, and it's not my place to tell you which it is. But that being said, I will tell you that I hate him right now, and the fact that he's done this to you makes me want to claw *his* eyes out."

Mel laughed again. She couldn't help it.

"Did you eat anything today?"

Mel shook her head.

"Well, I'm guessing you want to lay in this bed and wallow more than anything. And if that's the decision you make, that is entirely acceptable."

"But—"

"But, Harper is coming over," Grace said, sitting up. "I'm going to make dinner and we're going to drink a lot of wine. A lot. Of. Wine. You can cry, and scream, and eat fifty pounds of chocolate, and for your information I'm making my raspberry mousse. You can do whatever your heart desires. But I'm going to be here, Harper is going to be here, and Jax is, too, for whatever use he's going to be. My point is, you aren't alone, Mel. You never have been, and you never will be, no matter what happens with the idiot fucker who's making you cry. Got it?"

"Got it." Mel couldn't have stopped the small smile that turned up her mouth.

* * *

"Where's Mewanie?" June looked around the hospital waiting room for someone who just wasn't there. The way June pronounced Mel's name had always made him smile before, but now it was a feat that bordered on the impossible.

Bennett had to pause for a second before he answered the

little girl. Hearing Mel's name was like pouring lemon juice on a cut. It was painful and made him wince.

They were done. He knew it and it hurt, for many reasons.

He loved her, more than he'd ever loved anyone. And he knew it. He knew it beyond any reasonable doubt. But ever since he'd walked into that hospital room almost five days ago and seen the strongest man he knew bent and broken, he'd known he couldn't do it. He couldn't go through something like that with Mel. He'd watched Cindy, seen the pain and anguish on her face for days, and he wasn't strong enough for that.

How was it that after everything Danny had survived, this had happen? He'd come home and left the war behind him. So how? How could it happen?

Bennett couldn't do it. He couldn't dedicate his life to Mel and then have some freak accident pull them apart. Destroy their lives. Destroy everything. Destroy him.

Maybe he was a coward. No, he definitely was a coward, and he knew it. Mel was right; he wasn't the man she thought he was. But the thing was, he *knew* she was everything he thought she was and more. So much more. That was why he had to walk away.

Really, he shouldn't have started anything in the first place. It wasn't fair to her. He was never going to let her in completely. He was never going to let *anyone* in completely. But how the hell was he supposed to, when in the blink of an eye that person could be ripped out of his life? No, it was better this way. Alone. He couldn't get hurt when he was alone.

It took Bennett a second to answer, but he looked at the little girl and told her the truth.

"She went home, June Bug."

"Why didn't she say 'bye bye?"

She hadn't said good-bye because her every instinct had probably told her to get the hell away from him. He didn't blame her. He wished he could get the hell away from himself at the moment.

"She left?" Cindy asked, looking at Bennett.

He nodded.

Cindy looked confused as she studied him, and he knew for a fact she had about twenty questions on the tip of her tongue, but she didn't say anything more on the subject.

"I'm going to take them to dinner," Cindy said, grabbing June's tiny little hand. "We'll be back in a little bit."

"Okay." He watched the four of them walk down the hallway before he headed into Danny's room.

The doctors said his vitals were strong today, and they were optimistic about him waking up. Well, at least someone was optimistic, because Bennett sure as hell wasn't.

* * *

Mel was stationed firmly between Grace and Harper on the couch. They were about four bottles in, and though Mel's heart was still clearly ripped in two, the pain was dulled. Only just slightly, but still dulled.

Jax had gone into his and Grace's bedroom to give the girls some privacy, but Mel had liked the fact that he hadn't vacated the house.

"Your husband is good people," Mel said to Grace.

"My almost husband?" Grace clarified.

"That was what I meant. You know he let me cry on his shoulder and he didn't even finch."

"He didn't turn into a bird?" Harper asked.

"*Flinch*," Mel said. "He didn't even *flinch*."

"I can't believe you guys are going to be married in less than a week," Harper said.

"We don't have to talk about that," Grace said quickly.

"Shit." Harper covered her mouth with her hand.

"Just because I'm sad and pathetic doesn't mean we can't talk about Grace getting married," Mel told them.

"Mel..." Grace shook her head.

"You're getting married this week to the love of your life, I'd be a horrible friend if I got upset about that. If anything, you have more of a right to happiness than I do to my misery."

"What do you mean by that?" Harper asked.

"You and Jax have been something for pretty much your entire lives. Bennett and I...it's only been a couple of months. My short-lived relationship with him doesn't even make a dent in what you and Jax have."

"Mel, that's not fair," Grace said. "You love Bennett. So, I've loved Jax for a longer amount of time, but that doesn't make my love stronger or more powerful than yours. Love is love. It has a strength all its own, a strength that can't be ranked by time. Don't let anyone diminish how you feel, especially yourself."

Mel looked at her friend and couldn't help the small little flicker of hope that was flaring up in her chest. "I won't."

"Good."

"Life's too short," Harper said.

Those were the words that Mel had repeated over and over again all those months ago.

"Yeah it is. So what about you?" Mel asked, nudging Harper with her elbow.

Harper waved her free hand in the air and shook her head. "We don't need to get into that."

"Come on. I'm at the stage where I'm just intoxicated enough to not cry."

"The fact that you used the word *intoxicated* was pretty impressive," Grace said.

"Yeah, I would've just said *drunk*," Harper added with a nod.

"Stop delaying. What's going on with you and the blond Clark Kent?"

"Mel, really, we don't have to talk about it."

"Can you two stop it? At this exact moment, I'm okay, because of the two of you. And I'd really, really like to hear about something that's making you happy. This is the distraction I need. Please," she begged.

Harper looked at Mel for a second before she started talking. "Brad is good. He took me to dinner last Sunday—a dinner that was perfect, I might add. We talked the whole time, no awkward silences. He's sweet and charming and not pushy at all. He walked me to the door, told me he had a good time, said good night, and then went home. He didn't do that whole *wait two days* thing before he called, either. No, he called me five minutes after he left, and we talked for two more hours."

"Harper," Mel said, grabbing her hand and squeezing it tight. "That's great."

"He took me to lunch twice this week. And then dinner again last night."

"Still no smooching?" Grace asked.

"Yeah...he, uh, broke that barrier last night."

"Goooood?" Grace held out the word for entirely too long.

"Perfect," Harper said, glancing at Mel. She must've seen something in Mel's face. Longing, probably...and maybe a little pain. Okay, a lot of pain. "I knew I shouldn't have said anything," Harper sighed.

"No." Mel shook her head. "If anything, you two talking gives me hope. Not for Bennett to figure things out." She waved her hand in the air and dismissed the thought. "But for life to figure things out. For *me* to figure things out."

"Well, cheers to that," Grace said, holding her almost empty wineglass in the air.

The other two women clinked their glasses to it before

they took a sip. They'd shared many insights throughout the night. With each one they'd had a little toast, thus the dwindling wine.

"You're shockingly okay at the moment. Level-headed," Harper said, studying Mel.

"It's 'cause you two are here, and I'm pretty drunk. Plus, I don't think I have any more tears in me at the moment."

"That's understandable," Grace said.

"I'm going to be okay. If I can survive what happened last summer, I can survive this."

Harper grabbed Mel's hand and squeezed. "Sweetie, you don't have to be okay today."

"Oh, there's absolutely no chance of that. It's going to be a while. A very long while, but there's light at the end of the tunnel. I can't see it yet, but I'm pretty sure it's there."

Mel closed her eyes. Light at the end of the tunnel? God, she was speaking a load of bullshit. She just wanted things to go back to how they'd been a week ago. How could things have changed so much in only a few days? How could everything just fall apart?

She wanted him back. She wanted the man she loved back. She wanted to spend the rest of her life with him. Why was that so much to ask for? Why couldn't she have him?

It was stupid.

The whole thing was so incredibly stupid. And right at that moment she felt beyond stupid to want that man so desperately. A man who obviously didn't want her and was able to throw away their relationship like it had meant nothing. Like she'd meant nothing.

Mel's eyes started to water, and the tears started to fall.

Apparently she wasn't all cried out. Nope. The last couple of hours had been just a little lull, the calm before the real storm. Because now Mel really lost it. Harper grabbed the glass out of Mel's hand, and Mel lay down in Grace's lap. A second after that, Mel's legs were pulled into Harper's lap. Grace ran her fingers through Mel's hair, while Harper rubbed Mel's back. And that was how they stayed for the next couple of hours.

It was after midnight when Grace and Harper helped Mel into bed. But they didn't leave her alone. Nope. Both women crawled in next to her, and Teddy joined them, curling up at the foot of the bed.

* * *

Bennett hadn't really slept since Mel had left. When she'd been there, he'd been able to relax enough to sleep for more than eight hours. He'd gotten four hours of sleep the night before, and he'd done it sitting up in the chair next to Danny's bed. Yeah, his back and neck were still sore. But that was the kind of sleep he was going to be in for tonight as well.

Bennett could pull the chair out into the semibed thing it made. But after the last two nightmares he'd had, he didn't want to chance it. It was eleven o'clock on Monday night, and exhaustion was beginning to overtake him, so he leaned his head back on the chair and closed his eyes. It took about a second for Mel to come to the forefront of his mind.

It had been about thirty-eight hours since she'd left. Yes, he'd been counting, not that it'd done him any good. For the last couple of months, the longest Bennett had gone without speaking to her was a few hours. There was this void from the absence of her that he'd never felt before, a void that he had no clue how to deal with. But he was just going to have to deal.

It should be easier to get over her now as opposed to later, easier for him to just move on, but at the moment he couldn't think of anything more difficult.

Bennett opened his eyes and sat up. He was in the middle of a packed church, light streaming through the stained-glass windows as someone played the piano. The song changed and everyone around him stood up and turned. Bennett followed their lead, and when he turned around he stopped breathing.

It was Mel.

She was wearing a wedding dress. The top was molded to her chest, and the dress flared out at her waist, making a bell shape. Her curls were pinned up all around her face, and a veil dropped from the back of her head, flowing past her shoulders and stretching down her back. She was beaming as she looked down the aisle, a smile on her face that Bennett had never seen before.

Bennett turned forward and tried to see who she was looking at, but he couldn't see the guy at the end of the aisle. He didn't know who Mel was marrying, but it wasn't him. He had to get out of there. He was choking, suffocating, and he needed air. He reached for the tie at his neck and started to pull it off as he tripped over people on his way.

When he got to the doors at the back of the church he pushed them open and was immediately assaulted with a blast of desert sand in his face. Gunfire erupted and a bullet went through his shoulder. He fell back onto the ground and stared up at the blazing sun. He touched his shoulder and held his hand in front of his face. It was covered with blood. Something exploded near him and the blast knocked him unconscious. When he opened his eyes, Danny's face was floating above him.

Bennett was being dragged through the sand. The ringing in his ears was too loud to hear anything, but he could just make out the words Danny was mouthing: *I've got you.*

Bennett woke up, practically jumping out of his chair.

Shit. He didn't need one of these again. But the routine was second nature at this point. He leaned forward and put his head between his knees.

"I see you're still getting panic attacks," a raspy voice said.

Bennett's head shot up. Danny was awake.

* * *

Bennett stood at the edge of the room as doctors poked and prodded Danny, asking him a hundred questions while they did it. Cindy was standing by Danny's side, holding the hand that hadn't been broken with tears streaming down her smiling face.

The doctors were hopeful about Danny's recovery, but only time would tell, and there would need to be a lot of time.

It was after one in the morning before everything settled down. And Danny was in desperate need of some morphine and sleep.

"I'll be back in the morning. I'm glad you're awake, man," Bennett told Danny before he turned and headed for the door.

As was Bennett's routine lately, he went and walked around outside for a little while. He needed some air. He'd snapped out of the panic attack he'd been having pretty quickly after he'd seen that Danny was awake, but he wasn't quite over it yet. Just thinking about that dream had his heart rate going up.

He'd told himself so many times in the last two days that he just needed to move on from Mel. What he hadn't thought about was her moving on from him.

God, he was an idiot.

What did he expect? For her to forever pine over him? To never be with another man? Mel deserved every happiness in the world. She deserved to find a man who was going to love her every single day for the rest of her life.

The thing was, whether they were together or not, Bennett would love her every single day for the rest of his life. He knew he'd never get over her.

By the time Bennett got back to his hotel, his fingers were numb. Cindy had taken the kids over to her parents' room, so his room was empty. He didn't even bother changing. He just pulled off his boots and climbed into bed. The pillow he was using smelled vaguely of Mel; it was just a soft lingering touch of her. He buried his face in it and breathed deeply, searching for her.

But she wasn't there.

He flew backward as the bullet blasted through him. He touched his shoulder, then held his hand in front of his face. It was covered with blood. The explosion happened a second later and he blacked out. But this time it wasn't Danny's face hovering over him when he opened his eyes.

It was Mel.

She was kneeling over him, pressing her hands against his wound.

"Bennett, it's going to be okay," she said calmly. "Understand? You're going to be fine."

"Okay," he whispered as he looked up into her face.

"Stay right here, Bennett. I've got you. I promise."

He closed his eyes for just a second, and when he opened them he was back in the church again. The music was playing and Mel was walking down the aisle. She was passing right in front of him, but she didn't look over.

No, her eyes were intently focused at the end of the aisle. And the look on her face made him ache. He wanted to reach out and grab her, to stop her, to tell her that she was marrying the wrong man. That he'd made a mistake.

But as he went to reach out the scene shifted, and he was behind a wall of glass, looking out. He couldn't reach her, he couldn't stop her, couldn't talk to her, couldn't tell her he was sorry, tell her he loved her. His heart broke. He broke.

The pain in his shoulder came out of nowhere and he reached up, touching the wound. His hands were covered in blood, but it wasn't his shoulder this time. No, it was chest. His heart. This is what it would be like without her, bleeding out.

He woke up to sunlight streaming into the hotel room. His heart was pounding hard, but it had nothing to do with a panic attack.

Bennett had to get to Mel.

* * *

Mel stayed at Jax and Grace's house until the morning of Christmas Eve. She had spent the entire previous day watching Christmas movies with Grace and Harper. They sat on the living room floor making table decorations for the reception, drinking spiked eggnog, and eating more bags of potato chips than any of them could possibly count.

But after an entire day of wallowing around and trying her hardest to ignoring certain things, Mel decided it was time to get back to her life. Or at least *try* to get back to it.

Both Harper and Grace insisted that they would go back with her and stay the night, but Mel said no. She needed some time alone, she needed some time to regroup, to adjust to how things were now.

Besides, her family was getting back in town after a short trip to visit Mel's aunt in Mississippi. Mel was going over to their house on Christmas Day, so she was going to have to face the inquisition in about twenty-four hours. She needed to prepare herself, because breaking down in front of them wasn't an option.

When Mel and Teddy walked into the house, she had to pause for a moment in the hallway. It was cold and quiet. It felt hollow. She felt hollow.

Teddy was sitting in the living room, looking at her with his head tilted to the side. He apparently didn't understand what she was doing. Well, he could join the club because she had no freaking clue, either.

She took a deep breath before she stopped stalling and headed for her bedroom.

"First things first," she said as she dropped her bags at the door.

She walked straight over to her bed and grabbed the teddy bear. She had to get rid of it. Throw it away. Never, ever see it again. She went into the kitchen, her intentions clear, but when she got to the trash can she stopped. She looked down past the open lid, into the trash that she'd forgotten to take out before she left.

She couldn't do it. She couldn't throw something that meant so much to her into the garbage.

She took her foot off the pedal that lifted the lid and it closed with a clang. Mel reached up to the cabinet above her head and shoved the bear in there, right next to the Tupperware bowls.

Then she headed back down the hallway, passing a

clearly confused Teddy, who followed her around the house. She stripped her bed of the blankets and sheets and hauled them all off into the laundry room. And when she closed the lid on the steaming hot water, she started to cry.

It didn't matter what she did. Nothing was going to wash him away.

Chapter Twenty

Something I Need

Danny was asleep when Bennett made it back to the hospital. Cindy was sitting by his side reading a book.

"How's he doing?"

"Good." She smiled as she stood up and stretched. "He was up earlier, but he was in a lot of pain, so they gave him some more morphine. He was asking for you, though. He wants to talk to you."

"Well, I'm not going anywhere. No plans."

Cindy nodded, biting her lip as she studied Bennett. "What happened?" she asked.

"With what?"

"With you and Mel?"

Everything in Bennett froze. How was he supposed to explain that he'd flipped his shit and done the stupidest thing of his life?

"To be honest, I'm not exactly sure." He ran his hand along the top of his head and town the back to his neck. "I kind of lost it and took it out on her. I told her to leave."

"You love her."

It wasn't a question, but he answered anyway. "Yes, I do." He knew the pain in his voice was evident.

"She loves you, too."

"She told you that?" Bennett asked.

"Not in so many words. But she drove up here to be with you. She wanted to take care of you."

"I don't need to be taken care of."

Cindy just laughed and shook her head pityingly. "Just because you're a big, strong man doesn't mean you don't need to be taken care of. We all need to be taken care of at one point or another."

"I guess."

"No, we do," Cindy said seriously. "Bennett, I know what you're scared of. You're scared of letting somebody in and then losing them. You think there's going to come a day when that person won't be there anymore."

"You don't know what you're talking about."

"Bennett, did you forget for a second that you're my husband's best friend and that I know everything about you—including everything about your birth mother?"

He shook his head. "This isn't the same thing."

"You're right. Mel isn't the woman who walked out on you."

"I'm not scared of her walking out on me."

"No, you're not. You're scared to love and be loved back. You're scared to have that in your life. You were scared after the accident three years ago, and you're scared again after what's happened to Danny. You've seen how easy it is for someone to get ripped out of your life, and the thought of it being Mel is more than you can handle."

Bennett stood there, stunned. Apparently Cindy knew exactly what she was talking about.

She crossed the room and stopped right in front of him. She reached up and cupped his jaw with her hand.

"Stop hiding. It's not worth it. Danny almost died. But

you better believe that over the last week I didn't doubt being with him for a single second. There was never a moment when I thought it would've just been easier had I never been with him. He's made my life better. Loving him has made my life worth more. If you walk away from Mel, it isn't going to make your life easier. It's going to make your life harder."

She patted his cheek a couple of times before she pulled his face down to hers and she gave him a kiss on the other cheek.

"I pray to God you figure it out, Bennett. Because I know she's hurting just as much as you are." She pulled back from him. "Now you stay and sit with my husband and think about that while I go get us some breakfast." And with that she walked out of the room.

When Bennett turned to look at Danny's bed, his friend's eyes were open. "She's right, you know."

"Is that so?" Bennett asked, raising his eyebrows.

"Yeah. Don't tell her this, but she's usually always right. Come here." Danny raised his good hand and beckoned.

Bennett crossed the room and stood at Danny's side. Danny held his hand out and Bennett grabbed it. Danny's grip was weaker than normal, but still stronger than Bennett had expected.

"I can't thank you enough, man."

Bennett shook his head. "It was nothing."

"No, it was everything. Cindy told me everything you did." He let go of Bennett's hand and motioned to the chair next to the bed. "Sit down. Stay a while."

Bennett couldn't stop the small smile that turned up his mouth as he took a seat.

"What's with the panic attacks?" Danny asked.

And with that the smile disappeared. "Don't waste time before you start the interrogation, do you?"

"Nope. So what's going on?"

"They happen every once in a while."

"Did Mel ever see you have one?"

"Two days ago."

"Haven't the two of you spent every night together for the past three months or something?"

"Yeah."

"And you didn't have any panic attacks then?"

"No." Bennett sat back in the chair, more than a little shocked. How had he not made the connection? There had been no panic attacks ever since Mel had been around. He'd almost had one the night that stupid article had come out, the night of the anniversary of the crash. But he'd woken up with Mel in his arms and he'd gotten past it. *She'd* gotten him past it.

"What's going on, Bennett? What are you doing?"

"Are you kidding me?" Bennett couldn't stop himself from laughing. "You're lying in a bed, half-broken, and you're asking *me* what's wrong?"

Bennett didn't think it was possible for Danny's face to get more serious. "I might be broken physically, but that's nothing compared to being broken mentally. I told you not to fuck it up with Mel."

"That you did."

"Why didn't you listen? Cindy told me everything Mel did, too. Did you know that she went back to our house and got all of the kids Christmas presents so they'd have something to open tomorrow? Did you know that she arranged for Santa Claus to come see my kids tonight? Did you know that she arranged and paid for meals to be brought here every day so that they didn't have to eat McDonald's? Did you know that she sat and talked to my wife for hours and comforted her? That she took care of my family that she barely even knows? That she took care of them because of how much she loves you? Did you know all of those things?"

Bennett sat there, stunned. It took a moment for his brain to make his mouth move. "I knew a few of those things."

"That should've been enough. Don't ruin it, Bennett. Don't ruin the best thing that's ever happened to you. I almost missed out on my best thing, and I thank God every day I didn't. Go to her. Go get her. Apologize for being an ass and beg that woman to come back into your life. You both deserve to be happy."

"What if she doesn't take me back?"

"Do you love her?"

"More than anything."

"Then you try. You fight. You get off your ass and you get down there and you get on your knees and beg that woman for forgiveness. What is this *what if she doesn't take me back* bullshit? You *get* her back. You do everything in your power to make that woman realize you are the only man for her. Do you want to look back on this, on her, and realize that you made the biggest mistake of your life? You see it now, so fix it now. At the moment, you've already lost her. So what else have you got to lose? Your pride?"

"No." Bennett shook his head. "That's long gone."

"Good, because it's going to take some massive groveling, my friend. But if it works, it'll be worth it. Do you know why?"

Bennett nodded. "Because *she's* worth it."

* * *

Mel sat on the floor and stared at her Christmas tree. She'd dragged Bennett out to get one the day after Thanksgiving. It was right around when their relationship had started to change.

Bennett had spent a good hour fixing the strings of lights she had. A lot of the strings were only half-working, so he'd sat on the floor switching out fuses until he could get a whole strand to light up. Then they'd decorated it together, laughing and purposely brushing against each other as they went back and forth for ornaments.

Mel had spent the whole day trying to remove Bennett from her house. She'd put all his things in a bag and shoved it in the trunk of her car. But she couldn't bring herself to move the presents from under the tree. She just couldn't do it. She'd tried. She'd reached for them, held them in her hands, but she couldn't pull them away.

No, she'd wound up plugging the lights in, putting on a thoroughly depressing CD by one of her favorite musicians, pouring herself a glass of wine, and sitting down in front of the tree. And that was where she'd sat for the past hour.

It was dark outside, had been for a while now. The sun was long gone and Mel was cold. She'd grabbed a blanket a while ago and wrapped herself up in it.

The presents weren't the only thing she hadn't been able to pack up. She was wearing his gray air force T-shirt. It was the same one she'd worn after the first time they'd had sex. The same one she'd worn more times than she could count. Bennett had laughed at her because she'd pretty much steal it the second it came out of the dryer. He'd given up all claims on it months ago.

Just like he'd given up all claims on her.

Damn, she was pathetic.

Teddy was lying down on the floor next to her, his little head resting on her thigh while she trailed her fingers through his fur.

"I think I need more wine," she said, looking down at him. "I'm starting to feel sorry for myself again."

Teddy stood up when Mel shifted. As she got to her feet, he stuck his butt in the air and stretched his paws out in front of him, yawning. He followed her into the kitchen, sat, and patiently waited for a treat that he knew was going to come.

But before Mel could get one for him, his head perked to the side. He stood up and left the kitchen, heading down the hallway with his tail wagging.

"I just let you out. I'm not going out there again—it's freezing!" she called out after him.

Mel grabbed her wineglass from the counter, went back into the living room, and sat on the couch. She was tired of sitting on the cold, hard floor. She took another sip of wine as Teddy whined at the front door. "It's too cold. I'm not standing there while you play around in the leaves."

But Teddy didn't stop. Instead, he got worse, getting up on his back legs and scratching at the door.

"Fine. Fine," she said as she got up off the couch and put her wineglass on the coffee table. She slipped on her fuzzy slippers and pulled the blanket tighter around her. "I'll take you out, but I swear, if you don't do something productive I'll…I'll…I don't know what."

She opened the door—and that was as far as she got. Bennett's truck was parked in front of her house. He was just getting out and slamming the door shut.

He stopped when he saw her standing there, and just stared at her for a few seconds before he said anything. "If you never want to talk to me again, I'll completely understand and I'll leave you alone."

It took her a moment to remember how to speak. "I… I…um."

He'd been holding his breath, and his whole body showed relief that she hadn't ordered him away.

"How's Danny?"

"Awake and coherent. He's going to be okay."

"Thank God," she said, feeling a little relieved herself.

"Can I come up there and talk to you?"

She nodded, unsure of what to say or do. He quickly crossed the space to her and mounted the steps. The porch light illuminated him. He looked exhausted. It was etched all over his face, especially in those icy gray-blue eyes that she loved so much. He stopped a few feet in front of her and the distance felt like miles.

"I messed up, Mel. I screwed up so bad that I don't even know where to start. Telling you I'm sorry doesn't seem like it's enough. It won't ever be enough. Those two words can't even begin to express the remorse that I feel. I was an ass. A colossal moron." He took a step forward, but just one.

"Mel, you've changed everything for me. I didn't think it would happen. When this started between us, I'd found that list of yours, of all these mottoes you wanted to live by, of all these things you wanted to do. These adventures you wanted to have. I wanted to be a part of them. I wanted to experience them with you. And in the process of doing all of those things, and in doing none of those things, I fell in love with you." He took another step forward.

Mel couldn't breathe. She couldn't properly formulate words or remember how to move her mouth. She was dreaming. She had to be.

"I didn't think I'd ever find someone that I'd fall in love with. But it happened. And it scared me more than anything else ever had. I didn't know how to deal with it. When everything happened with the helicopter crash, when my life was torn apart, I let this overwhelming fear stop me from truly living. And then you came around, and I started living again.

"And then Danny's accident happened, and I saw what the worst-case scenario was. He's my best friend, and I didn't know what I was going to do if he didn't make it. And then I thought of you. Of losing you." He reached out and caressed her arms. "All I could think about was that I wouldn't survive. I wouldn't survive losing you like that."

"What changed?" she asked in a voice that was barely above a whisper.

"In my mind all I could think about was losing you like that, to some freak accident. But the thing is, I can't survive not being with you at all, either."

Mel wouldn't have been able to stop the tears streaming down her face if she'd tried. Bennett gently pulled her to him. He brought his hands up to her face and swiped his thumbs under her eyes.

"You have to let me in," she said as she put her hands on his chest and balled up his shirt in her fists. "You have to let me be a part of the good *and* the bad. To be a part of everything."

"I know."

"Do you really? You scared me up there. I didn't know who you were or what was going on, and it was because you wouldn't talk to me. When something happens you can't push me away. You can't say you don't want to talk about it. You have to tell me. This, *us*, has to be more than one-sided, because I can't do it this way, Bennett. I can't do it alone."

"I can't, either," he said. "Mel, if I were to write a list of everything I wanted to do, spending the rest of my life with you would be at the top. Without you in my life, none of it would mean anything. I stopped living before, but with you? With you I can't stop living. You're my big adventure. The best adventure I'll ever be on."

He leaned in and pressed his mouth to hers. His hands dropped from her face and he wrapped his arms around her, holding her flush against his body.

"I love you, Melanie," he whispered against her mouth.

"I love you, too."

He pulled back and looked into her face. "Enough to marry me?"

She froze. "Are you asking?"

In the next moment Bennett was dropping to his knee in front of her, reaching for her left hand and holding it in both of his.

"You want to know my 'I Didn't Kick the Bucket List'? I want to wake up next to you every morning, even when you're cranky and caffeine deprived. I want to come home to you every day. I want to have a handful of kids with you. I want to grow old with you. I want to spend the rest of my life with you. But the key in all of those things is *you*. I need you, Mel. I need you to be able to do *any* of it. I need you to be able to do *all* of it. So, Melanie O'Bryan, will you marry me?"

"Yes."

"Good. Now I can give you this." He reached into the pocket of his jacket and pulled out a small box. He flipped up the lid to reveal an antique ring. It was white gold with a cushion-cut diamond and two diamond filigree leaves on either side.

"It was Jocelyn's mother's ring. She gave it to me years ago so that I would have it when I found someone. I never thought in a million years I'd ever give it to anyone. But you changed everything for me." He pulled the ring out of the box. "I don't know if it's going to fit." He slipped it onto her left hand.

But it fit.

"I guess Jocelyn's mother had thin fingers, too." Bennett grinned at her.

"Get up here," she said, pulling on his hands.

Bennett complied and got up off his knees. He pulled her into his arms and kissed her hard as he walked her backward into the house, Teddy following behind them. Bennett shut the door with his foot before he locked it. Mel grabbed his hand and pulled him down the hallway to her bedroom.

She turned to him when they were in front of the bed, and she let the blanket fall from her shoulders and puddle around her feet. As Bennett held her close, Mel reached up and grabbed his face.

"Don't ever do that to me again. It hurt too much. I can't do that again, Bennett."

"Not ever. It's you and me, Mel. I've got you. I promise."

Epilogue

If We Only Live Once,
I Want to Live with You

Bennett had another dream that first night back in Mel's arms:

He was in that church again, but this time he wasn't sitting in a pew. No, this time he was standing at the front, and she was walking up the aisle toward him.

She was wearing that white dress, and the sunlight streaming in from the windows lit her up and made her radiant. Her smile was more than anything he could've imagined, and the look in her eyes almost had him falling to his knees.

She loved him, and the pure joy she felt from it was evident in everything about her. He knew the feeling because that was the exact same way he felt about her.

When she got to the end of the aisle she reached for him, and his hands instinctively reached out for her. He drew her into his arms.

Bennett woke up, this time not breathing hard, not freaking out, not on the verge of a panic attack. No, he was calm, and as he looked down at the woman in his arms, he was unbelievably happy.

He was going to marry Mel. He was going to spend the

rest of his life with her, and he was going to make every moment count.

He couldn't wait for the day that she did walk down the aisle toward him in that white dress. And on the day of Jax and Grace's wedding, Bennett might've not been all that prepared for the little preview he got.

The girls actually spent the night at Mel's house the night before the wedding. Bennett hadn't been too thrilled about a night away from Mel, especially so soon after they'd fixed things, but he'd sucked it up and dealt with it. If anything, not getting to see Mel at all before the wedding made the experience that much more real.

All of the groomsmen were stationed with Jax at the front of the church, and the bridesmaids would be walking down solo. The church was filled with people, green and white flowers decorated the end of every pew, and piano music played from the corner.

Paige was first down the aisle, then Harper. Bennett took a deep breath. Mel was next.

"I think you're more nervous than Jax is," Shep whispered under his breath to Bennett.

"I wouldn't doubt it."

And then there she was, standing at the end of the aisle. She wore a sleeveless dark green dress that streamed behind her as she walked. It was most likely the exact same dress that the other two women had worn, but Bennett hadn't really seen it on them. Nope, he only saw it on Mel.

Her curly hair was pinned up on her head, her face glowing, and her smile directed straight at him.

Bennett couldn't stop the tears that came to his eyes. The next time he stood in a church like this, Mel would be walking down the aisle to marry him.

Things Paige Morrison will never understand about Mirabelle, Florida:

Why wearing red shoes makes a girl a harlot

Why a shop would ever sell something called "buck urine"

Why everywhere she goes, she runs into sexy—and infuriating—Brendan King.

Please see the next page for an excerpt from

UNDONE,

Book #1 in the Country Roads series.

Chapter One

Short Fuses and a Whole Lot of Sparks

Bethelda Grimshaw was a snot-nosed wench. She was an evil, mean-spirited, vindictive, horrible human being.

Paige should've known. She should've known the instant she'd walked into that office and sat down. Bethelda Grimshaw had a malevolent stench radiating off her, kind of like road kill in ninety-degree weather. The interview, if it could even be called that, had been a complete waste of time.

"She didn't even read my résumé," Paige said, slamming her hand against the steering wheel as she pulled out of the parking lot of the Mirabelle Information Center.

No, Bethelda had barely even looked at said résumé before she'd set it down on the desk and leaned back in her chair, appraising Paige over her cat's-eye glasses.

"So you're the *infamous* Paige Morrison," Bethelda had said, raising a perfectly plucked, bright red eyebrow. "You've caused *quite* a stir since you came to town."

Quite a stir?

Okay, so there had been that incident down at the Piggly Wiggly, but that hadn't been Paige's fault. Betty Whitehurst might seem like a sweet, little old lady but in reality she was as blind as a bat and as vicious as a shrew. Betty drove her shopping cart like she was racing in the Indy 500, which was an accomplishment, as she barely cleared the handle. She'd slammed her cart into Paige, who in turn fell into a display of cans. Paige had been calm for all of about five seconds before Betty had started screeching at her about watching where she was going.

Paige wasn't one to take things lying down covered in cans of creamed corn, so she'd calmly explained to Betty that she *had* been watching where she was going. "Calmly" being that Paige had started yelling and the store manager had to get involved to quiet everyone down.

Yeah, Paige didn't deal very well with certain types of people. Certain types being evil, mean-spirited, vindictive, horrible human beings. And Bethelda Grimshaw was quickly climbing to the top of that list.

"As it turns out," Bethelda had said, pursing her lips in a patronizing pout, "we already filled the position. I'm afraid there was a mistake in having you come down here today."

"When?"

"Excuse me?" Bethelda had asked, her eyes sparkling with glee.

"When did you fill the position?" Paige had repeated, trying to stay calm.

"Last week."

Really? So the phone call Paige had gotten that morning to confirm the time of the interview had been a mistake?

This was the eleventh job interview she'd gone on in the last two months. And it had most definitely been the worst. It hadn't even been an interview. She'd been set up; she just didn't understand why. But she hadn't been about to ask that question out loud. So instead of flying off the handle and losing the last bit of restraint she had, Paige had calmly gotten up from the chair and left without making a scene. The whole thing was a freaking joke, which fit perfectly for the current theme of Paige's life.

Six months ago, Paige had been living in Philadelphia. She'd had a good job in the art department of an advertising agency. She'd shared a tiny two-bedroom apartment above a coffee shop with her best friend, Abby Fields. And she'd had Dylan, a man who she'd been very much in love with.

And then the rug got pulled out from under her and she'd fallen flat on her ass.

First off, Abby got a job at an up-and-coming PR firm. Which was good news, and Paige had been very excited for her, except the job was in Washington, DC, which Paige was not excited about. Then, before Paige could find a new room-mate, she'd lost her job. The advertising agency was bought out and she was in the first round of cuts. Without a job, she couldn't renew her lease, and was therefore homeless. So she'd moved in with Dylan. It was always supposed to be a temporary thing, just until Paige could find another job and get on her feet again.

But it never happened.

Paige had tried for two months and found nothing, and then the real bomb hit. She was either blind or just distracted by everything else that was going on, but either way, she never saw it coming.

Paige had been with Dylan for about a year and she'd really thought he'd been the one. Okay, he tended to be a bit of a snob when it came to certain things. For example, wine. Oh was he ever a wine snob, rather obnoxious about it really. He would always swirl it around in his glass, take a sip, sniff, and then take another loud sip, smacking his lips together.

He was also a snob about books. Paige enjoyed reading the classics, but she also liked reading romance, mystery, and fantasy. Whenever she would curl up with one of her books, Dylan tended to give her a rather patronizing look and shake his head.

"Reading fluff again I see," he would always say.

Yeah, she didn't miss *that* at all. Or the way he would roll his eyes when she and Abby would quote movies and TV shows to each other. Or how he'd never liked her music and flat-out refused to dance with her. Which had always been frustrating because Paige loved to dance. But despite all of that, she'd loved him. Loved the way he would run his fingers through his hair when he was distracted, loved his big goofy grin, and loved the way his glasses would slide down his nose.

But the thing was, he hadn't loved her.

One night, he'd come back to his apartment and sat Paige down on the couch. Looking back on it, she'd been an idiot, because there was a small part of her that thought he was actually about to propose.

"Paige," he'd said, sitting down on the coffee table and grabbing her hands. "I know that this was supposed to be a temporary thing, but weeks have turned into months. Living with you has brought a lot of things to light."

It was wrong, everything about that moment was *all wrong*. She could tell by the look in his eyes, by the tone of his voice, by the way he said *Paige* and *light*. In that moment she'd known exactly where he was going, and it wasn't anywhere with her. He wasn't proposing. He was breaking up with her.

She'd pulled her hands out of his and shrank back into the couch.

"This," he'd said, gesturing between the two of them, "was never going to go further than where we are right now."

And that was the part where her ears had started ringing.

"At one point I thought I might love you, but I've realized I'm not *in* love with you," he'd said, shaking his head. "I feel like you've thought this was going to go further, but the truth is I'm never going to marry you. Paige, you're not the one. I'm tired of pretending. I'm tired of putting in the effort for a relationship that isn't going anywhere else. It's not worth it to me."

"You mean I'm not worth it," she'd said, shocked.

"Paige, you deserve to be with someone who wants to make the effort, and I deserve to be with someone who I'm willing to make the effort for. It's better that we end this now, instead of delaying the inevitable."

He'd made it sound like he was doing her a favor, like he had her best interests at heart.

But all she'd heard was *You're not worth it* and *I'm not in love with you*. And those were the words that kept repeating in her head, over and over and over again.

Dylan had told her he was going to go stay with one of his friends for the week. She'd told him she'd be out before the end of the next day. She'd spent the entire night packing up her stuff. Well, packing and crying and drinking two entire bottles of the prick's wine.

Paige didn't have a lot of stuff. Most of the furniture from her and Abby's apartment had been Abby's. Everything that Paige owned had fit into the back of her Jeep and the U-Haul trailer that she'd rented the first thing the following morning. She'd loaded up and gotten out of there before four o'clock in the afternoon.

She'd stayed the night in a hotel room just outside of Philadelphia, where she'd promptly passed out. She'd been exhausted after her marathon packing, which was good because it was harder for a person to feel beyond pathetic in her sleep. No, that was what the following eighteen-hour drive had been reserved for.

Jobless, homeless, and brokenhearted, Paige had nowhere else to go but home to her parents. The problem was, there was no *home* anymore. The house in Philadelphia that Paige had grown up in was no longer her parents'. They'd sold it and retired to a little town in the South.

Mirabelle, Florida: population five thousand.

There was roughly the same amount of people in the six hundred square miles of Mirabelle as there were in half a square mile of Philadelphia. Well, unless the mosquitoes were counted as residents.

People who thought that Florida was all sunshine and sand were sorely mistaken. It did have its fair share of beautiful beaches. The entire southeast side of Mirabelle was the Gulf of Mexico. But about half of the town was made up of water. And all of that water, combined with the humidity that plagued the area, created the perfect breeding ground for mosquitoes. Otherwise known as tiny, blood-sucking villains that loved to bite the crap out of Paige's legs.

Paige had visited her parents a couple of times over the last couple of years, but she'd never been in love with Mirabelle like her parents were. And she still wasn't. She'd spent a month moping around her parents' house. Again, she was pathetic enough to believe that maybe, just maybe, Dylan would call her and tell her that he'd been wrong. That he missed her. That he loved her.

He never called, and Paige realized he was never going to. That was when Paige resigned herself to the fact that she had to move on with her life. So she'd started looking for a job.

Which had proved to be highly unsuccessful.

Paige had been living in Mirabelle for three months now. Three long miserable months where nothing had gone right. Not one single thing.

And as that delightful thought crossed her mind, she noticed that her engine was smoking. Great white plumes of steam escaped from the hood of her Jeep Cherokee.

"You've got to be kidding me," she said as she pulled off to the side of the road and turned the engine off. "Fan-freaking-tastic."

Paige grabbed her purse and started digging around in the infinite abyss, searching for her cell phone. She sifted through old receipts, a paperback book, her wallet, lip gloss, a nail file, gum...*ah*, cell phone. She pressed speed dial for her father. She held the phone against her ear while she leaned over and searched for her shoes that she'd thrown on the floor of the passenger side. As her hand closed over one of her black wedges, the phone beeped in her ear and disconnected. She sat up and held her phone out, staring at the display screen in disbelief.

No service.

"This has to be some sick, twisted joke," she said, banging her head down on the steering wheel. No service on her cell phone shouldn't have been that surprising; there were plenty of dead zones around Mirabelle. Apparently there was a lack of cell phone towers in this little piece of purgatory.

Paige resigned herself to the fact that she was going to have to walk to find civilization, or at least a bar of service on her cell phone. She went in search of her other wedge, locating it under the passenger seat.

The air conditioner had been off for less than two minutes, and it was already starting to warm up inside the Jeep. It was going to be a long, hot walk. Paige grabbed a hair tie from the gearshift, put her long brown hair up into a messy bun, and opened the door to the sweltering heat.

I hate *this godforsaken place.*

Paige missed Philadelphia. She missed her friends, her apartment with its rafters and squeaky floors. She missed having a job, missed having a paycheck, missed buying shoes. And even though she hated it, she still missed Dylan. Missed his dark shaggy hair, and the way he would nibble on her lower lip when they kissed. She even missed his humming when he cooked.

She shook her head and snapped back to the present. She might as well focus on the task at hand and stop thinking about what was no longer her life.

Paige walked for twenty minutes down the road to nowhere, not a single car passing her. By the time Paige got to Skeeter's Bait, Tackle, Guns, and Gas, she was sweating like nobody's business, her dress was sticking to her everywhere, and her feet were killing her. She had a nice blister on the back of her left heel.

She pushed the door open and was greeted with the smell of fish mixed with bleach, making her stomach turn. At least the air conditioner was cranked to full blast. There was a huge stuffed turkey sitting on the counter. The fleshy red thing on its neck looked like the stuff nightmares were made of, and the wall behind the register was covered in mounted fish. She really didn't get the whole "dead animal as a trophy" motif that the South had going on.

There was a display on the counter that had tiny little bottles that looked like energy drinks.

NEW AND IMPROVED SCENT. GREAT FOR ATTRACTING THE PERFECT GAME.

She picked up one of the tiny bottles and looked at it. It was doe urine.

She took a closer look at the display. They apparently also had the buck urine variety. She looked at the bottle in her hand, trying to grasp why people would cover themselves in this stuff. Was hunting really worth smelling like an animal's pee?

"Can I help you?"

The voice startled Paige and she looked up into the face of a very large balding man, his apron covered in God only knew what. She dropped the tiny bottle she had in her hand.

It fell to the ground. The cap smashed on the tile floor and liquid poured out everywhere.

It took a total of three seconds for the smell to punch her in the nose. It had to be the most fowl scent she'd ever inhaled.

Oh crap. Oh crap, oh crap, oh crap.

She was just stellar at first impressions these days.

"I'm so sorry," she said, trying not to gag. She took a step back from the offending puddle and looked up at the man.

His arms were folded across his chest and he frowned at her, saying nothing.

"Do you, uh, have something I can clean this up with?" she asked nervously.

"You're not from around here," he said, looking at her with his deadpan stare. It wasn't a question. It was a statement, one that she got whenever she met someone new. One that she was so sick and tired of she could scream. Yeah, all of the remorse she'd felt over spilling that bottle drained from her.

In Philadelphia, Paige's bohemian style was normal, but in Mirabelle her big carrings, multiple rings, and loud clothing tended to get her noticed. Her parents' neighbor, Mrs. Forns, thought that Paige was trouble, which she complained about on an almost daily basis.

"You know that marijuana is still illegal," Mrs. Forns had said the other night, standing on her parents' porch, and lecturing Paige's mother. "And I won't hesitate to call the authorities if I see your hippie daughter growing anything suspicious or doing any other illegal activities."

Denise Morrison, ever the queen of politeness, had just smiled. "You have nothing to be concerned about."

"But she's doing *something* in that shed of yours in the backyard."

The *something* that Paige did in the shed was paint. She'd converted it into her art studio, complete with ceiling fan.

"Don't worry, Mrs. Forns," Paige had said, sticking her head over her mother's shoulder. "I'll wait to have my orgies on your bingo nights. Is that on Tuesdays or Wednesdays?"

"Paige!" Denise had said as she'd shoved Paige back into the house and closed the door in her face.

Five minutes later, Denise had come into the kitchen shaking her head.

"Really, Paige? You had to tell her that you're having *orgies* in the backyard?"

Paige's father, Trevor Morrison, chuckled as he went through the mail at his desk.

"You need to control your temper and that smart mouth of yours," Denise had said.

"You know what you should start doing?" Trevor said, looking up with a big grin. "You should grow oregano in pots on the window sill and then throw little dime bags into her yard."

"Trevor, don't encourage her harassing that woman. Paige, she's a little bit older, very set in her ways, and a tad bit nosey."

"She needs to learn to keep her nose on her side of the fence," Paige had said.

"Don't let her bother you."

"That's easier said than done."

"Well then, maybe you should practice holding your tongue."

"Yes, mother, I'll get right on that."

So, as Paige stared at the massive man in front of her, whom she assumed to be Skeeter, she pursed her lips and held back the smart-ass retort that was on the tip of her tongue.

Be polite, she heard her mother's voice in her head say.

You just spilled animal pee all over his store. And you need to use his phone.

"No," Paige said, pushing her big sunglasses up her nose and into her hair. "My car broke down and I don't have any cell phone service. I was wondering if I could use your phone to call a tow truck."

"I'd call King's if I were you. They're the best," he said as he ripped a piece of receipt paper off the cash register and grabbed a pen with a broken plastic spoon taped to the top. He wrote something down and pushed the paper across the counter.

"Thank you. I can clean that up first," she said, pointing to the floor.

"I got it. I'd hate for you to get those hands of yours dirty," he said, moving the phone to her side of the counter.

She just couldn't win.

* * *

Brendan King leaned against the front bumper of Mr. Thame's minivan. He was switching out the old belt and replacing it with a new one when his grandfather stuck his head out of the office.

"Brendan," Oliver King said. "A car broke down on Buckland Road. It's Paige Morrison, Trevor and Denise Morrison's daughter. She said the engine was smoking. She had to walk to Skeeter's to use the phone. I told her you'd pick her up so she didn't have to walk back."

Oliver King didn't look his seventy years. His salt-and-pepper hair was still thick and growing only on the top of his head, and not out of his ears. He had a bit of a belly, but he'd had that for the last twenty years and it wasn't going anywhere. He'd opened King's Auto forty-three years ago, when he was twenty-seven. Now, he mainly worked behind the front counter, due to the arthritis in his hands and back. But it was a good thing because King's Auto was one of only a handful of auto shops in the county. They were always busy, so they needed a constant presence running things out of the shop.

Including Brendan and his grandfather, there were four full-time mechanics and two part-time kids who were still in high school and who worked in the garage. Part of the service that King's provided was towing, and Brendan was the man on duty on Mondays. And oh was he ever so happy he was on duty today.

Paige Morrison was the new girl in town. Her parents had moved down from Pennsylvania when they'd retired about two years ago, and Paige had moved in with them three months ago. Brendan had yet to meet her but he'd most definitely seen her. You couldn't really miss her as she jogged around town, with her very long legs, in a wide variety of the brightest and shortest shorts he'd ever seen in his life. His favorite pair had by far been the hot-pink pair, but the zebra-print ones came in a very close second.

He'd also heard about her. People had a lot to say about her more-than-*interesting* style. It was rumored that she had a bit of a temper and a pretty mouth that said whatever it wanted. Not that Brendan took a lot of stock in gossip. He'd wait to reserve his own judgment.

"Got it," Brendan said, pulling his gloves off and sticking them in his back pocket. "Tell Randall this still needs new spark plugs," he said, pointing to the minivan and walking into the office.

"I will." Oliver nodded and handed Brendan the keys to the tow truck.

Brendan grabbed two waters from the mini-fridge and his sunglasses from the desk and headed off into the scorching heat. It was a hot one, ninety-eight degrees, but the humidity made it feel like one hundred and three. He flipped his baseball cap so that the bill would actually give him some cover from the August sun and when he got into the tow truck he cranked the air as high as it would go.

It took him about fifteen minutes to get to Skeeter's and when he pulled up into the gravel parking lot, the door to the little shop opened and Brendan couldn't help but smile.

Paige Morrison's mile-long legs were shooting out of the sexiest shoes he'd ever seen. She was also wearing a flowing yellow dress that didn't really cover her amazing legs but did hug her chest and waist, and besides the two skinny straps at her shoulders, her arms were completely bare. Massive sunglasses covered her eyes and her dark brown hair was piled on top of her head.

There was no doubt about it; she was beautiful all right.

Brendan put the truck in park and hopped out.

"Ms. Morrison?" he asked even though he already knew who she was.

"Paige," she corrected, stopping in front of him. She was probably five foot ten or so, but her shoes added about three inches, making her just as tall as him. If he weren't wearing his work boots she would've been taller than him.

"I'm Brendan King," he said, sticking his hand out to shake hers. Her hand was soft and warm. He liked how it felt in his. He also liked the freckles that were sprinkled across her high cheekbones and straight, pert nose.

"I'm about a mile up the road," she said, letting go of his hand and pointing in the opposite direction that he'd come.

"Not the most sensible walking shoes," he said, eyeing her feet. The toes that peeked out of her shoes were bright red, and a thin band of silver wrapped around the second toe on her right foot. He looked back up to see her arched eyebrows come together for a second before she took a deep breath.

"Thanks for the observation," she said, walking past him and heading for the passenger door.

Well, this was going to be fun.

* * *

Stupid jerk.

Not the most sensible walking shoes, Paige repeated in her head.

Well, no shit, Sherlock.

Paige sat in the cab of Brendan's tow truck, trying to keep her temper in check. Her feet were killing her, and she really wanted to kick off her shoes. But she couldn't do that in front of him because then he would *know* that her feet were killing her.

"I'm guessing the orange Jeep is yours?" Brendan asked as it came into view.

"Another outstanding observation," she mumbled under her breath.

"I'm sorry?"

"Yes, it's mine," she said, trying to hide her sarcasm.

"Well, at least the engine isn't smoking anymore," he said as he pulled in behind it and jumped out of the truck. Paige grabbed her keys from her purse and followed, closing the door behind her.

He stopped behind the back of her Jeep for a moment, studying the half a dozen stickers that covered her bumper and part of her back window.

She had one that said MAKE ART NOT WAR in big blue letters, another said LOVE with a peace sign in the *O*. There was also a sea turtle, an owl with reading glasses, the Cat in the Hat, and her favorite that said I LOVE BIG BOOKS AND I CANNOT LIE.

He shook his head and laughed, walking to the front of the Jeep.

"What's so funny?" she asked, catching up to his long stride and standing next to him.

"Keys?" he asked, holding out his hand.

She put them in his palm but didn't let go.

"What's so funny?" she repeated.

"Just that you're clearly not from around here." He smiled, closing his hand over hers.

Brendan had a Southern accent, not nearly as thick as some of the other people's in town, and a wide cocky smile that she really hated, but only because she kind of liked it. She also kind of liked the five o'clock shadow that covered his square jaw. She couldn't see anything above his chiseled nose, as half of his face was covered by his sunglasses and the shadow from his grease-stained baseball cap, but she could tell his smile reached all the way up to his eyes.

He was most definitely physically fit, filling out his shirt and pants with wide biceps and thighs. His navy blue button-up shirt had short sleeves, showing off his tanned arms that were covered in tiny blond hairs.

God, he was attractive. But he was also pissing her off.

"I am so sick of everyone saying that," she said, ripping her hand out of his. "Is it such a bad thing to not be from around here?"

"No," he said, his mouth quirking. "It's just very obvious that you're not."

"Would I fit in more if I had a bumper sticker that said MY OTHER CAR IS A TRACTOR OR ONE THAT SAID IF YOU'RE NOT CONSERVATIVE YOU JUST AREN'T WORTH IT, or what about WHO NEEDS LITERACY WHEN YOU CAN SHOOT THINGS? What if I had a gun rack mounted on the back window or if I used buck piss as perfume to attract a husband? Would those things make me fit in?" she finished, folding her arms across her chest.

"No, I'd say you could start with not being so judgmental though," he said with a sarcastic smirk.

"Excuse me?"

"Ma'am, you just called everyone around here gun-toting,

illiterate rednecks who like to participate in bestiality. Insulting people really isn't a way to fit in," he said, shaking his head. "I would also refrain from spreading your liberal views to the masses, as politics are a bit of a hot-button topic around here. And if you want to attract a husband, you should stick with wearing doe urine, because that attracts only males. The buck urine attracts both males and females." He stopped and looked her up and down with a slow smile. "But maybe you're into that sort of thing."

"Yeah, well, everyone in this town thinks that I'm an amoral, promiscuous pothead. And you," she said, shoving her finger into his chest, "aren't any better. People make snap judgments about me before I even open my mouth. And just so you know, *I'm not even a liberal*," she screamed as she jabbed her finger into his chest a couple of times. She took a deep breath and stepped back, composing herself. "So maybe I would be *nice* if people would be just a little bit *nice* to me."

"I'm quite capable of being nice to people who deserve it. Can I look at your car now, or would you like to yell at me some more?"

"Be my guest," she said, glaring at him as she moved out of his way.

He unlocked the Jeep and popped the hood. As he moved to the front he pulled off his baseball cap and wiped the top of his head with his hand. Paige glimpsed his short, dirty-blond hair before he put the hat on backward. As he moved around in her engine his shirt pulled tight across his back and shoulders. He twisted off the cap to something and stuck it in his pocket. Then he walked back to his truck and grabbed a jug from a metal box on the side. He came back and poured the liquid into something in the engine and after a few seconds it gushed out of the bottom.

"Your radiator is cracked," he said, grabbing the cap out

of his pocket and screwing it back on. "I'm going to have to tow this back to the shop to replace it."

"How much?"

"For everything? We're looking at four maybe five hundred."

"Just perfect," she mumbled.

"Would you like a ride? Or were you planning on showing those shoes more of the countryside?"

"I'll take the ride."

* * *

Paige was quiet the whole time Brendan loaded her Jeep onto the truck. Her arms were folded under her perfect breasts and she stared at him with her full lips bunched in a scowl. Even pissed off she was stunning, and God, that mouth of hers. He really wanted to see it with an actual smile on it. He was pretty sure it would knock him on his ass.

Speaking of asses, seeing her smile probably wasn't likely at the moment. True, he had purposefully egged her on, but he couldn't resist going off on her when she'd let loose her colorful interpretations of the people from the area. A lot of them were true, but there was a difference between making fun of your own people and having an outsider make fun of them. But still, according to her, the people around here hadn't exactly been nice to her.

Twenty minutes later, with Paige's Jeep on the back of the tow truck, they were on their way to the shop. Brendan glanced over at her as he drove. She was looking out the window with her back to him. Her shoulders were stiff and she looked like she'd probably had enough stress before her car had decided to die on her.

Brendan looked back at the road and cleared his throat.

"I'm sorry about what I said back there."

Out of the corner of his eye he saw her shift in her seat and he could feel her eyes on him.

"Thank you. I should have kept my mouth shut, too. I just haven't had the best day."

"Why?" he asked, glancing over at her again.

Her body was angled toward him, but her arms were still folded across her chest like a shield. He couldn't help but glance down and see that her dress was slowly riding up her thighs. She had nice thighs, soft but strong. They would be good for... well, a lot of things.

He quickly looked back at the road, thankful he was wearing sunglasses.

"I've been trying to get a job. Today I had an interview, except it wasn't much of an interview."

"What was it?" he asked.

"A setup."

"A setup for what?"

"That *is* the question," she said bitterly.

"Huh?" he asked, looking at her again.

"I'm assuming you know who Bethelda Grimshaw is?"

Brendan's blood pressure had a tendency to rise at the mere mention of that name. Knowing that Bethelda had a part in Paige's current mood had Brendan's temper flaring instantly.

"What did she do?" he asked darkly.

Paige's eyebrows raised a fraction at his tone. She stared at him for a second before she answered. "There was a job opening at the Mirabelle Information Center to take pictures for the brochures and the local businesses for their Web site. They filled the position last week, something that Mrs. Grimshaw failed to mention when she called this morning to confirm my interview."

"She's looking for her next story."

"What?"

"Bethelda Grimshaw is Mirabelle's resident gossip," Brendan said harshly as he looked back to the road. "She got fired from the newspaper a couple of years ago because of the trash she wrote. Now she has a blog to spread her crap around."

"And she wants to write about me? Why?"

"I can think of a few reasons."

"What's that supposed to mean?" she asked, her voice going up an octave or two.

"Your ability to fly off the handle. Did you give her something to write about?" he asked, raising an eyebrow as he spared a glance at her.

"No," she said, bunching her full lips together. "I saved my freak-out for you."

"I deserved it. I wasn't exactly nice to you," Brendan said, shifting his hands down the steering wheel.

"You were a jerk."

Brendan came to a stop at a stop sign and turned completly in his seat to face Paige. Her eyebrows rose high over her sunglasses and she held her breath.

"I was, and I'm sorry," he said, putting every ounce of sincerity into his words.

"It's…I forgive you," she said softly and nodded her head.

Brendan turned back to the intersection and made a right. Paige was silent for a few moments, but he could feel her gaze on him as if she wanted to say something.

"What?"

"Why does buck urine attract males and females?"

Brendan couldn't help but smile.

"Bucks like to fight each other," he said, looking at her.

"Oh." She nodded and leaned back in her seat staring out the front window.

"You thirsty?" Brendan asked as he grabbed one of the waters in the cup holder and held it out to her.

"Yes, thank you," she said, grabbing it and downing half of the bottle.

"Who were the other interviews with?" Brendan asked, grabbing the other bottle for himself. He twisted the cap off and threw it into the cup holder.

"Landingham Printing and Design. Mrs. Landingham said I wouldn't be a good fit. Which is completely false because the program they use is one that I've used before."

Now he couldn't help but laugh.

"Uh, Paige, I can tell you right now why you didn't get that job. Mrs. Landingham didn't want you around Mr. Landingham."

"What?" she said, sitting up in her seat again. "What did she think I was going to do, steal her husband? I don't make plays on married men. Or men in their forties for that matter."

"Did you wear something like what you're wearing now to the interview?" he asked, looking at her and taking another eyeful of those long legs.

"I wore a black blazer with this. It's just so hot outside that I took it off."

"Maybe you should try wearing pants next time, and flats," he said before he took a sip of water.

"What's wrong with this dress?" she asked, looking down at herself. "It isn't that short."

"Sweetheart, with those legs, anything looks short."

"Don't call me sweetheart. And it isn't my fault I'm tall."

"No, it isn't, but people think the way they think."

"So Southern hospitality only goes so far when people think you're a whore."

"Hey, I didn't say that. I was just saying that your legs are long without those shoes that you're currently wearing. With them, you're pretty damn intimidating."

"Let's stop talking about my legs."

"Fine." He shrugged, looking back to the road. "But it is a rather visually stimulating conversation."

"Oh no. You are *not* allowed to flirt with me."

"Why not?"

"You were mean to me. I do *not* flirt with mean men."

"I can be nice," he said, turning to her and giving her a big smile.

"Stop it," she said, raising her eyebrows above her glasses in warning. "I mean it."

"So what about some of the other interviews? Who were they with?"

"Lindy's Frame Shop, that art gallery over on the beach—"

"Avenue Ocean?"

"Yeah, that one. And I also went to Picture Perfect. They all said I wasn't a good fit for one reason or another," she said dejected.

"Look, I'm really not one to get involved in town gossip. I've been on the receiving end my fair share of times and it isn't fun. But this is a small town, and everybody knows one another's business. Since you're new, you have no idea. Cynthia Bowers at Picture Perfect would've never hired you. Her husband has monogamy issues. The owner of Avenue Ocean, Mindy Trist, doesn't like anyone that's competition."

"Competition?"

Mindy Trist was a man-eater. Brendan knew this to be a fact because Mindy had been trying to get into his bed for years. He wasn't even remotely interested.

"You're prettier than she is."

Understatement of the year.

Paige was suddenly silent on her side of the truck.

"And as for Hurst and Marlene Lindy," Brendan continued, "they, uh, tend to be a little more conservative."

"Look," she said, snapping out of her silence.

Brendan couldn't help himself, her sudden burst of vehemence made him look at her again. If he kept this up he was going to drive into a ditch.

"I know I might appear to be some free-spirited hippie, but I'm really not. I'm moderate when it comes to politics," she said, holding up one finger. "I eat meat like it's nobody's business." Two fingers. "And I've never done drugs in my life." Three fingers.

"You don't have to convince me," he said, shaking his head. "So I'm sensing a pattern here with all of these jobs. Are you a photographer?"

"Yes, but I do graphic design and I paint."

"So a woman of many talents."

"I don't know about that," she said, shaking her head.

"Oh, I'm sure you have a lot of talent. It's probably proportional to the length of your legs."

"What did I tell you about flirting?" she asked seriously, but betrayed herself when the corner of her mouth quirked up.

"Look, Paige, don't let it get to you. Not everyone is all bad."

"So I've just been fortunate enough to meet everyone who's mean."

"You've met me."

"Yeah, well, the jury's still out on you."

"Then I guess I'll have to prove myself."

"I guess so," she said, leaning back in her seat. Her arms now rested in her lap, her shield coming down a little.

"I have a question," Brendan said, slowing down at another stop sign. "If you eat meat, why do you have such a problem with hunting?"

"It just seems a little barbaric. Hiding out in the woods to shoot Bambi and then mounting his head on a wall."

"Let me give you two scenarios."

"Okay."

"In scenario one, we have Bessie the cow. Bessie was born in a stall, taken away from her mother shortly after birth where she was moved to a pasture for a couple of years, all the while being injected with hormones and then shoved into a semi truck where she was shipped off to be slaughtered. And I don't think that you even want me to get started on that process.

"In scenario two, we have Bambi. Bambi was born in the wilderness and wasn't taken away from his mother. He then found a mate, had babies, and one day was killed. He never saw it coming. Not only is Bambi's meat hormone free, but he also lived a happy life in the wild, with no fences.

"Now you tell me, which scenario sounds better: Being raised to be slaughtered, or living free where you might or might not be killed."

She was silent for a few moments before she sighed.

"Fine, you win. The second sounds better."

"Yeah, that's what I thought," Brendan said as he pulled into the parking lot of King's Auto. "How are you getting home?" he asked as he put the truck into park.

"I called my dad after I called you. He's here actually," she said, pointing to a black Chevy Impala.

They both got out of the truck and headed toward the auto shop. Brendan held the door open for Paige, shoving his sunglasses into his shirt pocket. His grandfather and a man who Brendan recognized as Paige's father stood up from their chairs as Brendan and Paige walked in.

Trevor Morrison was a tall man, maybe six foot four or six foot five. He had light reddish-brown wispy hair on his head and large glasses perched on his nose. And like his daughter, his face and arms were covered in freckles.

"Hi, Daddy," Paige said, pushing her glasses up her nose and into her hair.

Brendan immediately noticed the change in her voice. Her cautious demeanor vanished and her shoulders relaxed. He'd caught a glimpse of this in the truck, but not to this extent.

"Mr. Morrison," Brendan said, taking a step forward and sticking his hand out.

Trevor grabbed Brendan's hand firmly. "Brendan," he said, giving him a warm smile and nodding his head. Trevor let go of Brendan's hand and turned to his daughter. "Paige, this is Oliver King," he said, gesturing to Brendan's grandfather, who was standing behind his desk. "Oliver, this is my daughter, Paige."

"I haven't had the pleasure," Oliver said, moving out from behind his desk and sticking out his hand.

Paige moved forward past Brendan, her arm brushing his as she passed.

"It's nice to meet you, sir," she said, grabbing Oliver's hand.

Oliver nodded as he let go of Paige's hand and looked up at Brendan. "So what happened?"

Paige turned to look at Brendan too. It was the first time he'd gotten a full look at her face without her sunglasses on. She had long dark eyelashes that framed her large gray irises. It took him a second to remember how to speak. He cleared his throat and looked past her to the other two men.

"It's the radiator. I'm going to have to order a new one, so it's going to take a few days."

"That's fine," she said, shrugging her shoulders. "It's not like I have anywhere to go."

Trevor's face fell. "The interview didn't go well?"

"Nope," Paige said, shaking her head. The tension in her shoulders came back but she tried to mask it by pasting a smile on her face. He desperately wanted to see a genuine, full-on smile from her.

"Things haven't exactly gone Paige's way since she moved here," Trevor said.

"Oh, I think my bad luck started long before I moved here," she said, folding her arms across her chest. Every time she did that, it pushed her breasts up and it took everything in Brendan not to stare.

"I don't think it was Paige's fault," Brendan said and everyone turned to look at him. "It was with Bethelda Grimshaw," he said to Oliver.

"Oh," Oliver said, shaking his head ruefully. "Don't let anything she says get to you. She's a horrible hag."

Paige laughed and the sound of it did funny things to Brendan's stomach.

"Told you," Brendan said, looking at her. Paige turned to him, a small smile lingering on her lips and in her eyes.

God, she was beautiful.

"Things will turn around," Oliver said. "We'll call you with an estimate before we do anything to your car."

They said their good-byes and as Paige walked out with her father she gave Brendan one last look, her lips quirking up slightly before she shook her head and walked out the door.

"I don't believe any of that nonsense people are saying about her," Oliver said as they both watched Paige and her dad walk out. "She's lovely."

Lovely? Yeah, that wasn't exactly the word Brendan would have used to describe her.

Hot? Yes. *Fiery?* Absolutely.

"Yeah, she's something all right."

"Oh, don't tell me you aren't a fan of hers. Son, you barely took your eyes off her."

"I'm not denying she's beautiful." How could he? "I bet she's a handful though and she's got a temper on her, along with a smart mouth." But he sure did like that smart mouth.

"That's a bit of the pot calling the kettle black," Oliver said, raising one bushy eyebrow. "If all of her experiences in this town have been similar to what Bethelda dishes out, I'm not surprised she's turned on the defense. You know what it's like to be the center of less than unsavory gossip in this town. To have a lot of the people turn their backs on you and turn you into a pariah," Oliver said, giving Brendan a knowing look.

"I know," Brendan conceded. "She deserves a break."

"You should help her find a job."

"With who?"

"You'll think of something," Oliver said, patting Brendan on the shoulder before going back to his desk. "You always do."

Jax has been protecting his best friend's
kid sister, Grace, since they were young.

Now that they're all grown up,
they insist there's nothing between them—
until one night changes everything...

Please see the next page for an excerpt of

UNDENIABLE

Book #2 in the Country Roads Series.

Prologue

The Princess

At six years old there were certain things Grace King didn't understand. She didn't understand where babies came from, how birds flew way up high in the sky, or where her father was. Grace had never met her dad; she didn't know what he looked like, she didn't even know his name, and for some reason this fact fascinated many people in Mirabelle.

"What's a girl bastard?"

Grace looked up from the picture she was coloring to see Hoyt Reynolds and Judson Coker looming over the other side of the picnic table where she was sitting.

Every day after the bell rang, Grace would wait outside on the playground for her brother Brendan to come and get her, and they'd walk home together. Today, Brendan was running a little late.

"I don't know." Judson smirked. "I think bastard works for boys and girls."

"Yeah." Hoyt shrugged. "Trash is trash."

Brendan was always telling Grace to ignore bullies, advice he had a problem following himself. Half the time she didn't even know what they were saying. Today was no different. She had no idea what a bastard was, but she was pretty sure it wasn't anything nice.

Grace looked back down to her picture and started coloring the crown of the princess. She grabbed her pink crayon from the pile she'd dumped out on the table, and just before she started coloring the dress the picture disappeared out from under her hands.

"Hey," she protested, looking back up at the boys, "give that back."

"No, I don't think I will," Judson said before he slowly started to rip the picture.

"Stop it," Grace said, swinging her legs over the bench and getting quickly to her feet. She ran to the other side of the table and stood in front of Judson. "Give it back to me."

"Make me," he said, holding the picture up high over her head as he ripped it cleanly in half.

Grace took a step forward and stomped down hard on his foot.

"You little bitch!" Judson screamed, hopping up and down on his uninjured foot.

Grace had one second of satisfaction before she found herself sprawled out on her back, the wind knocked out of her.

"Don't ever touch her again!"

Grace looked up just in time to see a tall, freckled, red-haired boy punch Hoyt in the face. It was Jax, one of Brendan's best friends, who had come to her rescue. And boy did Jax know what he was doing, because Hoyt fell back onto his butt hard.

"And if you ever call her that word again, you'll get a lot more than a punch in the face, you stupid little scum bag," Jax said as he put himself in between Grace and Judson. "Now get out of here."

"I'm going to tell my father about this," Hoyt said. This was a legitimate threat as Hoyt's father was the principal.

"You do that." Jax shrugged.

Apparently the two eight-year-olds didn't have anything else to say and they didn't want to take their chances against a big bad eleven-year-old, because they scrambled away and ran around the side of the building and out of sight.

"You okay?" Jax asked, turning around to Grace.

It was then that Grace realized the back of her dress was covered in mud and her palms were scraped and bleeding.

"No," she sniffed before she started to bawl.

"Oh, Grace," Jax said, grabbing her under her arms and pulling her to her feet. "Come here." He pulled her into his chest and rubbed her back. "It's okay, Gracie."

She looked up at him and bit her trembling lip. "They called me names." She hiccupped.

"They weren't true," he said, looking down at her.

"What's a bastard, Jax?"

Jax's hand stilled and his nose flared. "Nothing you need to worry about," he said. "Grace, sometimes dads aren't all they're cracked up to be."

She nodded once before she buried her head back in his chest. By the time she'd cried herself out, Jax's shirt was covered in her tears. She took a step back from him and wiped her fingers underneath her eyes. Jax reached down and grabbed the two halves of her picture from the ground.

"We can tape this back together," he said, looking down at the paper. He studied it for a second before he looked back to her. "This is what you are, Grace. A princess. Don't let anyone tell you different. You understand?" he asked, lightly tugging on her blond ponytail.

"Yes." She nodded.

"All right," he said, handing the papers back to her. "Get your stuff together and we'll go wait for Brendan."

"Where is he?" Grace asked as she gathered her crayons and put them back into the box.

"He got into trouble with Principal Reynolds again."

Grace looked up at Jax and frowned. She really didn't like the Reynolds family. Principal Reynolds wasn't any better than his son.

"No frowning, Princess. Let's go," Jax said, holding out his hand for her.

Grace shoved her crayons and drawing into her bag. She grabbed Jax's outstretched hand and let him lead her away.

Chapter One

The Protector

The nightmares felt so real. They always started off the exact same way as the accident had, but then they morphed into something so much worse, something that haunted Jax even when he was awake.

As a deputy sheriff for Atticus County, Jaxson Anderson was no stranger to being the first person to arrive at the scene of an accident. What he wasn't used to was being the first to an accident that involved two people he cared about. That day it had been Grace and Paige King. Grace was the little sister of Brendan King, one of Jax's best friends. Paige was Brendan's wife.

It had happened over six months ago. Violent storms had raged across Mirabelle for days, and the rains had flooded the river that ran through the town, making the current swift and deadly. By some miracle Jax and been driving right behind Paige and Grace. Jax and his friend Bennett Hart had watched as the SUV the girls were in swerved off the road, crashed through a barrier, and disappeared down to Whiskey River. The only thing that had stopped the car from being swept under the water was a tree growing out of the bank. The tree was barely strong enough to hold the car back.

That day Jax had experienced a panic like no other. He'd gone into the river desperate to pull them out. And that was when the second miracle of the day happened. Brendan, along with Nathanial Shepherd and Baxter McCoy had shown up. It took the efforts of all five men to pull the girls out of the car before it was swept under the water. It had been just a matter of seconds of getting them out before the tree gave way.

Jax went over those moments, over and over again, replaying everything from what he'd said to what he'd done. The one thing he was absolutely sure about was that getting those girls out of that river alive was miracle number three.

But Jax's nightmares didn't play out like the miracle. No, in his nightmares he watched as Grace died.

When the accident happened, they had to pull Grace out from the car before Paige. In the nightmare, it was Grace who was pulled out second. Paige was safe in Brendan's arms, and Jax would go to get Grace, but the tree would snap right before his hands touched hers. Jax would scream her name as the river dragged her away and she disappeared under the surface of the water.

Jax woke up, Grace's name still on his lips. He was breathing hard and drenched in sweat, the sheets sticking to his skin. He blinked, his eyes adjusting to the darkness as he slowly began to realize that what he'd seen wasn't real. That it was just another nightmare. That Grace wasn't lost. She'd walked away from the accident with a dislocated shoulder and minor scrapes and bruises.

Jax lay there and when he got his breathing under control and his heart stopped pounding out of his chest, he turned to look at the alarm clock. It was ten to five in the morning. He didn't need to be up for another hour, but it was pointless for him to even attempt to go back to sleep. Whenever he had a nightmare about Grace, he was on edge until he saw her and knew she was okay.

So instead, Jax threw back the sheets that were tangled around his legs and sat on the edge of the bed. He rubbed his face with his hands before he got up and padded into the bathroom. He brushed his teeth and splashed his face with cold water. He looked into the mirror as water dripped off the end of his long, freckled nose. The hollows under his eyes were tinged a light purple.

Mirabelle had a whopping five thousand people in its six hundred square miles, half of which was water. The little beach town made up sixty percent of Atticus County's population, and boy did those five thousand sure know how to keep the sheriff's office busy. Deputies worked twelve-hour shifts. Two days on, then two days off; three days on, then two days off.

Jax had worked only the first day of his three-day shift, and he'd had to deal with plenty already: a kid who'd stolen his mom's car to go joy riding with his girlfriend, more drunken college kids on spring break than he could count, and three house calls for domestic disturbances, two of which had ended in arrests. He was also investigating a string of burglaries that had been going on in Mirabelle. Five alone in the last two months, and they all looked to be connected.

The day before had been a long one and he left work exhausted. For normal people that would mean sleep would come easier, but that wasn't the case for Jax. For Jax, deep sleep brought on his nightmares. He'd been having nightmares for as far back as he could remember, and at twenty-nine years old, that was a long time. It was hard not to have nightmares when you grew up in an environment that was less than friendly.

Haldon Anderson was one mean son-of-a-bitch, and he took great pleasure in making his son feel like shit as often as possible. When Haldon wasn't in jail, he was out on a fishing boat making money to drown himself in a bottle of liquor and whatever pills he could get his hands on. And when Haldon got on one of his benders, there was absolutely nothing that was going to stop him. Whether Haldon used his fists or his words, he knew how to make a person bleed.

Haldon had laughed when Jax became a deputy seven years ago. He'd thought it was one of the greatest jokes of his life.

"This is perfect," he'd said, wiping his fingers underneath his eyes. "A worthless boy doing a thankless job. Working for justice my ass, you're not going to do anything to make this world a better place. The only thing you could've possibly done to achieve that was to have never been born."

Yup, Haldon Anderson, father of the *fucking* year.

As a child, Jax couldn't understand why his mother let his father get away with all the abuse. But Patricia Anderson wasn't a strong woman and her greatest weakness was Haldon. She hadn't protected her child like a mother should. Actually, she hadn't done anything that a mother should do.

Jax shook his head and pulled himself out of the past. That was the last thing he wanted to think about.

He put on a sweatshirt, a pair of gym shorts, and his sneakers before he headed out into the chilly April morning. He stretched for a minute before he hit the pavement and attempted to run from his demons.

* * *

Grace King inhaled deeply as she pulled out a fresh batch of Bananas Foster muffins. The rich smell filled her nose before it expanded her lungs. She smiled as she set them on the counter to cool. These muffins were going to sell out with the morning breakfast rush.

Grace didn't care if she was making cookies, pies, or cupcakes; she never got tired of it. One of her first memories was sitting in the kitchen at her grandparents' house while she watched her mother stir chocolate cake batter. Grace's fondest memories of her mother were the two of them baking together. Claire King had lost her battle to breast cancer almost fourteen years ago. But before she died, she'd passed on her love for baking to her daughter.

Grace had been working in her grandmother's café since she was eight years old. Now, at twenty-four, she helped her grandmother run Café Lula. The café was a small, brightly painted cottage out on Mirabelle Beach. The promise of freshly baked food kept customers from all over town and the county pouring in no matter the time of day or the season.

The day promised to be a busy one, as Grace had to fill up the dessert case with fresh goodies. She'd been experimenting with cupcake recipes the past couple of weeks. She'd wanted to make something amazing for her sister-in-law's baby shower. Grace had eaten dinner at Brendan and Paige's the night before, and she'd been the one in charge of dessert. For fear of disappointing a sassy pregnant woman, she'd brought her A-game and made two different types of cupcakes.

"I think my favorite is the Blueberry Lemonade," Paige had said as she'd rubbed her ever-growing belly. "But Trevor seems to like this Red Velvet Cheesecake one. I think he's dancing in there."

Trevor Oliver King was supposed to be gracing the world with his presence around the middle of May. Grace couldn't wait to meet her nephew. Paige was over seven months pregnant, and she was one of those women who still looked beautiful even though she was growing another human being inside of her. If Grace didn't love her sister-in-law dearly, she would've been fifty shades of jealous. As it was, she was only about twenty shades.

But really, Grace couldn't be happier for her brother and sister-in-law. Brendan was going to be an amazing father. Much better than his or Grace's had been.

Neither Brendan nor Grace had ever had their fathers in their lives. Brendan's dad had gotten their mother pregnant when she was seventeen. When he'd found out, he promptly split town and never looked back. But while Brendan at least knew who his father was, Grace had no idea about hers. It was one of the great mysteries, and a constant source of gossip in Mirabelle.

There were many things in life that Grace was grateful for, her brother and Paige topping the list. They were a team and they worked together. They loved each other deeply. And Grace envied that stupid dopey look they always got on their faces. She wanted that. And she knew exactly who she wanted it with. It was just too bad for her that the man in question was stubborn and refused to see her as anything besides his best friend's little sister.

Grace took a deep breath and shook her head, bringing herself back to the muffins that she had to take to the front of the café. There was no need to concern herself with frustrating men at the moment. So she loaded up a tray with an already cooled batch of muffins and went to load the display case before the eight o'clock rush of customers filled the café. But when she pushed her way through the door she found the frustrating man in question on the other side, staring at her with her favorite pair of deep green eyes.

* * *

Jax's whole body relaxed when he saw Grace push through the door from the kitchen. The moment she saw him her blue eyes lit up and her cupid's bow mouth split into a giant grin. She'd always looked at him that way. Like he was her favorite person in the whole world. God knew she was his.

"Heya, Deputy. Let me guess," she said as she put the tray down on the counter, "you came here for coffee?"

No. He'd come here to see her. He always came here to see her. But coffee was a legitimate enough excuse, especially since he hadn't gotten that much sleep and was at the beginning of another twelve-hour shift.

"Please," he said, drumming his long, freckled fingers on the counter.

"Did you eat breakfast?" she asked as she pulled a to-go cup off the stack and started pumping coffee into it.

"I'm fine."

"Hmm." She looked over her shoulder at him and pursed her lips. "You know that isn't going to fly for a second. I got just the thing to go with this." She put the steaming cup and a lid down on the counter. "Go fix your coffee while I bag up your breakfast."

Grace turned around and pushed through the door to the kitchen as Jax grabbed his cup and went over to the end of the counter where the sugar and milk was.

Since Jax was four years old, the King women had been feeding him. Between them and Shep's mom, theirs were the only home-cooked meals he'd gotten after his grandmother died. If it hadn't been for them, he would've gone to bed with an empty stomach more nights than most.

Patricia Anderson wasn't much of a Susie Homemaker. Between her long hours working at the Piggly Wiggly, and drinking herself into a stupor and getting high when Haldon was on parole, she sometimes forgot to stock the freezer with corndogs and mini pizzas for her son.

"Here you go."

Jax turned to find Grace by his side. She hadn't gotten

the height gene like Brendan. She was about five-feet-four and came in just under Jax's chin. Her petite stature and soft heart-shaped face inspired an overwhelming urge in him to protect her. She'd always inspired that feeling in him, ever since her mother brought her home from the hospital all those years ago.

"They're Bananas Foster muffins and they're fresh out of the oven," she said, holding out a bag.

"Thanks, Princess," he said, grabbing the bag and letting his fingers brush the back of her hand.

God, he loved the way her skin felt against his.

"Anytime, Jax." She smiled widely at him. A second later she stepped into him and grabbed his forearms for balance as she stretched up on her toes and kissed his jaw.

It was something Grace had done a thousand and one times before. She had no concept of personal boundaries with him, and she was wide open with her affection. And just like always, when her lips brushed his skin he had the overwhelming desire to turn into her. To feel her lips against his. To grab her and hold her against him while he explored her mouth with his.

But instead of following that impulse, he let her pull back from him.

"Eat those while they're hot," she said, pointing to the bag.

"I will," he promised.

"Do you need something for lunch? I can get you a sandwich."

"I'm good," he said, shaking his head.

"Really?" she asked putting her hands on her hips and narrowing her eyes at him.

He couldn't help but grin at her attempt to intimidate him.

There was no doubt about the fact that Grace King was tough. She'd had to grow a thick skin over the years. Even though Jax, along with Brendan and Shep, had done everything in their power to try to protect her, they couldn't be there to shield her from everything. So Grace had done everything to even up the score with whoever tried to put her down. She wasn't a shy little thing by any means, and she'd tell anybody what was up without a moment's hesitation.

"I'll stop somewhere and get something," he said.

"Or I can give you something now," she said, exasperated. "I'm getting you a sandwich," she said, turning on her heal and walking back into the kitchen.

"Grace, you don't have to do this," Jax said, following her.

"I know," she said, looking over her shoulder as she opened the refrigerator. "But I'm going to anyway."

Jax watched as Grace filled a bag with two sandwiches, a bag of chips, a cup of fruit salad, and his favorite, a butterscotch cookie.

"This should last you till dinner."

Jax didn't say anything as he pulled his wallet out to pay for everything.

"Oh, I don't think so," Grace said, shaking her head. "You are *not* paying."

Before Jax could respond the side door in the kitchen opened and Lula Mae walked in.

To the casual observer, Grace and Brendan's grandmother wouldn't strike a person as someone to be feared. She had a kind face and bright blue eyes that, when paired with her ample stature and friendly disposition, inspired a feeling of warmth and openness. But Lula Mae was fiercely loyal, and those blue eyes could go as cold as ice when someone hurt anyone she loved. Lula Mae had declared Jax as one of hers over twenty-five years ago, and she'd marched down to his parents' house more than once to give them a piece of her mind.

Jax had spent more nights sleeping at the Kings' house than he could count. It was one of the few places he'd actually felt safe growing up. And even now whenever he saw her or her husband, Oliver, he had that overwhelming feeling of being protected.

"Jaxson Lance Anderson," Lula Mae said, walking up to him, "what in the world is your wallet doing out? Your money is no good here."

"That's what I just told him."

Jax turned back to Grace, who was wearing a self-satisfied smile.

"Your granddaughter just gave me over thirty dollars' worth of food," he said, indicating the stuffed bag on the counter before he turned back to Lula Mae.

"I don't care," she said, shaking her head. "Now give me some sugar before you go and keep the people of Mirabelle safe."

"Yes, ma'am," Jax said, leaning down and giving Lula Mae a peck on the check.

"And next time I see that wallet of yours make an appearance in this establishment, you are going to get a smack upside that handsome head of yours. You understand me?"

"Yes, ma'am," Jax repeated.

"Good boy." She nodded, patting his cheek.

"Thanks again," he said, reaching for the bag of food and his coffee. "I'll see you two later."

"Bye, sugar," Lula Mae said as she rounded the counter.

"See you later," Grace said, giving him another of her face-splitting grins.

Jax headed for the door, unable to stop his own smile from spreading across his face.

* * *

Grace stared at Jax's retreating form as he walked out of the kitchen, and she appreciated every inch of it. He had a lean muscular body. His shoulders filled out the top of his forest green deputy's shirt, and his strong back tapered down to his waist. His shirt was tucked into his green pants that hung low from his narrow hips and covered his long, toned legs.

And oh, dear God, did Jaxson Anderson have a nice ass.

Though her appreciation of said ass had only been going on for about ten years, the appreciation of Jaxson Anderson had been discovered a long time ago. He was the boy who saved her from bullies on the playground. The boy who gave her his ice cream cone when hers fell in the dirt. The boy who picked her up off the ground when she Rollerbladed into a tree. The boy who let her cry on his shoulder after her mom died.

Yes, Brendan and Shep had done all those things as well, but Jax was different. Jax was hers. She'd decided that eighteen years ago. She'd just been waiting for him to figure it out.

But the man was ridiculously slow on the uptake.

Grace had been in love with him since she was six years old. She loved his freckles and his reddish brown hair. His hair that was always long enough to where someone could run their fingers through it and rumple it just a little. Not that she'd ever rumpled Jax's hair, but a girl always had her fantasies, and getting Jax all tousled was most definitely one of Grace's.

Jax was always so in control and self-contained, and so damn serious. More often than not, that boy had a frown on his face, which was probably why every time Grace saw his dimpled smile it made her go all warm and giddy.

God she loved his smile. She just wanted to kiss it, to run her lips down from his mouth to his smooth, triangular jaw.

Grace sighed wistfully as the door shut behind him and turned to her grandmother.

"You get your young man all fed and caffeinated?" Lula Mae asked as she pulled containers out of the refrigerator.

"I don't know about 'my young man,' but I did get Jax something to soak up that coffee he came in for."

"Oh, sweetie," Lula Mae said, looking at Grace and shaking her head pityingly, "that boy did not come in here for coffee."

"Hmmm, well he sure didn't ask for anything else," Grace said as she walked over to the stove and started plating the rest of her muffins.

"Just give it time."

"Time?" Grace spun around to look at her grandmother. "How much *time* does the man need? He's had years."

"Yes, well, he'll figure things out. Sooner than later I think."

"I don't think so. To him, I'm just Brendan's little sister."

"There's no *just* about it," Lula Mae said, grabbing one last container before she closed the fridge and walked back to the counter where she'd piled everything else. "He doesn't have brotherly feelings for you, Gracie. I've never seen anyone fluster that boy the way you do."

"Oh, come on, Jaxson Anderson doesn't get flustered," Grace said, shaking her head.

"If you think that, then he isn't the only one who's blind."

"What's that supposed to mean?"

"You see, Gracie, you've never had the chance to observe him when you aren't around."

"And?" she prompted, gesturing with her hand for her grandmother to carry on.

"He changes when you're around. Smiles more."

"Really? Because he still frowns a whole lot around me."

"Well, that's usually when some other boy is trying to get your attention, and he's jealous."

"Jealous," Grace scoffed. "Jax doesn't get jealous."

"Oh, yes, he does. Grace, you need to open your eyes; that boy has been fighting his feelings for you for years."

And with that, Lula Mae went about fixing her menu for the day, leaving Grace even more frustrated than she had been the minute before.

* * *

"Holy hell, that girl can bake."

Jax bit into his second muffin and chewed slowly. He hadn't realized how hungry he'd been until he'd taken that first bite, and then he'd promptly inhaled the first muffin. This one he intended to savor. He let the warm richness of the bread rest on his tongue for a moment before he swallowed and took a swig of his steaming coffee.

It was amazing how much better he felt with food in his stomach, or maybe he just felt better because he'd seen Grace. He *always* felt better when he saw Grace. She made everything so much brighter, so much *more*. Like swallowing a warm liquid that settled in his stomach before it shot out to this fingers and toes and made him feel like he could take on anything.

The power of caffeine had nothing on Grace King.

She was loud and vibrant, and it was almost impossible to escape her enthusiasm. She'd always had the ability to draw whoever was around into her atmosphere and keep them there. She'd drawn Jax in when she was a baby, and he'd been hooked ever since.

Though how he was hooked had changed in recent years. It hadn't been a slow gradual change, either. It had been about as subtle as Grace. Jax remembered the day vividly. She'd been eighteen years old; he'd been twenty-three.

He'd stopped by the Kings' house for dinner one night and Grace was out in the yard, washing her vintage yellow Bug. She had the radio blasting music so she hadn't heard him pull up on the street. She was wearing short cutoff blue jeans and a bright blue bikini top, the strings tied around the middle of her back and around her neck. Her light blond hair had been up in a ponytail, but a few strands had escaped and were sticking to the side of her neck. It was then, as Jax studied the slope of her neck, that he felt it. He'd wanted to come up behind her and put his mouth to that neck, taste her warm skin against his tongue.

He remembered stopping so suddenly at the thought that he'd almost tripped and landed on his face.

Grace was Brendan's little sister. Jax had watched her grow up, been there when they'd brought her home from the hospital, heard her first laugh as a baby, watched as she'd taken her first steps, sang happy birthday to her as she blew out candles on every single birthday. This was Grace, the girl he'd always thought of as his little sister. But damn if every single one of those brotherly feelings was gone.

Every. Last. One. Of. Them.

And then he'd watched, paralyzed from the revelation, as she turned to dunk the sponge in her hand in a bucket of soapy water, and he got a glimpse of her side.

"What the hell is that?"

Somehow he'd found his tongue and his voice had carried over the beat of the music.

Grace looked up and turned to him, her usual grin spreading across her face. But he'd only had a moment to register her smile because his eyes darted back down to her side where a blue swallow about the size of his hand was tattooed on her upper ribs. It was diving down; one of its wings spanned her side, the other wrapped around to cup under her right breast.

Jax had never thought much of Grace's breasts. They were small, not even a handful. But now? Now he wanted to know what those felt like, too. His fingers were itching to untie those straps.

What the hell was wrong with him?

"Why, Jaxson Anderson," Grace drawled, "are you staring at my chest?"

Jax looked up, and he could feel the flush coming to his cheeks. But he was determined to play this off, because he would go to the grave before he admitted to wanting one of his best friends' baby sister.

"No, I'm looking at that tattoo on your side," he said, letting his anger boil over into his voice. "What the hell did you do? Does Brendan know about this?" he almost screamed at her.

Why the hell was he so pissed off?

Because that tattoo was sexy as hell and he didn't want anyone looking at it. Or God, touching it. Touching her.

Her smile disappeared in an instant and her blue eyes turned icy. "He was there when I got it a month ago," she said, narrowing her eyes at him.

"He let you?" Jax asked, incredulous.

"Brendan doesn't *let me* do anything," Grace said, crossing her arms under her chest. It made her small breasts more prominent.

How had he not noticed how amazing they were before that moment?

"In case you hadn't noticed, I'm not a child anymore, Jax."

And that had been precisely the problem, because he *had* finally noticed. And it had tortured him every single day for the last six years.

Jax sighed before he took another bite of his muffin, because boy did Grace ever like to torture him.

Grace's friendliness tended to come off as flirting, and nothing got under Jax's skin more than when he saw Grace flirting with some little schmuck. He'd had to watch as guy after guy paraded through her life. Okay, so there hadn't been that many guys who'd gotten past the flirting stage. But none of them had been good enough for her, not a single one.

Jax wasn't good enough, either, so he'd resigned himself to doing what he *was* good enough for, watching out for her. And man was watching hard.

THE DISH

Where Authors Give You the Inside Scoop

♥ ♥ ♥ ♥ ♥ ♥ ♥ ♥ ♥ ♥ ♥ ♥ ♥ ♥ ♥ ♥

From the desk of Kristen Ashley

Dear Reader,

When the idea for LADY LUCK came to me, it was after watching the Dwayne Johnson film *Faster*.

I thought that movie was marvelous, and not just simply because I was watching all the beauty that is Dwayne Johnson on the screen.

What I enjoyed about it was that he played against his normal *The Game Plan/Gridiron Gang* funny guy/good guy type and shocked me by being an antihero. What made it even better was that he had very little dialogue. Now I enjoy watching Mr. Johnson do just about anything, including speak. What was so amazing about this is that his character in *Faster* should have been difficult to like, to root for, especially since he gave us very few words as to *why* we should do that. But he made me like him, root for him. Completely.

It was his face. It was his eyes. It was the way he could express himself with those—*not* his actions—that made us want him to get the vengeance he sought.

Therefore, when I was formulating Ty Walker and Alexa "Lexie" Berry from LADY LUCK in my head, I was building Ty as an antihero focused on revenge—a man who would do absolutely anything to get it. As for

Lexie, I was shoehorning her into this cold, seen-it-all/
done-it-all/had-nothing-left-to-give woman who was cold
as ice.

I was quite excited about the prospect of what would
happen with these two. A silent man with the fire of
vengeance in place of his heart. A closed-off woman with
a block of ice in place of hers.

Imagine my surprise as I wrote the first chapter of this
book and the Ty and Lexie I was creating in my head
were blown to smithereens so the real Ty and Lexie could
come out, not one thing like I'd been making them in
my head.

This happens, not often, but it happens. And it happens when I "make up" characters. Normally, my characters come to me as they are, who they are, the way they
look, and all the rest. If I try to create them from nothing,
force them into what I want them to be, they fight back.

By the time I got to writing Ty and Lexie, I learned
not to engage in a battle I never win. I just let go of who
I thought they should be and where I thought they were
going and took their ride.

And what a ride.

I'm so pleased I didn't battle them and got to know
them just as they are because their love story was a pleasure to watch unfold. There were times that were tough,
very tough, and I would say perhaps the toughest I've ever
written. But that just made their happy ending one that
tasted unbelievably sweet.

Of course, Ty did retain some of that silent angry man,
but he never became the antihero I expected him to be,
though he did do a few non-heroic things in dealing with
his intense issues. And I reckon one day I'll have my
antihero set on a course of vengeance who finds a woman

who has a heart of ice. Those concepts never go away. They just have to come to me naturally.

But I had to give Ty and Lexie their story as it came to me naturally.

And I loved every second of it.

Kristen Ashley

♥ ♥ ♥ ♥ ♥ ♥ ♥ ♥ ♥ ♥ ♥ ♥ ♥ ♥ ♥

From the desk of Anna Sullivan

Dear Reader,

There's a lot more to being a writer than sitting at a computer and turning my imagination into reality. Of course I love creating characters, deciding on their personal foibles, inventing a series of events to not only test their character but also to help them grow. And that's where everything begins: with the story.

But every writer does her share of book signings and interviews. As with every profession, there are some questions that crop up more often than others. Here are some examples—and the answers that run through my mind in my more irreverent moments:

Q: Why did you become a writer?
A: Because I like to control the people in my life and the only way I can do that is to invent them. (And

unfortunately, I still don't have much control; it's regrettable how often they don't listen to me and get into trouble anyway.)

Q: Those sex scenes, huh? (This invariably comes along with a smirk, waggling eyebrows, or a wink.)

A: I have three kids, you do the math. And please don't wink; it's almost never cute.

Q: Where do you get these ideas?

A: I used to ask my children that after they did something…unexpected. They'd usually come up blank. So do I, so I'll just say I don't know where the characters come from, but they won't leave me alone until I write them. I think there may be a clinical diagnosis and prescription meds for my affliction, but what kind of fun would that be?

But seriously, I hope you enjoy my second Windfall Island novel, HIDEAWAY COVE, as the search for Eugenia Stanhope, kidnapped almost a century before, continues.

Now Holden Abbot is joining the quest for truth, justice, and the American way…Wait, that's Superman. Well, Holden Abbot may not be the man of steel, but he's tall and handsome, and his smooth Southern accent doesn't hurt either. And even if he can't leap tall buildings in a single bound, Jessi Randal is falling head over heels in love with him. She may be Eugenia Stanhope's long-lost descendant, though, and that puts her life in danger, along with her seven year-old son, Benji. Holden may have to do the superhero thing after all. Or he may only be able to save one of them.

I had a great time finding out how this story ended. I hope you do, too.

Anna Sullivan

www.AnnaSullivanBooks.com
Twitter @ASullivanBooks
Facebook.com/AnnaSullivanBooks

♥ ♥ ♥ ♥ ♥ ♥ ♥ ♥ ♥ ♥ ♥ ♥ ♥ ♥ ♥

From the desk of Rochelle Alers

Dear Reader,

Writers hear it over and over again: Write about what you know. I believe I adhered to this rule when continuing the Cavanaugh Island series with MAGNOLIA DRIVE. This time you get to read about a young Gullah woman and her gift to discern the future. As I completed the character dossier for the heroine, I could hear my dearly departed mother whisper in my ear not to tell too much, because like her, my mother also had the gift of sight.

Growing up in New York City didn't lend itself to connecting with my Gullah roots until I was old enough to understand why my mother and other Gullah held to certain traditions that were a litany of don'ts: Don't put your hat on the bed, don't throw out what you sweep up after dark, don't put up a new calendar before the beginning of a new year, et cetera, et cetera, et cetera. The don'ts go on and on, too numerous to list here.

I'd believed the superstitions were silly until as an adult

I wanted to know why my grandfather, although born in Savannah, spoke English with a distinctive accent. However, it was the womenfolk in my family who taught me what it meant to be Gullah and the significance of the traditions passed down through generations of griots.

In MAGNOLIA DRIVE, red-haired, green-eyed Francine Tanner is Gullah and a modern-day griot and psychic. She is able to see everyone's future, though not her own. But when a handsome stranger sits in her chair at the Beauty Box asking for a haircut and a shave, the former actress turned hairstylist could never have predicted the effect he would have on her life and her future.

The first time Keaton Grace saw up-and-coming actress Francine Tanner perform in an off-Broadway show he found himself spellbound by her incredible talent. So much so that he wrote a movie script with her in mind. Then it was as if she dropped off the earth when she abruptly left the stage. The independent filmmaker didn't know their paths would cross again when he made plans to set up his movie studio, Grace Lowcountry Productions, on Cavanaugh Island. Keaton believes they were destined to meet again, while Francine fears reopening a chapter in her life she closed eight years ago.

MAGNOLIA DRIVE returns to Sanctuary Cove, where the customers at the Beauty Box will keep you laughing and wanting more, while the residents of the Cove are in rare form once they take sides in an upcoming local election. Many of the familiar characters are back to give you a glimpse into what has been going on in their lives. And for those of you who've asked if David Sullivan will ever find a love that promises forever—the answer is yes. Look for David and the woman who will tug at his heart and make him reassess his priorities in *Cherry Lane*.

Happy Reading!

Rochelle Alers

ralersbooks@aol.com
www.rochellealers.org

♥ ♥ ♥ ♥ ♥ ♥ ♥ ♥ ♥ ♥ ♥ ♥ ♥ ♥ ♥ ♥

From the desk of Jessica Scott

Dear Reader,

The first time I got the idea for my hero and heroine in BACK TO YOU, Trent and Laura, I was a brand-new lieutenant with no idea what deployment would entail. I remember sitting in my office, listening to one of the captains telling his wife he'd be home as soon as he could—and right after he hung up the phone, he promptly went back to work. He always talked about how much he loved her, and I wondered how he could tell her one thing and do something so different. And even more so, I was deeply curious about what his wife was like.

I was curious about the kind of woman who would love a man no matter how much war changed him. About the kind of woman with so much strength that she could hold their family together no matter what. But also, a woman who was *tired*. Who was starting to lose her faith in the man she'd married.

Having been the spouse left at home to hold the family together, I know intimately the struggles Laura has faced. I also know what it feels like to deploy and leave my family, and how hard it is to come home.

I absolutely love writing stories of redemption, and at the heart of it, this is a story of redemption. It takes a strong love to make it through the dark times.

I hope you enjoy reading Trent and Laura's story in BACK TO YOU as much as I enjoyed bringing their story to life.

Xoxo

Jessica Scott

www.JessicaScott.net
Twitter @JessicaScott09
Facebook.com/JessicaScottAuthor

♥ ♥ ♥ ♥ ♥ ♥ ♥ ♥ ♥ ♥ ♥ ♥ ♥

From the desk of Shannon Richard

Dear Reader,

So UNSTOPPABLE had originally been planned for the fourth book, but after certain plot developments, Bennett and Mel's story needed to be moved in the lineup to third place. When I dove into their story I knew very little about where I was going, but once I started there was no turning back.

Bennett Hart was another character who walked onto the page out of nowhere and the second I met him I knew he *needed* to have his story told. I mean, how could he not when he's named after one of my favorite heroines? Yup, Bennett is named after Elizabeth Bennett from Jane Austen's *Pride and Prejudice*. Don't scoff, she's awesome and I love her dearly. And *hello*, she ends up with a certain Mr. Fitzwilliam Darcy…he's my ultimate literary crush. I mean really, I swoon just thinking about him.

And I'm not the only one swooning over here. A certain Ms. Melanie O'Bryan is hard-core dreaming/fantasizing/drooling (just a little bit) over Bennett. Mel was definitely an unexpected character for me. It took me a little while to see that she had a story to tell, and I always like to say it was Bennett who realized her potential before I did.

Both characters have their guards up at the beginning of UNSTOPPABLE. Bennett is still dealing with the trauma he experienced when he was in Afghanistan, and Mel is dealing with getting shot a couple of months ago. Mel is a very sweet girl and she appears to be just a little bit unassuming…to those who don't know her, that is. As it turns out, she has a wild side and she lets Bennett see it in full force. Bennett and Mel were a different writing experience for me. I was discovering them as they discovered each other, and sometimes they surprised me beyond words. They taught me a lot about myself and I will be forever grateful that they shared their story with me.

Cheers,

♥ ♥ ♥ ♥ ♥ ♥ ♥ ♥ ♥ ♥ ♥ ♥ ♥ ♥ ♥ ♥

From the desk of Lauren Layne

Dear Reader,

I am a hopeless romantic. For as long as I can remember, I've been stalking happy endings. It started with skimming Nancy Drew and Sweet Valley Twins books for the parts about boys. From there, it was sneaking into the Young Adult section of the library way before my time to get at the Sweet Valley High books—because there was kissing in those.

By my mid-teens, I'd discovered that there was an entire genre of books devoted to giving romantics like me a guaranteed happily ever after. It was the start of a lifetime affair with romance novels.

So it shouldn't come as a surprise that as I was stock-piling my book boyfriends, I also did a fair amount of thinking about the future hero of my own love story. I had it all figured out by junior high. My future husband would have brown hair. He'd be a lawyer. Maybe a doctor, but probably a lawyer. He'd be the strong, silent type. Very stoic. He'd be a conservative dresser, and it would be strange to see him out of his classic black suit, except on weekends when he'd wear khakis and pressed polos. We'd meet when I was in my mid-to-late twenties, and he'd realize instantly that my power suits and classic pumps were his perfect match. Did I mention that in this vision I, too, was a lawyer?

Fast forward a few (okay, many) years. How'd I do?

Well…my husband has brown hair. *That's the only part I got right*. He's an extroverted charmer and wouldn't be caught dead in a standard-issue suit. He's not a lawyer, and I've never seen him wear khakis. Oh, and we started dating in high school, and were married by twenty-three.

I couldn't have been more wrong, and yet…I couldn't be more happy. Although I am a "planner" in every sense of the word, I've learned that love doesn't care one bit about the person you *think* is your perfect mate.

In my Best Mistake series, the heroines learn exactly that. They have a pretty clear idea of the type of person they're supposed to be with. And they couldn't be more wrong.

Whether it's the cocktail waitress falling for the uptight CEO, or the rigid perfectionist who wins the heart of a dedicated playboy, these women learn that being wrong has never felt so right.

I had a wonderful time wreaking havoc on the lives of Sophie and Brynn Dalton, and I hope you have as much fun reading about the best mistakes these women ever made.

Here's to the best of plans going awry—because that's when the fun starts.

Lauren Layne

www.laurenlayne.com

About the Author

Shannon Richard grew up in the Panhandle of Florida as the baby sister of two overly protective but loving brothers. She was raised by a more than somewhat eccentric mother, a self-proclaimed vocabularist who showed her how to get lost in a book, and a father who passed on his love for coffee and really loud music. She graduated from Florida State University with a Bachelor's in English Literature and still lives in Tallahassee, where she battles everyday life with writing, reading, and a rant every once in a while. Okay, so the rants might happen on a regular basis. She's still waiting for her Southern, scruffy Mr. Darcy, and in the meantime she writes love stories to indulge her overactive imagination. Oh, and she's a pretty big fan of the whimsy.

Learn more at:
ShannonRichard.net
Twitter, @Shan_Richard
Facebook.com/ShannonNRichard